Smiling ON A TROUBLED PLANET

IN A SHADOW OF TIME

DAVID O. IDAHOSA

To order additional copies of this book, contact:
Bookwhip
1-855-339-3589
https://www.bookwhip.com

I would like to dedicate this book to my
late mother, Veronica Idahosa. I miss you, Mom,
and no other woman in life can take
your place in my heart

Chapter 1

It is in the middle of summer, in between spring and autumn. It is the time when young people take advantage of the first and last rays of the afternoon sun to play at being birds flying into rivers and swimming pools; this is also the very time the sun is at its northernmost point in the sky, appearing at its highest altitude above the horizons; the time when the days are their longest and the nights are their shortest, with day length decreasing as the season progresses after the solstice; this time all radiant in the sky, radiant, as we observe conscientiously and perspicaciously how the day and night embrace each other, and clarity and love emerge between moon and sun. It is the very time when one could have plenty of time for making memories and having fun—very relaxed fun when the trees swing back and forth, to and fro, and beautiful colored leaves dropping down; the time also for sunshine and sunglasses, good time and silliness; time for different outdoor sports and activities, such as volleyball, lawn tennis and table tennis, basketball, water skiing, surfing, beach football, soccer, water polo, swimming, cricket, biking and so on. Yes, this is also the time, the very precise, desirable, favorable, and most convenient time for someone to pick up a good book and read to acquire knowledge.

At this time of summer, as Kadosh sits on the bank of a river which flows among woodland such as ash. He is sitting and watching thoughtfully, watching heedfully deep inside the soul of the river; he is watching as it floats behind, the wind blowing from one direction to another; he remains still, and could mentally listen to hear a message from the gods with whom he communes appropriately. As the river flows, it is flowing inside of him, and the sound is a sound of silence accompanied by fury, destruction, darkness, and shadow of death. Instantly, he could sense something, something strange and inconceivable coming. He fancies from a distance how the whirlwind blows, benevolent celestial beings without wings falling down from heaven to the Earth to lay tentative architectural plans for mankind to keep up, to understand, and to walk along with to a new beginning of life, without the intention to arouse the wrath of the gods and goddesses to a greater extent.

Kadosh watching still as the river floats, consciously could not he take in meaning of what he is experiencing, or where he is, or what is occurring around him. His head he lifts up to turn his attention around where exactly he is and what indeed he is doing, only to see, in an exact manner from a short distance, a young, tall, and beautiful blonde girl, nude, lying on top of another young and good-looking boy, also nude. They are both kissing, smooching, romancing, and mimicking on the bank of the same river where he sits. Could not he possibly hold a belief of what he sees that no other person dares to dream. Without delay, turns he to look to the other side in an effort to keep out of sight of the thing. He sees a group of young men and women joyfully chanting and clapping hands, yielding sounds of high volume and intensity, and, looking to his back side, could see he another group of youths with cans and bottles of beer, whisky, gin, and other alcoholic beverages. Not far from them are couples playing with their kids. Could not help he comprehend why he is where he is, having no awareness of the surroundings, his own existence, his sensations, nor his thoughts. In an altered level of consciousness, he sees himself. Could not help he regain his senses, bring himself back to life to be who he used to be before coming to sit near the river. Without an intermediary, he notes what he sees is beyond his imagination, beyond his invariable imagination. It is something closely related in form, position, and degree to what is most excellent to be declared formally as a vision. A vision is what it is, nothing, but a vision. This vision is conceived by his own imagination, nurtured, and has become fruitful. It is a mystical power for sensing and seeing things beyond humans—a strange power not bestowed upon many for the reason not everyone could hold in mind how potential is the power he or she possesses.

Looking up, his gaze moves straight to the direction of the many trees and flowers surrounding the river, to the singing birds flying in the sky, to the float of the river, and ultimately, to the other plants and animals. Could see he the natural impacts they are having on that environment. Falls he in love with it; falls he in love with nature; falls he in love with creation. Very deep becomes his belief in the existence of a supernatural being, solid, secured, established, and marked by great physical power. Curiously looking forward to see the people around who are virtually naked. Seeing how splendid and joyous it is for him to bear witness to this, senses he the end of the world is imminent. Ascertains he man has brought a curse upon himself, and the wrath of the maker is about to be observed and attested, the consequences of greed, want it all that man has put upon himself is about to explode into something characterized by pain, sorrow, misery, severe affliction, and destruction. How could he make this comprehensible to his fellow humans? In which way would not he be depicted a cynic who has lost his faith, his beliefs, and his trust in humanity? A cynic, a cynic, perhaps what he sees himself become. For long ago he has lost his faith, trust, and beliefs in humanity. He has seen evil becomes the ruler mankind has chosen to let rule over it, rule over and control its very soul, at a time when this evil comes to consume and absorb this soul. Now that the soul has been destroyed and ravaged, is there any need for intervention? Or is there anything in which to intervene? Definitely, nothing, nothing will be done to revive the soul, nothing will be done to save this soul because it is doomed, doomed already, and anything hold upon to impart new spirit to this soul, to get it restored, would, thus inflame the whole situation and causes it to be more calamitous. The soul must die, it must die, the soul that has committed atrocities must die, the soul of man must die to be reborn and converted to a different soul, a new soul, a new soul that could testify of the destruction of the first soul, and will pledge to a solemn oath never to take the same path that will set him in a position in which he will be behaving in the most reprehensible manner in a way the first soul did. A cynic he is, a cynic who affirms to be conscious of the way to bring mankind back to life, revives the soul before dawn, because when it is dawn, the soul which already has been seen gradually dematerialized, would cease to exist.

Chapter 2

Kadosh, who in point of reality, is not holding in his brain any practical knowledge of where he is, or what he is doing, could himself see how he maintains an upright position from the bank of the river where he sits and observes carefully the river and everything surrounding it. Could neither believe he what is transpiring, nor could apprehend he the event that passed through his mind. He intends to walk away from where he is. He intends to leave there to return back to where he lives—his little haven. But the instant he walks and glances expressively around him, he could still see the many jolly and delightful youths and grown men and women who are thrilled with the wonderful lives they live. They are showing recognition of the quality of nature and its existence still untouched and influenced by the so-called civilization that is steering mankind to its destruction.

Walking, while at the same time emptying his mind of thoughts and fixating his attentions, he endeavors to recollect what indeed has happened to him and the chief reason he feels so exhausted. His strength and energy are gone from him that he could not fathom how it has all come about. He recalls it is a vision, but why him? Why him, Kadosh, a young African, who, in not less than two years, has embarked on a formidable struggle tending to cause his own death? For twenty-five days on top of the Mediterranean Sea, water blowing out of the storm, the wind blowing through, and the dreadful, monstrous waves of the sea moving up and down. Inside the small boat have been more than thirty people—men and women—teenagers and adults. Reaching the middle of the sea, with intense screaming and whistling blasting out simultaneously from different directions around him. Could certify he how the boat in a gradual manner, is capsized and sank. Could do he not-a-thing about it, solely to continuously devotes himself to how the boat sinks and how everybody inside are unceasingly screaming and diving into the large deep water of the Mediterranean Sea in-between Libya and Italy.

Three days after the event, he sees himself in a hospital on an Island in Italy, called Lampedusa. Lampedusa—an Island in Italy that has become a harbor for every migrant from Africa to Europe by sea. He has been given medical treatment and later returned to the refugee camp. Perhaps, he attempts to question the doctors and nurses in the hospital on what brought him there. But not a soul is in a position to utter any explanation to him. Could not he recall what in actuality has come about, and how he has come to be seeing himself lay in bed in hospital—-and to his profound state of wonder, sees he everybody surrounding him is white, white people quite dissimilar from the white people he has lived with in Libya for two years. As he continues to recapture his memories of life, the only thing he could summon back to his awareness is when he witnesses the boat capsizing in the middle of the sea. Without lapse of time, he apprehends with certainty and clarity where he is, what has brought him, and the main purpose he lay in bed. But yet, he longs for someone to at least do a little explanation on how it has all come about. Unfortunately, for him, due to his current state of health, no one is prompt to unravel the tremendous life story and the horrors he has unconsciously encountered at the time of the dreadful and tragic not-to-tell event. Rather, he is sent a doctor who has come to issue to him some advice, drugs to help relieve the anxiety and depression, and brings him back from the state of shock he has fallen. He is exhausted of strength and energy, once again, and swiftly returns back to sleep.

For four days Kadosh is in hospital where he is attended to by a variety of doctors and nurses, including psychologists and psychiatrists. A severe situational anxiety and depression he undergoes, trying to recover from the shock. But after, he is sent to live with his fellow refugees in a camp built for them that is topically contained to the fullest extent with immigrants mainly from Africa and the Middle East, where people are being traumatized by the atrocities of war events, and the rates of poverty are high, leading to a situation whereby many youths—men and women, are being dispelled and compelled to travel by land and seas to Europe in attempts to proclaim the success of avoiding hunger and poverty and death.

Seeing the many immigrants inside the camp, Kadosh quickly discerns he is in Europe, and it is Italy—which signifies how his dream has come to reality. Sees he how tears of joy run from his eyes down to his cheeks. It is joy, the joy of fulfilling his sole and longtime dream, his longtime self-imposed dream of coming to live the rest of his life in Europe, a continent he supposes civilization is at its best, and freedom is at its noticeable way. In his heart there is confidence he has arrived in heaven, and there is a conviction for this, seeing how he is been treated when admitted to the hospital. The assumption that if it has been in Africa where their boat capsized and sank, he might perhaps be dead. His heart is in Europe, for he deems the Europeans as being able to succeed in finding a practical measure for eradicating any condition of having no food, money, or a place to sleep for their citizens. Europe is heaven to him; so excited and overjoyed he is, believing his future is going to be bright and cheerful in this new heaven he finds himself—the heaven he has constantly with his heart seems to battle to agree to the desirability to live and die.

And it came to pass, after he is sent back to live with the other refugees in the camp. How he has been rescued by the Italian Navy and Coast Guard is later disclosed to him. Twelve people out of a hundred and twenty-five people are said to have survived the wreckage of a long inflatable boat, also known to them as a 'zodiac' —a boat actually built for less than fifteen people. He is also informed when he is rescued by the guards, he has been unconscious and lifeless, and his body found on the shore of the sea.

Staying indoors all the time, and not wanting to see people outside the camp, causes his health to deteriorate gradually. The memory of how he has been rescued is haunting his reverie. He could not help the very situation to place himself in a position whether to persist in shedding tears or be showing himself pleasure like other refugees who are as happy as people having won a lottery and are to receive the money that will last them for a lifetime. What he could not help bring to his heart is the idea to wonder whether to live in Italy if eventually he is issued a stay there, or to leave to another part of Europe. Perhaps, long before even he has decided to start to conceive of the idea of traveling to Europe, and holding in his heart the peril to travel across many other African countries to get to Libya, and from there, sneaks into a distressed, inflatable boat owned by some Libyan smugglers who receive the sum of 1,500 euros from everyone who boards the boat. Knows he Italy's economy is in a mess, recurrently shrinking; the economic crisis is affecting them and the immigrants, forcing many to flee the country in order to build a better future for themselves in other European countries, the U.S., and Canada with better economy and job opportunities. A truly desirable man in nature and admirable by many, a man also possessing personal qualities needed and lauded by his neighbors. On top of that he is having knowledge and spiritual insights. He could read and write and is very much aware of everything going on around the globe. Knows he he has succumbed to the endurance of evil and death to reach where he is—but moving further to get to a destination where his soul could repose is much more of a fascination to him than relaxing to see what heaven has for him in Italy, or perhaps he thinks he could return to his homeland where he has been born and bred, where he has lived all his childhood with a contented spirit, and has been much more determined to arrive one day at the top...and become part and parcel of the new generation to erect and champion a better way of life for his country and the people he loves and cherishes so much. But how could he do that with all he has come up against while growing up? It is a society encompassed with intense and extreme unhappiness, poverty-stricken conditions, and most severe of it all, wars—radical Islamic groups imposing strict forms of Sharia laws in many of the regions—kidnapping, intimidating, brutalizing, and killing innocent citizens who have refused to abide to their laws, taking in violent manners what they feel are their rights, claiming others are enemies of Islam, claiming others are infidels and deserve to die.

How could he even think of returning to his country, Somalia? Of what good will it yield, returning to a place he has recently fled due to how he has been beaten and almost knocked down by rifles and handguns of these dangerous terrorist groups. Two days after he succeeds in leaving that region, he is told his mother and two sisters have been shot dead by the same people. Given the present circumstances, what would he do in that country? What kind of life would he live there? No, he shall see heaven since hell is not the right place for him to be. He shall live, he shall also live to see his own children, and children's children. Has commenced he with this tough and deadly journey of life that is self-imposed, regardless of what comes the consequences of his every action and movement, he must endure to the end, he must let his soul be free—and to do that, he must proceed with this journey of life to prosperity.

Chapter 3

And coming here for long Lakota, who has consistently wanted to be a writer—a prolific and successful writer. Now could see he his achievement of desires come about; coming to a fulfillment his dreams that many like him have; with joy he is overwhelmed; and is in a state of excitement that he has never was since birth.

Fire and brimstone it takes to get a book written, external punishment voluntarily to be endured. But, to many writers, a wonderfully pleasant experience that is, and effortless it is, and nothing in which to complain. To get the book commence and come to reach a climax, it appeases and solaces them. Joyous it is, a dream accomplishing, expressing yourself, expressing your emotions through art, of your lungs pushing air out to others to inhale and feel, your voice expressing and your messages spreading to many as you can that you can not reach, see, or unable to speak to; telling stories, and as well, with the Universe communicating, and your soul communing. Inside, seeing yourself possessing that beauty of life never you have thought exist is positively the most excellent aspect of it. Hence, being a thoughtful and committed soul, in your mind to formulate how lives of others around you, you could be amplifying your impact, inspiring, and strengthening your lead for them to follow.

Unarguably, more tormenting writing is, when actually badly off you are and worthless—and more and more, being disregarded you are and loathed around you by folks, for the fact that fathom they all on a project you are working relentlessly and intensively not a soul could get to the bottom of the whole thing of what the project is all about to know the plain truth. Then you are on the brink of getting the book published; this is the first time you have written a book and as a published author you are about to see yourself. Thence come again, perhaps your mind you open. You look deep, and yourself the inception of weighing to see if there is any effective feasibility to swiftly get things done. In your instincts and intuitions you are trusting the book you have written is about to have an impact on an ongoing election campaign in a country with the largest economy in the world, the most powerful nation, a country believed and known to be the founder of the modern day democracy, America.

And during all this time, going through Lakota's most bizarre process of computations. ' "Money rules the world,"' they say. Of course, money rules, and, ' "Money is the root of all evil,"' they also say. Without money, to be found, you are nowhere. The strongest man you can be. The most intelligent man you can be. The most beautiful man you can be. The most honest and sincere human being you can as well be. But I tell you, there is not a need for a skepticism if you remain poverty-stricken and still experiencing a desire for food. But this is the world we live in today—a world that undermines meritocracy, a world where many do not merit what they possess, or rather do they deserve praise for their deeds. In this same world, the vicious alone relishes the good things in it while the just suffers and dies beautifully in silence.

In his inmost heart Lakota comprehension of the consequences of failure, presumably not able to put this dream of his into a reality. Knows he he would not have to fail, but if he could acquire some patience, that would be the one notable solution—some patience to proceed further in his journey of life. He would have to be patient. But for how long? Has he not been thinking he could change the world to make it a more peaceful place to live? Why the patience if, inevitably, he is unable to influence people on an ongoing election that could turn over power to the wrong hands, and moreover he could do it for his late mother who has passed away at the very time he is writing the book. Tears upon tears he has shed writing this book. Tears he is never going to see his mother again, and he is not there to bury her with his other brothers and sisters. Tears he is poor, and the sole remedy is to eradicate that poverty.

To many of his friends, he has once said, ' "something in life you all need to know that you do not know yet is, if you do not take poverty seriously and meditate day-in and day-out of how you could eradicate it, it will take you seriously and make of you his servant for life."'

In an overmuch rush, he is to get things done. Money he needs, which is the only solution. He could do whatever he sets up his mind in doing, he has built a constant thought. Thence takes he the little money left with him to feed and pay his bills, calls he a publishing company. A deal with them he makes and instantly, all the manuscripts he sends to them, oblivious as to what is necessary for him to do—reviewing again and again that all the words are correctly spelled and written.

It is not long the manuscripts he has submitted for publication are later sent back to him for an approval. It is then he clearly notices the presence of the many obvious, and not-so-obvious errors, in his own writing. To correct them, more money is demanded by the company—which is half of what he has previously paid for the publication. He is about to relinquish his every efforts. Henceforth, walks into his spirit of consciousness, the conception he is being defeated, defeated by his unknown foes, who literally are his envious neighbors. It is awful for him to accept this defeat because his suspension of disbelief is not to let the pride inside of him be overturned by shame. To him, it is like he is about his gods to be let down, and that he could not do. Could neither he fool his instinct, nor would he allow his gods be brought upon by shame and humiliation; this is against his will. Though, it is sadness and grief that are left for him as he lacks the necessary power to overcome the misery, and at the same time, lamenting his own existence.

Unable to concentrate much on properly reviewing the manuscripts, he approves of it and signs for the publication. After some weeks, he receives an email from the Publishing Company the book is been published. He is sent a copy of it, which he never sets eyes on.

Yes, after much struggles, futilities, and impossibilities, he Lakota sees the publication of his book carried out. He is overwhelmed with joy; a certain and remarkable thing inside of him to an extreme degree is delightful; a certain glow of life which is beautiful and wonderful, pushing him to be so confident of himself, confident his dream is becoming reality.

After the contest and concordance of his soul with these many challenges for the past several days and weeks, under a necessity, he is for a fully merited a state of tranquility. But one thing, is his quest only for glory and fame? Or is it for mere survival and for enlightening humans on the signs of the end of the world?

But, so far, as the society is interconnected with the Universe, he refuses to rest his mind, for it is been snatched by the unwillingness to allow him. Needs he to accomplish his self-imposed mission to move his world forth, shame his foes, and heal humanity after all the knowledge he thinks he has accumulated from his childhood till the time of his adulthood to become one of the most exquisite mind in the history of mankind. And this silly thought of his is nothing than sheer lunacy, sheer lunacy, because he is not truly who he is even if he is having the belief and faith he is the one to lead humanity back to the gods and goddesses that control the Universe and want to see humanity turn back to them after a very long time of walking too far away.

Chapter 4

In becoming a writer, thinking you could easily and sensibly peer into a prosperous future by breaking the chains of poverty and exterminating the demons controlling it, there is an excellent reason for you to rethink. In good faith, you have to rethink, for the fact writing is just as easy as walking a doorway to poverty, or viable as death, and not recount how your heart and soul have both been tortured and menaced. The mystery surrounding the life of an artist is incomprehensible, inexplicable, and unquestionable. Creativity is his vocation, putting talent and imagination into practice to arrive at a particular result. The more reflections, speculations, and association of different ideas, henceforth, enormous research, and brain development, an artist finds himself arriving in a state of self-shaping and self-fulfillment. What follows is transcendence—that means he is surpassing other humans. And this is the ingenious reason why virtually all artists think of themselves to be peculiar and unique. Yes they do. The artists always see themselves to be different people with higher powers derived from knowledge and wisdom; they believe they could see what others are unable to see; they see themselves as immortal—like gods and goddesses.

A true art is not to be accompanied by wealth, for that is not what it is all about. It is meant to serve a purpose more than material wealth. It is an extraordinary power physically applied by man to draw humanity closer to its Universe. True art could be described as losing something in you to acquire something more extraordinary, a gift that cannot be purchased, except giving birth inside of you. This gift actuates you to redefine yourself and also redefine others, then setting you as a role model for the people around you. The gift brings you back to life as it is transformed into a natural force only can be controlled by the Universe; the gift metamorphoses you to become immortal—a god or goddess. You see yourself in the true human form—you see yourself possessing that power to move the world forward—that power to heal humanity.

The intrinsic truth is when artists commence in exploiting themselves, losing something in them to acquire that extraordinary gifts, and doing it purposefully for the benefits, not looking up to see if there is any accordance with their soul and the Universe. That is when you see them become failures. They fail consciously because the gift in them is not natural. It has to be natural. It has to be with a powerful emotion, a desire, fire, or passion. Of course constantly it is rewarding if done well—that is if done with a truthful heart, not merely for the benefits. Art has to be from the heart, and by only that will it be seen as natural and will be seen as art: the ability to create, the expression of thoughts and feelings. Although many artists who are not driven by this force of nature may be opportune to make huger advancement when it comes to wealthy possessions in life more than those driven by it. But one thing in art most artists decline to instill in their hearts is leaving a great legacy is worth more than the wealth: being an inspiration to the generations to come. Artists, in reality, could be seen as people who lay not up treasures for themselves on Earth—and that is what makes them immortal. How much these people have to render—their lives to save others, to lure them into the life that has been long prepared for humanity to live. It is bitter, but it is out of a sense of obligation in as far as they are capable of carrying this burden given to them by their unknown gods and goddesses, who also have entrusted them this power in their ponderous hearts, impelling them to start to think wisely and differently from the people around them. The talent for creating is derived from the deep area of the artist's organic lifestyle—whereby, thriving in the process appears to be conspicuously virulent and carcinogenic.

This is the unsatisfactory situation Lakota finds himself dancing around and not knowing a way out. To be a prolific and successful writer he has wanted. Good, ultimately written the book and published he has, and for the good return he waits. In the book, about his past life he has written, and the life he is living in present time as he progresses with the writing. About his family. But basically and feelingly, his late mother whom he has written very well. Notwithstanding, the book is substantially all about politics around the world. It is what literally draws his attention to come to supply to the fullest extent in him, a motivation to begin to think of fulfilling his desire to write, his willingness to spread his messages around the globe. Reading is a thing from which he uniformly derives pleasure, but undermining his capability of becoming a writer he has always seen himself. However, instantly, when he commences with the book, inspiration has been pouring in; his heart is filled with a source of great excitement. He is unstoppable in spite of the many adversities and obstacles to thwart his progress. He experiences within him as this healing energy to create is powerfully and invariably propelling him to write and get the book published. His life full to the brim with the feeling of cheerfulness. He becomes lively once again like a normal human being. He sees himself regaining his lost confidence. Who he is, he notes. He also understands he is having the ability to see beyond, to imagine, and to formulate indispensable ideas for originating the necessary tools to destroy evil and bring humanity back to reunite with its Universe. In this book, has written he about the need for a change in the world, how few a people tend to own and control more than half of the wealth in the same world where he lives. Has written he about power, greed, and lust. Has written he also about oppression, jealousy, and vendetta. He sees how people possess power and others strive for it. Those who possess it are not in accord with their hearts to show sympathy and sorrow. They detest to be compassionate and share among their neighbors this wealth that they possess so humanity could be healed. In lieu, they are intolerable and gleeful. With tranquility and calmness, they manipulate and steal from those who own nothing. This is unbearable to him. There are things to be done for a modification of what he witnesses. To bring about a cessation of this unpleasing way of life that causes damages to the number ten times more than half of the total number of the living, he must be possessing a knack that could enable him turn water into wine. That knack to possess is not a thing to put upon to act in a rush. He must be patient because patience, he believes, is a driving force, a might blowing power in addition to a brainy plan well arranged to fight evil—that is to say, he is to await more time and years, he is to await for the next decade.

To him, even tomorrow is still a long way off. There has to be an end to this. His heart he perceives, is wounded. It is bleeding, bleeding for the sake of humanity. How could this be happening in the world while he remains speechless? A world created for all beings and animals and plants and other creatures to live in peace and harmony. Better for him his heart he could tear out and feed to the wild beasts, rather than sit and conduct an observation of the manner in which the beautiful world torpedoes. The most trivial, yet fierce, thing to do to save a life of a fellow being would be noted as the most reasonable to do in the sight of the unseen creator—the originator, and ruler of the Universe, the Universe itself. Sacrifices have to be made to save the world. Many their lives have to be rendered to please the Universe, to revive and rehabilitate humanity. Saints have to die in the fight for reconciliation with the Universe. If none are in readiness to pay a price to heal others, all, in the end, would be destroyed. How could people tend to see the light shining, yet, perpetually hold to a conception of walking away from it into darkness? What promises will they fulfill, seeing themselves there, if not imminence of danger and hopelessness and death?

Chapter 5

And there he is, Lakota. After having his book published. The same publishing company, every day him they call. They send emails of different marketing proposals for him to take up. Knows he not which of the proposals are authentically stronger and would be successful, being that it is his attempt to be in a special place. And it is not a grueling responsibility if, in actuality, he is not demanded more money, almost three times the amount he has paid for the publication. Although, prior to any agreement for the payment of publication and how he is to send the manuscripts to them, and also approve of it, more explanations, simplifications, and justifications have been laid out for him on a variety of book proposals by a variety of publishing consultants. Thence he is assured the publication fees is absolutely to do merely more than what it is intended, and also get the books marketed and sold. Later on, when more money is demanded from him, he is unable to put questions to his own faculty of thought and reason. He is unable to ask himself why he has become an individual victim of a deliberate deception by some licensed professionals working under a corporate company. Instead, he takes to the counsels of the marketing consultants, which pierce like a sword into his ears, then to the heart, and send his spirit aloft. However, penniless he is, and could not afford his rent to pay, not to mention that himself he could feed. He is exhausted and thoughtfully wants to run away from himself in order to save his soul. But his soul and body are attached to one another—so there is never a way for him to set them apart and send them on a different errand to render his life what attunes to it most. Phone calls are coming from the different men and women working in that same publishing company located in the United States.

At this very time when it is not up to six months he lost his mother. The woman he loves so much he so believes no other woman would be able to take her place in his heart; the woman he has seen once for more than fourteen years since he has left her in his country to travel abroad in an effort to seek a better future, seeing the possibilities of his future looks dim and doomed in his own country where he has been born and bred.

Lakota has not been having much contacts with his mother for the fear of not able to talk to her well, but has seldom sent her money to feed and also to spend on medications for diagnosed diabetes that later resulted into an exigent and grim form of hypertension vascular damage. With the thoughts and loss of his mother, and her ghost coming to haunt him, thence comes he is also starting to experience eyestrain, which is producing eye discomfort and headaches. It is causing severe pains on every part of his head like someone tightening a giant vice around his head and hitting it with a hammer. That pain he feels as it cut through his head to the brain. After several surgical operations on one of his eyes, still notices he a reasonable doubt of ever to sight and scan with the eye that has suffered tremendously the experience and effects of a retinal detachment eye disorder. Furthermore, pressures are mounted on him to not fail the payment on the marketing proposals designed for him by his marketing consultants. More awful news—an ultimatum is given to him.

At this very time of hopelessness and the arising fear that he will die sooner or later, there comes a lad who he never sets eyes on aforetime. In their country's embassy he has with him encountered. Perhaps, quickly, and full of trust they become good friends. At first, Lakota is unable to look to his attitude to even develop a conception in his mind he is about to align himself as a partner to a young African, who is indecent, with unclean hands, blessed with a knack of trafficking drugs around Europe, and is equipped with a medium that serves as exchange in every human needs, or as a measure of values. The lad is rich, but filthy and appears to be marked by a lack of intelligence or wisdom. When people say it is wisdom that yields wealth, it is absolutely nonsensical and deserves an encouragement for people to disbelieve and rebel against any religion they cast their faiths, because it is unjustifiable to see this happening and no intervention from the deity they worship and pray to every day and night.

Lakota is outraged, bearing witness, a manner in which his new friend lavishes money and doing it unwisely. Firstly, he believes it would be of a good notion to lecture and help him plan what would be best for him to invest. It is like, ' "Are you the one to lecture me of how I should be spending my money? See how wise you are, and still, you remain very poor?" ' In spite of the fact that the qualities and functions they both possess and exhibit in life are immeasurable afar from each other's own, but, between them is a close confidentiality and friendliness. There are calculative thoughts drifting directly and untouched down into Lakota's central nervous system, and they are to be reserved for future use. Being the good lad, he would have preferred to exert more pressure upon his friend so he could think better of how his money should be invested, but it seems any time he tries, he becomes a laughing matter to his friend and the people surrounding his friend, who in fact, are all lauding their friend for the excessive expenses.

And it came to pass, that the days of the strongest and fullest of trouble are over for him. This is the information Lakota, in a good commencement, transfers from his heart to the brain, and back to his heart as days come and go, and he is still unable to confront his own serious problem, the inability to pay for the marketing of his book. Yet, ecstatic he is, having the strong belief every a dream of his he is going to make a reality, every tribulation and uneasiness he will overcome without doubt.

Many a time, Lakota is invited to meet with his new and rich friend, who is extremely quiet and dangerous, like a dull blade that cut easily. They would drink a variety of alcoholic beverages and smoke joint of marijuana and argue over issues, that he, Lakota could see as comprehensively irrelevant.

For long, has he not taken a tough decision to quit smoking anything related to drugs, or cigarettes? Yes he has, and he has made many attempts in every way, at a time, he is becoming successful, perhaps, because it is making him spend his little savings indiscreetly, putting him into more stress and difficulties. Now, that anew he encounters a friend who purchases everything, even when he gets drunk and intoxicated with the drugs and wants to quit, they will mock him, they will do a lot of names calling. When he tries relating his callous situation of life to his new friend, for sure he is shunned and told to face life, and not to be a coward who will retreat from the wars already set for the world to fight. Thence he starts to think of a way out of this absurdity of life, devoting himself to finding the true meanings of everything he has experienced. He realizes he will never awake from the nightmare, and no matter how he tries, he could not. Perhaps, is it not he who earlier has seen himself as the man possessed with power, that power to fantasize, that power to visualize, and also to realize goals?

After many days have passed, Lakota is steady at that crucial moment to depart thence from the country where he is allowed to reside indefinitely, to go live in another country. Though penniless, though mentally and emotionally devastated completely in no way able to bear with his self-imposed tax. And so to say, it is also at this very moment his rich friend calls for him…to seek his counsel on which place would be more of a provision for environmental, physical, and financial comforts for them. To his friend, life is not about fighting, but winning, and it is always winning, and winning. As a plan is made for him to leave the next two days ahead of them to join with another lad who is providing himself with earnings by selling drugs on the street in Switzerland.

For long, swore to himself and to his gods he has, to never in any unlawful act engage. For many a time he has done it and has come to also welcome the consequences and remorse. How could he return himself to live in that world where villains live and dwell? How could he see what he sees that he wishes not to be seeing, that causes his heart to burn? How he sees the world already in chaos, and instead of walking the path that leads to healing it, he is in a plan to making more contributions to the chaos scene. Is this what he has previously planned to do after writing his book? Or, is the book not written to spread messages to others of how humanity could be redeemed?

Arrives enduringly when a night before the day set for him to leave with the small amount of money he has scrambled and tussled to get hands upon, he is contacted and convened by his friend once more, for more information on how to reach, and more lectures of what and what not to do and to do. In the context of this lecture, thence brings to light a secret his friend has long been afraid to temper with. Not minding how often Lakota has observed his friend purchasing a dog for a young teenage girl born and bred there in a country south of Europe, and also providing the food and everything for her and the dog. Or to say, how he is asking him to fetch him women of different sizes of nipples and bodies, and squandering money on them. Frankly, he has never with his own heart lend him a penny, probably because he never demands, knowing he is to be a man for himself, he is to think of how to make life for himself, not depending on anyone. To speak genuinely, his every thoughts and inventive skills are to find a way into his friend's pocket in order to remove the money. Thus, whatever he is encountering during all these many a time when they are together, he is turned into a server, a drudge, an attendant, and an assistant, he holds firmly and steadfastly to his purpose. He declines to relinquish, knowing time will come when it will be a story to be told, when it will be a laughing joke among themselves, how he has fooled and belittled himself to a stark illiterate who is unable to spell his first name, thinking he knows it all, thinking he is the boss, for he has made money selling drugs on the street.

People like that he has seen before and apperceives what they are capable of: they relish to be seen, they show a tremendous admiration for everyone nearer to them, and most in particular, to women.

Not so surprising, when this special friend of his lay down an offer for him, asking if he would be able to swallow three hundred grams of cocaine and travel to meet the friend he has previously introduced to him, who lives in Swiss. Could refuse he not to accept this offer, seeing it is of a prodigious opportunity for him to swallow them and divert it to another place for a good and reasonable sales. So, he accepts in a prompt attempt. Meanwhile, another offer has also been brought to table. His name and surname are demanded. But he has to question the motive for this—which he is made aware someone in Swiss will be sending some money to them to be used in the effectuation of their new planned deal. Being the lad is undocumented, he needs to use Lakota's name, who is legal in the country, to collect the money.

Within him, Lakota's heart is overwhelmed with intense and exultant happiness, casting his vision into his future, believing the Universe to be in control of his life once again, believing the gods and goddesses to be attentively listening to all his cries and clamors. Sees he from a distance as he stares deep and deep, the darkness becoming light, and all his troubles washing away.

The next day, not far from the morning time he is phoned by his friend to get himself prepared to meet with him to collect the money. He is told to come to his house for them to go there in company. This Lakota agrees to. And he goes straight to meet with him at home. Believing they are leaving without delay to go collect the money. But, surprisingly, notices he how his friend is rolling another joint of marijuana to smoke. He, Lakota, is calm and still, in a pretense he seems not to be in a hurry. Perhaps, when the joint of marijuana is passed to him to take a puff, he has to reject it. He has to reject it, because well enough he knows he is on a dangerous mission that could also alter his fate, which, inevitably, is necessary for him at that particular time. He waits for his friend to be done with his smoking. Far downward in his heart, he is poised to confront whatever obstacles that would cause him to give up his tentative project. Therefore, he waits, waits, and waits, and all of a sudden, he could perceive as his friend arises from the sofa, where he sits, waving for him to come with him outside. Reaching outside, he is told he has called him out for other people out there no to get to any understanding of the adventurous game they are about to set out on to play. And immediately that is said, they depart thence.

At the money transfer agent's office, they are told it is not the right place. They are given a different address to collect the money. Meanwhile, his friend who has never mentioned the little girl he has sympathetically and keenly lavished money to alter her bad and poor life situation, is also going to collect another sum of money for him.

At this instant, when Lakota's friend becomes held in fatigue, being unable to think with clarity, which person he would have to confide in to finish the task with a favorable outcome—the teenage girl or Lakota? Perhaps the lad is in a bounteous favor of leaving Lakota to the task alone due to how much trust and confidence and reliance he has built on him. So he leaves him and goes to meet the teenage girl in a different place.

Lakota, seeing how this lad has placed upon him reliance and trust, leaving him to do the execution of the task all alone by himself, with nobody watching and following him in order for him not to steal the money. His heart becomes subjected to repeated beatings; his heart is set in a convulsive fit of shaking, quivering, and vibrating—that he could no longer move his feet. To him, he has aforetime given up every of his objective to take on this action, being that he is followed by his friend every little step, every little move he makes, with no little space. Now, it is that same person pinning his hope and faith on him to swiftly get everything done and come show him the result. He could not believe his eyes, as he walks along the street, speaking in tongues to himself till the time he arrives at the very address he is told to go look for, he is barely unaware.

As he enters into the office and demands for the money, he is told the numbers are incomplete. He phones his friend to inquire and told to wait for him. But to Lakota, waiting for him would be to say he is the stupidest among the many insane and clever peasants who are not quite different from the silly buffoons living their lives and dying in the many prisons around the globe. How could he ever be able to deal with this episode and live with it, even, as doubt enters into his consciousness? What is the conviction he has to offer the gods and goddesses who guild him and have offered him with a wonderful opportunity as this, for not taking a chance and making good use of it? Either he would have to set things in estimation to let this chance for an advancement slips away, or simply and mildly and pleasantly accept this as a priceless gift from a considerable distance in which the Universe watches him.

Knowing his friend will be there shortly, which will tell the end of the whole story, Lakota takes a good look at the numbers again. He adds one more number to it, which is nine. The form he fills out. He submits it to the cashier, who looks very closely and carefully, doing a thorough checking and stamping the form, then handling over a bundle of euro notes, which he could not wait to know if it is the exact money. Not even watching his back, he sets out. He walks straight away to take the underground train. And there he is, on the train, with his pocket loaded with a bundle of money, his heart flipping and flopping, and his soul lost in the wilderness, unfound.

However, successfully and boldly, at some later time he has made it home. Straight, he goes into his room after greeting his roommates, who sit on the sofa, watching soccer after gambling their money on games. The door of his room he locks from inside. He brings out the money and starts counting. Looking at the money in his both hands—the fresh smell of the banknotes are beyond what is ordinary. He proceeds with the counting. When he is done, knowing it is the exact amount he expects, he sits down, picking up his phone which he has long switched off. He phones his friend, who, at that very time, fathoms he is inevitably in a six-foot grave dug by himself. He tells him to be calm, and that things are in order. He tells him to wait for him in his house while he hurries to meet with him. The phone he drops down, gets himself in the course of opening his one big handbag and another bigger piece of luggage. All his belongings, he packs inside. As he is about to leave the house, his friends, he quickly makes aware he is traveling to visit his girlfriend whom they always refer to as: "Never-before-seen-by-anybody."

He sees how they are still debating, as their voices produce sounds of high volume, he leaves, closing the door behind him.

Meanwhile, two of his roommates, who depend on him for supports and financial assistance, for some days before that day, have both come to the conclusion to keep with a plan for manipulating him, believing he is always the cheerful giver who will not relent. They have insulted him, called him names, and demand he pays the bigger share of their expenses. This he only finds obtuse and not graceful when he starts to reflect on the different approaches he has taken to get them out of the innumerable struggles and troubles they have seen themselves prior to this time. There is not any mentioned way a man could pass, or any code of some excessive hardship he would break to release his fellow humans from confinement— that they still will not at the same instant see him as their worst foe. If it has happened to Jesus, the man who has come only because he thought he could see the people he loves, suffer and die as a consequence of their many sins and evil deeds, thinks he could save them. They refuse to accept him, and what next?—Nail him to the cross and grant freedom to a robber who will vandalize their houses, rape their women, and take from them their money, or even slaughter them. It is not a good thing to be too good every time. It is not also that to be good is not good. It is that many, many a being do not in point of fact deserve any a kind of assistance from their fellow being for an improvement in life; they do not deserve it, instead, what they wish for, is what should be given to them—and that which they wish for, is always ignoring them when you see them drowning and are at the points of getting into their graves, simply because, that is certainly what they deserve. And so also to say, there are very many out there, who with sincere and authentic hearts, will appreciate any favor rendered to them, yet, they never would be able to come across such a favorable circumstance. And some, who are very appreciative and do have the opportunity and grace, and are being lend a helping hand, would encourage the man with a good heart to continue doing all that is good, not regarding how he is to be repaid. It is not that there are still no saints. There are very many, but, in a world today we now live—a world where evil dominates and the good and beautiful hearts are being burned into aches, we hardly practically pick the good pictures to be able to distinguish between the vicious and the saints. But in all, well, we must keep doing good things. We must keep helping others, for the more we do, the less burden we are to carry in our hearts, and moreover, the happier we become steep down.

Chapter 6

Immediately, as Lakota leaves the house with his hand luggage, including his small laptop computer. Takes he a bus directly to the capital city of the country, since it is not far from the city he lives. This he has done deliberately, due to the fact knows he he would hardly be seen by his compatriots who might recognize him. There finds he a very cheap hotel, one of the cheapest in the city, and stays for the night.

Not quite long after he has checked into the hotel, then receives he text messages—threats of death and many abusive words from his friends around the city—these people, who, in point of fact, are not the owner of the money, and are totally unaware of how the whole issue is given birth, but they are extremely intense and longing to meet with him for their shares of the money. This he is unable to penetrate the meaning of, why a grievous risk he would have to take to render a compensation to others for the sake of being more powerful and vicious. Could not help he get to the bottom of what is amiss at this very moment of his life. Could look he aback how the friendship with his friend all started with trust and alliance—the promises he has made to help the lad expand his drug business and also develop and figure out what possible and easy business they could both invest in if eventually they arrive with a sweet smell of success by being able to raise and accumulate the funds. Could look he aback how they used to laugh, smoke, and drink, while steep down he has been with a machination to steal from him, to steal from him to execute his own plans. Could see he he is virtually ill-natured and mean, even more than these people he has for so long decried and counselled against who are leading the world into a state of separation from humanity and the Universe wholly for them to champion the notion of letting greed dominate their every plans. Could see he he is playfully malicious and a wicked wit who counsels one thing and does another—a hypocrite, a Pharisee—pretending to be what he is not, advocating and attacking the reputation of the leaders around the globe for possession of the qualities of greed and power. Now, himself he sees as one of them; himself he sees as the real evil that lives among men and must be eliminated.

Then he switches off his phone and takes time to do a thorough check of his heart to see to it. He rapidly comes to a conclusion to return the money to his friend. Knows he that is the sole remedy, the possible way out for him to take away the burden in his heart and fortify his soul to progress with his journey of healing, rather than causing havoc.

Coming to a conclusion to return the money, then also evaluates the worth of the banknotes he holds, and preeminently, his rational motive for stealing the money at the initial time. If not he needs the money for an enormous problem in need of an urgent and effective solution. In his book, he has written money should not has to be a curse, instead, it has to be a blessing—all these, are due to a manner in which, he has suffered, and money has later come to his rescue in reaching his objectives. Now that he is holding this bundle of money and thinking what to do with it—whether to return it to the rightful owner, or to spend it on his planned project, he discerns the reason the love of money is said to be the root of all evil. Unarguably, it is. There is a rite of confirmation by every soul if truly we want to utter the truth and think we will be able to heal our wounded world.

And, as Lakota's heart uninterruptedly beats and arrives at a non-stopping juncture, he observes how some unknown voices advance and wander about this heart of his, disputing between themselves. Thence remains he silent and calm a bit, to pay careful attention to this natural event inside him. He acknowledges two abnormal creatures give birth in his heart, and both are in conflict with each other. One of them is calm, has a smiling face, advocates compassion, love, hope, and forgiveness—while the other, is aggressive, worried, and advocates revenge, anger, ego, fame, pride, and all the evil things in the world. Lakota knows these are the voices of the unseen and unknown gods and goddesses—and he knows it is between evil and good. Which way he is to follow, and this would ultimately define his future.

Not to come to a quick conclusion that will wrongly land him into a more sympathetic awe and obliquity more than the one he is previously swimming and drowning in with no possible hope of climbing out. Knows he has to reconsider it to desirable, a good, proper, close, and careful examination. He throws a question at himself:

'"Returning this money to the owner, where else would I ever get the money to market and sell my book?"'He is quiet for a moment before responding: ' "Nowhere, absolutely nowhere."' Then, pauses he for a moment, and adds another question, ' "Am I evil for being too passionate about life and writing a book? Is this what life is all about, for humans to choose passion for their professions over compassion for their fellow humans? Is this not greed in the sight of the living God, the Creator and beginner of life that lives in the hearts of us all and always available to speak to us exclusively if we are willing to put our ears down for him? The essence of passion over compassion, is it not what is destroying humanity that we factually do not seek to arrive at a comprehension?"' Then again, he replies, ' "Yes, this is the problem of the world—materialism has sunk into our hearts and blood to a degree it now becomes a culture and makes us no longer care for our dying fellow humans—and this is greed which has become a natural state of man by his own will. And it corrupts us, ruins lives, and steals from us. Now, to us it remains, to find a way to eliminate it from our minds, and from our society, if indeed we will ever think of losing our senses of possession. And to say, the real differences between these two—passion and compassion, is that one will lead you to poverty if you are not careful enough, while the other will liberate you from that poverty and welcome you to a world of possession and power. So, it is up to you which way you wish to walk along."'

With much contemplation on what is necessary for him to do next when after he has sat and stood and sat and stood for a while, commences he to recall how he first met his friend and a lot of unnecessary explanation did he to him his every critical situation to see whether there is any way he might be influenced by something to make him possess that spirit of empathy to render him a help. On the contrary, what did he gain if not drinks and drugs and humiliation and degradation? Thence, suddenly, as he is still in his thought process, with tears streaming out of his two eyes, knowing even if he is not fighting to revenge, but the money he does need to work out a solution to his problem, and he needs it more than the moron who is addicted to lavishing. And moreover, he thinks it will be of a good idea if in actuality he hesitates to return the money to the lad, as per say, the lad is a man with the nature of vice, not only to make money, but also to destroy anybody close to him. This he knows when the lad tries to lure him to swallow cocaine and travel with it to another country. He was about to make afresh of him a drug trafficker once again—a life he has long quit and vows never to return to live. Lakota is in a state of lamentation and very much regretful of the actions he is about to embark on, for he has constantly thought it to be right for a man to do all that is kind to mortality, and now it is he, again, trapped in a circle of greed. But, is it not the greatest opportunity imaginable offering itself to him? Yes, it is. There is a need for him to accomplish his longtime dream, the dream to help win the world back and give humanity what it deserves. Yes, it is the time, the only available and precise time, and he could see himself in a crossroad where tough decision is needed to be taken, one that would either become a hindrance to his future, or smooth the path for his dream to materialize. And when this decision is being made, there shall be no going back. So, it is a charge for him to make the proper decision.

After much thoughts, Lakota counts the money once again. Seeing it is 3,000 euros. Of which, literally, he is in necessity of 900 euros to get his book into marketing—a course he believes would change his life forever. Thence swiftly he leaves the hotel he is to stay for the night, and with his luggage, walks he straight to a money transfer agent where he did send 2,500 euros to his sister, who is living in the northern part of the country, near France. After that is done, the money has been sent, he walks to the bus station where he purchases a bus ticket and departs that very night, forgetful of the money formerly paid to stay for the night in the hotel.

To his vast surprise, he sees himself in a different city after having slept for four hours on the bus, and is much more delighted for not having met anyone known to him before, from the beginning of the trip to when he arrives there. That he counts as a progress on the account no one would inform his friend, who has become his greatest foe, and is hunting for him, dead or alive.

Lakota arrives at the bus station—with some of the money he has stolen, which are still in his pocket. Without patience, enters into a café and orders a cup of coffee and a spicy deli-style salami sandwich, which he pounces on and munches hungrily and pleasurably, sipping his coffee conscientiously and mildly. He eats to his satisfaction, or even more so, and leaves some uneaten. Thence, he makes a call to his elder sister who lives there, the same person he has also sent the larger part of the stolen money. He tells her he would be in the city sooner or later, and that he is traveling to another city, but has decided to pay a one hour visit before he would have to proceed further with his trip. That she is heedless of the mission her brother has contained and incorporated himself, she welcomes him to her house any a time he feels is necessary. Perhaps, he is still there at the big luxury café, eating all sorts of categorized sandwiches and drinking coffee and other beverages to digest everything. At the café, he stays, stays, and is never tired of throwing the money, which have to be his, generously in purchasing and eating and eating. Delightfully impressed with all his efforts for having stolen the money, although the troubles, which are inevitable parts of life that would befall him in time to emanate. He has never had any thought about it. He has never had any thought about it, for he has never formulated in his mind if his friends would ever be able to have a contact with him or anyone related to him.

In his sister's house…soon after at the final point, he is able to disclose what he has come upon and how the whole money is in her possession at that instant. Finally, in a position of let-what-will-be-to-be she holds. Later after when the money is successfully given to them by the money transfer agent, there comes merrymaking and an attitude of no remorse. It gives the impression of how money is to be a solution to every human problem, experiencing how easily he is able to convince his own sister and comes to win her supports and encouragements. They all need the money for many reasons, and it is principally for him to finance his projects, and also to assist their family in Africa who, in accordance with truth, are very much in lack of financial assistance. According to what genuinely he is to be preoccupied with, the condition and situation of his family back in Africa, who wholly are living below poverty line, and it is causing his heart to break every a day and every a night. This naturally has been from the beginning of his life, a priority, and it is the chief reason he has departed thence from his own country to travel abroad in an effort to search for a better future for himself and his family at home—his brothers and sisters. Not that he has not attempted everything, in every way, in his best effort, to do what is needed to be done to assist them and clear the way of poverty from their lives. But the more attempts he makes, the more they demand, at a time his heart and soul have become so feeble and ill, as they have brought upon themselves the curse placed on the ignorant family Lakota also finds himself. That the woman he has loved so much is dead, the woman who is also his angel and goddess whom he worships every day—his mother. This has been sad and unfortunate for him, so, this has led him to hang onto a thought there is never a need for him to put on himself any blame for not taking responsibility for these people's adverse fate. The most severe of it all is, he could see his own father who possess very many land properties worth millions of his country's currency, and thousands of dollars—and these properties he could share among the children, and they would, significantly, become rich and not experience a lack of financial stability again. On the contrary, the old man, who thus lives on, way beyond his hundred year. Even when he is in a very bad state of health, yet, in every possible way, he is striving to possess the ability to preserve his land properties for who no one knows. The more this old man endeavors to preserve these properties, the easier it is for people from outside the family, who are richer and influential, to ruthlessly steal them, and they do it with impunity. To some of the old man's children, it is insanity, while, to others, it is greed. Howbeit, to Lakota, it is both. It is insanity, and it is also greed.

He sees the old man, the man said to be his own father who he has once loved during his childhood, so dearly, even more than his own mother, when in actuality, life is still very like a fairytale to him, when at that very early age in life he is lacking the necessary power to perceive with intellect the intent and purpose of life; at that time in life when he is still not in a position to be able to distinguish between fiction and reality, nor could he be able to distinguish between evil and good; it is at a time in life when he could see his mother to be of an impediment to his every success in life, merely because she is harsh and cruel and is always unwilling to be of any good assistance to tolerance, trying to prevent him from walking closer to danger, while he is enamored by his father love of his passion for anything he sets his sights on doing, and doing it perfectly.

Henceforth, it is this old man he comes to deem a miser, a man who would have enough to feed the world and yet, would be starving to death and not admit it. The most unfavorable fact of the story is, after a while that Lakota's mother departed to the land of the saints and never will be seen again by any human born of a woman, he has painfully regretted not being too close and having frequent conversations with her—the woman no woman in life, he believes, could take her place in his heart. Painfully regrettable and devastating is the loss of that woman to him, which has made him vow the sole, viable means for her to renounce her anger against him and not send her ghost to haunt him for the certainty she has loved him more but never has been able to have a good contact and communication with him. From thence onward, solemnly Lakota has pledged to maintain a constant availability for taking measures and supplying means of subsistence for the family, most specifically, his father, and also to be in a good contact—all to appease his dead mother wherever she might be.

Frequently he phones is father and shares memorable times and jokes with him in an attempt to alleviate the grief and sorrow of his lost wife. With the little interaction he has with him, he never hesitates to send him some money and also offers hopes and courage for a better time promising to meet with him sooner when things get better for him, and also tearfully pleading for him not to be fretful about the situation they are. Albeit, his father has never for a day made up his mind to come forth with the discussion of his worthy land properties that might create a better opportunity for the entire family and give a chance for a new life to begin. And, Lakota is never in a position to come up with such a question, for he neither would assume something similar to that, nor would he not hold to doubt when informed by another person. He proceeds with these supports and assistance until the actual day the news reached him of how his father's eldest son, born to him by his first wife, has been able to convince someone to purchase a very small part of the properties and earned a very reasonable amount of money for himself. Although this lad, who is the eldest of all the male children and the mostly favored—a crook who has later become his father's best friend on the basis of strongly affixing himself to his father's will to be initiated in the same secret society with him—in truth, he formerly has come to fix in his mind most of the properties are to be willed to him naturally, according to their native laws and customs after his father might have passed away. Nevertheless, impatience finds a way into his life, seeing the properties taken from them by different people, and besides, their father is beginning to lay complaints to them, instead of doing that to the police force or suing them. And by so doing, putting their lives in peril, by urging them to go fight for him. They all become fed up and lost interest in this issue. Every a day their father would not cease to complain about his poverty, and yet, would not think of helping himself with the properties he owns that are about to be looted away by people who strongly believe they are having a clue of the worth.

At a time so contradictory and unexpected, when Lakota is provided with the information by his sister of what has transpired, it is a nightmare from which he could not wake. He could, in swiftness, recall how his father grumbles, while expressing feelings of his dissatisfaction for not being properly cared for, due to the fact he could not, by himself, afford a cell phone. He, Lakota, could not accept to believe the information that is being passed into his ears that would change the course of his life, and incline to his own will, but not to the will of others.

Lakota patiently listens for some minutes in awed silence to his sister, in a manner in which she utters the words out of her mouth, while his own psyche takes a journey aback to how he and his other brothers born to his father by his mother. At the time their father is engulfed by debt and could not find a way out, they have taken to their will, with obligation, with no remorse, laid down their lives to work day-in and day-out on the farm with their father to cultivate those lands—and that is precisely the opportunity thrown to the old man to secure and preserve these valuable land properties. Not that he finds fault with his father's conception to continuously preserve those properties for the future, but for how long would he be fighting a persistent battle for land properties? The old man is ill, even at his point of death, and thus far, he would not show any a sign of relenting. Is it insanity, or is it greed? This is a question in which he could not find an answer. In all perspectives entail, he deems his father to be a destroyer, not a builder. In his heart, he could hardly find a place in it for any exoneration for the old man; he could not, because he could not; he could not because the old man is in a true and faithful manner, setting a war for the children after he might have died.

A will, which is said to be a legal declaration of the way a person wishes his or her properties and possessions to be disposed of after death. Even if this is written, it would serve as a no-good purpose when you have been placed in a position of having many children to whom you cannot cater, or marrying more than one wife and making them live somberly. How is it ever going to end if not without doubt the whole children would be at war with each other? And this de facto has been a weighty and pressing issue that never has been addressed or attended to by these Africans in order for them to start to engage in experiential practices and seek enlightenment to rewrite and update these traditions and customs that are not heading to prosperity or peace, neither are they leading to cooperation within family members. It is always wars within families and communities in Africa for no other reasons to be explained rather than fighting over land properties left for them by their parents or ancestors. If it happens a man cannot build and live in his house with peace amongst his family, then how would there be any possibility to see men build and live in a community with peace amongst all households?—to live and share meals and accommodations together, showing no detestation and malignity among themselves? How will it ever occur, any possibility, to see in any history of man, in a way men will be able to live and build a nation with love and peace afloat, or not to mention worldwide? The world is doomed—humanity is doomed—we are all doomed, if we still cannot find a common ground to put aside little differences and rebuild heaven here on Earth. It is not that we are fully to blame for all our actions, in the sense the generations before have brought this upon us. They have made us believe we must strive for everything to survive, we must treat ourselves with hatred and no compassion, and believe we own things that belong to our neighbors and never allow them to be in possession of them. They have made us believe in differences amongst ourselves by placing material things amid us in which to fight— thereby prompting us to loathe and despise each other. Those who can see clearly and are wise enough to discern the true significance of this ideal, have come to find a way to repeal it. To the favored, this ideal, is to them, a conception of something in its absolute perfection, a thing regarded by them as a model of excellence, a goal we must strive to achieve, a desired object, a worthy principle to be seen as guidelines to follow to perfection and achievements. This ideal, which in afterward, does establish and place power on some very few people, making them fearless and stronger than the rest. This power becomes an instrument for controlling others, and it is wrongfully attained by these same people, who instill fear in the hearts and minds of those they wish to control. But, it is those who are wise enough that have come to observe this conspicuously as a way to lure us into materialism; they have come to see a substantial reason to arbitrate and put in preference another way far less destructive that serve for the good purpose of humanity. These wise ones have foreseen this ideal and fathom it is to lead humans into creating enmity amongst themselves; so they have come to refrain from it—refrain from an ideal made to strive for a main purpose to live a life more gracious and deluxe than our neighbors. As we live and relish this ideal, we watch our neighbors dying and we mock them. The bitter and unpleasant part about this ideal is it is created and designed not to favor everybody, but the few, amongst which majority, if not possessing quality of being morally bad, they will be striving to. And, come to look at the most perturbing side of it, in striving to take little of what belongs to them with all their passion and much focus and relentless hard work, the good people, everything they have worked for from the beginning to where they are, crumbles and fades away, and then they become a whisper, a ghost, a memory, and are seen no more. How horrible and terrible it is to observe and affirm how an ideal destroys people and you cannot, in any way, get rid of it?

In a precise description, this equates to the intentions of Lakota's father, to create amongst his children a future with disputes and hate. It is this in which Lakota realizes, he must refrain. He has to refrain in order to live a different life and be very far from them all. But first, he has to refrain from his father, not even bringing to mind the some of his own documents of the properties his father possesses and helps him protect, which he has never sought his permission before the attempts.

Later that afternoon, the second day he arrives in his sister's house and is in a jolly mood with her and his two beautiful and lovely nieces. The house is replenished with food and drinks in addition to what his sister has purchased forthwith she is informed about his visit. Life is always splendid and worth living when liquid assets get involved. His book marketing consultant, with a celerity he phones, and when he is asked the reason for the call, says he to them he is primed to make the payment for the marketing—which sends a sign of joy straight to the heart of the consultant, since for long they have almost given up hope he would be unable to afford it. Perhaps, he too has given up the notion of placing himself in a situation where he is sadly attempting to paint a beautiful picture of clear and marvelous expectations in future, but the situation is with no excusable circumstance, aligned with frustration, grief, and sorrow. It compels him to send a stern warning to them to stop disturbing him with the frequent phone calls, knowing he would never get the money.

After when all were done, the payment is felicitous and could regard he himself triumphant, who has exercised a quantum leap to send his ghost to the land where he wishes it to be. There in his sister's house, from death arises celebration to life. They celebrate in a manner so tranquil and unheard of by the nearest soul sitting closer to them. Then, of course, a message is reached to his nervous system. He recalls his proposed course to send money to every of his brother and sister. With no delay, stands he and is very much relaxed, after a formidable task having put to execution and implementation an attractive and fascinating history to rewrite—that would later turn to become mournful in the end. He runs with no hindrance straight to an agency for money transfer where he sends 300.00 euros to his family.

Returning to meet his sister, who also is a bit worried about his brother leaving the house to meet up with his old friends and showering them with money. He informs her of how he has sent to their family in Africa some money. She is profoundly delighted, and at the same time delightfully profound, expressing her gratitude as if there is a lump-sum of benefit she is to derive.

In some minutes, at a later time than when all the calls to Africa are made and the money is been shared among his brothers and sisters, and as well, his father, he leaves for the city center to pick up some clothes in a boutique. He also purchases a clipper for cutting his hair. Later that evening, even before imparting to his sister any information he would be leaving the country the next day, he purchases a flight ticket to travel to Belgium.

Astonishment and bewilderment successfully find a way to arrive in his sister's heart promptly as she is notified of the trip. She is worried about this. She becomes worried even more than he, who is traveling to a place he knows nothing about, or rather, if he has somebody there to house him in the new country. As there is no way she could bring about a conviction to make him stay in the city and spend the remaining part of the money wisely and not send himself into an impoverished world once again, she wishes him the best of luck in life and advises him to leave some of the money so he could always call from anywhere, anytime when he is in need. This he has done. That same night, he picks up his luggage once again and leaves to take the bus to travel to the capital city where he could board a flight to Brussels, Belgium.

While in Belgium, after having committed himself to multitudinous trifles and strenuous efforts, and afterward, that he comes to see himself through, he rents a room in an apartment owned by another African in the city of Liege. The apartment which is filthy and always having an unpleasant odor, indeed, is a place he comes to proudly appreciate. No matter how much he pays, it is quintuple the worth of the room and the entire apartment. He sleeps, wakes up, and leave for the city to find a job. Soon after, he would reappear at the place he calls home and sleep. Even though he has to pay a lot for everything but, he is glad he found a place to live and pays monthly, after having spent three days, paying for a hotel, which is twice as expensive as the monthly rent. So enraptured he is and more hopeful to achieve his objective in the country, seeing how things move gradually in a planned way. Perhaps, there is this other thing, he also fathoms things are moving well and smoothly thanks to the money in his pocket.

At this very point in time, suddenly comes a wave of mystery and threats of death into his life. When would life, for once, be fair to him, or be pleasant for him? When would the day come when he is going to enjoy the desirable things in life and never fret about the next day to be deeply encountered with tremendous misfortune and unhappiness? Why is his fate entangled in a series of conflicts and unending miseries? Why is he always the unwanted one by the people of the world? Or is it that he has long offended the gods and goddesses for them to lay a curse upon him? Or is it that the Universe has created and composed his fate this way for a purpose in the future? If so, for what purpose would it be—that he is been denied of any valuable thing hidden in human life, prompting him to come also denies the existence of a true world, a true world where one shall fancy and recognize a family of his own, where one shall fancy and recognize his children growing up with him, a world where a woman shall place around her waist his arms and place around his neck her two arms and hold him so closely and kisses him softly and tenderly? When shall he ever experience that world, that true world?

And it came to pass, this very hour when his elder sister, with who he has left some money and has departed from her house to another country on the path to seek a possibility of getting a job, since, in the country where he could legally work is turning into a city even the teenagers born and bred there are fleeing for their lives to other countries, for they are in an escape of hunger and starvation after an economic turmoil which is almost about to tear the country into pieces.

When his sister phones to unveil the stress and strain she is undergoing due to the many threats and intimidation posed to her from the friends he has lived with before in the same apartment in the capital city, where he has stolen someone's money. He could not consider it true; everything he is detailed—his roommates are skillful and shrewd enough to stumble upon one of the phone he has dumped in a garbage can. They have inserted a SIM card to find his two sister's phone numbers. They are phoning and threatening to deprive her of life if ever she is unsuccessful to provide information on her brother's whereabouts.

To Lakota, when the names of the people posing these threats are mentioned, he is startled and disappointed. Thus, for the sake of healing humanity, some time ago he has rendered his last penny to keep them alive. Now, he has successfully deceived someone else and stolen his money, they all fancy he would become the Good Samaritan once again, as he is always trained pretty forwardly to be. And as he has placed them all in unfulfilled expectations, they all want a piece of him, they all want a piece of his flesh. Despite that he is running to avoid all these distortions and uncomfortableness, he still is able to send two of them 100.00 euros. But why is it always so the people you love so much and fight for, are also the ones to persecute and prosecute you? They will perpetually acquaint themselves with you, making you think of them as true friends, but elimination is always their machination.

As many a call of threats reach his two sisters to provide him—dead or alive, so too are calls and emails reaching him from his publishing company in the U.S., for him to sign and fax papers and documents existing in various forms to them. Not only to say what has turned out for him is a misfortune, but that more difficulties arise, as the money he has left in his account in care of his sister is seized by the Central Bank for having failed to pay his annual income tax return for some years passed.

Right, and behold, in reality, everything becomes extremely frightening since he is starting to develop inside of him the feelings of aversions and becomes upset with his own soul for having brought his family into a dangerous incident like this. Their phone numbers he demands and rings the lads, using his phone number in Belgium, insulting their intelligence and asking them to come get him in there. All these he has done in order to calm them, and divert their attentions from his family to himself.

With all these drama and commotions, he comes to perceive the wonderful mysteries behind the world of art, the challenges faced by artists and what drives them to madness, and most to an exceptional degree the parts of their spirit, soul, and body that are being exploited and extracted from them, by them.

"'There is something about this book,'" he says to himself. ' "There is something beyond his own explanation and the human comprehension, and it is mysterious. It is mysterious—a book that is written under an adverse condition, as an epic story of himself, which he is the protagonist, and also the antagonist, who is in opposition to other protagonists who are leading the world into a state of disorder and chaos. It is a book in which he has taken all the converted heat inside of him and mixes it with ill-feeling, humiliation, cry for justice, and all the struggles and scuffles he and other less privileged people have experienced, and afterward putting them into writing. The book is mysterious because, as he writes and is being guided by his guiding angels, inspirations are pouring in as many terrifying events and crisis unfold around the globe. And he laments at a time his mind is in a general state of alarm, but he is more concerned and sympathizes with humankind.'"

At this particular time, his mind he would have to draw away from the thought of yielding to the fear he has come to realize. Rather he, this fear he overcomes, or dies he in it. Grasps he everything so quickly, knows he, it is the time, the precise and accurate time to move forth. Thereupon, after from his sister having been able to secure some money to purchase a ticket, takes he all his belongings and departs thence to the nearest country, Holland—where spends he three days and leaves eventually to return to where he has previously run away, a place he becomes scared of, a place crime is becoming so rampant for the lack of job and financial assistance. It is a country in South Europe, it is Italy. But never will he make the stupid mistake the capital city to return to where he once lived. Instead moves he to live in another city with one of his old pals.

With his old pal who with another lad, is also residing and flourishing, there, they are all with one accord, paying the rent together and going to their various employment destinations, or whatever they wish to go do outside. While, at later on, he gets baffled, as every a day he wakes up and sees the two lads enter their car and drive to purchase used cars they would then load with clothes and other electronic equipment to send to Africa. He would watch them purchase more cars, clothes, and electronic equipment, and then question them on how he could get involved in the business. He would then be delivered a lecture on how the business is done and instructed on the manual labor aid he should offer them to contribute to the effectiveness and improvement of the different business activities in which they are engaged. He observes them cautiously as he peers into their eyes, trying to discern what their actual plans for him genuinely is. Hence, he becomes certain they are mocking him, mocking him for having stolen an overwhelming amount of money and not knowing in what to invest. They probably mock him for the fact one of them possesses the money being paid in a business transacted with Lakota long ago. Notwithstanding, the lad, in earlier time, has his explanation on how the whole thing has flopped, and he, Lakota, is forced to believe, hence he is not there at the final hour the deal is negotiated and carried out.

Lakota spends a great deal of time with both friends, squandering the little money in his pocket, feeding them, with promises of paying him back as soon as their goods are sold in Africa. Once again, he arrives in a position of inadequate quality and is unable to cater to himself and figure out what is amiss. Once again, he finds himself miserable and pathetic, analyzing the past and present, and desiring a reversal that could design and contrive his life.

The two foolish wise men, who have been, amusingly, clever enough to have gulled and later conveyed him into wretchedness, are now spontaneously becoming enemies of themselves, fighting and commissioning in altercations, and also divulging their illicit acts to others. The more the feuds continue, as they wrangle amongst themselves, the more Lakota becomes aware how they have met with their fortune to enjoy the good life they live. When at the end one of them unveils how his other friend has been spending the money Lakota has worked hard for with his friend some months ago, like in a state of mental meltdown, he finds himself. And the more he speculates about it every day, the more he becomes depressed with boredom as he thrusts into solitude. Knowing well he has consistently attempted to give of wisdom and cunning a proof, he is beginning to question himself, if in a matter of fact, he does merit to be treated in this manner by friends. At the same time, recollecting all the past memories how he has dealt with another friend—the one he has stolen from—whether it is untrustworthy, or at least inhumane. However, he is more engrossed in deep thoughts, and an ability to puzzle out why, he, Lakota, is fated to be poor and sympathetic, presumably, it is the work of the Universe. While in this insane and solitary latitude and longitude, he could visualize a fatal crash between the gods and goddesses living above humanity, and how it has come about he is experiencing a mortal blow in his head by one of the gods for having bestowed upon himself an uncalled for task. Before long, perceives he, in certainty, a sacrifice he needs to make, and for no apparent reason whatsoever he needs to think twice, solely to roll the dice and be free, be free like a bird to fly, to fly so high to a different world unknown to humanity.

Chapter 7

And there is a beautiful and small local tiled road—tiles with glossy surfaces to reflect light coming from the sun, neither hot nor hurtful to the body; walketh along this road few more a people, wearing orchid purple silk robes, and are all they like priests and priestesses; walketh they towards a very big, purple house fenced round with designated black painted wrought-iron fences—compared to those in Buckingham Palace—the beautiful, wide compound provideth trees with green leaves and are spaced between one another like a park; from the grass carpet cometh clouds of purple smoke, as walketh around all they beautiful people, holding hands, chanting, and chatting happily and humorously; glory comes in existence, so is splendor, so is beauty, so is majesty, but above all, is love and compassion amongst they all; understanding they shareth, and with each other there is certitude, and they are stabilized, as talketh they politely—some baskets holding they full of variety of fruits unknown, and shareth with each other, laughingly; a good place to live, it is, a good place so ever to live and dwell. It is splendid. Everywhere turneth ye thy eyes, are lights—pure white lights, coming from nowhere. The people all, same height, almost the same age. There are neither old, nor are there young. However, all in the same form with grey hair. Men are in a different form from women, but in togetherness are all without separation or segregation, and living happily under the warm temperate weather. They, some ye see playeth harps whilst on a cloud lyeth, whilst they some ye see playeth, standing, and others they sitteth. The most satisfactory and best observation and understanding of it all is there is no night...but it is all the same with a glamour sky that yields a beautifully bright spring day.

The entering of every a person into this compound, and later into a very big hall, quietly and amicably, are carried through without pride or prejudice. There are men and women showing the way to the lord and master of the house, who, stands upright and watches meticulously and solicitously, surrounded by some hundreds of celestial beings. Then bows he to welcome every a soul to a kingdom meant for all—the kingdom known as "The Kingdom of the Immortals."

While sits everyone around El gran maestro, with eagerness to listen to his doctrines, what emerges from one of the unsealed and cleared room, a white dove that, in some seconds, transforms into a light that shines far and wide and altering the place to become clearer and illuminated.

Many who are there a new are swept off by the wind of consternation; hopes of everlasting dreams by many are steamed with poisons and salt altogether; truths become lies, and lies become truths; eagles fly far from above to set free the little dangerous mouse trapped in human hearts—and courage is restored and administered and questioned.

Among these many celestial beings, are Lakota and Kadosh, who on the outside of simplification and skepticism, are thunderstruck and speechless to attain any ability to derive any rational motive from anyone who would be willing to utter a word to them. This inability to discern their complex situation is shooting out from a gun, some bullets, and directing them to their heads, making them swim afloat in a pool of blood; and their brains become practically inconsistent.

Words, there are none to characterize this unanticipated process of transformation or ascension into an outstanding magnitude. Momentarily, not one soul amongst all these many celestial beings like them, could be excused to be edified of any reason the assembly is held, why they have all come where they are, or what has brought them there—which in entity, should have been the first question thrown out, since it is more meaningful and also in stand for the meanings of the previous questions.

Lakota and Kadosh, they could see all around a scene of wonderment and unsoundness of mind—the very place where life both begins and ends. This is a place one fetches up, with mucho gustos, and congeniality, be seeing himself très heureux and never would fancy a time calling for a departure. Perhaps, we fancy to build and structure a world that is pleasantly secure in comfort and liveliness, and by so doing, all of a sudden we find ourselves in the world long anticipated. In actuality, it is not that this appear to be a surprise, nor that we are fortunate. It is merely because we have dreamed this dream and keep dreaming it in our hearts all day and night. As we dream it, we patiently operate and put ourselves in this process of arriving in this wonderful world. It is so facile and proper to say a man dreams to become a thief and a killer, then he has first went to purchase a gun. Of course, that man is walking closer to his everyday dream. With a little difficult exertion of will, he might achieve his every dreams. It is a cosmic force which describes to us the existence and true meaning of the stars in the night sky. It provides us with knowledge of how to apply our universal and ethical principles. It is quite as easy to grasp what we want is what we get. In another way, many might seek good to arrive at bad, but it is true they have never done it with a sincere heart. For if they do, they would persevere no matter the many predicaments that come with a distraction to compel them to alter their minds, and they will work their way up the ladder.

This beautiful land full of wonderment and fascination which Lakota and Kadosh, both joyously drop themselves in curiosity. There, they pray to inhabit all the rest of their lives. It is a place they have constantly dream of as heaven supposed for the people with the goodwill to heal humanity; a place where angels, also known as gods and goddesses, dwell. Methodically, at this very time, when they are there, they never fancy participating in events and activities. Neither any of these has come close in occurrence to them in their lifetimes.

Latterly, a voice, like a stealthy sound pops out from nowhere, gradually becomes loud, speaking to everyone. "O' ye children of the living God, hear ye now that ye might be able to spread these words that ye hear this day! For ye are the ones to lead humanity back to where they ought to be...that is, the place designed for them all! As ye hear these delightful and appealing words and instill them in hearts ye carry that are already troubled on how to save the world from the iniquities and deviltries that plague humanity and is about to fall upon their heads like a hammer on the head of a nail to be driven through a hole! Ye know the truth and ye have spoken all to them from the beginning of the world, but they lend not their ears to thy words! Know it now there is a more formidable task for ye to do to accomplish the mission and purpose of the reason ye are the chosen ones! Ye are the chosen ones equipped with weaponry to fight this evolving battle! Well, ye shall fight with all strengths, truly I say to ye, ye shall prevail and set them all free from a bondage they have trapped themselves! Ye shall fight it courageously, for it is of necessity a battle ye must fight, and with certainty, ye shall revert them to their creator—the Universe! Ye shall do these things mounted upon ye to do, and ye shall do it wholeheartedly and unremorsefully, for it is ye who have promised solemnly to undertake these services willingly, with no benefits attached to it! But know ye all who contend and strive vigorously and resolutely for humanity, afterwards, shall be like us! And, as ye fully engage in this protracted struggles and walk into the inevitable darkness of life to quest for a demolition of that perilous vault dispensable in order to heal all of mankind on Earth, so the gods and goddesses here fight all that is falsehood and spiritual battle that also requires sacred and divine power! Know this arduous and mortal battle will not be effortless in achieving victory! But also know victory is ye! Victory is ye, and victory shall always be ye, though ye might be unsuccessful in the battle, but ye already are victorious, ye are victorious in the sight of the living God, the Universe! Ye are victors, and ye are the pioneers, the leading light with volitional consciousness to lead humanity and trail the way back to the maker! And then ye will be fully indemnified and proclaimed saints by popular acclamation, and thence ye will ascend into darkness, back to light and finally to that which is above the firmament and become immortalized, crowned gods and goddesses! Behold, I say to ye, go ye into the world now and set loose the string that binds mankind with transgression and death! Set loose that string and bring them back to the place particularly created and designed for them to live! Set loose that string binding them with all the horrific magic of imminence of danger accrued and maneuvered to possess some flamboyant threats to attract humanity to failure, and make it see its doom! However, if they cannot spit out the blood of their transgressions, then they shall, without delay, be forcibly made to inhale the air of agony and affliction and threats, or, if they wish, they might exercise their discretion to drink from the wine of repentance and abide to the true ideal design for them to live harmoniously! Hence, they tend to remain who they are and cling happily to their old and odd beliefs and prefer to swim progressively in their transgression till they become breathless, and be thrown into an inferno to be burnt to ashes!"

"Nevertheless, I motion and require from ye to do the part laid down for ye! Ye are required by morality to create more harmony among all, and to make certain a domain bound with more mutual respect for all, and do in all possible way to tempt and attract them to develop the mental, moral, and social capabilities for them to be in time to time able to appreciate and learn from one another and not yield every a time the desire to engage in too much extreme competitiveness! And for all practical purposes, show them love and light as the way to walk along! So! Now that ye all have become aware of this practical reason, and have reach to a conclusion to be active in this battle that entails considerable risks, I exhort ye to do so with a steady and sincere heart, and focus! Go ye all to fulfill these tasks set for ye to win the hearts of all brothers and sisters! Profess to them of the way that leads to the restoration of all mankind! Behold, bestowed upon ye is the sacred and divine power to overcome and conquer every scoundrel and barricade! Go ye! Go! Go!

> Man tends to be good, man tends to be vicious
> When darkness arises, hope to no avail fled and lost
> Thy soul thou sleepest to death, on the verge insanity cries in bliss
> The curious internal commitment thou seekest not a discernment
> Practically and willfully thy maker thou hast contrary befit and affix
> For this an incentive bonus for mass production and wealth
>
> Seest thee this as a hope of deliverance
>
> Since down in the deepest and darkest filthy stratum
> Thou hast found sanctuary and pleasure, eating sugar plum
> Carefully, as thou observe other's tears tremble with fears
> Seest not in a moment the woe that betide thee
>
> O' my world give to me things that art rightfully mine
> That art thou take and live to not technically undermine
> If all possessions never will thou live and die to constantly attain
> So why the crippling and the so much blood for power to retain?

Chapter 8

All this while, at a time when every a man and a woman there listens with attentiveness and passion to the voices and messages, calmness creeps into all souls, and the wind of hope blows around the cloud through darkness into light, sending a clue for the liberation of humanity. It is utterly assumed, by many, to be a new beginning of a significant and outstanding battle in a campaign to heal the wounded soul of humanity. How this would begin and carry through to completion would, be the cross-question thrown to each and every one there by their own souls. Perhaps they all are completely aware of a mission approved that they are about to embark on—an arduous mission that absorbs them completely and has broken apart the structure and nature of their being as humans, transforming them to become celestial beings. It is a mission with no certainty to clasp a possession of any capability to arrive as triumphant. But undisputed amount of ascertainment to come up with the trust they previously built in their relation with the Universe, to lead them through their darkest hours. As they plunge into wonderment about this mission, audacity and certitude begin to lay a new foundation of bricks and stones in the middle of their hearts.

"'Victory will always be ours," they mutter stealthily to themselves.

And it came to be at the very moment when all have been said, the voice that has popped out from nowhere and spoken from everywhere has, ultimately, ceased; El gran maestro has left the hall, walking along with the vast number of other celestial beings, as many as five hundred of them, leaving behind as few as ten, who, indeed, are unable to think with clarity what, in effect is happening. Before leaving these few ten, everyone is provided with a sufficient time to hug and cherish one another, and it is desirable; it is harmonic; it is substantial; it is pleasant; it is enjoyable by both souls with the warmth of the hugs; and it is the real world—the eternal world full of light, bliss, compassion and love.

Anon, in not quite a longer time, the few ten are led out of the hall and compound to outside of the gate by one of the celestial being, who in a polite manner, instructs them on what and what not to do. From the outside gate, they spectate meticulously as the other celestial beings, including El gran maestro, wave hands at them, bidding farewell.

Among these few ten left to embark on this mission that would, inevitably, be fascinating, and at the same time, baneful, are Lakota and Kadosh and eight others, who are all for the first, and only, time, seeing and acquainting themselves as they walk in reverse along the road that leads to the compound from which they have departed. After then, the woman leading them out into this complicated and hazardous journey back to Earth, where, literally, still is home to them, commences she to share his spiritual and intellectual insights. First, she establishes an acquaintance and presents every a person to another. And, finally, she presents herself to them as the goddess of penitence.

Lakota and Kadosh are the first people she presents to the group, follows by Hussein, then, Helen, Michelle, Lao, Shiromi, Osagie, Aadita, and Tyson—all, whom are of different social, cultural, and economic backgrounds.

The goddess of penitence, who, after the presentation, is in a transformation into a human form. When others glance at this transformation, all of a sudden, they too are in their own transformation. Immediately after the transformation into human form, but dress like ancient Roman Empire legionaries fighting wars and are possessing no weapon of a kind; and spontaneously, come to distinguish their human form from the celestial, they grasp in certainty who they have been while living on Earth.

"Pas de temps à perdre," declares the leader of the group. "Pas de temps," she repeats, as she marches like a vengeful warrior stepping back into a war front. Hence, as she does so, she instructs them to march along with her to where they grasp not if it is to be heaven, or hell. Perhaps, while they march, the goddess of penitence proceeds with her doctrines and enlightenment that tend to be a purported sign from the living God— the Universe. "Very much indeed sure I am everyone here is a good and fortunate witness to every a thing that has come to pass. Thou shall, in later time, be willing to partake in the sharing of these testimonies to every a part where dwells mankind! Yes, all thee I credit with veracity, for this hast chosen thee thy Universe," she responds, without waiting for any of them to speak a word of whether they are to be affirmed witnesses or not, and, continues she, "What hast been administered to thee that thou hast perceived with thine eyes, thou hast attest. To mankind all, that thou knowest and seest, shall thou speak; to accept it as truth, it is thy commitment and the sermon preach thee to all of mankind; to mankind preach of this remarkable and outstanding experience; those who tend to lend their ears to thee and seek a way to turn to this belief, saved from the transgression those shall be. But all they who say he is bluffing, he has come to lie and deceive, condemned they all have themselves beforehand and need no one to subject them to a worse situation."

She ceases to utter words and stares down to the valley, the valley they are about to descend to return to Earth; the valley of the shadow of death. She takes a heed and quietly stares deeply down into the valley, trying to explore its spirit and discern its thoughts while, at the same time, raising her head up and staring deeply into their eyes, the ten of them—glancing through to see into their every thought. She glances to find their hearts and takes it aback to be in possession, for she perceives, with no doubt they are all drowned in fear and are about to withhold any conviction of walking through this valley, the very valley of the shadow of death.

"No hay que perder tiempo, hombres. Nos tenemos que hacer los que tenemos que hacer. Nos tenemos que ir ahora! Ahora! Nos vamos ahora mismo," she clamors, and as she does so, she is not waiting for any question that might require elucidation. So, she goes onward with her marching and journeys on, placing in maintenance her extraordinary strength to walk briskly, and at the same time, talk boldly with no time for any shattered illusion. "La vida es demasiado caro! Je dis la vie est trop cher! Pero, es la muerte que es más caro! Yo digo a ustedes este! Si no estoy seguro de lo que estoy haciendo, yo no voy a llama a ustedes para venir conmigo a esta camino del miedo! El camino es esta! Es el camino del miedo que siempre se vuelve hacia el camino de la felicidad en el paraiso!»

There is not a soul prepared to be left alone there, for it would be heedful for them to walk along with the goddess of penitence than to falsely retreat and be left to decide their own fate of what is appropriate for them, which, on the contrary, would become a decision to help them see their fates eaten up by unseen tragedy itself. With no delay, they all run swiftly to meet up with her.

"The primary basis for this valley to be named and reputed 'the valley of the shadow of death,' is unambiguously because it has served immensely as the battle ground between good and evil; it has served purposely for death to become life, and life to become death; it is the ground that helps yield the catalyst for the transformation of being into deity; it is here the divines tend to engage in the last battle between themselves—the good would have to confront the evil, and if able to obtain a favorable outcome, will rule the earth again and bring mankind back to the maker, the Universe."

She remains true and firm to herself, as she walks without turning back to show any awareness of the people she is to be their guide. However, they all that are her followers are poised to proceed behind her, expressing a thoughtful assessment, not to question her instinct. It is a funny and silly atmosphere replenished with amazement and inspiration. The fact the goddess of penitence is stimulated with craziness and, at the same time, humor, but she is also having the quality of a great leader to whom every a person would look up to; she is full of vitality and eager to explore and smooth the path for those with virtue and morality to be regarded and honored; she is lissome, strong, active, and acutely in her self-confident manner, and is prepared to trample every evil on her foot.

Then it is the time when they walk trembling down the valley of the shadow of death—which is mostly filled with some groups of timber and iroko trees grown together in some parts, olive and oak trees grown together in other parts, and then pine, elm, and red maple grown in another part. The valley is with a possible threat of eruption and displays a place many battles have been fought some time ago. While you walk and tremble, you trample on rotten skulls and bones of dead humans. These different types of trees, which are said to be trees that usually do not grow together, but do in this valley and are healthy and far from an untimely demise, with the leaves fresh, breathing life to nature.

They descend further into the heart of this forest and concentrate their attentions, this forest, which seems to be christened "no-way-for-survival," where hopes and life are crunched and fear and turbulence become the sole owners of their hearts. Likely when they unceasingly walk downward and inspect closely the floating water bubbling out from the ground, they see the water emerges and floats downward. Colonies of different species of bats, including vampire bats, flap their spread-out wings in and around the night sky. Black owls hooting at the bright shining stars and moon, the clouds moving gradually, closing and reopening. It is incommunicable to them and is sending their ghosts to scuffle in the middle of horror, portraying to them a picture of casualty, and a manner of dying.

Seeing they are stormed by fear and awake to the reality of transformation of god to human, the goddess of penitence then brings to a halt her movement, turns back to address them of the instance of peril they have come to see themselves.

"Ye I must remind, in this journey to return to Earth, there is no turning back! Worse ye are to come across. Whence ye do, ye knowest ye hast been inclined to be active in participating in these events! It is ye fate that hast caused ye to be here for a work meant for ye to bring to fulfillment! Never will it be so effortless, or will it be amusing, or will it be fascinating! But it will be cataclysmic and accompanied by awe and sorrow. Perhaps, in the wake of evil and their strengths, ye hearts bleed and call for submission, but ye shall be strengthened to prevail over evil and return to Earth where ye shall be engaged in the true and actual battle over there while the gods and goddesses do their part of the battle for the victory of humanity to be proclaimed! Ye hast seen this to come before ye, but ye knowest there in ye hearts that the Universe is with ye, and ye fearest no evil!" When she finishes saying this, she turns back to face the journey, with no time to get involved in any further discussion. Meanwhile, to her followers, there is an urgent need for a discussion and questionings on the matters at hand that have been left incomprehensible.

They consider thoughtfully, not to bring a curse upon themselves by questioning her ability to play a guiding role. She is energetic, keen on taking decisions, and portraying herself as a role model. But to understand and believe her is like getting blood out of a stone. Reasonably, it would have been a sensible and suitable thing to do, to raise a question on the situation so dreadful and filled with preposterousness, which they found themselves. It seems all the same to them she is never properly aware they hold within them the power to make her do a better and viable interpretation and explication of the many events and activities they have seen themselves participated and undergone. It is a mystery. It could not be explained on how indeed they are susceptible to falling for her every wish.

At the time they resume with their marching in alignment with her, each and every a person is on his or her moment to play in a suitable manner, as well to prove to be a follower with importance and sensitivity. While marching on fallen leaves and climbing trees that have toppled over across the tiny roads due to gale-force winds and severe thunderstorms and rains, all thoughtfully waiting for one another to be in the front role to express an opinion.

That Shiromi could not wait any longer for the others to speak up, so he leaps on a sudden decision with an assumption to take responsibility for whatever might be the outcome. He calls to the goddess of penitence from behind, "O' goddess of penitence, my apology if I am going across my boundary. But I suggest it would be essentially good if we are edified."

"You are more than free to put any question to me," replies the goddess of penitence, turning to recognize the identity of the person speaking. At that moment, takes a move around to find a comfortable place to sit and also demands all of them to do the same.

While sitting, she pulls two small, shiny stones out of her small purse. She strikes them against each other to produce fire on the leaves she has gathered on top of some dead and dried wood she has gone to fetch; this allows fire to chat into the night since it is a bit cold, and a bit dark. As they sit, relishing the warmth of the fire, she demands of Shiromi, "What is your question, please?"

"I was about to ask if, at any point, it will appear one day the living God, who you allude to be the Universe, and maker of mankind is a mortal being or a supernatural being? Besides that, why is that living God not revealing himself to mankind so for all to be aware of his existence and find a way to draw closer to him? It is so apparent what I have observed and come to hold to be true is El gran maestro is also the living God. If that conforms with reality, it simply denotes I have seen the creator of heaven and earth, and all things within them," says Shiromi, looking down, drawing on the ground with a stick of wood that he holds, not bothering to raise his head to the rest of the group.

"Ha, ha, ha, ha, ha, ha," the god of penitence let loose a loud guffaw, then proceeds: "You see, you all here have failed to satisfy my expectations and have proven worthless of possessing the ability and capacity to carry out a task bestowed upon you. I have said so, for the fact you, as my followers, look upon me to be something too superior, not as a goddess I am that you have seen yourself transformed into, and later back to beings you appear to be now. When the Jews said to Jesus, 'For a good work we stoned thee not; but for blasphemy; and because that that thou, being a man, makest thyself God...'" and in muteness, looks around her, hoping someone would help her finish the scripture. But no one does. She continues, "Is there anyone who will help me to finish this scripture written in the Bible?"

Instantly, continues Shiromi from where she has stopped: "'Jesus answered them, is it not written in your law, I said ye are gods? If he called them gods, unto Him the word of God came, and the scripture cannot be broken; Say ye of him, whom the father hath sanctified, and sent into the world, thou blasphemest; because I said, I am the son of God? If I do not the works of my father, believe me not. But if I do, though ye believe not me, believe the works; that ye may know, and believe, that the Father is in me, and I in Him.'"

"Good, and wellstated," saysshe, the goddess of penitence, as her eyes cut through his, straight into his heart and something transpires between the both of them. It is a strong feeling of affection. It is love. "From this day on, ye have been notified, that ye all are gods if ye do the will of thy father—the maker; ye are gods and goddesses if ye work to elevate the ideology to bring mankind back to the maker; ye are gods if ye see in every human what ye see in thyself; ye are gods if ye believe man is his own God. From the question thrown to me before by Shiromi," for one more time, she gazes at him, admiring his spirit, but, not the face, "he has thought he has seen the living God—the maker—the creator. He has thought El gran maestro is the living God, also known as the Universe. But that is not true. There is no creator and there is no God."

"Whoa," they all sigh and look at her like a people afflicted with mental derangement.

But never mind, she continues, "There is no God that created you in his own image, but there is a God you all created in your own image in your hearts, and that God is the universe. It is not a human being, neither is it a supernatural being, it is the Universe that dwells in everyone's heart, calling for you to do the goodwill, to do all that is required and essential to uplift the spirit of humanity, to create and develop the energies of love, compassion, kindness, joy, happiness, light, and whatsoever that is agreeable to the spirit that dwells in each and every one. There is no God the way they say, neither is there a true religion; the truest of all religion is you. Your God is in you, the way it is in every other human. If only we could listen to the voice coming from it and live with its instructions. No man has ever seen God, because there is none. The universe, or God, as you may call it, is the place where the soul roams when it leaves your body; it is in you, and you are in it; it is not a female, neither is it a male; it is a spirit that dwells in you and controls your every thought and action. The only reason many become evil and want to destroy instead to build, is merely because they are not willing to follow the instructions protruding from that voice, that spirit; they incline to something far different from this—they have chosen their own destiny, thinking it is to liberate themselves to attain happiness; they champion ideals to benefit; they loathe that concept of free will to think and engage in activities meant to assist their fellow beings, not to say they wish to live morally, instead embrace the will to commit atrocities and reap benefit from the chaos; they encounter humors in the misfortune of others because they choose their way, crediting themselves with veracity, maintaining and considering it to be their own free will; you all are the universe and are from the Universe; he who comes from the Universe is a universe; the stars are all from the Universe, and he who comes from the star, is a star—so it is, he who comes from God, is a god; he who comes from the star shines just as the star shines; he shines alongside of the moon; he shines and becomes a light upon the total darkness of the heart of the evil and morally bad and alter that heart to become a sanctuary full of light; and when others see, they follow; when the light shines—it makes the heart to be cheerful, joyful, and stimulating; this light is love; love is God; and God is love; so when go ye into the world, be the light and shine and let others see and follow; but know it that you carry with you a religion you must draw others to, a religion of the heart, but not of a place when being practiced—it is the truest of all religion. It is love, and you are God, God is love, and you are love. As you may know, El gran maestro is a god like every others, the greatest of all the gods and goddesses. But in this kingdom where the gods and goddesses dwell, there is no small or big god, there is no inferior or superior god because all are one of the same call, of the same assistance and usefulness; there is no king and there is no servant either; we are all one doing the work that is bestowed upon us to do to heal humanity; and I tell you we were all humans who later became gods and goddesses for having been the pioneers to prepare and open up the ways for others to follow to see that evil does not pull mankind along to destructiveness, and this we did and have been disapproved of, mortified, and executed—not knowing they have helped to bring about the transformation of our mortal being into immortality; now we remain immortal and are never returning to being mortal, but will always be of immense assistance to all who are also in this struggle to bring humanity back to its maker, in as long as they provide the necessary cooperation."

After having said all this, she stands while her eyes goes straight back up to Shiromi, who also is very much aware of what in the initial time has transpired between the both of them. Afterward, says she again, "And for the voice that you all have been hearing speaking in our kingdom, that is the voice inside of you; it is not coming from the dove that descended from the Universe, it is in you, and have all been listening to it deep down inside of you, and it is God in your imagination, the Universe."

"Whoa," sigh all again, as they lift themselves from where they sit and proceed with the journey along with the goddess of penitence, who aforetime is marching on with anticipation, without deliberately looking aback if they are following or not.

Shall it not be said to be a falsehood and outrageous if we do not allege and put forward these practices to conform ourselves and create the world that is more free and enjoyable for us to live? Instead, we do what we desire that is of great benefit to us and stare into potential danger.

Of time from the beginning, firm faiths hath these many sheep.
A super spirit, a deity ye believeth hath ye originated and breath in ye breathed.
Hath these sheep, before now lost in adoration, lost in devotion, lost in communion;

Myriad come, myriad go, unaltered beliefs and faith and ways;

Hence, uniformly boring and swept off hope, ye lay and sleep on;

Herewith, aptly and deservedly, men, power attained and gained and appraise;

Power to rule, power to impose, power to control, power to destroy.

Yet, of no option abideth these a many sheep and feigned ye enjoy.

Ponder not, ponder not, play no game pour le changement;

And pains, and agony, and danger live ye and die in real.

Time after time that hath passed, similar in kind, similar in degree.

Now, await ye more hours from sleep to be awake?

Oh, the good sheep I tend; there's a call, a call for me to be awake.

Wake up my world, and not to be laid to sleep.

Chapter 9

They descend inch and inch the valley, murmuring words within themselves about the exhortation being delivered to them by the goddess of penitence, who literally is not in a state of preparedness to await more questions to be raised. On the spur of the moment, there come the grumble and growl noises from the powerful thunderstorm, expanding current of compressed air that creates loud and booming burst of more fractal and turbulent noises. Their stresses become elevated due to the heavy sound of rain making everything around them accompanied by more tumultuous noises; intense and overpowering fear drives along their bloodstreams.

Owls begin to hoot, and bats increase their feeding buzz and flapping their wings around, moving steadily in almost the same direction. As the day fades away and night comes into existence, they could neither walk along the narrow road norreduce the intensity to keepmarching and find a place to repose and mellow out—for it is the fear of the bats and owls and the sounds of the rain and thunderstorms that create a scenario where they all seem doomed.

Without notice, there emerges from nowhere, swarms of angry bees that viciously attack them. While the bees angrily attack them, they seem to be unaware they are in peril and are to run for their lives. In preference, like a troop of baboons, in fearful manners, they utter aloud piercing cries and stay behind, permitting the many stings from the bees. However, as this takes eventuation, the goddess of penitence swiftly and sensibly grows her wings and becomes an angel. She is seen hovering in the mid-air and instructing them to bend as far forward and run downward.

"Bend down your heads and run! Run! Run! Do not wait to be told what to do! Run! Just run! Run to anywhere!" She keeps shouting.

It is then they all involuntarily set into motion and speedily dash down the valley, stumbling in partial blindness against trees and down into some bog-hole brimmed with skulls and bones of human and smells of rotting flesh dead long ago. After much scuffling, they are able to come out and get on with the experience with more stings from the bees, constraining them to keep running and dashing their bodies down the valley—meanwhile, the goddess of penitence, who has previously grown wings and has been hovering around, expeditiously snatches Shiromi away unseen by some like an eagle snatches a chicken away, and keeps holding a firm grip on him, wrapping her arms and legs around him with great cordiality and hospitality, exhibiting demonstrations of what flying angels looks like in the air.

After much exhibition in the air, the goddess of penitence is able to get very far from the forest to a place, and eventually swoops to the ground and is able to drop Shiromi on a beach along the coast of a mighty ocean and leaves him there. She kisses him with such tenderness to revive him. Then she flaps her wings and flies into the air to continue with the search for others who have been thrown loosely about in different directions and have lost their ways. She flies into the air and into the forest. She searches everywhere, calling their names loud and wild. Although they have all lost their ways and are scattered around everywhere. Howbeit, with exertion, cooperation, and wittiness, they are all able to practically guarantee a reunion after having called each other's names—seeing the red and swollen faces developed by the venomous sacs left after the stings of bees—which are also very itchy, and many other wounds around their bodies derived from the stumbling. They are all wet and smell because of the rotting flesh of dead bodies and human skulls and bones they have fallen into. Some unfortunate ones are faced with more injuries, broken legs and arms. They are unable to move over and take steps along with the group without being aided by their peers and fellows. They are badly hurt and suffering a great deal of pains and distress. But they decline to relinquish the struggle, the struggle to return to Earth in order to encounter more struggles to bring mankind aback to its maker; it is a struggle; it is a battle—a battle that needed to be won, to be better won than to be lost because if lost, it would be the end of a tale, and a new chapter would commence; a new life would begin, and it shall be called a new beginning for mankind.

Sighting the mighty ocean from a distance, not too far away, they all acknowledge it is to their best intention and interest to get closer and rest on the beach, despite having undergone all the afflictions they have muddled through. Not too far away from them, at the other side of the forest, the goddess of penitence keenly penetrates every corner and angle to see if a soul could be found. That she does so. She unceasingly calls out their names and whistles her rhythmic songs said to be meant for the survivors of battles—a song that only could be understood by the immortals. As she proceeds further with her search and whistle, hovering around the air, moving up and down, to and fro, repeatedly several a time, till she becomes feeble and is unable to fix in her mind how exactly she is to put up, or not mention where she is. Yet, she acknowledges her vision is going black and her heart is losing strength, and all she could do is refresh and go for a relaxation. To do this, she is required to slowly flap her wings and land on the ground. Lastly, when she landed, seems done by a mechanism her both wings abruptly disappeared from her body and she collapses to the ground and falls asleep.

At that instant, after much carefulness and endeavor, as the group eventually arrive at the beach, solely to meet Shiromi, who lay sleeping, totally unconscious, not interrupted and tends to lack feelings and sensitivity. It startles them to encounter him in such a horrible situation that it virtually triggered their hearts to be buried in a more unanticipated despondency. A sentiment reaped from bereavement is the flood that washes panic into their nervous system controlling many numbers of autonomic functions, transferring trends of atramentous and fluctuating messages of monstrosity and craziness to their cerebral aqueduct and the thalamus in all of their brains. It could not be said they have lost him, or they have also lost the goddess of penitence, their guide, who in actual point, they are clueless of her whereabouts. They are veritably unsatisfied with a situation that engrosses them—which she has made them to be; they are on a verge to relent and not forward their journey, since they are on a suicidal mission to feed their own hearts to the demons that dwell in the forest equipped and poised to hunt them down wherever they will intend to hide so to bring them to justice. Although, they have been warned before of how arduous and horrible this journey back to Earth would look like, but, on their own volition, have all solemnly declared and committed themselves to it no matter the endangerment that lay ahead. This is the time to put to test all their faiths—whether in humanity or in deaths.

They continue to scream and dash themselves to the ground, mourning over the death of their comrade who lay down. Mourning his death is one thing, but could they mourn for the goddess of penitence who is nowhere to be found? For dead she is, or alive, they know nothing. Perhaps, they are all greatly fatigued and consumed by the ghosts of the unsafe surrounding they see themselves to incline their souls. To abscond from it and ingress themselves into a new world where they might encounter peace and tranquility, that which becomes a fantasy that would not, in any time, by mechanism be altered to become reality. Yet, they would not refrain from that state of mourning, despite bleeding and suffering from the wounds and bruises they have attained in an attempt to escape from the dangerous bees and the abundant horrors attached to the forest; they mourn and weep. They continuously in adversity, mourn and weep— wandering around aimlessly from one side of the beach to the other, with their minds thrown into a maelstrom of perplexity, complexity, and impossibility.

In the intervening time, Shiromi, who is pronounced dead, has joyously ascended into a different world; a beautiful and wonderful world. A world where he finds, in emplacement, his soul in acceptance of a meeting and mingling with the soul of the goddess of penitence—and it is the greatest and most pleasurable moment ever has he experienced from the time he is given birth. In this frame of mind he is delightfully hopeful, seeing himself rest on the bosom of the goddess of penitence, and she gently strokes the back of his head, runs her hand over his body, and caress every delicate area of it. When he lifts his head up to look into her eyes, she commences in trailing kisses—first all over his body, and then extending to his lips, tenderly, very softly, slowly, and sweetly, letting her soul melts into his soul, uniting the souls to become one; the spirit leaps about excitedly and rejoice.

Moving him closer to her body, she wraps her arm around him. He does the same. They both caress each other's body, while she whispers words of wisdom, words of encouragement, words of affirmation, words of hope, and words of love, all into his ears. She maintains her course of progressive caress and love for him. It is going to last forever, he thinks, forever and ever. He so much wants it to be so—for both to entangle their souls and wrap themselves together; it is a world so blissful. It is the true meaning of life to him...and the reason humans live; he wants to live in that world and never revert to the world he has abandoned.

Regardless of the fact some of them sight the goddess of penitence grows wings like an angel and hovering in the air, instructing them to run for their dearly lives, but what still lurks within their hearts is a most profound and radical doubt she is still living and within that environment. She might have flown back to the world of the immortals—the world where the gods and goddesses live, some are beginning to put to assumption. Thus, they wander aimlessly and mourn and wail and shed all the tears in them out to the ground, but none are able to come up with a proposition, setting out to look through everywhere around the forest in an effort to find her. Yet, they love her, or indeed, think they do.

And when she hears the cries and sounds of a garish noise connected and extended into some kind of peculiar noises that become songs sing to the gods and goddesses. The goddess of penitence, in a flash, keenly refrain from her kissing and mimicking, in an effort to keep her ears to the ground to hear the songs of resurrection, which enables her a complete comprehension of what has befallen the both of them. She senses they are both unconscious and being mourned by their comrades, for they are under the impression they are dead. In spite the fact she would never die—for she is an immortal goddess, and nothing, nothing would ever take her life, for she has entrusted her soul to the Universe, the living God. However, she is not in a position to cause any delay for Shiromi to return to those who mourn over his passing; she needs to put into fulfillment the great task set for her by the Universe. So, in a swift motion, she kneels down and pleads to Shiromi, a mortal she has come to love and is willing and incline to love and keep safe wherever he would be. She pleads and instructs him to return to life for the good of humanity, and for the mission set forth for them to accomplish. What has transpired between them will forever remain something divine and sacred, for it is a union between a human and a god—between mortal and immortal.

Surprisingly, all of them who stand staring at the dead body of Shiromi are engaged in deep speculations whether to dig a grave and bury him, or take the body with them back to Earth; they see the same person supposed to have been dead and has been motionless for some hours, now shakes his body. It seems to them a dream or a nightmare that what they observe is far beyond their imagination as though their instincts has lied to them.

Soon after, one of them, after much consideration, reacts immediately as he reaches a conclusion to take a step closer to the dead body. And to his good sense of protracted astonishment, he finds Shiromi waking from death. Before he could cry out loud, he sees him stoops up on his feet, staring at everyone, who see a perilous reality of life, and, not knowing what else to do, commission themselves in a contest and relish an unwanted and unexpected race to flee from the dangerous environment. They want to flee to elude the ghost, they want to flee from themselves and be wherever they wish not to be, merely not to be a witness to what they have seen themselves bump into. It is freakishly bizarre and create an environment where evil is said to be in existence and the sole remedy is not to seek of how to destroy this evil, but to elude it. By then, where were they heading to that they fancy to be a sanctuary safe and strong? Or do they even know the way they have taken to get there or to get out?

As they continue to scamper off and spurt recklessly, carelessly, panic-stricken, and flee into the forest where they have once escaped and rejoiced they are able to do so until they come to find Shiromi lay dead. As they hold onto their race contest, scrambling, screaming, and shrieking, Shiromi relentlessly runs after and calls them by their names, beseeching them to wait for him to analyze his motive for coming back to life and what indeed has transpired. But would they make any effort to hear a word from him? Would they ever confide in someone thought dead to be alive and want to hear him details his experience? Would they not see death if they turn back to look at him? So, they proceed further to a place not known to them, but inclusively race on without restraint, dash their bodies to the trees and not poised to bring about a cessation of the unwanted race.

And it is so, while they run in a custom invariable for their lives in an effort to elude the harm of the ghost—the ghost of a friend so dear to them. Someone they have lost in a struggle to save the world. At that moment, come unexpectedly in a rush, some colonies of vampire bats, flapping their wings and coming towards them. Consternation creates a way; death appears to be of no delay; hope from men flee to a disarray; trust not that you pray; trust not your ego to escape a prey; run to defeat or while the sun shines make hay.

Now, it is up to them to flee from the forest once again, or confront the vampire bats already clinging and preying upon them and poised to drill holes into their body and drill the whole blood out. They all recapitulate the fight against the bats with their hands and legs and heads and bodies; they continue to do whatever it takes to set themselves free as the bats continue to cling and prey on them and have discovered every means to penetrate their teeth into their skins and get the blood out to feed themselves. They continue to fight the bats, with no faith, they run from the forest aback to the beach where they have left to escape a ghost of a one-time friend whom they have come to fancy as a foe, seeking to destroy them. Perhaps, as they flee, with blood splattering everywhere from every part of their bodies from the bites of the vampire bats. All of a sudden, sparkles of living light flashes brightly from the sky through the dark night all over the entire forest and all they steadily observe is a manner in which the vampire bats turn into ashes, and the more the flash of light reaches them, the more the bats are turning into ashes, while the others fly away into the dark forest. While this is in progress, they hear a voice come from the sky and says to them;

"For I am with thee! The Universe is with thee! Fear not!"

And that is all they could hear and never see anything; neither do they hear more of what the voice has to say.

Coming out of the forest with all damages and harms done to them by the bats and the dashing of their bodies to the ground and the big and mighty trees in the forest—bleeding as though having fought with lions. In coping with the adversity and pains, they all still possess the strength to cluster together. With cooperation, they are able to locate one another and bring themselves back together to make a huge amount of a profound progress in achieving victory to exit the forest known to be the forest of evil. Still in that gloomy state of mind, when they approach the beach to find a place to reduce their intensity and recuperate, from a distance, they ascertain Shiromi is sitting close to the ocean, staring deeply into the water as it floats to and fro. That they would have to run again, which is to say they are to render themselves back to the forest of evil that would be of no good to them. But because the choice is left for them now—an alternative for them to eliminate one of their two mutually possibilities for a survival—to meet with the ghost of their one-time friend, or run back to the demons that dwell in the forest of evil. This they need to conclude in a way that makes sense, not for one person, but for the whole; they are not in a situation to put up with the repeated encountering of danger, instead they are to draw a sword of gladiator to fight once and die, or die as many a time before their final death. They are exhausted and lack the strength and capability to keep running for their lives. They are accessible to a new way of pondering the burden once and for all. After all, has a voice not spoken from the sky to alert them the Universe is with them? All these information imparted to them, is it to be taken for granted? Do they not fathom the mission set before them, if it is more than what they would be able to accomplish, would have not be set by the Universe that controls everything below and above?

Left with one alternative to survive, they all walk closer to Shiromi, quietly and cautiously. Immediately he turns his face from the water he is staring into to look back to the forest, he sees his comrades approaching. He jumps up, rejoicing for the reunion and walks towards them in a mood full of blissful harmony. When they see the way in which he rejoices and walks towards to reunite himself with them, a base of optimism, good fortune, and assurance like a bright star stalks in their hearts and they are genuinely convinced he is still the same person and not a ghost. With faith and the power of positivity binding their hearts, grace waters their blood, and with words of wisdom cautiously and judiciously administering to them of the need for a reunion with Shiromi, they all walk faster and closer to embrace him.

For minutes, it is laughter and joy, and later, displeasure and remorse they share. They hug, cry, and recollect all the adversities that have betide them for the past day, but also the wonders they have driven deep to encounter, and the inner enlightenment that lies within them, which they have rediscovered and need to nurture. However, their prospects seem dim and yield no confidence, but in no sense seems to perpetuate the present in weakness and obscurity merely because of the situation they find themselves slide into. They will overcome and adhere to the factors that incline them to a unique belief meant to heal humanity. They have to proceed further with the journey to return to Earth in order to carry out the task set for them. Humans live and die, but the gods and goddesses live forever, they are immortals that live eternal lives and never die, so they are already seeing themselves.

Menschen leben und sterben, aber die gotter und gottinnen zu leben fur immer. Sie sind unsterblich, die das leben ewigen Leben.

For at a time when they have finished with the hugs, cries, and the recalls of memories, Shiromi stands in front of them to relate how he has seen the goddess of penitence, whom all of them think has returned to the world of the immortal. He recounts how he has met with her in another world—that is strange to him or seems strange he thinks. How they have talked and laughed. But to detail all what transpired between the two of them, that he is unwilling to let out. Although, they all conceive everything he never wants to disclose to them; they are fully aware both are in love, and that has been the principal reason the goddess of penitence has to save him first before anybody. Indeed, they are also unaware she has come to rescue him at the time of their predicament. As a matter of fact, none of the misprepared to put down his or her ears to be told what has occurred, apart from being informed of how they are to leave that dangerous environment to return to Earth. Yet, Shiromi continues in his narration and would not come to a halt. He tries in every aspect, and by every means necessary to generate the discussion to a level when others might join in and ask how they might be able to do a thorough search for the goddess of penitence—his lover and savior. However, when the responses from them is not strong enough in which to comply, his heart becomes troubled. He is unable to conceal his anger—which actually impels him to live with discontent and bitterness. He stands in muteness, observing every one of them, warily, and waiting for someone to utter a word—to say it is better for them to search for his lover.

It happened that none of them turns out to speak or come about what is basically essential for them to do next. And this is driving him mad and creating more space in his heart to be enraged, to be unsettled, and to be confused a good prospect will relieve them. And when this anger continues to fill his heart, he becomes more enraged. Then, there is no way he could control it, and this anger, which lights a fire inside of him, the fire to fight the demons in the forest of evil, to struggle, to encounter vicissitudes and futility, and overcomes them. He wants to go to fight the demons; he wants to see the love of his life; he wants to hold her and never let her slip away again; although, he could visualize a forlorn acknowledgement of failure if he tries, but he also knows he is possessing that relentless energy to fight and become victorious. How could he live without her? How could he ever live his life not hearing her whispers words into his ears? How could that be? He needs to go and look for her, to advance the development of their intimacy, the meanings and reasons of their mutual relationship—a deity and a being.

Confused and disappointed by his comrades, Shiromi takes a step closer to the ocean, sitting down, folding his legs, and staring towards the wide and endless water as it floats. Just how the air is to the bird, the water is to the fish, so she has been to him. He understands he has to embark on this search. She means everything to him, everything, everything that he needs to be happy, to enjoy pleasure and satisfaction; he needs the warmth and love she has constantly offered to him which he would live for and makes him carry on.

After having spent some minutes there, he returns to his comrades. He throws a question to them:

"Is there any one of you willing to take this journey with me to the forest to look through in an effort to locate the whereabouts of the goddess of penitence?"

But no one respond. Maybe they ponder in their hearts it will be more satisfactory for each and every one's mouth to be kept shut: that it is not in any one's best interest to arouse another person's anger; it is better to let the sleeping dogs lie and not discuss the matter further.

Still taking a firm stand that they are to go in search for the god of penitence, Shiromi raises his voice, and it is extremely high they are all appalled when he expresses his thoughts and feelings. "If you are not standing for anything, you will only see yourself falling for everything at the end, and it will become so bad at the time your life is already in peril." And after saying this, he stares round to see if anyone responds. He finds none. Then he proceeds, "It takes amount of integrity and courage to first think, and secondly, put into action a war with the demons. Running away from a jeopardous situation like this is only a means for us to endanger our lives. Things need to be done with dexterity to avoid being trapped in an unhappy medium."

But before he could finish addressing them of what is right and what is wrong, asserting to be a leader, solely because he is passionately in love with a goddess and would do anything to find her, a voice from behind comes from where he stands.

It is the voice of Lakota. "Shiromi, we all know you are in love with the goddess of penitence. We are not kids to be tricked to acquire your desire to find her. We know thoroughly well when someone is in love, he or she will do everything, all the crazy things, and you can even lay down your life for that person with no remorse. No one is stopping you from doing what you wish. But I tell you, I am not going back into that forest. I do not know of other people, but as for me, not to that forest of evil anymore because I am done with it. I am not going back until the light shines on that darkness, that darkness that breathes air into that forest for the demons to live."

"Thank you for sharing your thoughts and feelings, most of all, for being open-minded about everything." This, he says, as he walks closer to his friend, Lakota, touches him by the shoulder, and presses on with his teachings, "I know you might think I am on the brink to lose my life for her because she is my lover. Of course, that is true. But assuming it is to be any of you, trust me I would do the same. I would do anything to see we are not losing anybody."

Saying this, it touches them in their very hearts as they watch him speaks and later stands mute. They know what he is saying is true. They understand well and believe firmly they ought to be there for each other, no matter what.

But Shiromi continues with his teachings. "We will not see well in darkness if we are not blind. We will not live if we are not dead. To see in the dark is to be blind; to live is to be dead. No life is saved by anyone except by the grace and order from the Universe. I am in love with a goddess. You might not comprehend that yet. I have been taught a lot...a lot of things that will take all of you years to gain knowledge."

Then after much contemplation and floods of thoughts being pondered, they all inexorably arrive at a conclusion to expose themselves to that instance of risk and plunge into that forest, the forest of evil created from the valley of the shadow of death.

Themselves they cordially assemble once again; with their feeble selves formerly suffering from strain and detriments, they set on a quest for the goddess of penitence who has been their guidance and has presently become absent in their midst. The elusive eagerness to find her wherever she might be, is written in their hearts and a thing to capitalize on, to do whatever it would take to bring her back to life, even if discovered dead. They are all cogent and conclusive, strongly considering it to be truth in their hearts they are possessing the power to bring her back to life. It is faith leading them, it is instructing, and it is driving them to take upon this noxious risk, with the gravity pulling them to the goddess.

As they march on and on and advance towards the rooted heart of the forest of evil, they chant songs and sing praises to the goddess and accelerate their march as they undoubtedly draw their spirits to the other spirits said to be evil, inhabiting the forest.

They move on and on, blowing away from their hearts doubts and cautions that may pave the way to revulsion and trepidation. And at this same time, the goddess of penitence is long awake and looking around. At least she is able to discern she is in the valley of the shadow of death that leads to the forest of evil. Still, the manner she arrives there is what she tries to recall in memory; she might still be in a dream she thinks. She wants to see this dream pass while she returns to her real world where she could have her life back and see herself wrapping her arms around the only man she has ever loved and dreamed of. If only the dream could be altered into a reality. If only she possesses the power to change the whole situation back to where it begins when she is spending her life with her beloved.

In a sudden moment, a light from the sky shines through the forest to the exact location where she lay down, exhausted; where she is aspiring herself of a kind of heroine she would be to alter dreams into reality, or to say, alter reality into dreams—she is fantasizing on whether at that instance if she could bring the past back to the present, and make the present become past. But who is she to possess this power to alter the fate of mankind? Is she not a mere goddess, even if she has been chosen by the

Universe to lead, to guide, and to return them home—these beings who are to engage themselves in activities of a mission to bring mankind back to the maker? Of course, she is a goddess, but not the Universe itself, the maker who is in control and command of everything.

As the light continues to shine in her face, she feels some power thrown unto her, an energy inside her that appears to move around every part of her body, drawing more energy from the sunlight, enriching it with the air she breathes, and sending her soul far away to where Shiromi and the other eight chosen beings are marching, accelerating deep towards the demons who are all asleep because the god of joy and the goddess of truth have driven them to go back to sleep for them to pass by easily without being fiddled.

Then swiftly sends she her ghost to reunite with her body. And when reunited—the soul and the body become one. She sees herself rises from the ground, intensely, fully energized, and is in readiness to embark on her journey again. She flaps her wings and flies into the sky, hovering around the sky, on top of the trees in the valley, then to the forest, descending to where the people she is to be their guidance march and chant and sing. Albeit, already paralyzed with the prospect of being able to situate the whereabouts of the goddess. It becomes a life not conformable to their wishes. It would have been said that they feel so remorseful for having attempted, at first, to set on this particular search to arrive in an atmosphere of misery and fear, which might as well has hampered everything in which they have dreamed, everything that could lead to the outset of enthusiasm to reach mankind with their doctrines. There is a veracity if not valid, but is in a way close to it, that their minds are all set on fire, intoxicated with the peril that would befall them.

To their astonishments, the goddess of penitence eventually lands on the ground close to where they are, flapping and continues to flip-flopping with her wings. Before they could utter anything or come closer to her, she waves to them and utters words for them to stop walking towards where she stands.

"Do not walk past where you are, please," she hollers at them as her wings gradually transform back to the same human form.

When Shiromi first spots her appears, crying tears of joy he commences, rightly thinking it is necessary for him to restore his emotion. Intrinsically, he is overwhelmed, overwhelmed with joy and happiness. And so she is. To control this emotion in the presence of the other people around is like giving up their lives. They want each other, they need each other to acquaint and feel that warmth again, to experience that reality they have both envisioned when they seem cling to each other.

As they both watch themselves, staring at each other's eyes from an intervening space, everybody around watch as well. Shiromi leaps from where he stands, staring at the goddess, and without questioning, advances with great haste towards her, and touches her. Without intervention, she responds and a scene of love affair occurs—a meeting and mingling, with passion, with tenderness, and with a gross and safe capacity of love. Others who are around and are in observance, grasp it is desirable and favorable for the enhancement of the relation between humans and gods. As this thought peers into their hearts, something surprisingly good and preeminent transpires. It is said that a white dove descends from above, and on top of them both, hovering around, and all of a sudden, the whole forest becomes very bright as if a ritual is performed on them to attempt to produce something supernatural. They are both seen transformed into something unlike, in nature—light is seen reflecting from them, and the color of the light is pure purple like it has been when they have first seen themselves as gods and goddesses. It happens that the overwhelming reaction, which has educed from their longtime emotional chastity is seen to be replaced with calmness and stableness.

Later that day, after they have all engaged in a festivity to welcome the reappearance of their guide, the goddess of penitence, for they have been able to walk through the forest of evil to go back to the beach where they are to set sail through the ocean to return to Earth. For all, that is the real moment of optimism.

Along the way, they are given a brief account by the goddess about what is to happen there in the forest of evil—a battle to be held between the demons, who are being put to sleep at that very moment by the gods and goddesses. It is said to be a battle between good and evil to determine the fate of man; it is said to be a-not-to-be-experienced battle, or else they might get caught in the crossfire. So, for this, it is advantageous, necessary, and advisable that they, in swiftness, discover and acquire a means to traverse that ocean and be at the other side of it. It is to be done, and done in a hurry.

They have all engaged in distinctive activities: cutting down trees with machetes, which they know nothing about how they have come to be in possession—all with the influence of the goddess. These trees are sliced into woods, with and without skills, been transformed into a vessel. They have done it. They have formed the logs to become a mighty sea craft.

Anon, it is for them not to carelessly consume more time than they have previously did—whether they lack the interest, energy, vigor, or enthusiasm, but it is absolutely prudent if they would get on board the big canoe and sail off to wherever they wish, in as much it is an environment far from where they are.

"Get on board and let us leave this very zone the demons have established," instructs, the goddess as she raises her voice, trying to get them informed of how dangerous the place is, and a need for them to speedily disappear.

Hearing this, they all jump into the big canoe, rapidly and energetically, with their paddles. They set on and propel the vessel through the ocean. Meanwhile, after they have left, they could, from a considerable distance, see the very place they have just departed from looks like it has been hit by some torpedoes. There are fire burning everywhere. There is smoke going up, and from that distance, they could perceive by ear a sound like bombs exploding.

"I guess you can all see to the reason I have wanted us to leave that place earlier," says the goddess to them, standing up, putting both hands on her waist and watching while the canoe shove off being paddled by the rest of them.

"Have the demons awaken and commence in a battle with the gods and goddesses?" demands Tyson, who is said to be the oldest of all, but is constantly very quiet and calm—a result of literally how timorous he has been, experiencing what seems to him to be so fictitious.

"Tyson, you get it right," responds the goddess, stepping towards where the love of her life is, staring into his eyes as if she needs words from his soul to respond to questions thrown to her. Thereupon, she proceeds, "What has transpired there that we can attest to is the beginning of the battle I have long indoctrinated all of you. It is the battle of the good and evil." Looking around to see if in fact they are in a concerned manner paying attention to her doctrines, she proceeds, "Immediately as we have left that place, the demons are awaken from sleep and they have bumped into the fact they have been put to sleep by the god of joy and the goddess of truth. They tend to be consistent with anger and wrath; they are furious and rise to chase after us to make certain we are all captured and killed. It is saddening and aching in their hearts, and besides, it is humiliating to them, for they have seen all of you coming towards where they have stationed an ambush to ensnare and kill everyone. They have yearned to feed on everyone, they have wanted you to quench their thirst for blood because for long they have not thirsted any blood of any human. These people who are both in human and animal forms. The demons dwelling in that forest of evil. They are all giants and as big as those mighty trees in that forest. Some time ago, they have fought so many battles with us, and are still fighting. We would not relent until we win this battle and ensure a future for humanity to live in peace and harmony, to return to their maker, whereby they will, in every moment, in every second, show loyalty and appreciation for having been freely endorsed with gross opportunity to inhabit the planet and relish the life on it. These demons have chased after and virtually caught up with us when the goddess of truth and the god of joy fly to become the cause of a derailment to them on their way. And it happened that about twenty of them valiantly get engaged in a dubious and catastrophic battle with the god and goddess, who, in actuality, have not been featured or attributed with the kind of special power to fight a battle as tough as that. Though, enough power has been entrusted to their care, which they possess deep down in the murkiest part of their souls, but not meant to be in use at that very particular time. All they have, are intended to show the ability to heal and promote peace—and for that motive they have come. They attempt in every feasible way to let peace predominate, but also to be able to thwart the demons' evil plans to get us killed. But these demons would not reason in accordance with the peace deal, in contrast to that, they make efforts to use their powers to overpower and maliciously ravage the god and goddess. So, it happens there arises an altercation from one of them who is known for being too malicious and always thirsty of blood. It has led to irksome and coercive disputes amongst them. When the Universe acknowledges that, it knows there is something urgent to be carried out in order to invalidate this plan of theirs. For that, it solely appeals to the god of justice to present himself, and to be wholly and justly in active in this battle. Thence, when indulges himself in this battle the god of justice, he is not to undergo any mental or physical strain, only to send some invisible torpedoes so destructive to obliterate them all. To crush them. To demolish them. To make sure none are spared, and that is accurately put into effect—just what we are fully knowledgeable of from observation."

Chapter 10

Wherefore, as they assail upward across the ocean, they unceasingly do so with pious hope they would reach to the end of the ocean. While, the paddling they do with technical skills persistently and with meager energy. But rumbling and troubling in their hearts are the facts they would not in any moment, cease to meditate upon this story being narrated to them by the goddess. They are exhaustively stunned in awe and troubled about what might have occurred if they have not exhibited their shrewdness, heedfully lending their ears to the goddess with no demand for elaboration on the reason why she so badly wants them to hurry to board the canoe. Hence, at that very moment of time, they lack the aptitude and effectiveness to immerse themselves into this task. They excellently perform the first task of building the canoe, and since they are all weak and weary. They have wanted so much to settle upon how they could stay to repose and refresh themselves before anything else. Instead, they have expeditiously jumped into the canoe and paddle briskly to traverse the ocean. With that, they have all been able to elude the evilest race of men and demons, they have eluded death that is nigh.

Then appear unanticipated mighty waves in the ocean as they sail across. The waves are seen traveling hundreds of miles before reaching the unseen land and returning to where they are. The lightning strikes, storm lingers, and thunder rolls, all in the middle of a warm afternoon. As the waves in progression rise, and the lightning and thunderstorm increase their strikes and lights and cries, the light coming from the soul of the sun becomes dim, the day becomes dull, getting darker, and darker. They continue to sail, gripping the paddles—some fallen and getting back on their feet to make certain they do not relinquish the paddling. The goddess lauds them all and continues to raise her voice, instructing them to be balanced with their faiths and hard work. They need to under-gird their canoe if they hope to keep it from sinking or breaking apart in the violent wind blowing sideways. The silent rock of energy in their hearts is seen exploding, constraining them to manifest their abilities of persistence; they begin to see they are entangled in a series of dangerous assignments and acknowledge the severity of the situation. Though drown in terror and evil thoughts playing across and daunting their personal emotion, they contend, they preserve, they persevere.

In this troubled time when conflicts are in everywhere outside, deep inside them consternation augments and the prospects for survival is bathed away to an extreme end of the unknown world. But hearing the goddess' instructions, they tend to look up to courage, holding onto their paddling. Thence, there arise more storms and winds, from the sky, descend upon the large vessel and tear it apart, sending them to the ocean to forcefully launch themselves into swimming in an ocean that seems to have a beginning, but no ending. And at that very moment, a fiery-faced monster arises from under the ocean. The monster is a giant, thirty times bigger and taller than any of them. It is seen as more human, as it has two legs, but deceitfully, it has eight big hands: four on each side and the face appears to make him look like a dragon. From afar, it could expectorate fire from its mouth, and the fire when is dropped in the water, instantly, becomes stimulated and burns from the top of the ocean, downwards. In frankness, there is no terse comprehensiveness of how this has come to be feasible. It is peculiar as saying man made man and breathed life into him to exist and live with him as a fellow human, but it is also possible to be literally scared to death, and yet engages oneself into fighting a battle with the unknown spirits, or design and build an atomic bomb, knowing the consequences if detonated.

Swimming helplessly and desperately to reach the shore of this cosmic ocean believed to be Earth, they lengthen in duration, exerting their energy and might even as the ocean shows signs of menace. But to them it is an irreversible momentum; it is an irrevocable decision to head on with the swimming and not await a second no matter what, let it be they become breathless.

Meanwhile, the mysterious monster advances towards them as fast as it could, still expectorating fire to destroy each and every one of them—including the goddess of penitence. It is seen that the better their intentions and determinations to improve their swimming skills and accelerate faster than they are, the closer the vicinity of the portentous monster. For every time it moves its foot is likened to thirty times that of a normal human being. And this monster is genuinely poised and eager to render physically worthless every being in that ocean; it is its fury that technically is the driving force bringing the steadiness and inevitableness to substantiate its conclusion and destruction—it is an objective, and at the same time, emotive.

As the goddess of penitence simultaneously swims and offers prayers to the Universe for some powers to tackle these many circumstances that have erupted at the same moments. She seeks for the extraordinary power to confront this immense danger that lay in front of her. Before long, she continues to offer her prayers invariably while she swims and inhales a reasonable amount of water, drowning and proceeding with the swimming.

It came to pass her prayers are lastly heard by the Universe, who notifies some other gods and goddesses of what good fortune and misfortune that have overtaken them in the ocean of death—which would, in turn, muddle the many formidable problems that have long engulfed the world and humanity living in it. They need to be set free from this mode, this circumstance in which they now exist; they need to be saved from these demons that have long become a hindrance to man's will to seek his own destiny. Instead they have begotten these many evil doers to rule over man on Earth. They have battened, vitalized, and stabilized them to be potentially able to exercise their power over others. They have gifted these evil doers with power, wealth, fame, and influence to conquer and place humanity in bondage and never permit its return to its maker.

For this, the Universe, the other gods and goddesses, bring into reality and agree to make an affirmative decision for some of them to be sent there to assist the goddess of penitence and her crews, to offer them an obstinate resistance, and also destroy that demon known to be one of the greatest of the twelve most mischievous and parlous demons that are said to have begot the evildoers on Earth, and have done so to encumber humanity from returning home to its maker. Though, its real name is said to be "Akulupus." But the gods and goddesses have preferred a distinctive name for it because its evil deeds have created more calamities for every soul that pass through that ocean without being mercilessly and completely crushed. For that reason, they have come to name it "Kalamuto," which means "calamity."

As they swim towards the shore in despairs, persistently, unceasingly they swim. Albeit, chasing after them, Kalamuto the fiery-faced monster. Catching up with some, strangles them, pulling off their heads, and the blood floating it spits and drinks. To quench its longtime thirst it drinks and drinks. More fire and fire it expectorates from its mouth. Arrive there on the scene the god of justice and other gods and goddesses; and around the monster's head, hovering and fluttering in the air; a commutation of fire to fire, and also spitting and splashing out water to snuff out the fire. For many a time and oft, more a fire and a fire protrude, more a fire snuff out; time creates and opportunity forcibly grabbed; Meanwhile, the goddess of penitence and some of the comrades still alive swiftly out of the ocean of death swim to reach the shore, while, fervently and heedfully inspect the remains of the bloody flesh on top of the ocean; wherein the fiery-faced monster elevates, lifts itself, and ascends into the sky. It grows wings, flies and hovers around, still sending fire from above to destroy them.

More fire as well as more water to extinguish the fire. More arrows, hotter than fire, from the gods and goddesses, all coming. Alas! They all have a war declared on Kalamuto the giant, Kalamuto the monster. As they are placed in a position of furtherance and progression, bombarding the monster in the air, a terrible weakness it develops and cunningly, away it flies.

"Justice must be served! Justice must be served!"...these utters loudly the god of justice, ascending higher and flying as he speedily chases along with the monster to fully assure it is hunt down for a penalty to be inflicted. Granting, it is said the god of justice has intermittently aforetime ruined and eliminated a variety of these demons, as many as equated to the total numbers of all the other gods and goddesses, on which simple reason he is been christened the god of justice.

When he persistently chases after the monster, in astonishment, he sees it turns around to engage in a battle with him. To destroy the parlous demon, he would need some more effective and potential powers to do it. How could he attain that power to defeat it without the aid of his comrades? That becomes a task, sighting, as the monster advances towards him in the sky.

"'Mataratata! Mataratata!'" The god of justice cries out loudly to the Universe. Forthwith, as he does, the Universe sends to him a sharp and shiny blade sword as sharp as the devil himself. The sword he pierces directly into the heart of the monster as it advances to grab and crush him into pieces. All of them afar a bit from the scene, watches the manner in which a mighty giant monster falls down from the sky, producing a noise, ' "Boooooom!"' as if the tallest building in the world has collapsed.

At the time they are able to reach the shore of the ocean where they come to detect the high level of what has occurred, how disastrous and dangerous the battle has been. Ultimately, they notice they have lost four of their comrades, among whom are Michelle, Osagie, Lao, and Helen. On the spur of moment, they all burst into tears, mourning and weeping, seeing that never a time would they meet with these people again, these people that have lived with them all this while and have entrusted themselves into the same arduous journey to return to Earth so to engage in a task with them to heal humanity; they mourn and weep for their comrades; more, they mourn and weep for themselves as they reflect widely and conscientiously on the circumstances that might develop promptly. But, in not quite long, a dove descends from above and all they could hear is the same voice that has constantly spoken to them in a time when they are in a state of affliction.

The voice is saying to them, "Mourn not, weep not! Mourn not, weep not for these people. For if you do, you do for nothing. Verily, I say unto you, these people seen dead are being perpetuated as immortals. They have become gods and goddesses. Rejoice now and be happy all, for thy brethren who are humans have been immortalized. That is a splendid achievement; it is a great privilege; it is a reputation; it is honor because it seldom happens. It is to be celebrated and regarded as one of the happiest days for the immortals, for they have seen the light shining from above, and they have come to actively accept the profound and divine truth in understanding and interpreting the words of the Universe that have long been prophesied to them, which many more are cheerfully willing to take on this cause to heal humanity, knowing their rewards are merely to live in the kingdom of the immortals. This has happened this day to bring about a fulfillment of that prophecy."

And after the voice has finished saying these words to them, in company, they congregate themselves, conceiving themselves to be one and showing restraint for a value of diversity. All who are able to survive the tragic situation become one said to entail in this struggle, to uphold of it, and bear the burden. At that very moment, a kind of a supernatural power comes in to fill their hearts. It is a power of fortification, it is a power to take them wherever they wish to go, or whatever they wish to do to build and heal. Thence, there is a spontaneous freshness, an awareness, and promises all wrapped up in a vision to proceed in conquering the Earth, with no fear or favor, all for the good of humankind.

Far in a distance from where they stand on the shore, they could catch a glimpse of a very high mountain. It is a beautiful mountain covered in snow all along to the peak.

"What is that we are seeing?" demands, Aadita, who is said to be the youngest of all the mortals there.

The god of justice, raises his head up from the deep trance he has fallen into. He says to them, "Yes, it is a mountain said to be the great mountain of fire. There, you all have to climb to reach. From there, you ought to throw yourself down to Earth. I tell you, do not cause yourself to be distressed about how you will survive and pass through to return to Earth. No! Do that not. Eradicate from your hearts that feelings of aversion. Do so because you know you possess that extraordinary power of fortification, the power to help you survive any critical situation. I tell you, for any a burden never meant for you to bear, should not have come to you. But because you have been given the power to overcome, so, all these you will experience, and yet, will still survive them and return to Earth in order to carry out the task set for you by the Universe. Yes, I say to you now, you shall undergo a series of difficulties as you approach the most terrifying and precarious aspects of life. You will come across these malaise and vale of sorrows humans have bestowed upon themselves for the sake of greed. You will see the horrors and qualms and deaths they have inflicted on themselves. And you will also see how pitifully and anxiously they seek to be liberated from the bondage."

For a while, the place they stand and stare at the mountain is marked by absence of sound or noise. Anon, it seems they have all plunged deep-seated in a trance and none respond to the other. But all of a sudden, there is a unicorn, a horse with single straight spiraled horn projecting from its forehead. It is a white unicorn. It is seen descending from the sky and comes running slowly in the air towards them, accompanied with colorful flowers, birds, and fairy infants. However, reaching where they stand, the unicorn, spontaneously transforms into a celestial being, and it is el El gran maestro. Seeing him, they hurriedly advance towards where he lands and embrace him one after the other, while the butterflies, birds, flowers, and fairy infants hover around, pouring magical stars upon them.

At that time, it is El gran maestro standing, beset by some other celestial beings and humans. He wears a white and blue robe around his body, looking about to see if everyone present is directing his or her attention to him. He is poised, eloquent, and in a commencement of delivering his sermons to them—the one said to be the finest and premium of all the sermons before they could return to Earth.

The first thing he does is to put in order the closing of eyes by every person as he comes up with a prayer for their fallen peers, as a tribute to their devotions and sacrifices for the general good of humanity. They are asked to utter prayers and gratitude to the Universe, for having accepted and chosen them to become part of the immortals, to have permitted a transformation of these humans to become gods and goddesses.

When this progressively eventuates, they all proceed with their prayers silently. First, for their dead comrades, later, for their setting to return to Earth.

Kadosh, one amidst them who perfectly remains in quietness and calmness, not following what others do, for his mind has departed from him to meet with ponder on the basis and motive on why prayers are needed. Frankly, it seems to him madness is perpetuating them, or they are perpetuating madness—all of them. Madness is preparing them to meet with the demons that have once fought with them and relent. It is madness, he thinks, nothing, but madness. He sees the emphasis placed on the word ' "prayer"' as to be a factual fact to exhibit madness. For reasons that one has to strain his mind or voice, or cast a burden upon oneself to utter prayers to unknown deities in efforts to gain grace and good fortune, not to mention the time and energy being practically exhausted. It is sheer madness to him—sheer lunacy, a very horrible condition of being mentally deranged.

After when the prayers are said, El gran maestro, who, genuinely, could see into the hearts of everyone present—humans and celestial beings, for he has been ordained and gifted with the power to do so by the Universe. He walks slowly in a peaceful manner and, thrusting closer to Kadosh, wraps his arms around his neck. Instantly, he kisses him softly and moderately on the cheek. He kisses him, looking into his eyes. Kadosh's heart weeps in tears, as he experiences this, reflecting on how Judas has kissed Jesus before selling him out to the Romans to be arrested. He quickly comes to the assumption it is a kiss of deception, it is a kiss of betrayal. He admits this and speaks loudly, unknowing others there are hearing. It is bewildering and prodigious all who hear it. While to Kadosh, he is acutely ashamed and repelled he has been caught in a betrayal of allegiance towards the rest of them.

Standing beside him, El gran maestro speaks loudly for everyone to hear. "Prayer, as you may understand it to be, is a communion with the divine—it shows a kind of devotion, it helps us to confess our deeds (good and bad) to the divine. Or, let me put it this way so you all might get the picture of what I am indicating. Prayer draws the soul closer to the divine; it is an intimate, a secret communication between the soul and the divine. Most of all, it enables us to share feelings deep down inside, and also to praise and thank the divine. Here, the divine, we see as the Universe that people represent pictorially in their hearts as the living God. When we pray, we are, in a sense, trusting in something beyond that is unseen, which I may refer to as having faith in something. No one—mortal or immortal, who is absented from this thing said to be faith. Even scientists do. They believe in something far from what others can see. Only they can see this, not with their naked eyes, although with their hearts and minds—whether some say they possess intellectual ability or aptitude. So it is with the Jews,

Christians, Muslims, Buddhists, and other religions and sects. Those who worship idols see more abstractly than anyone else. They make sacrifices and whisper some sort of strange incantations to their gods and goddesses being represented with images and some that are invisible. And all these you see to acknowledge a bit of the peculiar things about faith. It is to gratify our feelings. We believe in things we have not seen for certainty, and since indeed we believe because we have heard, then we grow with it and intend to pass it to the next generation and to another. Perhaps, we can see things that are real and not use our powers of reason to know what we are seeing is real. Yes, we believe in things unseen, for we need guidance to lead us to our various destinations since we cannot undertake all things on our own. Now, in this aspect, it is quite different with the immortals. As for the gods and goddesses, it is our power of reason that is vital. We see the Universe around us. We see nature. We see humanity. And we know all we see is real and part of existence, part of us. It is only the divine in every one of these we seek some power far beyond us, which the Universe owns, being the controller of all. We pray to the Universe to show our gratitude for permitting us these opportunities to see with the light shown to us, for the knowledge and wisdom we have acquired, and then, for the force of energy so generously spread around the four corners of the Universe. We draw strength from the light, from the knowledge and wisdom, from the force of energy, to fight the evils that dwell among us; to heal humanity; to make nature reconcile with us again. Do we not see these wonderful things around us and ascertain there is power beyond us that controls them? The flying birds, the talking seas and oceans, the beautiful smiling moon, and the stars sprinkling their astonishing faces in wake of man's inner bliss? The great and mighty Sun with its warmness? Do we not see the lions and tigers and other wild animals in the forest, living and dying just like man? Do we not see all the blooming flowers sing songs and worship nature and also praying to the Universe? We see these things, so why then do we doubt the existence of a power beyond? To our observations and understandings, life, to everyone, is essential in any way we might see or find it. It has made us strive every day for something—a want, a desire, not only for pleasure, but also for building our spiritual and mental being. Therefore, it is necessary to achieve this want and desire, and to do so, we must compel ourselves with strange attitudes into some strange world we know nothing about. Prayer might be ineffective and only superstitious, but it also helps us in many ways to arrive at an atmosphere of hope. Hope is vital to humans. Without hope, we are lost, lost in sight, lost in a process, or in a course. Yes, I tell you, the intrinsic truth is we cannot live without hope. It is what keeps us alive. It helps us rebuild ourselves. We only wish to see something happen, be true, or think it will, and it becomes a belief that helps us to strive to arrive at our destinations, making it become a reality. Thus, I say to you all, without hope we are lost. Hope, which is based on an expectation of positive outcomes. It is an optimistic attitude of the mind. When this hope is gone, there is nothing left for us, and then bad things happen. So many might disagree with this theory, asserting they might not be in need of hope, perhaps, for they are not lost. But, believe me if I briefly state that humanity, as a whole, is lost. And since they all belong to the society and are included in this, so I formulate in my mind they are all lost. So to say, all they need is hope to outlive and to outlast. Again, I repeat, to arrive at this atmosphere of hope, we need to pray to that which we believe in and cannot see; that which is the Universe, the divine within, the supernatural being living within us that some refer to as the living God. Yes, that is the name for it. That is the actual name for it. And that is all we are. We are God, and surely we are powerful beyond measure, and we are way bigger than our ignorance and stupidity, we are limited, we are the thinking form."

Kadosh is stunned and sees himself in a different mental formation, apparently unaware of where he is. He lacks sensitivity to external stimuli. There comes the element so mystical and fanciful playing a significant part in his inner world. This energy which he has never felt, comes unexpectedly, uninvited. He looks a great depth into that strange world and see things not there. He looks deeper into it and see things that appear to be having intensely bright colors. They are there, and at the same time, not. He certainly could not see through these bright colors, he certainly could not destroy the completeness of it. Hence, he remains stunned while his heart burns and freezes. He is delusional, watching, as his spirit lifts up from him and rests in the air. It is mystifying, it is an incomprehensible mystery, it is madness, and it is a consequence of his doubts, his thoughts of not trusting in the words of the immortal administered to them by El gran maestro. He knows right away, he knows his doubts is dragging him to testify of what he has seen. But he wants to be set free, he wants to be who he used to be, he wants his spirit to return to his own body, and vows never to doubt the words from the immortals. How could he be punished for things he thinks he knows nothing about?

El gran maestro comes closer to Kadosh and touches him again. At that time, he sees himself free from a bondage, his own transgression, his own doubts, and is becoming himself again as his spirit return to his body.

Looking directly and deeply into his eyes, not uttering a word, El gran maestro proceeds with delivering his sermons. "Thou will climb that great mountain of fire successfully and thyself throwest down to Earth from the peak…believe it or not, not a needle shall thee be hurt. Climbing the mountain will be a bit stressful and terrifying and dangerous, but believe it, the Universe is with thee. Reaching Earth, know that thou hast to love and treat every human in a selfless way, showing dexterity, the same way thou ought to do to thyself. That is the greatest of all the rules. To be close to the Universe and show the willingness to heal humanity for the power to be given unto thee. Thou must do that, which is pleasing to thy lord, thy maker. Teachest thou the people also what thou hast been taught. Armest them with wisdom and understandings, feedest them with knowledge, and nurturest them with love and compassion. Verily, I say to thee, there is nothing to be done which they can doest not. Thy lord, God hast set thee on a journey of life to bring humanity back to him. Doest it in any way, but doest it, breakest thee the code and unveilest the secret to the world. Let thee humanity out from the bondage to be saved." And immediately after he says this, he is seen ascending back to the sky as he has arrived, accompanied with the same colorful flowers, birds, and fairy infants.

There remain the god of justice, the goddess of penitence, and the other gods and goddess who have accompanied them to win victory over the giant monster, which has almost sent them to their graves. Although the mysterious monster has propitiously send some of them solely to aid in their earlier transformations to become gods and goddesses.

Soon after, there is Aadita, also Hussein, Tyson, Lakota, Kadosh, and last of all, Shiromi, who would have been more favored to be transformed into a god for a major basis to live the rest of his life peacefully in eternity with the only woman he has ever loved, and come to desire so much. He has indubitably considers it preference, even when it seems outlandish. But he has consistently been oblivious of the many battles said to be engaged in in the future between the immortals and the demons. In accordance with fact, no matter what trouble shall come after him, but yet, it would have been far preferable for him to live with her, to have her, and simply, to never lose sight of her, for she would, in certainty, be the victory he intends to fight for; she would be the world and everything to him.

It comes time for them to depart from the gods and goddesses and forge ahead with their complex journey to return to Earth. After many embraces between every being, god, and goddess, Shromi and the goddess of penitence look into each other's eyes again, wishing they have never acquainted with each other, or seen each other, regretting what has transpired that has led to love being the outcome. They would have been better than other people, they would have been free and feel better just like others. Why have they started a journey as complex as that? They stay staring at each other, tranquil, one waiting for the other to utter a word. Both are tied with a bond in muteness, how they both long for the immeasurable fulfillment of the relationship, the inner wondering to become a thing that is real and firm. They keep staring until a time they move closer to each other and begin their mingling and tender love affair once again in the presence of all, while the rest cheer and clap for them, setting on their expedition, leaving them both to decide which way to choose—to remain there or get back to their errands.

Chapter 11

And it came to pass when the gods and goddesses have all left them to their faith and cause. Shiromi climbs the great mountain of fire with his comrades while his heart, already owned by the goddess of penitence, sings hymns composed for the sake of intimate love. Kadosh is recovering from the great shock he has undergone. He regains his strength to climb the mountain. Meanwhile, wrapped around his mind is a clump of different conceptions, leading to many thoughts and wondering. He is faced with another problem of a code said by El gran maestro that is needed to be broken to unveil the truth to the world. Likewise, there are also some speculations about the great mountain of fire and the reasons it has been portrayed with a name so frightening. He sees the climbing as so easy and adventurous in a situation where one would be filled with pleasure, performing activities, exerting physically and mentally to develop fitness or perpetuate it. It would be amusing and frolicsome.

As they continue to climb and engage in discourse with themselves, they attempt to inspect and interpret what exactly they have experienced, how they are to successfully implement those plans set for them by the Universe, and attain fulfillment. Without premeditation, they come to a realization that they are in a place quite distinct from where they ought to be. The weather there gets colder, and colder, to arrive as forty times cold as it has been prior to when they arrived. It is twenty degrees below zero. They could neither descend nor ascend to reach the mountain peak, which is as far as where they have started. They have to do whatever it takes to reach the peak since it has become the possible option. The more they strive, the more they thrive. Invariably, they climb and ascend to the peak. Thence, the colder it becomes, and what is left within them is hopelessness and only to assume freezing to death. Death is nigh in every way to their hearts, it is nigh, nigh in the option to revive them and is possible, probable, preferable, and also favorable. Pendant plus de ciquante minutes ils étaient encore dans ce temps très froid, ils sont gelés et ils se lamentent, their feet covered with sandals and bodies with robes meant to sustain very hot weather. It is at that time Kadosh is able to recall in memory of the true reason it is named the great mountain of fire. He knows that is probably the beginning of the terror and horror set to plague them, he knows the actual significant of the mountain is fire, and he fancies it burns like hell previously inside his own heart, and the more it burns, it produces hope from within to keep him warm, to overcome the situation, and to stay alive.

Start they in an instant to develop positive thinking—that which, in a mechanical manner becomes an energy to which also is the strength for them to fight, to withstand, and to overcome their current situation. Although, it is said that energy has protruded from the heart of Kadosh and is broadened to instill itself into every one of them. Thus, when Kadosh thinks of this, he remembers how he has doubted El gran maestro. All of a sudden he could drench himself into a chain of unfortunate, deep-seated thoughts to draw more inspirations, and besides that, to acquire more knowledge.

After they have all suffered the terrific and horrific situation that imposed on them a complex task, impelling them to engage in a battle with their hearts to persistently survive and see themselves in a fresh and lively world once again. It is a sacred battle. It is said to be a metaphysical thing, based on speculations and abstractions in reasoning, which has led to a healing. This, which is said to be the law of opposite connections by merely using a thought to alter a situation. It might be very well said that it does not work for every a being. But to conform to truth and be realistic, it is the remediation of all mankind's predicaments if truly mankind could see into its own potentials. It is a free gift that should be possessed by every individual and not to be purchased with gold or silver. Howbeit, man has constantly underestimated his own capability and, in contrast, decided to witlessly and preposterously walk along with his fellow man to be taught everything: how he could eat, how he could shower, how he could live—to a degree, he has been taught how he could die. It is not science or philosophical theory or whatsoever, it is common-sense that only need purity to attain and to be put in use. To hold comprehension of this theory, it is simple as plunging into thought and recalling in memory of the opposite of any state of affair. It is using the good times to confront the bad times, while also using the bad times to confront the good times. As humans we are obliged to familiarize ourselves with hardships and challenges in life. We are bound to experience the good and the bad times no matter the class of life we might find ourselves. In attempting to meet with our material needs, this is inevitable and undeniable. We meet up with good and bad hours, good and bad people—the people who mock us, who steal from us, who beat us, who shame us, who drag us, or even, try to terminate our lives. Then again, we also meet up with people who assist us, elevate us, cheer us, laud us, or even want to lay their lives down for us. This indicates how life consists of various aspects, various directions, and it is up to us which one we find ourselves turning to. In perfect pretext, these aspects and directions might be based mostly on both—the good and the bad. It is true as we grow older, life becomes more interesting, more difficult, and more terrible. So, it happens that when we powerfully commit ourselves to one particular aspect or direction and come across any practical problem along the way, we thence have to think deeply on a manner in which to develop and maintain that ability to sort out effective and genuine solutions to that practical problem. This, which literally is to look back to the past events that have been so joyful, harmonious, and successful. And, immediately that thinking begins a movement to proceed to fill our brains, then to the minds, and finally, to the hearts, we become positive. Positivity or positiveness, is that which authentically is said to be the affirmations for moving forward in a right direction of increase and progress. That is the energy that has been uncovered and drawn to us, and that brings a practical solution to that practical problem. But the pervasive problem is that, many a fellow have seen this long ago from the very time man has been first put into existence and has been permitted the ability to make his own decisions. However, man has been so forgetful and failed to acknowledge the fact that it is also contrary, so as to say, that this logic could also be applied when he is in a jolly and playful mood and everything seems glamorous. Then, is it not his duty to also look back to the past events when things have been so totally miserable and tragic? This has constantly and will continuously be a tremendous problem of the people of the world that definitely necessitate a viable solution. When a man and a woman purposefully commence in a family life and everything seems sweet and pretty, they become oblivious of the perils and misadventures that await the marriage in the latter days. So also is the people of the world who have innovated, created and invented everything—good and bad, not knowing there might be consequences, or they pretend not to know, or they have no intention of wanting to know—since, better let us live for the moment and enjoy the huge benefits, the good things that we have, and let tomorrow take care of itself. Perhaps, there is a factual fact, and it is of infallibility that there is no beginning without an ending, or an ending without a beginning, there is no good without evil, or evil without good, or say there is no birth without death, neither is there death without birth. It is the law of opposite connections, whether we tend to like it or not, or say it is an ordinary theory stated by an individual who is merely expressing his own opinion. Wherein, there is a mathematical formula to which, for long, we have been permitted access and have declined so fatuously, for we think we know, whereas we know nothing of our own if we are not taught. And, intrinsically, we have always underestimated ourselves in conveying a terrible havoc within and placing the blame on those who are ruining our lives and driving us into misery. We complain of our governments when we are not in any manner, or in any a time poised in a struggle to change the system by ourselves, to ensure a brighter and sunnier days for ourselves and for our children and the next generations to come. We lament of the lives we live that we see clearly that are unsuitable, perhaps, we aid and build more supports for those who prompt the cause of our afflictions. Yes, that is what we do. We do it, and we cling to that same motive of how to fortify them by all means to be more constructive and destructive with their course of actions.

O' brethren, how long do we seek the things that are not there?
How long shall we have to play the games that bringest us to loss?
How long will we be blindfolded by our greed and ignorance?
O' brethren, how long?

In accordance with fact, we must employ our sights to various directions to accumulate more information from different sources and then pick out which is best for us, better than walking in one direction with same rules that causes predicaments day-in, day-out. Whereby it would be greatly advisable for us to look in that direction of a driving dynamism. So to say, if we aware of the significance and meaning of life, we would at least create a method that fit our social structure...that we see to be approving to us and also to our neighbors, purposefully to avoid stirring up strife and enmity which might as well ingenerate hatred, social disorder, violent conduct, and conflicts among ourselves. Granting, if we look to these different directions, we would be able to grasp everything in precision and accuracy that has been briefly explained in the law of opposite connections. The mathematical formula is simple, and it goes like this when we access it from a negative situation. -1+2=1. When we access it from a positive situation, then it goes like this...+2-1=1. Which indicates every number from the right, plus the number from the left will absolutely bring us to a whole number that is exact to 1. The number (1) is always positive. And when we are doing this, we do not have to yield to skepticism. We just do it, trusting in our inborn intuitive power.

Climbing continuously, ascending towards the peak of the mountain. Straining themselves, endeavoring to make their journey back to Earth, becomes fact, rather than a fiction. With great anticipation of victory that requires more strenuous efforts, they imagine the peak of the mountain to be in a not-too-far-away intervening space from them. How they could arrive there and plummet into jubilation and commemoration becomes a dubious undertaking.

On spur of moment, all they could see are flakes of fire falling unceasingly from the sky. They are falling, and falling on everywhere, to a certain extent there is no space left for any of them to place their feet. The flakes of fire, as they rain down, they burn the fields where they walk and roll. Absurdity is tearing their hearts to be judged. Their pasts are reinvented as their presents disappear, and reappear, and disappear repeatedly, while their pasts seek to judge the presents, and leaving behind the future. It is strange, and the worse ever, it is filled with danger, inviting despairs for a voluntary participation.

Kadosh, who beforetime has discovered a talent to confront every pugnacious condition like that, swiftly raises up his head and screams, uttering loudly for all who are with him and far away from him to hear. He shouts to them thrice, "The law of opposite connections! The law of opposite connections! The law of opposite connections."

When they heard, they plunge into thoughts for the second time. They are thinking of the cold that almost freeze and truss them with death. They continue to think of it, and in that moment, they all become cold and feel like they are dancing in the rain, as it contrast sharply to the flakes of fire. It is splendid and enjoyable as they walk happily, easily, and slowly to the peak of the mountain of fire, exhausted, but with jubilation and commemoration. It is said to be the happiest time each of them has ever experienced, seeing themselves about to return to Earth, seeing themselves about to be reborn, seeing themselves about to face an arduous journey to be judged, and destroyed to become immortals. It is pretty cool and fascinating, standing on the peak of the mountain, all of them, and staring back to Earth that is unseen except for the cloud in the sky.

There is jubilation, there is commemoration—shedding of tears for their lost comrades. Howbeit, some are also utterly remorseful for not having been the victims that melancholy has befallen. Since becoming an immortal is what far and away would be preferable rather than having to embark on more arduous journey that would, indubitably, be overwhelmed by more sadness, more misery, and more suffering back on Earth. Yet, they all relish the very moment of what life has brought to them, they all recognize the magnitude of the task that is bestowed upon their souls and hearts, they all value the aptitude in them that has brought them to a call to heal, to heal humanity of the damage, of the woe, of the laceration inflicted on them by the demons and their advocates—their undercover agents. In a matter of fact they are all full of hopes and delights, they are all full of desires to do the will of the Universe, and bring about an accomplishment.

After much thoughts and jubilation and commemoration, they could all stare into the bright and shining sun that yields and throws joy into their unsoiled hearts, enabling them to merge with each other, standing in unison, preparing to throw themselves from the peak of the mountain down to the Earth with love and no intention to outwit one another. It is love, the love they have for each other that fuse them—that fuse their hearts; it is love, and that love is an opened door for them to enter into eternity, to aid them in all the missions set before them.

Chapter 12

I t is a dark night inside one of the deepest subways in the heart of the city of Paris. It is midnight. Deep inside the subway, is an extensive secret and deep rock tunnel, organically dry and darkness brims it and decayed bodies and blood stained the walls, inviting the ghosts of the long lost souls inside to guard and protect the cardboard cartons lying on the floor, and as well the wretched bodies lying on top of them. The only light that seldom protrude to reveal life is that of the drug addicts lighting and smoking their powdered cocaine with ice pipes, injecting their skins with syringes—all French citizens—black, white, and Arab descent.

It is in this very place Lakota sees himself lying amongst other tens of frustrated, homeless, illegal immigrants living and feeding and roaming the streets of Paris every a day, every a night. He is not at the initial time aware of what in life he is doing in a place like that, nor has he grasped a real motive that could be stated if demanded by anybody from him. Everything to him seems to be a nightmare, which jocularly is not a thing afar from realness, a positive fact.

This becomes so heavy in thought for him, venturing to do whatever is possible to ponder the questions in order to see how he could come up with a clear response. A careful thought, and this he is doing repeatedly. Granting, there is no one to throw a question to him since others lying beside him are in a state of inactivity, slumbering peacefully after having roamed the big city of Paris throughout the day, either searching for a job, trying to get shelter, or eat something to earn more energy in order to proceed with their daily struggles. If that is to happen, probably he would be unable to give the details of what in actual fact has transpired. But if he ventures to give a narration of what he has experienced in the land of the immortals, in a strange world where his soul, for a time, has journeyed and wandered to come back to him, no one on Earth would incontrovertibly not label him a lunatic. Or, say he has a response, explicitly precise, he would say:

"'I am insane, and I request a psychiatrist to help me, to get me out of this insanity. The problem relating to this insanity has totally swept me away from what veritably is real, and still, it is dragging me to my grave.'"

Wherefore, he is able to remind himself of every a thing which he has experienced in that strange world. Not preoccupied he is in this afflictive situation, he starts to see he is been called—a call in which he must not refuse to respond, a call of duty to serve and protect humanity, which he so love and cherish, to protect them from falling into a bottomless pit. He sees everything so transparently and dreary, he sees the reality so very far from vision, and they are all there in the eyes of the ghouls that haunt him, coming from the various directions of life, deep down inside the somber dangerous tunnel; they are there—the ghouls with their fiery hair are there, they are screaming and advancing sluggishly towards him. So he thinks, looking into their eyes and seeing faith in religion replenished with polluted air and proliferated across the globe, politics playing games with shrewdness and blood hanging around their throats and mouths, true values of humanity robbed off and taken away to be set ablaze, regardless of how the divine signature of nature itself burst into tears to inherit despairs, endeavoring to obtain clemency, but all to no avail, more and more, humans creating, inventing, and destroying that which is so exquisite, that which is so extremely beautiful and pure and purposeful, while so, the vulnerable birds flock in the air in search of their daily meals with their iridescent colors of feathers... blue, red, green, yellow, pink, purple, black, white, grey, all broken and become fractions burned to produce a chemical substance meant for benefiting, and also for a sabotage.

And when Lakota conclusively returns to his senses, sighting and monitoring the drug addicts in the vicinity; the very way they engage themselves in conversations, engage in feuds, engage in fights, engage in smoking and drinking, engage in singing, and engage in sex—all seem to him like it is a ritual, and at the same time, virtual, outstanding, cruel, and far blunter.

Inside the deep somber tunnel, everything is going on—there is sex, rape, boxing matches, contests, and violent conducts. Some days ago when Lakota has first arrived, another homeless Romanian teenage boy, with whom he is acquainted, out of empathy, voluntarily, has come to show him the place. They have been confronted by a group of drug addicts, people with a constant motivation of doing wrongs, embracing vicious and mischievous purposes. They have initially thought they have some money with them, making attempts in performing their duties of extortion. But when they discovered afterwards they are penniless, in the context, in rage, they viciously pounce on the Romanian teenage boy, who is also rude, assertive of his rights and holding his ground with a mindset that France is created for the harboring of every human being from every part of the planet. This, which is contrary to the beliefs of the drug addicts, who assert to be French citizens, and the rightful people permitted to enjoy the facilities and resources of their country, by quoting to them the national motto of France: "Liberté, Egalité et Fraternité, c'est pour les Françaises, cette ne pas pour les étrangers."

While they have engaged in that quarrel, Lakota is doing everything in his power to ease the tension, pleading for both sides to be calm and to understand they are all the victims of the system, a mechanism for enriching the privileged and creating more space for the peasants to ramble, stumble, and bubble inside poverty and hopelessness. Perhaps, they utterly decline to lend their ears to him. Only what, at last, he comes to witness, is one of the drug addicts, a light-skin black man originally from Martinique, brings out a penknife from his trouser and viciously attacks and stabs the teenage boy thrice before Lakota and some other lads could rush over and separate the fight. It is stunning to the highest degree, practiced to be unexplained. He, he alone could see the ghost of his dead mother combating the ghouls eager to intervene in these events. She is fighting the ghouls, and, simultaneously, calling for him to single out which path he is to walk—move on to create a continuous healing energy for humanity, or create a world designed to encompass wrongdoings and wretchedness.

Knows he Lakota he is to spring from his present situation to a better one, to move on to ensue something greater than him and his power, to live up to his dream of alerting the world of the danger of too much material developments and advancements in every society. It may be he has more problems of his own, but he has come to believe helping people sort out their problems makes us to be oblivious of our own and later come upon the strength to sort out the ones engulfing us. He has to do it. It is a call he needs to answer even if there are going to be so much pain for no gain. Perhaps it would be that it is for his love for mankind. How do we help heal humanity? Or must we not see ourselves be remembered for something good, something that would help shape a better future for the next generations to come? These thoughts, thus contrasting and contradicting within him, are encompassed in a shade and shadow of a mixed of complexities and troubles.

He recalls how it all happened he is at that moment taking a responsibility to having to shelter himself inside a deep somber tunnel. He remembers how he has left another country in Europe after writing a book that causes him to express his own regrets. He has left the country with his vision being his best friend, his only friend. It has traveled with him wherever he has been and has coupled itself with him, gracefully in readiness to take that journey with him to the end of time.

He has moved everywhere like an owl at night, flickering and wandering from one tree to the next, darting instinctively to reach the right place where there is enough for him to feed and composed to rest. He has traveled to Switzerland once again on a bus and has been caught by the border police who have debunked the proxy passport he possesses and about to swiftly deport him back to Africa, after making some numbers of phone calls to the immigration in the country he has left to come there. They have expressed their regrets for having anything to do with him and show a strong confirmation, ordering the Swiss police to get him out of Europe. At the later end, he has been pardoned by the Swiss who have finally dumped him on the border between Switzerland and France, a small city called St. Julien. There, it occurs he is penniless and has to walk around the city and sleep in the street for five days at the very time winter is at its edge, and the place is as cold as hell. After when he has lost his bag where he has all his good clothes, shoes, cream, and all he has bought not long before he departs from Italy.

He is later sent some money by his sister, who, prior to the time this dejection and desolation have come to be his sanctuary, has issued a warning for him to rest in that country no matter how tough the situation might be.

When in the course of time he is able to purchase a train ticket from this small city sharing a border with Switzerland and arrives without exception in Paris, a city in which he has long dreamed, a city he is affectionate with that he dreams would be a heaven, for some years back when he passes through there while traveling to Italy from Holland. His love and affection for the city grows forthwith he starts to see people of different races—working, eating, living, and dying there.

And now, here he is again, homeless and wrapping himself up with a carton. For two days he has been sleeping there and enjoying it, experiencing every good aspect of life, how poverty is transformed into inspiration. He begins to put some questions to himself:

"'If he is rich, living in a mansion, eating palatable food, and riding in a beautiful and expensive car, would it ever occur to him that people are begging to sleep in a tunnel? Or is he saying it is a good idea to generate for someone to be living wretchedly deliberately to experience life and derive meanings from it? Beyond the shadow of a doubt, strange it would be to be told to undergo suffering in order to discover and attain virtue and morality. Anyway, it is true that the beauty in life is not that one has to have everything he desires so much. And, in an attempt to achieve our objectives in life, everything could be given to some freely, while to others, it could cost them everything.'"

Lakota's attention and perception are carried along a whirlwind blowing from east to west, and he fathoms he is effecting and arriving at the most important discoveries of his pursuit to become a prolific and renowned writer, the most important discoveries of his life. He sees these peasants live happily with love and compassion amongst themselves, and it is in the practical equations of this love, the natural forces guiding this love that is strengthening them, giving them hope and life. This, in essence, propels him to see life distinctively—helping him to ascertain certain things about life and uphold a belief—that to bring more meaning and satisfaction into our lives, is not by acquiring all our desires, but by being positive and increasing that mood, making attempts to wipe out sources of displeasure, and allowing that pleasant emotion in us to range from contentment to intense joy and harmony. He understands it is a good thing to do, and not fret too much about our situations or problems in life. For, if to be happy is to acquire all desires, many wealthy people would live forever without seeing death. But, these people who drink and smoke with no hope for better days, are as happy as people with millions of dollars. It baffles him anyway, it baffles him.

At about 5:00 a.m. when the first underground train is to pass through the train track, which is not more than some meters away from where they lie. All of them are far awake, preparing their cartons and hiding them in a hidden corner to be used the next day. They walk along the train track to the outside of the tunnel with their phones and lighters serving as lights.

Lakota, at that time, is perfectly aware of a mission set for him to accomplish. He acknowledges he has to do the right thing, push himself forward and believe predominance will come to his side, since good always predominates over evil. He grasps in his mind with certainty that for him to bring all this into reality, he must take the initiative of making connections with his instincts and look for his compatriots, since that would be the only thing to enable him take the plunge into success in the new land he has seen himself.

When eventually, with ingenious plans and carefulness, it appears they have all succeeded in getting themselves out of the tunnel. They see themselves meet face-to-face with the subway security guards who know erstwhile from where they are all coming, but decline any interference in their lives and simply open the gate of the subway for them to pass to their varying destinations. That is Paris. Who really cares what you do with your life, or who really minds if you are not abiding to the laws, as long as you are not caught stealing or robbery—who cares?

That afternoon, after when Lakota has left the tunnel to engage in his insignificant daily routine due to how he roams all day with his other homeless friends without direction or objective. Beautiful and marvelous day it is, dining at varieties of soup and food kitchen where food are being offered to them freely. Going to shower and changing his outfits in public bathrooms that are in everywhere around the city. And that is a good start he usually could have a place he could eat every day—which brings him to uphold the notion of a government that provides for the hungry and homeless people.

Admittedly, in Paris, it has become a sickness. It is demoralizing, seeing how some of the French citizens and immigrants who are legal and documented, capitalize on that and become oblivious of the need to search for job. France is a land of freedom and liberty, if the truth is to be said. They harbor immigrants more than anywhere in the world, they feed and provide shelters for them, but is it really enough when these people become like wrecked vessels that are unfit to rebuild themselves? How tremendous and amusing it would be if we live by our moral standard, if we create a world where there is an equal opportunity for all. However, it is already been written in the book, been classified, been inserted into the mindset of all, and has become a proportion of the system that all men cannot be equal. As it is also written that every man should be for himself. Then why do we in pretext, show with sincerity we worry too much about the predicaments betiding our neighbors, and still not putting in offer a solution to it when we can? Is it a style designed to mock them, to frustrate them, or assist them to advance towards achieving a better life? Which one it actually is, is incomprehensible. Bearing witness of all these and engaging in discourses with some of these homeless, whom many are French citizens, but minorities, there is this expectation of conflict in the later future, if not war. The complaints popping out of the mouths of majority of these confused and frustrated young men, it seems obvious and naughty that humans will not stop pretending. Who is to fix this system, which, genuinely, is broken? Or do we think it is not? Do we see things and continuously pretend they are not there? One day, our pretense will become a burden to us, to a degree we will dig our own graves without knowing it. We see in a way many countries, like the U.S. and other European countries, have become a place where human rights are being practiced when it comes to harboring immigrants fleeing wars, persecutions, and poverty in their homelands. But it would have been better to help them engage in activities in their country by investing on projects that can create jobs for them there, or help them resolve problems heading to conflicts, doing it with diplomacy. Instead we fuel wars inside these countries and manufacture weapons for them to purchase to destroy themselves. Hmmm. It is horrible.

It is said that Lakota could conceive a time of bitterness. Of course, if it all continues the way it is, as he fancies how he sleeps in sorrows and adversities and wakes up to see the world he loathes—the world he cannot help comprehend.

Later that day, giving details of his situation, he finds himself with another African man he has met while walking spiritlessly alone and tries to sell his wristwatch to him at a very cheap price, solely for him to have some money in his pocket. Despites the man's refusal to purchase the expensive, but-automatically-too-cheap-wristwatch, since he is totally broke and is in an urgent need of the money, the man has volunteered to show him a street called Chateau d'Eau in the heart of Paris—knowing he could find his compatriots there who would get him informed of what is necessary for him to do to help himself—which literally has been his initial intention from when he has arrived in the city, and he has longed for it. In realness, he sees agony breaking through to trouble his heart, and at the same time, creativity is creating and seeking a way to amend him, to amend his spirit.

Walking along the street of Chateau d'Eau, he meditates upon the reasons he is where he is. He perceives it is not a propitious place considered for him to be at that very time. He is not in Paris, a great city in France. Unspeaking, he stands, stunned and motionless, observing every a thing and outlining the meaning, sketching everything into images in his head. He wants to start writing about everything. He wants to paint the picture of the scene. He sees the charm and fascination of every event, and, as well, the opposite of that, he sees himself in some strange cities, in some strange countries, and in Africa. This is unimaginable and frightening to his well-being.

He meets with some lads whom, when he first sights them, knows he they are his compatriots, by surveying their attitudes and displays of self-importance.

"'They should be my compatriots,"' he says to himself, walking closer to where they stand and speaks to them in English. Of course, due to the way in which they responded, he feels a kind of energy enters his vein and runs via the blood to his heart and every part of his body. This is the first time he has seen a human being show a sign of acceptance to be his compatriot since he has entered the country. It is at the later end, after having witnessed himself become a part of the society, that he acknowledges very many of them see themselves twisted by a perception of how the new people entering to settle in the country are a burden for them to bear. And for that natural and plain proof, they all come upon the notion to be in denial of their identities and nationalities. It is not them that the fault lay upon, but society that has made this be an entity. It is the system, it will transform you, makes you despise your father or your mother.

Later on, he is shown a barber shop where he starts to learn how to become a barber. It is good that he starts. It is essential and helps him erase his past memories, even when they would not want to go away. He realizes the situation, looking back at how he used to live a good life. Perhaps he could hear voices from his own head inculcate in him an upright and gratifying lesson, letting him be aware that, sometimes, we do things that make us feel remorseful, but it is up to us whether to let that become an impediment, or learn from it in furtherance to build upon something to pave the way for a better future.

With hunger, threats, mocking, and, sometimes, happiness, after three months he grasps clearly there is no way he could possibly keep steady pace with the insults and abuses he undertakes from the young lad who is said to be his master. Despite this lad is not in any way close to a professional barber. He is uninformed, wayward, and seldom acts in jest. At some points, he gets in physical combats with his employer who owns the shop and is a good lad, and cunning when it comes to money. It is all about and how to make it. Lakota comprehends it is in his best interest to leave the lad and go in search for his own shop where he could cut people's hair and earn his own money so as to be able to, at least, care for himself, raise some money to move into an apartment that he could be share with other people, rather than going to eat in a soup kitchen and sleep in a homeless shelter every night. He is done with it. He is done with the notion of seeing himself drowned and not making any attempts to swim out of the sea. He fancies it an easy thing to do, seeing that others are coming in and not spending a week to learn before cutting people's hair and getting paid for it. He would have to uplift himself, he would have to grant himself a leave from suffering unpleasant experiences, changing the unpleasant situation to become a better one. He would have to move his world forward no matter what comes, he shall survive and read a success story.

Hence, when he leaves and has his own place to cut hair, he sees it is not meeting his expectations. Frequently, he engages in quarrels and feuds with the customers, and the employer, who actually has no choice, could not sack him, for there are many shops that are also looking for barbers. So, he proceeds with the work and begins to earn salaries and purchase whatever he needs. He thinks about the job very much, and inevitably, arrives at a junction where he understands for him to improve in it, he must learn the secret of it. Ultimately, he discovers, via this profession, that any sort of skill or talent can be created through the seriousness, passion, and more training. It has taught him that whatever a man is doing at any given time, he is physically and emotionally sending a message to enrich the mental state, modifying the brain to become better at that thing and becomes a professional. It is the more you practice and show devotion that helps you to arrive at the climax. Sacrifices are needed, very much needed.

Seeing himself as a man who has been sleeping in the streets and tunnels, and then, in the blink of an eye, has a place he could sleep that he pays for. Furthermore, he is able to purchase any kind of food he wants and cooks them in his own home. This, in accordance with fact, has in a way, compels him to envisage a strict liability action required by many individuals. It is exasperating and boring to him to see that society can do a lot to assist people to stand on their feet when tragic stories of life emerge. But to say that some people take advantage of the social assistance rendered to them and stuck in it, forgetting they would have to be "man enough" to change their own situation; it appears they are abusing it, they are exploiting others, and also contributing to the reasons many governments are not in support of rendering every citizen equal share of their benefits. This is what he, Lakota, witnesses take place in Paris, the proceedings by which many of these French citizens said to be minorities, indulge in criticizing and finding faults with their governments. Meanwhile, they too are tied up with hatred and disbelief in the system, which is steering them to find themselves in a situation so critical they are unable to surpass. If he, Lakota, who has come there with no penny and is illegal in the country, could find a way for himself, then what are these people doing?—grumbling and inflicting more agonies on themselves. Will that solve the whole problem? Sometimes, it is not society we punish if we decide to perpetuate misdeeds and become failure, which we should consider as our own responsibilities.

Lakota, by this time, is having the prospect of coming out victorious. He regards himself as a strong man, doing the things that are desirable, therefore, obtaining certitudes and convictions that would prompt him to set himself in a satisfactory state, thence, moves his world forward. He suffers looking for his own customers, cutting the hair, and proactively engaging in some serious and important conversations with them to add enthusiasm into the job while giving them his attention. The job, to him, is not tiresome, or requiring too much efforts, instead, it is pleasant, it is enjoyable, and it is relaxing. Not to say, how he could make more money by cleaning and tidying the shop, or the many young girls and women who come in and throw themselves to him, wanting to pleasure him with their physical beauty. He is a happy man again, particularly when it happens he is having access to enter the city's public library to borrow some books, even when he is illegal in the country. He loves France and he sees himself as someone to inspire people in France to embrace evolution, but also to extend it to the entire world. It could be said he feels disheartened with the French citizens, generally the blacks and Arabs, who happen to be in one of the greatest countries in the world and would not make notice of the great opportunities lay for them to relish and be happy. He, being that man with intellectual curiosity, has immersed into the world of literature and reading almost every book in the library written in English. Wherein he is starting to haul himself from a tranquil and calm life into plight, into danger, into a world that invites scrutiny from the French who are noted to practically believe in the ways of the French and displeased with the fact he is reading books in English. Of course, he does perceive this, he does note how he is attended to as an African, who is illegal and not complying to their rules and regulations that all immigrants are obliged to speak French. He would never desist from his mission purposefully because people observe his attitudes and try to know more about him and from where he is coming from. He is intensely ambitious, searching for an answer to a question never before been asked. His wandering quest for a meaning of life is noticeable by the public. His entire soul, which craves for energetic movements and sensations and desires, things unheard of, things that are exciting, things that are extraordinary. Every a thing he possesses inside is seen reflecting outside of him. He is burning with the flame, showing more ability to procure more and more knowledge from every source. At a time, he becomes a lone wolf, terrifying the French and their authority. They are scared of him, because of how he deems everything to be possible, even things that are not, because of how he seems a dynamic and courageous leader, and willing to prove it. Yet, he is very patient and witty. He fathoms the Universe to be a web of energy, extending it to him to purify his spirit—that certain purity of spirit which he lacks to become a great artist of any sort, to become an activist, to become a true evolutionist who is guided by love and the willingness to do everything peacefully with his heart and soul, not merely by words, but by his doings. The power for adaptation he could see is what he needs to survive, and he must survive, he must accomplish the mission set for him.

One sunny afternoon, at the time when slow spring comes each day and gradually until a night of warm wind appears and bring it suddenly and full. The time when winter is at its end and everyone wishing for spring, wishing to experience the festive joy and hope it brings. The time when everyone witnesses the mystery of how the sunny and calm weather creates attractive and connective atmosphere that permits us to inhale the air that has much to do with humanity and nature, and how they affiliate, seeing how the flowers bloom; this very time, while inside the shop where he works Lakota reads one of the novel he has bought from a bookshop— that is indeed, a book on religion, theology, and spirituality—all about mythology in comparison with other religious books like the Bible, the Koran, and the Torah. It is interesting and worth the money he has purchased it. Then, walks in a tall, light-skinned lass, who is as beautiful as a goddess and, to an extent, any man who sets his eyes on her would be poised to pay any amount of money to have her for one hour. She is eloquent when she opens her mouth to speak, having that respectful and benignant attitude, and moreover, she is honest, not showing if she has a higher status than others; that makes every man want to fall in love with her immediately she sits to talk.

The moment she first steps into the shop, Lakota thinks she has come in to fix her hair, since the shop is also serving as a beauty salon, where some African women dress and plait hair. In fact, it is astounding, and seems jocular when she requests for a barber rightly as Lakota is about to show her to one of the hairdressers whom they both work together and also his employer.

Thereupon, it is the Arab lad, who also is a barber, indubitably cannot even comprehend a word she speaks for the fact he doesn't speak English. Meanwhile, she too declines to speak a language others could hear—a language she understands quite well and what everybody there could speak—the French language. The other lad briskly seizes the opportunity to show her his seat so he could cut her hair. Lakota is furious, perhaps, not that he is going to allow that fury spoils his day, or make him forget about a mission on which he is about to embark that he has read in a book not quite long. It becomes more astounding when she walks closer to Lakota and requests if she would be permitted to sit in his seat so as to get her hair cut. Understanding very well that his co-worker, the other lad is better and is in the business longer than he, Lakota reckons it appropriate and wiser if the lad is given the job, for he has only learnt and worked at this profession for a short time, not even four months, while his colleague who is assisting and teaching him more of how to do this job and also how to handle some of these customers because he has stayed nineteen years doing this particular work, having too many customers, earning a lot, and lavishing on drugs and women.

After she sits and the robe is tied round her body, he picks up his clipper, brushes the dirt out of it, oils and treats it with some chemicals all to impress her that he is a professional barber—furthermore, he cares for her safety in aspect of health and well-being. Moving closer, he loves the smell of her and is ineluctably carried away by her beauty and sense of humor.

After more than ten minutes without anyone talking, but concentrating on listening to the music coming from the television he Lakota has placed there. Silence occupies the latitude and space inside the shop. It is then then she feels opportune to speak, and she says to him, "I have seen you reading a book when I first passed this shop. I have read that same book some years ago and know what it is all about."

"Wow! That is great," replies Lakota, trying to draw confidence from the conversation.

"You seem to like to read," she continues, trying to lift her head to see if her eyes meets with his. And she does as their both eyes fracas and smiles project of their both faces.

"I am a writer. Not long till I have published my autobiographical book."

"I know that from the first time I set my eyes on you while you read. I see you have strong passion for reading. The way you are serious with the book I grasp you are not showing much interest in your job like you are in that book. I understand you want to travel into a world far different from where you are, and that is the reason you always pick up books and read whenever there are no customers. By the way, how does it look like when you are writing? More specifically when you are writing a non-fiction book."

"I think it is easier and more emotional. When you commence in writing a story...you see that the beginning is filled with many emotions— excitement, inspiration, hope, and anticipation. Then comes a time when you really become doubtful and overwhelmed with the feelings of agitation and anxiety. But, in all, you broaden your perspectives of what is important in your life and how it could probably shape and play a vital role in your future and make you achieve the longtime dream you have been pursuing."

"That is so wonderful. How I wish I could write. I enjoy reading books, apart from the problem I am having, not actually knowing what to do to acquire this extraordinary talent for creativity."

"What do you do for a living," Lakota demands, wiping some hairs off the lady's body.

"As a matter of fact, I am a lawyer to many politicians in this country," she responds, looking around to see everyone there staring at her, even when she thinks no one, except Lakota, understands English.

"Wow! You must be filthy rich then," says Lakota, thinking of what to do to get more of her attention as he hears some of the women picking up a conversation with the lady.

"You're not kidding. The truth is that I am not rich. Are you going to charge me more because I have made you aware of the work I do?" she demands, laughingly.

"Of course, not," replies Lakota, engaging more in the discourse about politics.

He sees that she is pretty. She is a woman who deserves to be loved and cherished. He would want to lick her shoes if ever she would permit and request conduct like that. He is, at that very moment, recalling how he has always believed to meet the woman of his life, a woman who is to love him for whom he truly is, not whom he pretends to be. Hence, he has vowed to love such a woman, to accredit his belief that whatever any man wish to do for a woman, he should do it, please her, cherish her, adore her, and worship her, for she is like a mother to him. She has long given birth to him right before he knows her.

"I guess you must be very current—in politics, I mean," inquires Lakota, cutting the hair slowly and walking around to see if his employer pays any attention to what he does. Wherein his employer is passionately and stupidly in love with him despite she is married to another African and has borne him two kids.

"Politicians are the problems of this world," she unravels. "Since they have come to conceive they can easily ridicule and poke fun at us with their ideas, knowing we would undoubtedly succumb to their will. It is amazing how we, the people, still are reluctant in getting to make them change this view. On the contrary, many of us are proudly constituting to how we are being steadily manipulated and maneuvered by this people, seeing malnutrition in one hand, while obesity is in the other hand, seeing human beings getting stuck in abject poverty, and at the same time, some others are having enough to feed their pets and throw away. Is it not of our interests and concerns to query this ideals that have been created for the full benefits of the few?"

After she finishes uttering her speech, she breaks into silence likely as every other person there. It is completely blatant, seeing he, Lakota, has conceived a great reason to rejoice, for he has stumbled to meet someone he has long been searching for who would help him execute the plans he is been drawing in his head all alone. He ascertains there is not any need for him to proceed with the pretense of satisfying the wish of his employer rather than with his relentless pursuit of happiness, which is more akin to a mission set for him. However, he practically has no clue of who she is, or from where she has comes, yet he already affirms he is heading to a natural destination with her. He believes that it is destiny bringing her to him since, long ago, prior to their meeting, he has yearned for it. He has envisaged someone like her partaking in this mission. Naturally, weirdly engrossed in his life has been the force, the severity, and the condition of his vision, the vision to reach his word to the world, to enlighten the feeble-minded.

Not minding how the other women and the other Arab lad and his customers stare attentively at the both of them, they persist and resume with their conversation and express joy in it, regardless of who is there. It shows a kind of absurdity to others. But it is a belief that yields desirability and magnetism. What you await, also awaits you. When one patiently and wisely lumbers across the Universe, searching for that which is yours, believing so much in what you love and trusting in your hearts' desire, and you keep doing it and believing, only to come face to face with it. What would be others expectations? For you to relinquish all your dreams and relentless struggling and faith, solely because you tend to perpetually please others to displease yourself. Are there not things that are more essential to one's heart than of many more to fascinate and satisfy other's anticipations, specifically when it seems that no matter what you do to please these people, they are constantly poised to never lend their ears to you? So, will it not be more suitable and divine to accept that which is agreeable to your heart?—that which your heart truly desires?

They both would not wait for the people around to pass their judgment on them, for they know they are on the right track and are moving towards where their hearts are directed. Thusly, they proceed with giggling, and more giggling, and more giggling.

When the beautiful angel finally leaves the shop, she gives him her phone number, beseeching him to ring her on phone and perhaps meet to have a dinner together in one of the restaurants in Paris. It is great, an exciting feeling of wonder and sensation. It is what he wishes for that he sees himself come personally with. He would not fail to hit a chance to grab what has been offered to him by the Universe. In spite of the life that he lives, which is extremely more appreciable and superb, but he acknowledges it is also the appropriate time for him to make his word be heard—to spread the messages across the globe—that message for a change in the system of how humanity should be living.

Chapter 13

It is a man called Tyson. He has been born and raised in the city of Vicksburg, Mississippi. His father who has stumbled upon wealth, owning large farm land upon which he usually grows vegetables and mostly raising sheep, goats and cows. After their mother has passed away as a result of long-term pains and disability from lung cancer. She has also suffered from breast cancer three years and survives it two years before the lung cancer. Finally, when she died, the father becomes unfit to push ahead with the farming due to heart failure and the inability to cope with the loss of the dearest person to him. In this way he has also passed away a year after he has lost his wife, bequeathing to his two sons the sum of two million dollars, and also, a style of respect for hard-work, goodness, and modesty.

Two years after the death of their father, Tyson and his younger brother, George, could no longer see a situation that was in a proper condition for them to conform to each other. It has become typically apparent to other people, and also appalling, the manner in which George is troubling and battling his elder brother, Tyson, considering he wants his share of their father's wealth in order to move on with his life. At a time they have become two brothers who are far different, and that is challenging and engendering an indefinite numbers of furies and feuds and squabbles. In the course of time, when Tyson could no longer get along with the everyday battles, on apace, he arrives at a conclusion to waive his plans of tying bonds with his brother. He calls for George, and then settles the issue with their father's attorney, who has first argued it is a wrong decision for them to take. But, seeing what he is seeing at the very time he makes an effort to bring a settlement to the feuds, he wholeheartedly suggests it is the appropriate thing to be done. The wealth is split into two equal parts, the first with his own, follows by the other.

Tyson, presently, lives in New York, after investing his money as a stock-broker for five years, buying and selling stocks and other securities. He has become a billionaire and having everything he dreams—putting up more investments in real estate and care properties. There is money pouring in, and more, and more. Meanwhile, his younger brother George has seen himself struggling in the streets of Las Vegas, trying to find a haven, for he has gambled all his money on different spins of roulette, drugs, prostitutes, and luxury cars.

For many a time, Tyson could not bear the burden of living happily with everything he possesses in life while his brother suffers and wanders around the streets. He wants to reach out to him, lend him a helping hand, and also reestablish a close relation with him. On the other hand, George is so overcome with shame and guilt and regrets that he is unable to put in conducts any acceptance of his brother's assistance. He could not stand this humiliation—a consequence of his own failures. It conveys the impression of being classified as a failure—that is like a poison to his own nature. So, he rebuffs the offers, believing in his will and strength to destroy Goliath and becomes King of Israel. His massive ego, his own pride, is forcefully dragging him away from his blood brother into a disarray. He could do it on his own. He could venture to do anything to prolong and keep the ball rolling, but not with his brother's aid.

For many a month, Tyson has labored to locate his brother's whereabouts to no avail. He understands him better than anyone else. He comprehends it is ego playing his card on him. He has to let him go. He has to let him be free like a bird, to fly to wherever and however he wishes. He has to allow the water that boils to become cool simply by not snuffing out the fire. He has to do it that way—permit a chance for something unbelievable, something unthinkable, to become probable, and to become creditable. A miracle, which is what he awaits to see.

Some years later he watches on the television, the news on how his brother is abducted by a group of terrorists in the Middle East. At first, he dismisses the notion to accept it as true, that it is his own blood brother, George being abducted by terrorists in the Middle East with a threat they are going to behead him, except on a condition which accounts on the American troops being pulled out of their country. Like a dream, it is to him, a nightmare, it actually is. For, if it has been a dream, it might have been very sensible, but nightmares are tremendously horrible.

Perhaps, some weeks ago he has met with his brother who has become so devoted to his Christian faith prior to this incident. They have both talked about their pasts and dine and merry together. He learns that his brother is already working with the CIA, but he would never hazard a guess he will be traveling to a war zone where there are these monsters of ruthless cruelty to set out on an operation as so dreary and deadly as that.

When his brother declines his assistance, he also ceases to prolong the cause and renounces a claim to do what seems to be against his will, probably not to make him feel inadequate or embarrassed. Whereas, he has been later informed of how his brother joins the FBI and has been hired through their collegiate recruitment program. After that he is assigned to the many perilous and grievous tasks, and has been provided with information, authority, and power to stalk and harass people deem too dangerous to be allowed to live in the society. It seems so ghastly and unsafe when Tyson at the initial time hears his own brother is commending himself into the hands of these evil spirits seen every day in the streets of America. He perceives a potentially dangerous attachment to this profession, and he notes there is a need for him to consult his brother, to notify him of his worries and fears. Nevertheless, he is also excessively punctilious and considerate not to meddle in his brother's private affairs. So, he desists.

Hearing the news is heartrending and devastating. But, is there anything he could do to get his brother alive from the hands of the terrorists? Is there any way he could plead to the American Government to pull their troops back in order for his brother to live again? Will life be worth living after losing every member of his family? Is it how he has outlined to live his future, with lots of money and no one to share it with? What goodwill and admiration will it be to lose all that are precious to him, and unaffectedly relish his wealth all alone? He has thought of having a child of his own, but when his marriage has fallen apart, he has to pay a ransom amount to his wife who has filed a lawsuit to divorce him. It is a disappointment, a painful sense of dissatisfaction of how the system works. He has done everything for the woman—everything, probably, everything to please her. He has spent his money on her to get the best quality of education in the country and abroad. He has lavished her with a luxurious life and brought her closer to eminent and well respected people in the world. Whereby, the retribution is how his own wife commences in a sex affair with their cook. Thence, he, Tyson arrives home one day to meet them both having sex in his matrimonial bed. It is repulsive and provoking. If he is not highly cautious and tolerable, he is bound to commit double homicide. For that understandable reason, he has given up the notion to engage in another relationship so fast. Instead, he wants to wait for the right time, he wants a child with any woman, no matter where she comes from, but never involve himself in a marriage again. He has left his wealth under the control of a CEO and found peace in his heart to pursue and acquire knowledge, to study matter and phenomena in the Universe; he tends to be philosophical, religious, being able to give mythical explanations of the nature and structure of the Universe; he wants to be enlightened, to seek an answer for creation; he wants to know how man has come into existence and living on Earth.

It happened that at that very moment, it is him speaking to some unknown humans around the lonely territory he occupies all alone. For long, he has been deeply concerned about his brother's attitudes and lifestyle. He minds to alert him of the possible outcome. What if he does, will he ever pay any attention to him? He understands his brother is not afraid of anything, lest it be death. To avoid hearing how his brother has become one of the greatest spies and has been working for the Federal Government of his country, he has decided to focus more on his quest for the truth about creation. That, which positively distracted his attention, prompting him to become more absorbed in battling the complexity of life and man and his relation with the Universe. He sees in himself the wonderful compound of positivity and spirituality, leading him to his goal. He has been studying, philosophizing, exploring every possibility, yet he has been unable to abstain from his brother's affairs, he has been unable to give up on him, perchance, this has been the preeminent basis which has led to they both not able to get along with each other. His own brother, George, who has come to be what he is—bothering, contemplating, and speculating on everything—his brother's fortune his own misfortune, a misfortune that has later driven him into his inner discomfort, making every attempts to outpace him in the pursuit of recognition, in the pursuit of grandiosity. He has become what he becomes, involving and appointing himself in more competitive battles, inevitably bleeding tears of enviousness and crying joy to shroud his bitter dark heart, all because he tends to see his brother fall down to worship and submit to him. He wants to be honored by every a being, he wants to be more successful, he wants to be a national figure, he wants to climb to reach the climax—to see himself more respected and honored, then he would see himself as a true patriot who loves and contributes a perpetual support to his nation, regardless of where it stands; a hero who will die serving his nation, not a billionaire like his brother, a coward who could not harm a rat.

Tyson who grasps all what is going on, oftentimes says to himself, ' "why is it there are innumerable people among us who still, intensively, decline to accept the easiest truth—to fear what is dangerous and refrain from it? It is true, this many tend to do—to take interest in events and incidents that foment bereavement. They are quite gleeful and drown frequently in the habit of desiring to lay their hands in fire, merely to feel the pain. They are not petrified because of their strong beliefs in themselves, in their historical background, or in their governments. They believe they are to serve the purpose, dedicate their lives to the service of their governments and nations—all to attain different ranks and be presented with medals of Honor. They become so patriotic to render their lives for their nation, even when they are ordered to destroy every other soul seen as a disturbance to their nation. They do whatever it takes with no further inquiry or raising a question for why it is necessary. And that they rule out of fanaticism. In a practical manner, it appears to them that the terrorists are the ones to be labeled fanatics. They would decline to acknowledge their own faults, seeing that fanaticism is noted to be of different forms. Fanaticism which means wildly excessive or irrational devotion, dedication, or enthusiasm. Whether it is towards politics, race, sport, religion, or towards a nation—it is all the same. In accordance with fact, when people become so fanatic about humanity, then we will see that no one is hurting anyone. Then, we will come to realize that we are all one in a collective consciousness—known to be a set of shared beliefs, ideas and moral attitudes which operate as a unifying force within the society. Unless we defy the mindset to accept everything as it already is, seeing it as the law of nature, we will never achieve peace, we will never be free. It is so hapless, it is so pitiful, it is so distasteful, to see how blind we still are to be unable to draw into our intelligence and general knowingness, to not compass how we have imprisoned ourselves in some kind of religion, or race, or politics, or sport, or government, or whatsoever. By so doing, we have seen others not in the same track with us to be against us. We separate ourselves from them, we isolate ourselves, we forget that in this isolation of ourselves we come to a destruction, we come to our own doom. All these issues of religion, politics, race, and sport, are not essentially questions of beliefs, but questions of deep inner feelings, which tend to create identity in us. And when we live with identity in our hearts, we are in actual fact constituting the distinction between ourselves and others, proving our superiority. And that is a sense of power, a power to rule over them, a power to guide them to our own doctrines and making them loathe and put an end to theirs, to make of them a subordinate functionary. The pleasure we derive from this ideal is so strong it becomes so spiritual within us, it becomes a part of our everyday lives. In our continuous participation in this ideal, we will never incur or capture a point of relief. But, except on one ground, we could recover, and to do so, we have to reengage with humanity and nature, and to reengage, we must reform our ways and doctrines. For us to be able to breathe a fresh air of a new life, we have to teach and participate in loving and caring for our neighbors, accepting their dissimilarities and similarities inclusively as they are, sharing with them our love and compassion, and we have to start now. Then, we will see the light again. Then, we will experience that source of our power and strength and glory and paint the most beautiful picture of history.'"

Tyson grasps in his mind that, in no degree would he have the innate capacity, by means of entreaty, to convincingly demonstrate to the government of his country that there is a necessity for his brother's life to be spared while they return their troops home. There is no way he might be able to influence them for his brother's life to be saved. Albeit, he has been phoned by the CIA to be briefed the significant and insignificant parts of the story, and also meticulously advise him not to disclose to anyone of some of their laid out plans to redeem his brother from captivity.

Waiting, waiting, and waiting. Days and months passed and nothing effectively has been accomplished. Nothing in realness is to be lost if he dies for his brother. Nothing on Earth will enrapture or exult him more than having his brother alive. He loves him so much. He loves him, for he is the only person left in his whole life, so he has become a part of him. Money could not bring his brother back to him even when he has enough to lavish on anyone who might help save his life.

For all this while, he has forsaken absolutely all the projects he is been involved, that he has previously done a massive spending, not to mention the time committed. He wakes up one night, depressed, and unable to sleep, nor is he able to concentrate on any other thing he does. Assimilating much thought he arrives at one opinion—there is a reason for everything. He instantly grasps it would be equivocal, it would be faultless if he could leave off his wealth in search of some real meaning to life and the existence of man. He has to do it, for it is a call he has long be called for—which he has ignored perhaps for him not to lose his wealth. This is really the time, the exact time for him to put his studies into practice, for him to understand the true nature of the Universe better than he has. This, he expeditiously ascertains it is an obligation, an obligation to walk along the pavement of abhorrence and dejection. But he desires to do it, he yearns for it—to encounter turbulent mischief and mayhem and unhappiness.

After some few days the thoughts have come into him to go search for his brother, George, Tyson sees himself in the city of Ankara, the capital of Turkey, lodging in an extremely luxurious hotel of an exorbitant price of 20,000.00 dollars for one night. He decides to pay for one week, going outside every day to take a walk around the city, and, more specifically to find people who have been able to use their expert knowledge to become long-running smugglers from Turkey to the neighboring countries.

At last, after much searching and a brief bargaining he is been told to get himself prepared that same night to be hidden in a car, which will be driven into Syria. This he has done, first, paying another large sum of 30,000.00 dollars for the trip. When at some later time they arrive in the area where from a little distance he could hear the terrible sound of gunshots and screaming from the armies and the rebels who are noticeable for possessing a no-tolerance attitude towards anyone who is in opposition or in contradiction to their philosophical system and are bearing the responsibility of his brother's captivity. A frightful and malicious wind of gloom slips into his heart, danger casts its shades upon him and his face gleams with lights of incompetency, panic sprinkles waters of death and calling names he could probably not comprehend, his tendency overstates and overrules his motive, and not a word he could perceive with his ear, only to realize his own systema nervosum periphericum responding to the non-stop most widely violence shooting, and with the outcry and yelling and cheering of the word, "Allahu Akbar, Allahu Akbar, Allahu Akbar," recurrently from every corner, from every hidden and empty quarter. It is horrifying and revolting, hearing these cries and violence acts being partake in. He invisions himself come to seek his own death and to be reborn, and this very place is the right place, the right scene.

It came to pass that he has to bargain with some of the smugglers who have brought him to where he is, pleading for them to settle on a plan on how his brother might be set free, with a promise of a hundred million dollars. It is these smugglers' interest to carry out this plan by going to negotiate with the leaders of the terrorist group. Not that it would be acquired with ease because of the violence risk involved when tensions between the terrorists and the armies and other foreign troops remain so very steep. But the money bargained would be worth dying for. If they could have that amount of money at that hour, never in life will they cross the border to die in a war zone, or ponder in their heart on how to smuggle people into other countries. They want the money so badly, and they are desperate to do whatever it might take to achieve their dreams, to become rich...and live happily throughout the rest of their remaining lives on Earth. They have to lose their lives, or get the money.

They have been having contacts with the terrorists for long and come across them several times when some of their comrades delivering they to them across the border. Know they everywhere, and why should it be that all their lives they have to entangle in danger, why do not the right thing once and for all and from then on be free forever? They have to, they have to be the soldiers who die once before their final deaths. So, advise they him to be patient where they have concealed him in a locked room inside an evacuated house in a deserted area not far from where they will be going to negotiate with the men that matters, where gunfire are exchanged.

Of persistently inhabiting in a dark locked room, after twenty hours, no water, no food, showing restraint and bracing the noise of the falling rain, the loud noise of the wind turbine outside the house, indeed, not to mention the sound of the violence gunshots. Looks he at his wrist watch once again to realize it is 10:00 pm and becomes darker. Wants he to escape, thinking they have forgotten him there, or they are unable to meet with the demand, or perhaps, been killed they have already by the terrorists who might have declined to enlist in any kind of negotiation with anyone. Wondering he is and worried of what possible unsatisfactory situation that will evolve. It might be better if he tries to break the door open and escape, now for his own life. He could not maintain the continuity to bear the burden of his own brother anymore. He is done with it. He is done encountering dangers and falling into predicaments for his brother who is so adamant in refusal to alter his principles—his envious brother. He is done with searching for the true meanings of life.

As he is about to smash and shatter the door, he hears the noise of a car drives closer to the deserted house. And when some of the people walk closer to the door where he is locked in, fear bounces upon his chest. He persists and refuse to utter a word until someone ultimately comes to open the door for him to get out.

Reaching where the three of the terrorists who have come along with the smugglers to negotiate with him the release of his brother for money, bows he down to them and in Arabic, greets,

"Salam Alaikum."

"Alaikum Salam," they all respond.

At that moment, one of them requests: "Are you a Muslim?"

"No, I am not. I would not mind to become a part of any other religion someday, but as for now I am not having any religion until this episode my brother has landed himself," responds he, not even daring to look into the eyes of the questioner. "Alright," of them one says, and walks closer, holding his hand out for a shake with him. Baffles him it is to consider what he has vitally uttered out to be a kind of compliment instead of dragging along the dangerous line that yields a sheer provocation and stupidity—this being said to a person who is extremely religious. His anticipation is it would be decried, and more if not thoughtfully said, the counteraction would frankly be said that he has broken a taboo, and he, as the perpetrator would surely be inflicted a penalization.

When holds he his hand out to the man who demands a handshake, he expects a bruise on his face. On the contrary, the man shakes him and also walks closer to embrace him warmly. Stunning it is a moment in his life, a moment when he assures himself of the wonderful steps necessary for him to reach his destination, his discoveries.

"Your brother, George has formerly recounted everything about you before us. And I can see you are truthfully that same person he has mentioned. You see, I know you are on a quest to find the meanings of life. The meaning of life have become a recurrent theme which everyone of us who is possessive of this intellectual abilities and faculties. Hence, we are proud to perform greatly well in a struggle to question the reason for the conflict between man and his creator, or rather you say 'the Universe,' or cosmos. It is a philosophical and spiritual constant question that practically craves a culmination, Urim and Thummim. Although, many scientists and theologians have also have many speculations on their own about this subject matter, for it concerns them, it is of interest and importance to them. They have done their own exploration of the context and parameters concerning varying aspects of the meanings of life. People have come to arrive at distinctive answers, drawing from their conceptions, from their perceptions. It is not that we do not gratify the new way of life that civilization has betoken in man. Not that we are unkind and inconsiderate in the acceptance of a better way of life, or let's say we are hostile and always tending to destroy any time, any day. That does not consist of any fact in a manner in which they view and equate us. It does not conform to what we are. Before the westerners start to sense civilization, we the Arabs and some others referred to as "easterners" by them have long done so. We have had this rational value upon which art, science, and morals are all built. We have had great philosophers who see the Earth where we live to be a beautiful and wonderful place to inhabit, so we should preserve it. The Greeks, whose civilization has influenced other westerners to this day, assuredly, have sought it from the ancient Egyptians, ancient Assyrians, ancient Babylonians, and ancient Persians. These ancient kingdoms have sought to secure predominant influence around the globe. They have built museums and monuments, and have come up with new formulations uncovered in medicines to cure strange diseases. You see, blessed with the Koran as a religious guide, Mohammed Laila Surilalaila la…"

"Peace be upon the holy one," responds Tyson, lifting his head up to discover how they all turn their faces to see who has blurted out a word of Islam.

"That is splendid. It seems you have been involved in some studies of the Koran," demands, the terrorist.

"Yes, I have actually been doing a little of it prior to the time I decide to come here."

"Anyway, my name is Hussein, and I am the third in position of all the rebels. I hope you pardon me seeing that you are standing face to face with a man possessing a great mental power, a man with deep intellect and also showing compassion. A man like me being transformed into a monster"

"You seem more interesting than I have originally thought," said he Tyson, walking closer to Hussein and whispering in his ear, pleading for a loaf of bread and water.

"You are hungry and thirsty, and never mentioned it? Be not afraid of me. I know of you before you even thought of coming here," said Hussein, ordering for food to be brought and served to his new friend—Middle Eastern food, enriched with spices to make it more palatable.

The food after when served and they have both eaten to their satisfactions while proceeding with the earnest conversation from which they both derive intellectual pleasure as others watch and drink their tea and smoke shisha. For the fact that Tyson desires so much for the food to help curb his appetite, yet, he is much too perspicacious not to be oblivious of the basis of his self-committing adventurous journey…that has delivered him into their hands. But, it thus appears he is indeed vastly drifted into fascination, listening to a new friend presumed to be an enemy.

"I guess you will, in some ways, endeavor to discern everything we have put into discussion, to be able to see that both sides of the story have to be narrated, and after estimation and consideration before any judgment should be passed. A lot of people come to conclusion without first listening to the other man. Anyway, you see how they build roads and bridges and charge people for using that road. Then people would say the government is doing well. That is capitalism for you: a way of exploiting and making you work all your life until you become exhausted and depressed—it is a way of tying massive debts around our necks. What I am implying is they make life easier for you, and at the same time, more miserable. Civilization, in actuality, has taken humanity into a new world of activities and energy, but do we have to remunerate with our lives, our souls? Watching birds fly and doing it on our own, using machines in transporting people and goods from one city to another, is a great achievement in the history of mankind, but why has the pursuit of well-being ceased to be visible in the agenda of our rulers and governments? Where has compassion gone? Where has virtue gone? Where has fairness gone? Where has prudence gone? We believe with intellect, technology, and science man will obtain the greatest power in achieving immortality. It is true we have invented machines to make it feasible for us to acquire massive amount of knowledge, and advance more every minute and hour and day, but when shall we be knowledgeable enough to discern the reason of our existence—to know why and what we are truly living for as humans?"

Listening to Hussein speaks with conviction, seems though he could express himself better in speech than in any other thing. He is eloquent and thoughtful. But how could one not intrude in an affair so relevant to get through the globe? It is fascinating and arousing curiosity and basic cognitive process. It is precisely what he wishes he could endeavor to inculcate in these people labeled terrorists. Presently, it is one of them coming up with the subject matter. Then, why not admonish them of the proper rules needed to confront problems without having to participate in any violence act. He wants to teach, and also learn.

So says he to Hussein, "My brother...I do share your beliefs that humans are making every attempt to elude the very important issues to be dealt with. They substantively postulate that by eluding these problems they might be capable of advancing towards a stage of life where happiness is attainable. Yet, what they are staunchly oblivious of is that these problems await them no matter where they intend to journey to; they will revert, and the problems will be reestablished. You see, Hussein, to an extent, we humans have come to develop artificial intelligence, which is opposite of human intelligence, and also a rival. In a real sense, we are threatening humanity with new ideas and innovations. We see things that from afar that can guide us through a course to where our doom lies, yet, what are within a short distance from us that will guide us to eternity and posterity and prosperity, this we do not see, or we see and solely neglect them. It is baffling how we tend to live, how we tend to bring upon ourselves menace and destruction, which will last forever. We see global warming, we see the never-to-be resolved worldwide financial crisis, wars, and terrorism spreading across the entire globe, tornadoes, earthquakes, tsunamis, and more and more natural disasters, yet we tend to neglect these things which matters and ready to bring about failures to heal our world, to hamper our every single dream to live peacefully and joyously. See how we live in pretense, laying apart that same fear that we too have created. We firmly believe in our strengths to achieve our goals in life. We are believing in our governments to be at our assistance, so when they fail, we too fail. How glorious will that day be? How glorious will it be the day humankind will be set free from the bondage it is been locked in? How will it be when our adhering to love and compassion will be the rhythm we live to, when our hearts will bleed in confidence and exultation that yield benevolence?"

"Have you mention that, Tyson?" demands Hussein, resting for a few minutes before he could move onward with the discussion. "There you go!"

He goes on, "Would you concur if I say terrorism is a way people believe they could possibly break free from this system of capitalism?—this same system that champions a mindset that creates deforming behaviors inconsistent with who we are as human beings. These terrorists believe they are being oppressed, and the only way they can fight is to terrorize people. This system of capitalism uniformly, will, and shall project source cultivated in violence and destruction. It will steadily beget more competitive dynamics while banks increase in numbers and gain strength and fortunes. It will incessantly give rise to more wage slavery and inequalities. Intrinsically, when many of us have come to see to the reality of this, and we wish we have never plumped for this very unconventional lifestyle. We fancy a new way out, which naturally and guilelessly is to return to the ways remotely compared to primordial. It is a spontaneous movement into bliss, into contentment, into well-being. Nonetheless, we also have for long ago decried this same way that we see ourselves reverting to…to be so reprehensible—which was a motive for a rebellion at the first time—a way which helps us communicate with our creator, and also with the rest of humanity—that way is religion. Man used to think that religion makes people to be virtue, to be moral. So, when it happens that man no longer believe what he observes of religion and how it is supposed to be represented, so he has decided to choose to live differently, to eliminate fear and conflicts within himself, to create a different atmosphere of change and create his own reality. And now that he has arrived at an alternative which becomes more tragic and detrimental, he has decided on his own once again to retract and cling to the better of two evil. But all he could behold is others despising him, loathing him, and labeling him a fool. When it appears he is powerless and lacking the necessary authority to do as he wishes because of how he is been portrayed and classified, he must not tremble in fear, he must not be intimidated and be deprived of his right to make decisions that will be soothing for him. In preference, he will fight, he will shed his own blood and the blood of others to retrieve the dream taken away from him."

"Do you, without prevarication take time to ponder this subject-matter so as to surmise openly in the broad daylight, that by shedding blood, all will be resolved and demands will be met?" requests Tyson, attempting not to be rude. He wishes to be certain he is standing for the truth of the matter to be unveiled, basically on the term of religion, whereas he prays silently in his heart even if he never believes in prayers and perpetually maintains and advances the notion of people's thinking ability to be more potential in everything, and to continually abstains from the fantasies of the existence of the supernatural entities or entity, for, perhaps, he has seen much lack of evidence.

"I do absolutely consent to that credence which affiliates and upholds a positive outcome. I believe in a conflict resolution. I do hold to your perspectives of how matters should be handled. I understand that, via peace and non-violence, we will always attain freedom, independence, social changes, success, or whatever we wish for. Still, in every way, fighting is inevitable and necessary only if we do it right, if we do it to permit justice to be served and not to become the victims of hate by our neighbors for our wrongdoings." After he has said that, he stands mute, thinking of what else to do or say. "Would you mind if we both take a walk together to discuss more on these issues?" asks he Hussein.

"Yes of course. I welcome your suggestions, my friend," replies he Tyson.

"Anyway, I would prefer you call me a brother," adds, Hussein. "Like an old saying, that we should not trust the English because of their treacherous attitudes towards others in order to steal, so also I advise you to fear the Arabs because they are always dangerous and desperate to do anything that is terrible. What I am implying is, in this place we are, you must be mindful of whatever you intend to pronounce with your mouth, or could be dead at anytime."

When thence as they walk alone in the desert, leaving behind the other terrorists and smugglers who are supremely enchanted for spending enough time there rather than exchanging gunfire with their enemies. They are able to seize the opportunity by drinking tea and smoking all sorts of things. They are less concerned with what both men have to discuss. That is not a burden to them since it already has been concluded and confirmed that a million dollars is being deposited into one of their account in Switzerland. They have to commence with the merriment, while still hoping for the actual amount within some hours when George would be released from his hideout.

"I supposed you comprehend very well this should not have to be a culpability I ought to be meddled in. You see, I am exclusively capable of seeing myself and the world around me sparked and driven into a state of extreme confusion and agitation and violence, for the fact that all men now tend to believe more in power and wealth. Will it not be suitable and desirable if we share love, if we show empathy, if we are being compassionate to our fellow beings?"

"You are very right," says he Tyson, into his eyes looking directly to see if he could read his heart from there. "From how I see you, I sure would opine if you opt for something different—I ought to propound a better life which you honestly merit. Do you have to put upon yourself vengeance when, without doubt, you could even save humanity with your wisdom and knowledge?"

"It is not vengeance, if I must appeal honestly. It is God's will. And to obeys God's will, which is goodwill, we must inexorably ascertain that we are to deny and disobey our own will,—which is man's will, man's will of possession, possession of power and wealth, the will that permits greed to dominate our hearts," articulates Hussein, walking around Tyson as they converse.

Tyson himself is short of words when he hears his new brother, Hussein, gives his moral instructions in tedious manner. He is greatly troubled inside. Yet, he grossly underestimates his rational motive. He has this intuition it could have done him well if he has not plunged into a sort of martyr operation to be attached to a willingness to focus solely on the past and not letting it be history, history which verily will never be forgotten in all human history. In spite of that, he thinks it would be preferable to promote an idea that will insert into one's heart to graciously eradicate violence as a means of seeking justice, an idea that could conquer the demons in that desert and draw all of them to a succession. He loves him no matter what. He understands how the bitterness and resentments come to exist in him. Those who love you would surely do for what you are, not for what you try to be. Because, it is that which you are that you see the true self, and not who you pretend to be. He loves him, because he knows he will be willing to alter his beliefs and walk along the path that leads to peace and healing. He knows he could help him cut the fatal thread tying him to assist in possessing deadly weapons and fighting alongside these evildoers. He wishes he could get his brother freed and takes the man along with him to the United States to help change his life, to transform him from impotence to important, from evil to saint.

"Do you not see we are both connected spiritually and intellectually?" states he Tyson. "There is a saying that when two or more souls connect in recognition, the entire world goes silent, and the connection yields fruit that is a mechanism, either for building, or for destroying. Truly, ours is for building, for healing. I conceive you have found yourself not fit into this lifestyle. It is true that many great men like you have also encountered vulnerable situations like this, and in the process, they are transformed and rewarded with greatness. They first become blind purposefully to get a vision. I know what the problem here is. It is the westerners' notions to transform everyone to their own likeness; to spread democracy around the globe, and that is practically inducing others, who are not in accord with their ideals, to think of halting it before it gets late."

"You have it right my brother," rejoins he Hussein, taking his new brother's hand and holding him tightly with the confident panache of a brother, as well of one amante.

"Verily, I say to you." Holding him closer till at a time Tyson perceives, through that sense of touching, the heavy perspiration and odor coming from his body for not having showered for some days. They could both feel something inside of them connecting, reacting, and it is remarkable, phenomena in nature.

"You see, Tyson, I am quite vague here about your brother's assertion of you being a billionaire. I suppose if I would admit by evaluation that you seem to be unsuitable for that custom. You feel it is not convenient for you to be living an extravagant life, bathing in money when billions of people around the globe are starving to death. You seem to want to look for a way to escape from your own life...to adopt a new idea, to build, and most of all, to heal. It behooves the both of us to reflect on this theme. It is not a coincident this encountering has occurred, neither we are to say if our acquaintance, our affinity, our companionship are not destined. Our attachment to each other is also as I do sincerely aspire to, by belief in the possibility of its occurrence, is prearranged, solidified and required to be a detachment from the terrible iniquitous world. It is not an obnoxious day for us, rather, it should be considered a sacred day for consecrated life, and it is worth celebrating for the sake of humanity. And, if veritably, you do agree with me, I may in the awake of ethical consideration, take this journey with you to the land that is prepared for us to be. I will do so because I am under the impression that life is all about giving to receive; it is all about sacrificing, and when tremendous sacrifices are made, we are rewarded with things of greater values. For we to assure others of the reason we must turn to do what is right that we intend them to do, then we must introduce a way to emphatically succumb to their will—that which in all probabilities could be of a profound disturbance to our own consciousness. That is to reason as in alchemy first law of equivalent exchange which states that humankind cannot gain anything without first giving something in return. To obtain, something of equal value must be lost."

"Wow! You have it right," says he Tyson, snappily. "That is exactly what I was about to say. It reminds me of the end of the world, if we humans will not retrieve from our odd ways to move to the right direction, to heal our wounded planet, and to heal humanity."

"Very well said my brother. Then we must commence now before dawn, before it gets late." He relaxes and breathes heavily before proceeding, "I grow up in London, England where I have studied and obtain Master of Science degree in computer science at the University College, London. I wanted to work and be a part of society, lately to see myself scuffling here in the desert in the wake of gunfire and screaming and consternation. The majority of people labeled terrorists here in this battlefield are Arab children born and bred in the civilized countries like France, Belgium, Holland, Sweden, Denmark, Britain, United States, Germany, Australia, and Canada...while some few others are from Nigeria and Egypt. Others who have never set foot out of their country are said to be not very active in the fights because the grudges engrossed in them are incomparable and unparalleled with the ones in these foreign fighters, as they know us to be. We have lived our childhood and adulthood there in the west, yet we are classified to be second or third class citizens, and no matter how we try, we feel left out all the time. The more we try, the more we find it challenging to please them, to impress them, to satisfy their every need and want of us. It all becomes like jealousy, but it is not. We want to be parts and parcels of the societies where we live. We want to be able to fit in, to live like others and have equal rights and supports and privileges just the same way all of them do. Since they have already taught us how to live and fly and die, we intend to be like them, and all we hear and see them do to us is deprived us of everything and even mock, reject, and treat us unfairly, treat us with gross insensitivity, treat us with insolence, treat us with contemptuous rudeness. And when we endeavor to live our lives in a preferable way, in our own standard, in our own traditional style, they claim we are still far away from civilization, they claim we need their ideals to live. And when we are not abiding to these laws, then we extemporaneously become their worst enemies. Hitherto, they advocate freedom and liberty everywhere and never allow others to be free to do what suits them. It is hypocrisy, it is bigotry, and we have come to swiftly apprehend this, using our intellects. They say we are evil, and our religion and culture are polluted with blood and violence; they say we are ill-fated with anger and killings and everything about us is equated to a degree of obliteration and extermination, perhaps, in so many cities in America, what we see every time are volatile situations with troops and rioters eager for a confrontation. Then, where is the certainty that futurity will not be dazzled? Where is that certitude and conviction that the professed freedom and liberty, the professed civilization, will not be bewildered with chaos and violence? Do we not acknowledge how ignominy, how discrediting it is to see we are left without gentility, without refinement, without enlightenment, not to mention accomplishment? We adore and worship money as a god; we think about technology more than we think about our fellow humans. And we assert we know it all; we say we are "Mr. Perfect" who will lead the world to survival, while directly leading it to its doom. With the intentions of defeating the terrorists and making the countries in the Middle East become democratic, they invade all these countries and bombarding the people there, arresting suspected terrorists and taking them to Guantanamo Bay in Cuba to be imprisoned. Water-boarding and torture are conducted. Yet, all these people responsible continue to enjoy impunity. They infiltrate and make us fight against each other, saying Arabs are always fighting themselves. They do so believing most of our brothers and sisters will be fleeing to seek asylum in their countries and gradually brainwashed and converted to adopt a different belief, which will bring the downfall of the religion they condemn and do not want its existence. Although, they have forgotten it is another way for them to help us spread the religion to the four corners of the Earth. Because, once you are Muslim, a Muslim you remain. Some do automatically get converted, but majority are poised to stick with it and spread it to others who are of different religions."

Sitting down on the sandy desert, under tremendous heat from the sun, Tyson observes his new brother, Hussein as he delicately edifies him of what life is all about.

Learning is a good thing. You can get it from any source, from anywhere, from anyone, unless you are not willing to put your ears down to listen. Those who listen know what we know not that we think we know. The more they listen, the more their ears pick every word and meaning and reason them to see how useful it might be.

He listens attentively and does his own contemplation, drawing comparisons between what he learns and his own knowledge. He recognizes the magnitude of their convention. It is worth it.

"If I am to be frank with you, I have never anticipated this, but I have always knew before I set on this journey I would meet people like me on the way. My heartfelt gratitude. You might not know how delightful this experience is to me. It is a great honor to have this opportunity to meet and speak with you, and I admittedly accredit we have more to do together that has destined this convergence. But one question I would have to ask you."

"You are free to ask me any question, brother. Firstly, let me say thank you for the compliments. I am more than honored to be acquainted."

"If I may ask, why are these Arab dictators not concerned about the well-being of their citizens? I mean, why are they embezzling their countries' wealth and spending it alone on themselves? It sounds to me that Arabs lack unity."

"Thank you, brother. That is the truth you have uttered. Arab people are the most inconvenient people to live with. Believe me if I say this. They are more hypocritical than the westerners. However, they cease to realize what in actuality their problem is. None of them trust or believe in their blood brother, not to go too far to say their friends. For they all say they are Muslims and practice Islam as a religion, their hatred for each other is far grander, even more than they have for the Jews, whom they all affirm to be their worst foes. They struggle to outsmart each other every single minute. So, if you request for the head of their brother, surely, they are constantly in readiness to cut and barter it in exchange of something worthy, or presumably for money. Regarding how tensions always escalate when their rulers and politicians decline to compromise with the people: it indicates how power has come to restore overwhelming desire for more and barbarity in their breathing hearts. Their rulers are the most treacherous and materialistic amongst all of the politicians around the globe. They own estates, sports, and luxury cars while the youths in the country are foolishly ensnared in massive chalice of frustration and terrible nightmares, forcing them to abandon and flee their own countries in search of a better future in the societies not conducive for them to live in. Notwithstanding, these same youths are lured into jihad and fanaticism in the name of that same religion being used to deceive and mislead them. It is a form of betrayal; it is a mechanism for driving them around as devices for achieving their goals, using them to cut and shape everything to their own satisfaction. A pity it is to see people still very blind to see. More pity it is when you know you are being misled, and yet you claim to be a good servant. Woe unto that servant who tends to serve his master with dislikes and pretense. Another thing that you see is many Muslims, riot, demonstrate, and burn flags of western countries for drawing cartoons of the Prophet Muhammed, but the very next day, you see them shooting and killing themselves, fleeing their countries to go live in the same Europe, U.S., Australia, and Canada with the people they say they detest for mocking their prophets. Which is more precious and to be more treasured? A cartoon depicting a prophet who died long ago and is believed to have ascended into heaven, or a life of another human being. In evaluating the cause and effect of this problem, I am perfectly aware of the argumentation placed before others outside the religion. It is something that draws attention that when one tends to concentrate to clearly assess it, you come to believe these people to be abnormal. You see them as insane people who are being carried away with the knowledge they have acquired from the Koran. People would want to see Muslims value their fellow humans; they would want to see them value new ideas for invention and innovation; they would want to see them value and participate in activities like sports and arts. They would want to see them discuss climate change and how we can help solve the problems, instead of spending their entire lifetime killing themselves with guns and ammunitions produced and sold to them by the same people they label infidels and not worthy to live. It is a shameful thing to see this happening, and to put an end to it, these fanatics have decided to bring them together under one law of Islam (sharia) where people will no longer value material things more than they value the lives of their fellow beings. They yearn to be more compassionate and loving themselves and their neighbors. In the real sense, these people, these same people who are justifying their own killings to win back the hearts of their people, these same people are also committing atrocities; their hands are all stained with the blood of their victims. They too have come to portray themselves as evil. They have come to see themselves fighting for power, not justice that ought to have been their commitments. They read and reread history and think it is better to repeat it, to repeat the war between the Jihadists and the Crusaders. They want to fight. I tell you, they are poised to fight, and I am doing everything to halt the war they prophesized about, a holywar."

"Are you saying you are attempting to stop it?" Demands Tyson, standing in amazement, waiting for what his new brother is to say about his role in the terrorist group.

"Of course, I am. I am disguising, and sure you acknowledge the dangers and risks involved in this. Anyway, one thing I would never allow is the death of your brother to occur. I will try my possible best. There is something you need to understand about religion. People are being controlled by these institutions. Very true. Looking to what has occurred in the past when Christians are engaging in wars and torturing people for not believing, we would think it is the teachings of the Sermon on the Mount of Jesus Christ that inspires them. As for the Koran, I have read it, and I have come to see the reason why most people who believe in it, wrongly interpret it. It is a book you read and derive pleasure while acquiring great knowledge. But it is also a book in which killing is conveyed and treated with affection and tenderness if done to protect the religion from being disorganized. And it is for that discernment it is being firmly purported a radical book for radical people. From what I understand about these religious books: the Old Testament of the Bible, the Torah, the Koran, and other religious books—they are all books one has to take heed when reading and drawing inspirations. If Jesus Christ existed, I believe he has been the only one who preached and practiced forgiveness and love, which is the path that can lead us to peace. And another thing you must understand, if we could add some elements of truth to the whole perception, we will see that rebellion is something organic. Rebellion has modelled and rambled the world to where it is today; it has stirred and conveyed what we now call civilization; it has methodically perpetuated what we now regard as democracy. The British rebelled against the Roman Empire. So did the Americans, who rebelled against the British because they felt being oppressed and exploited. What about the French Revolution? Many great nations in the world today did it, and it confirmedly favored them. When one is not satisfied with the ideal being forced on him by his dictator, what he does is to rebel. Just as some countries in the former Soviet Union are unwilling to put up with the Russian' rules of conduct, trying in every way to break loose from them. But, for now, things have changed, laws and orders have been modified in order to restore peace. This, which have come to permit a criticism to be procured by the world. The truth is we must not force people to live like us. We must allow them choose which way is advantageous for them to walk along.

Chapter 14

Wherein, it happens that they watch the seconds, the minutes, the hours of the day passed away quietly. Night awakes in wonders and fears. Poised, they are to meander, to drift, to perambulate upon the dreadful journey to where angels are rendered blind and malignant spirits become visible, while saints dance along with the songs effusing from the voices of the evil spirits. In the hot, unsheltered desert disposed to discomfort and vulnerability, they all roll, drive—all they that have been banished from Earth and determination ventured them to set in to trespass hell. To the devil's preposterous addiction and inclination, they administer in a scuffling to reach under a curse placed besides them. If gain this battle comes you shall in vain await, you must in vain await. The truck which they drive they drive into the soul of a desert, then to the place where comes the darkest night with no pity, with no mercy.

There, they arrive in a dungeon carved out of a cave that trail deep down to the utmost part, the center of Earth where Jupiter and Mars lay their foundation to reach heaven from beyond. Inside the dungeon, the condition absolutely unbearable, absolutely filthy. They walk, they walk along in strange beliefs and memories black and minatory; they advance with dark conception as dark as the night itself.

"Let us assail more, let us assail so when we reach if ever we shall see where light smiles, seeing how the rain from the sky trembles down to amassed in a corner where every blood of the innocent victims which their souls hang around the walls to become as red as danger itself."

Nowhere to escape to, for the desert seems too hot and ruinous to permit any to reside. They walk, they walk, with the prospect of meeting and greeting hope, who stood afar, wisely prompting his foe, despair to be the guide. They walk into the pale of night as they listen to the horrific wind plays drum that holds back felicity, and is seized with torture and misfortune.

In the soul of the dark dungeon, the utmost part, to trust evil better than good as eclipse of the day turning so sensational. Let not thy will be a curse. Let no man inflict on himself pains and agonies leniently for the vengeance he seeks. They walk, they walk, and Tyson and Hussein souls fly very high to a world unknown, to a world where the gods and goddesses dwell.

When they arrive at the very place, Tyson and Hussein are faintly aware of how they arrived in there where they see themselves. For more than three hours of descending deep down the dungeon, their souls have both leaped away to the wonderland, to where they are being welcomed by the gods and goddesses and the Universe, who also has assigned them on a journey to return to Earth in order to come heal the wounded soul of humanity and return it to its maker. They have walked along with the other terrorists and guards and guides who indeed are unaware their both souls have journeyed far into another world and return.

Reaching there they come vis-à-vis with the most wanted human being on Earth, the caliph, the man responsible for the cause of world unrest, the man whose intention is to spread his wicked teachings he claims to be part of the Koran to all Muslims around the globe, to return them to their creed, and not permit the presence of civilization to rob them of it. And this he intends to achieve, using violence, which ipso facto is a means to draw them to himself in order to exercise his own volition. Thence, he has delightfully become a dreadful monster, terrorizing his neighbors, his families, his friends: he has utterly assented to the obscurity lurked inside his obscured heart; there is no turning back for him—no mere mortal shall save him from his doom; he has buried his soul under the depth of the sea of a midnight hour that have nurtured him from the beginning of time; yet, he is the happiest of all beings, enjoying the most delicate situation and joyous moments, witnessing himself surrounded with demons and ghouls that dine with him every dark night deep in the illuminated evil dungeon; he is more alert when it comes to satisfying his sexual desire with some of the most beautiful women born into the world; he is living in grace, living in glory, living for afterlife, securing a belief he is going directly to Heaven to meet with the prophets and his God. For what he does, he is doing for humanity, he is doing to save the world from its insanity; he says he comprehends everything better than anyone ever does, and enough is enough for all the garbage of civilization; he beseeches people to pass their judgment; he says he is done with polity, he is done with refinement, he is done with civility under hypocrisy while his race, his creed, his personality have all become a curse, and he, a victim of hate.

When in entirety, Tyson is introduced to the caliph by Hussein, who in accordance with fact, has become his brother, his comrade, his hermano, his frère, his bruder, his fratello; there comes the hope of him meeting with his blood brother, George, who has been held captive for more than a month. Except for the fact he could see in the caliph's eyes, a character indicating rage, and also indicating misfortune. He could use his own imagination to examine and grasp the atmosphere around where he stands and with whom he stands.

He murmurs to himself, "'See what they have made of a man, what has become of him. They have created from a being a terrible monster in the guise of a terrorist; they have transformed a human being into a beast, a hell-hound that has become a terror that rules and preys aloft their very soul, day-in, day-out.'"

Skepticism flies in the air as he looks into his eyes for a second time. He is overwhelmed by the enormous fear that have provoked deaths in that very desert; he is heedless and severely drawn to a world where future is unpredictable for humanity; he sees his heart bridged with sense of guilt, and of remorse. He wishes he has never been born on this earth, he wishes he has never been born to live. His glimpse for the inevitability of the end of the world becomes more factual than it is doubtful.

His psyche is on the verge of departing from him as he shakes hand with the man. He fancies Zeitgeist—the spirit of time, moves steadily, and too imminent, seeking a requirement to develop and issue a warning order that has long been utterly declined by the same humanity. How is he ever going to escape from this? That, which becomes a question unanswerable by anyone. He sees evil being portrayed; he blesses and curses within his heart, the very day man is created to live upon Earth. There is a consequence in every of our faulty measure that we have measured to others. In doing anything, either for bargaining or for the benefit of pursuing and realizing our objectives, we have to look ahead of what the outcome would be like. We do things and never fret over what the end result would become, for we detest the notion of being imperfect. We proudly secure our own prides. We claim and affirm we know everything more than others do. We refuse to submit to the law of Karma—that which controls the fate of humanity, which states that every action performed produces an equal and opposite reaction—that which directly influences our very existence.

"You are welcome to this world of iniquities where I live and reign. You are welcome to my world. I guess you have heard much about me. What a surprise it is for you to come face-to-face with me. Welcome to my world, Americano. Bienvenue à mon royaume, mon ami. It is a great pleasure, a great honor, and privilege to welcome you to my own world where the devil himself has come to build his own empire, or, if I may say, where saints have come to inhabit in the wake of the wonders on Earth. On the other hand, it is my heartfelt gratitude to witness this day you are being introduced to the monster created by the westerners and propped by the existence of a true and almighty God, and the illusion of the forgotten souls who live in Heaven. Not to drag you into any misconception whatsoever, this monster's sole interest is to bring an end to civilization and everything it stands for, so for the commitments of the general population to be reaffirmed, so as for the laws of God to be practiced and not to be reformed. You can see that we are both on the same quest for the true meanings of life, you and I."

After he says that, he instructs two of the kidnapped victims be brought out from the prison where they have been hidden and fed every day. Tout de suite, Tyson's heart leaps in rejoice, hearing he is about to see his brother's face. The news reinforces his hopes. He wants to see George again. He wants to see if only for once they could hug and have a word before anything that is bound to transpire.

When they are brought forward and untied from the ropes, Tyson waits for an order from the caliph, who cautiously watches as he smokes his cigarette and smiles. He eventually calls George by his name and demands of Tyson the money that has been previously bargained before there could be permission of him hugging and interacting with his brother.

In a few moments Tyson is able to make some phone calls to his CEO for the 2 million dollars to be transferred into one of their comrade's account who is living in Dubai. Then, finally, after all said and done, the money is confirmed. From where he stands, he sees George, his little wayward brother, walking towards him. He too advances towards him and they both hug and shed tears and reconcile with each other while others around observe in sympathy and sorrow, and also in a confusion of mind. The caliph, that he has compassion for Tyson having volunteered to launch himself in a risky trip to break through the boundary where death sings hymns, he thinks of allowing goodness result in this perilous mission of a love for a brother. He is prepared to witness a scene of peace and happiness and forgiveness. Howbeit, his dark heart would not permit it; his rage towards America would not permit him to be kind and forgiving whenever he sees a human being born American. His heart becomes stiff and is in a further disturbance, looking to his own present condition—the risks he has entailed to bring vengeance upon the very cause of his own unrest.

Seeing two brothers hugging and interacting, he walks closer to them and utters, "Are you both aware of how I honestly loathe and detest the westerners in the form they have transformed the world and the entire people in it into what they desire in their hearts? Anyway, if I use the world 'westerners,' it might seem like it denotes all white people from Europe. That is untrue. I am positively alluding to those who proudly substantiate a claim to be the smartest, in general, because if not them, we would be living a more peaceful and prosperous world. The word, 'democracy' is an American ideal. And in the name of that democracy, which they preach and never truly practice, they have turned the world into a living hell, bringing disasters and atrocities among every human being of every race, of every religion, of every ethnicity. They have done so with the aid of their allies, their so-called European comrades. Now, we no longer live in a world where virtue and morality pay. We no longer live in a world where honesty and sincerity are both virtues. They have intoxicated the minds of all the youths around the globe, knowing these little ones are our future. Do you know language is a communication? Yet, they have taught these little kids a language far from virtue and morality, in preference, arm them with weapons to engage in fights and battles with their parents and societies. You see, the language development of a child during his early age plays a vital role in all his entire life. They have decided to instill in them a language that will help them communicate with fear; they have created that fear in them, make communication to be very difficult for them because they inculcate them with a sense of duty, a doctrine that is bind with confusion and complication. The lack of skills in communication makes life difficult for us, specifically for the little ones. The inability for one to express his opinion, his interest, surely does cut off his potentiality for representing himself, for knowing who truly he is and what is essential for him to commit himself. That is to say, he is becoming insecure of himself. Fear becomes his very enemy, which indeed he himself has created or he is taught and forced to create it. And when this fear now absorbs his every thought, his neighbors become his enemies. To all intents and purposes, I do not know how to make you grasp my words, the morals I have instilled, and all the knowledge which also I have imparted through a lot of observations and studying. What I am saying is that if we have to teach our children something, we have to be decidedly cautious, we have to be wise enough to first apprehend, and after much examination of ourselves for quality and accuracy, before passing it forward to them. It matters a lot, but we do not know, or we all ignore what it is of the utmost importance. It should have to be an upright obligation that we do the right thing, that we feed our children and raise them with delicacy and nobility and purity. Because, a little child does an immense amount of learning and practicing during the years since he first become conscious of his surroundings and tries to fit into it, grasping the sounds, the words, the lifestyles and everything uttered and done as a paradigm that he has to accept and trail."

Everyone around stand mute as the caliph, the most wanted man in the world delivers his series of lectures. Tyson is astounded hearing all these from a man supposed, under his commands, some radical religious group have slaughtered and murdered thousands non-Muslims and Muslims.

"'How could a fanatic so dangerous be so enlightened?'" He speaks in a murmur to himself. ' "Or is it that he acknowledges what he is doing is wrong and still inclines to it, basically to respond to the west that he is against the will imposed on him, instead, he will foster and sustain his own will to bring an end to the spread of westerner's doctrines in the Middle East for the Easterners to restore theirs? Yes, there seems to be a multiple valued logic pertaining to what is happening around the globe, and perhaps, it comports a viable alternative to change the system designated and thrown to them to live with. That, veraciously is his logic, and it is the only viable way to come up with a solution for a problem that deems hypocritical, so he thinks. He is been buried in his will, and he will not relent. He will not, for any reason stays alive while his dream crumbles. He is going to stick to that will, his will—and his will which is drawing nigh; yes, it is upon that will he depends, upon that will he vehemently believes, upon that will he conceives and perceives his future, his exaltation. He has sworn an oath that has come to turn against his very bitter soul. It is vengeance displaying its aptitude in him. He quests for a way to take vengeance upon himself, forgetting there is also an aftereffect for his actions. On the other hand, why have the westerners chosen to enlighten others of how life should be lived when they themselves have not been able to learn how to live a life? Or, ethereally, their aims are to steal from others with the knowledge they have procured, since they fathom knowledge to be power, then they will use that power to rule, to govern them while they participate in the exploitation. It does carry a stigma upon the soul of mankind, if we cannot acquire the capacity of realizing how important every single day is, and how more important the next day will be. For that reason, we should cherish the day, and, as well, cherish our neighbors who freely join us to live it. We ought to treat those neighbors well and ensure they are happy and rejoicing with us. Because, with a troubled neighbor, we will never see a peaceful and happy day. See how humanity has chosen to seek its own downfall. Who would not understand that how we are being raised is a part of what reflects every day in the society? Who among us would say he is not having a discernment of how children are raised in this modern world we have labeled civilization? That children enjoy to interact with others—their friends and families. They try to give their attentions to the ideas of others and respond in their own manners. By helping them plan, helping them reach their needs and achieving some of their goals, doing it with love, reassuring them to be more devoted and passionate, it presents them with a sense of security and stability. It enables them to be wise and be useful and to engage in major life activities—moving from one task to another, without having to grapple with others instructions on what is necessary to be done. It means the very real difference between children working with guidance but under their own power rather than being dangled on a string like puppets, moving only as they are manipulated by their teachers or parents directions.'"

It seems he, Tyson, is still much asleep. He sees himself reproducing his youth time—the images occupying his memories are carried aback to the episode of how his upbringing has been like, how he has seen himself witnessed one of the worst human tragedy in history—when starvation and war were not the most awful cause of death, instead, it was lynching. He has witnessed the dark past of American history, he has witnessed in a variety of public events where black people are visually and satirically lynched—people cheering and singing as black males and females are hanged and set ablaze. Although, his own father, who has been strictly against these evil acts, has been able to seize that opportunity in giving intellectual insights to his children about the country's past history of how the black race has pitifully and starkly suffered in the hands of the whites. Not that it was not done to the Mexicans and the Chinese, but they were extensively focused on the blacks, on the ground that the plurality's opinion did favor the conviction, considering how they were still grudgingly incensed and could not help get over the issue of how they ought to be respected by other race not white. After the civil war and the emancipation proclamation, all these, due to the economic struggles and a startling wealth decline. To these people, their subject has been race. Race is connected to intelligence, race is connected to power, race is connected to justice, and race is everything. Granted, it has been all about superiority and beliefs, and is still what it is all about—a belief, a notion that men should rule over women, that the rich should rule over the poor, that white race should rule over other races. Presumably, that he was to be born black, he would have find it entertaining to smile or laugh with a person of white skin—for he will be seeing himself hypocritical, for having have to witness all these and forgive so easily. It is unbearable and displays an offensive remarks. There comes a subtle distinction between restoring his faith in humanity and losing it entirely. It is an obnoxious thing to do, to take discrimination as an agenda as some people would understand, for the fact that they are not the victims. Prejudice, bigotry, and racism in America explain it all to the outside world. It signifies what the American patriotism really is all about—hypocrites who preach of their good and upright deeds to uplift the good spirit of humanity, while silently eliminating their fellow citizens and mocking their neighbors for their rough poverty background, people plainly spouting hate and lashing out at anyone they deem illegal or unworthy of common human decency. They question these immigrants role in the world and reckon them devoid of wittiness and creativeness. Looking back to history, slavery was first abolished in France and England and other European countries prior to the time it was in the U.S. To this day, racism is still very pronounced in America, the land of the free. And, why is it so? The great Abraham Lincoln died for it. Martin Luther King Jr also died for it. John F. Kennedy as well died for it. And many more. You are likely to watch on television of how a black male is choked to death by some white policemen for illegally selling cigarettes, short while, another white, young fanatic, who, out of hatred, enters a black church to shoot and kill nine people, including the pastor who also is a senator, only to get a calm arrest and receives some free burgers from the white policemen who arrested him. Before the so-called terrorist has to set on his mission to eliminate these people inside the church, he has posted his pictures and a manifesto on a website. He has been seen burning the American flag and waving the Confederate flag, visiting slavery museums and criticizing the black race as inferior. Be that as it may, many were contrary to a motion to remove the Confederate flag from the state buildings. Looking back to history, Since the Nazis lost the war, they have been forbidden never to fly the Nazis swastika, either at home or in the state buildings. The Confederate flag, to the witty and pedantic Americans, they discern it is not simply for the promotion of slavery and racism, but also as a guide reflecting on the past, the war that intended to break and destroy the great country. It is about America saying, "No, we are not returning to where we have come from. We are one nation and proud of flying one flag which stands for our unity."

As for the flag, it belongs to the museum, and that is where it should stay. In another case, taking a thorough look at what is happening in the Middle East today, we are all convinced that the creation of the terrorist group, known as 'ISIS', that he, Tyson has come to meet personally with their leader, who has kidnapped his only brother, is a result of the invasion of Iraq by America and its allies. In the name of promoting democracy and luring them into their system, their world, and as well—for a permission to be granted for them to exploit the wealth of that country—perhaps, extract and refine the oil there. Albeit, they have falsely linked it with the terrorist attack in New York, which everyone around the globe acknowledge it has been a mechanism reserved to design a scenario quite different from what factually is the motivation. It all become a nightmare as the world awakes to realize the difficult equation brought upon all to solve. The terrorists, on the other hand, have clutched at every opportunity to encounter and treasure themselves in a commitment to vengeance, to seize power to govern themselves, and express their strong disapproval to foreign interventions and the corrupt and biased new governments who split and bargain the wealth of their nation with the westerners and themselves. As they ceaselessly capture and experience the division, the conflicts between themselves, they swiftly come to their senses. They fathom their only option is for them to accept the choices handed to them by their destiny to live in their own land with their own lifestyle, or die in the hands of the westerners and their missiles. They conclude they are being fooled and all that are not fit into their lifestyle have become a law forced upon them to practice. The fact that more and more public perception of people in the Middle East is clear and simple: they loathe and dread America and its allies. Rage and jealousy have become the outcome of living with the principles brought to them from strange lands. In their hearts they are filled with contempt, they are filled with uncertainties, they are filled with suspicions and mistrust for the westerners, knowing any a time they are coming to their aid, they are sacrificing to exploit and rule them, to exhibit their power and force it on them. Therefore, they commence with rebellion. At the beginning of this war the rebels are armed and paid by the Americans to oust the dictator, but when the caliph offered these people more money, they accepted and have become parts of the group that has become expanded and powerful. Some even joined the group, bringing with them the lethal ammunitions supplied to them. It is not that America has not done some extraordinary work to heal humanity, to bring everyone together for the creation of a world more stable and united. But, nevertheless, their motives, always for a gain, so many people believe. Furthermore, for a reason they are always proud to implement on others an ideal far from what is being demanded. They assert to play a role model. They fail to remember of how they have been unable to fix themselves into a rightful condition of life. That is where the problem lies—they are incognizant of the fact their lifestyle anticipations are way too far and high and require some adjustments. They refuse to think of giving themselves a final inspection and confirmation to know if they are on the right track before dragging others along. They assert to be other's role models. But what makes them consider themselves that? Wherein, they could legitimately and honorably be seen so, assuming they could eject pride and ego and jealousy aside, assuming they could cease to judge others based on their appearances, or their color of race, or their religion, or however anyone might wish to live a life. Role models respect and regard you in any way and precisely as you are. Even in a deep mood of unmanly misery, they still show you love, they still show you compassion. They restore, heighten, and fortify you to overcome any temptation and never withdraw at the very point when brood might seem too strong to persist. However, to see that humanity will ever be healed, we have to look up to America to still continue to lead the world. America remains the only hope for humanity to rediscover itself. The world cannot live without that nation playing a role model. Playing a role model does not mean you have to command, instead, it means you to lay plans and also listen to other's opinions. No one in the world would say he or she is not in love with how America entertains us, how they create, how they innovate, how they invent—make the world celebrate science and technology. If only the greedy politicians and those whose core beliefs are in fanatical patriotism—they see their fellow countrymen starve and become homeless and still want to support the too much spending in military for a reason so spiteful—seeing how their ambition and anticipation are to be found in how policing the world is an obligation. These people who decline to look to the consequences of wars—the many young men and women sent to fight in wars—many whose brains are being blown off, many who have become mentally and physically disabled due to injuries sustained. Is there any parent who would not want to see his or her child graduate from Harvard University, Yale, Oxford, Cambridge, Princeton, or Columbia? Yes, there is something to be included in facts-finding—when we can see the increase of chronic homelessness in America. America should be dealing with issues that matters most to them before leaving their home to dictate to others on how to live and die. America should be much more concerned about the increase in violence in the streets, the easy means that sophisticated firearms fall into the hands of radical Muslims and other mentally disturbed citizens who go out conducting experiments in mass shooting in nightclubs, places of worships, hospitals, schools, and along the streets. America should be preoccupied with youths disobeying law enforcement officers, organized and fortified delinquents and lawbreakers, racial tensions, increased bigotry, hatred and violence. Not that the money and ideas are not there, it is that people do not care if others sleep and die in the streets. Americans should be fretful of how their congress is being run by greedy politicians who never get anything done except to allow the strife for power hold them down to failure. The gridlock in Washington continually hurts the economy as it hurts the provision of a minimal level of well-being and social support for the citizens. On the other hand, who would want to follow the Russians, the Iranians, Chinese, North Koreans, Libyans, Nigerians, Mexicans, or the Saudis? To where will the world be led to? Not that to have a role model means you have to be dictated everything you have to do. To have a role models means to show good examples. If not the Europeans would be fit to be the role model the world yearns for. Because, in Europe, citizens are being treated fairly and better than anywhere in the world. Europe itself has failed in the sense they have given America the too much privilege to do anything it wishes. They forget America is a nation, who can fail at any given time, and when they elect a bad leader, who can take them on the wrong way, they will fail. And when someone you rely too much on fails, you too will fail.

While Tyson is set apart from his brother in await of the caliph's instruction to proceed with the hugging and interactions. All of a sudden, he notes how the periphery of the place falls in silence. He contrasts the coldness driving into his heart with the blood of a dog slain before a supposed ancient and holiest ritual practiced in the Middle East. He thinks he has seen a dog, whereas, he is seeing one of the kidnapped victims dragged down to the floor where everybody stand and being slain with a machete by one of the guards. In an instant, he could hear everybody, including the caliph, laughing and cheering.

Hence, this occurrence has sent his psyche far, far away to a realm of horrific condition. He could not help himself to resist it. So he burst into tears, he burst into flames. He cries the river in his eyes dry, he cries, he cries. As he weeps the sorrow of his heart full, he weeps, he weeps. Over the solid perilous wilderness, mountain ties to a complete loss of hope and faith for humanity, eagles fly and upon the smiling sky, hang. Who shall thy neighbor put to a blame for his affliction and misdemeanor when wild in grief he is begets?

When the caliph notes he is shedding tears, he instructs for more of the victims to be brought out, and in everybody's presence the guards proceed with the slayings. It is cowardice and appalling. Not what a man should experience and still be alive. Meanwhile, these murderers live in it every single a day, they are cooperating and taking interests in evil acts, splitting the blood of these innocent people all because they seek what is commonly known as "an eye for an eye," "a tooth for a tooth," like for like, measure for measure. Do we have to allow our emotions misguide us to commit ourselves in some kind of misconducts that will become a disaster to all of humanity, exclusively because we seek vengeance to destroy our few enemies? Do we have to bestow upon ourselves vengeance? Do we have to influence a sentiment of becoming evil to destroy evil?—for when one becomes evil and starts to act like them, it will require an unpleasant life attached to a great effort for the person to retrieve his life and truly stand for his cause—that injustice and oppression he is fighting against.

Within a brief preceding time, as more victims are brought out from their hidden places and slewed in the presence of everybody, nothing, no one to halt the course of action, for none is eligible to utter a word, or say, pledges himself to propose an interference. It is way too daunting, irreligious, and barbarous. Say a word, you will be burned alive.

Then appears before all that are there, a Jew, who has been caught with George. The reason for his abduction is that he pretends to fight alongside with them, but at the same time, obtaining information from them to pass to the Jewish government, pursuing his own interest in knowing their thoughts and plans to help his country engage in a battle with them. As claimed by the caliph, the man named Amram, for the time he has stayed and operated with them, has been living and hiding under a false name known as "Abdu-Bari." His Arabic language is so fluent, making him so eloquent. It is a perfidy, treachery, or high treason—worse than that, infiltration. He has gradually gained entrance, not into their territory, but into their every thoughts, into their ideas, which suggests the Israeli Defense Department is consummately aware of their every plan, their every move, and their every step. What they are to do in the future if possibly they are able to come off with flying colors in creating the Islamic State, all have been unveiled, let the cat out of the bag, not to other people rather than their worst and detestable open enemy, hostile force. The punishment for this is unpredictable to anyone.

"Let me say this: in all the predicaments that torment humanity to this day, the Jews are to be blamed. They are to take the culpability for everything. It is all their fault humans now see themselves as animals to be sacrificed to God. That is the basis for the action I took, ordering my guards to slay those men for all of you to feel it in your heart if actually it is an appropriate thing to do, if it is moral for innocent blood to be spilled. It is all about justice. It is all about people doing what is right, treating each other with love and compassion, rather than shedding blood. It is the Jewish idea for people to clutter life with too many obligations: to embrace a notion of self-confidence, self-improvement, self-respect, and other selves. And there is one self, which genuinely is the greatest of all selves, and as well the intensely controversial and destructive to mankind, and it is the self-efficacy—the measure of the belief in one's own ability to complete tasks and reach goals. That is when evil itself was created. In another way, some commonly advert to it as self-passion. I will be very much unfeigned with you in this. If man could allow the forgo of his self-passion to be reconverted to a soil of compassion that is watered every time by love, that soil will become so moisture and fertile and continues to yield any good fruit planted on it. What you ought to know that is concealed is the Jews who beforehand, come to feel this self of a cognitive content in their hearts, for a cause still inexplicable till this day. The Jews, with their too much obsession with identity have created a world from a world, a dissimilar world from a world they encountered. They have passed the spiritual and intellectual insights to the world; they professed a belief of a more supreme God than other gods and goddesses that have come before them and that were of other tribes. They have not only proclaimed this God of theirs to be so supreme and pure and divine, but they have also affirm solemnly and formally as the true children of that living God. They have come with countless scriptures full of invented stories about their God and their past prophets. Admitting, they have presented to the world the legendary and poetic records to beautify and glorify these stories. Then, heedlessly, the amazing mysticism behind this new divine God has conveyed the world to a new society, unlocks a way to modern science, and a new mindset of how the society, which we live in, can be understood and appreciated by possessing material wealth and physical comfort. From thence, materialism has become our lifestyle—conventional or unconventional. We have become obliged to living in a world where we find it unfeasible to live without money. Oh, money, it has become everything that man seeks, that man needs to outlive. Supposing that we make a retreat from our present day to the past, and reconsider how money becomes our treasured gift of life and also serving purpose of security and solidity: in early time, sacks of grain cereals, live-stocks, beads, cowry shell, and other attractive items were all used in exchange for more useful commodities. It was after when coin became a representation of exchange that it slipped into the hands of the covetous, the gluttonous, the unappeasable—people whom greed sunk into their veins and blood. They now have the excessive desire to possess and own everything on Earth, including the ones not needed and deserved. If you understand history very well, you will understand it is the Jews themselves who have traded their own soul to become what money now represent in the society. The invention of currencies has been mainly for a purpose of placing trust within the traders in external authority within barter exchange. But when the Jews took hold of it and have it in their control, it has become a curse upon humanity. Monopoly was invented for more gains to be made. Compassion and love were sold and bought by this representation of a currency. Federal Reserves and Central banks were invented around the globe to control this money, and all in the control of the same people with same ideas, only to profit."

"The banks, which, in point of fact, are not owned by the governments of the nations, are known to be independent institutions. Since the banks need more money and will always need more money, so wars must escalate to meet the greedy need. With this money, see how man has created a startled life that runs through the whole of humanity. The Jews who became the first to be aware of the potency humans possess with the too much knowledge they have acquired—migrating and extending away so very far and steering back, maimed, and humiliated to essentially reestablish and reintroduce themselves to the world, and also to rebuild their scattered temple. These people have suffered in the hands of many people in different empires and kingdoms who were more powerful and organized. They were enslaved and forced against their wills in these foreign lands. They were taught lessons that they learned from, and instead of turning those pains and miseries into grudges to continuously wage wars against their neighbors, they turned it into inspiration for enlightenment. It became a device inside them that serves brilliantly to energize them to shrewdly manifest their creative talents in writing the scriptures which are drawn from the myths of the ancient Greek, ancient Babylonian, and from some of the books they came across with while serving as slaves in Egypt, like the Book of The Dead, which was written by the Egyptians thousands of years ago. The fact that no proof of what eventuated when the Jews were in Egypt as slaves, the reasons the Egyptians actually treated them so maliciously, according to what their scriptures say. No one was there to narrate the story to our comprehension and acceptance. Thus far, some will suggest, maybe they came to realize the threats they were posing to them, seeing the progression they were making, their advancements in learning and procuring knowledge. For the fact these Egyptians were using them as slaves to build and develop their cities, they were also very much afraid of coming to live under their teachings and knowledge and be ruled by them in the future. They envisioned how witty and skillful they would be. So, they decided to derail them from departing from the country with those knowledge they have acquired from them and the ones they possessed as well. They grasp it was going to be too dangerous to allow these people stay close together without being separated. They saw everything, how the future would look like if the Jews are allowed to put their knowledge into practice. They wanted to stop it. But when the Jews eventually prevailed and arrived at their own destination, they were never oblivious of their history, believing it to be their destiny. When they became knowledgeable of what they possess, they transformed it into something different and extended their doctrines to the entire world. First and foremost, with a claim of a new living God who have bestowed power upon his chosen ones—his only children, the Jews of all people. And after then, when they considered what power means and how it influences human life and the society, they appreciate their aptitudes in handling and maintaining their course of wealth. Then, they resolved to settle with transactions, knowing money is the power to rule over men. From thence, they have become the controllers of money, which indicates how they with a fundamental and profound expertise have become the controllers of men. When madness of possession seized the notion of humanity, they took advantage of it, sold their pound of flesh for money, amass a great fortune, which they were later borrowing out for interest. They introduced the terms monopoly, monopsony, oligopoly and other -polies and -sonies. Since they control money, they became the controller of the Universe and everything in it. The struggles, the fights, the needs, and wants of money were then besieged with refractory and dilemma and became so filled with emotion, energy, keenness and fierceness. To secure and make money to be more valuable and estimable, they logically and shrewdly created a scarcity of it.

"Now, see how we have made money rule over us, make it control and dominate our lives, make it more meaningful in comparison to human lives, make it more influential and significant to nature, and even our maker. It has become a multisyllabic question without any answer how we could return to normality, how we humans will be able to retrieve our lost kingdom on Earth, how we could conceive a better future without money piercing into our hearts to cause a malicious mischief. In our hearts we have accumulated too much philosophy, too much mathematics, too much sensibility, too much postulation, too much credence, too much confidence, all in the name of achieving wealth, getting our share of the money, thereby distracting our attentions from what are of most importance...that we need to live a more peaceful and harmonious life. Money has become our sole source of excitements, and as well, our source of uneasiness. We are thrown into confusion and disorder, making us not know where to head to or what is ahead of us, for we think we have met something that makes us that has become the thing breaking us. We witness how a man can offer his own soul or that of his mother or father or brother or sister in exchange of money, in exchange for a favorable position in life so as to achieve his goals. We see all these and still formulate in our minds a realm of possibility and certainty to which we could aviate from to arrive in a succeeding lane where peace and love will excel. We humans are to be equated to a prank if we could still live in hopes and faiths after having brought upon ourselves a cataclysmic circumstance—destroying humanity and nature."

"Perhaps, we Muslims, to be honest, envy these Jews so much to a degree we, wholeheartedly, prefer to live with them as friends, as families who descended from Abraham, not as foes that we are at present. Meanwhile, the westerners will not approve of that proposal to be put into execution. We have fought with them for several years and come to realize the mystical power they possess. Things about them are seen peculiars, so we have come to a conclusion they are indeed the chosen ones. To that extent we were compelled to adopt their God as our God, using a different approach to reestablish the truth and validity of the supremacy of that same God. We love these people. That too much love is what resulted to a motive we now hate them. They will not open their hearts to welcome us in. They are so reserved and cryptic, and will not share their hidden power with others. They want everything for themselves alone. They carry a sturdy and secure interest in the idea of hidden powers. Yes, they do, and with that they intend to impose their dominion over the surface of the Earth. About these very people, we are all aware of how they began that persistent and harsh journey of life, how they wandered through the desert in return to the place they customarily assert to be their homeland. In real sense, we can see that they are still wandering and contemplating on why, with everything being placed for them in perpetual wonderment, and whenever they stop and try to assemble to live in oneness, we will be prompt to disorganize and dissociate them, if not, we would have to await the huge and instantaneous repercussions. Initially, it was like that: they have wandered around the globe to acquire wisdom and knowledge. They have wandered around the globe to put into accomplishment their vision. They have wandered to navigate the world into heaven, into insanity, into a belief to attain peace and arrive in a land of milk and honey. They have wandered from east to west and north to south. They have wandered from birth to death, and then returning from death to the birth of a new Adam—of a world fits for all humanity to live in. They staunchly believe they could solve the equation of death, restore the arithmetic of life, and find a meaning to the existence of death and birth. They heartily and emphatically champion a notion for exploration, for scuffling to acquire their lost treasures. They consider themselves to be the chosen people who comprehend the meaning and significance of life. They educate and enlighten us of the principles we must follow. The Greeks, the Romans, The Egyptians, The Babylonians, and many other empires and kingdoms, they all were having their gods and goddesses in a form of images prayed to, worshipped, and adored. But when the Jews intended to invent and create their own god, they made it to be an invisible god that could be worshipped spiritually. In the Old Testament, we understand that animal sacrifices were made to that God, then in the New Testament, they claimed that same God was aroused because of their continuous life of transgression and wickedness. For that reason he has to send his only begotten son to come into the world to sacrifice his own life for us—which why he was known as the lamb of the world. So, when Jesus Christ came into the world, there were no more sacrifices of animals to please their God, instead, it became a sacrifice of your every good deed on Earth so you might arrive in paradise after death. Amid all these, you are obligated to first be reborn: be born again."

For over one hour, they all sit on the floor and stare. The caliph has been very active and ardent with his speech—capturing everyone's attention with his discourse. As for Tyson it was fascinating. He could see himself in a process of gaining knowledge. He wishes he could hear more. No one dare interrupts the caliph, except there was a question to be raised, so he has demanded of any of them just before the commencement of the discourse.

Tyson, who possesses the eagerness to a consistent learning, rises to an upright position, and he says, "Please, may I demand of you the reason we have to sequentially and progressively blame the Jews of afflicting humanity with all these predicaments? It seems we are relying and attributing to wrong information that only helps perpetuate misconception."

"Are you indirectly stating we accuse the Jews, we show them a depth of distaste merely for no reason?" Demands the caliph, in response to the question thrown to him by Tyson.

"Nope, that is not what I intended. I, in effect, do propose we should be blaming our governments in all what is eventuating that we are witnessing. They ought to be held responsible for the danger they have placed the world; we all fathom how greed has crippled into all human's heart, not alone the Jews. If ever we are to confront the challenges enshrouding us, we must be heedful not to whine and moan and groan and accuse people wrongly, otherwise, all we strive for, all we pursue to bring about justice, will in our eyes fall in vain. The Jews I comprehend are money lenders, and have since submerged themselves into this very line of work, admitting it to be their sources of income. They have done it for too long we all do concur, and we all bear witness. In all conscience if I may disclose to you all. I am wealthy and live a very pleasant and enjoyable life because my father saved and left some money for us before he passed away. But, coming to this place and experiencing all these that have eventuated, and coming to understand how injustice and inequality have set the world apart, established divisions among humans, created hatred, which is in opposition to love and compassion that are indispensable for a progression of a wonderful and satisfying world. It sets my heart ablaze to see this as a world we ought to be living. It is so fortunate for me to be here. They say where fortune is, you walk to find it. It never comes to you. So it is, where danger is, you walk to find it as well. This is more than enough for me to explore to define life for myself. Seeing all these and learning them, I weep myself in my own pity, and I ask, 'Is it a pleasure for us to play the role of a hero when all that betide all is a woe?' I am not on the side of anyone when it comes to putting things right for the sake of humanity. Be that as it may, regarding the subject-matter of the manner in which the Jews are to be labeled a curse to humanity, I will say it is better we extend our views towards what is right and do it, and do it for once and for all. If we accuse the Jews of their functions in bringing the world into a situation where money now becomes a god, yes, I will, a hundred percent, support that motion. But, not to relate the scriptures they have written to the greed that dwells in their hearts. I may ask then if this ideal of modern democracy and wealth and capitalism are all derived from the early scriptures of the book written by the Jews. No, that is not true. The scriptures have been translated, transcribed, revised, rewritten, modified, rearranged, rephrased, polished, which then resulted in a misinterpretation—so for that, people have been misguided by the so-called prophets and philosophers that came afterwards to claim they comprehend the metaphorical meanings."

"According to your statements of how the Arabs love the Jews and aim to promote friendly relations with them, rather than engage in disputes,

I come to easily assimilate why it is so apparent the Koran is documented and scrutinized as a continuation of the Torah and the Old Testament of the Bible. In addition, other scriptures were written by the prophets to augment and upgrade the moral standards and conditioned it to their own appetency. Looking to the New Testament, the Sermon on the Mount of Jesus Christ, if we apply our practical ascertainment, we will see that the scriptures there demonstrate how we could believe in the saving of souls from the dark forces ruling our world, the dark forces disconnecting humanity from its maker; the scriptures make us believe God to be all-loving and all-powerful, and that Jesus of Nazareth, His son, was preaching and living love and has pioneered and pave the way for us to reach his father, and to live fully and abundantly."

The caliphisdaze dimmensely by the response coming from Tyson's mouth. He acknowledges in an instant he is about to be lost in the discussion, and he would be unable to withhold a defeat when it comes to sharing knowledge and challenging each other of the facts attached to the thesis. So, he swiftly adds to it to prove his own intelligence, to prove how much knowledge he has attained to arrive where he is.

"Tyson, are you insinuating the Jews never have the vision of ruling the world, trailblazing people to arrive under their own control of the Universe and everything in it? Thence, why were Europeans chasing them away from their countries? Why, at the initial time, do they proclaimed to be the chosen ones? Answer that question," standing upright and lowering his gun on Tyson where he is seated. "Answer me, or else you are to suffer for proving how much you know to me," he continues, still pointing his AK47 gun at him.

George, who, seeing his brother who has meandered across the oceans and seas and mountains and valleys and cold and heat, unaided by no one, for a reason to secure and maintain his extrication from the hands of some mentally deranged people who faithfully assert they could turn the world back to its past by torturing and fatally slaying and murdering people who stand on their way. He is conscious of what would emerge from this confrontation and menace that have fallen upon his own brother, Tyson, a man he has long despised and engaged in a contest with, willfully to gratify his ego of verifying his own potential. He thinks it is the precise time for him to recompense his brother for his forgiving nature, his benevolent heart to have still regard and think of him as a brother, and coming for him, after all he has done to hurt him in the past.

Thereupon, he arises from where he sits and advances slowly towards the caliph, pleading for him to spare his brother's life.

But, turning back to see who is pleading, the caliph, instantly, as he sees George, is startled and vents out his frustration on his guards, who hastily grapple George and pin him to the ground, with more than six AK47's pointed at him.

Then, intrudes Hussein, who has been so inactive and reticent, not venturing to meddle into the caliph's discourse, knowing what the outcome is going to look like. He walks straight to his boss who shifts his focus towards his trusted ally, thence, whispers something into his left ear. For a moment the caliph is tranquil and relieved from his tension, although his anger still very much on a high-level despite how he manages to control it.

"Tyson, I understand how your purpose is to be cautious and looking into both sides of every story before passing your judgment. As for the caliph, you have every reason to bring this accusation upon the Jews for their roles in the world affairs," says Hussein, gazing at Tyson, and also turning his gaze at the caliph and every other persons present in the scene. "All the same, we all here are on the same cause, with the same vision to engender a culture of change in our societies. As for the Jews, if they never have the vision of ruling the world and engineering people to lay on them faith and trust in respect of who they are, with their desperate minds and desperate motives so firm, which is to bring everyone into their own control. From the beginning of their existence, they have proclaimed themselves as the chosen ones of the living God, their god, our god. Unequivocally, it was because they knew what they are capable of, so they came with their visions, they commenced with their doctrines and extended everything beyond the surface of the Earth for all to believe. They cast their personal spells on us in an attempt to capture our minds and hearts. They wrote the New Testament, simultaneously proclaiming Jesus Christ to be the only son of the living God, the Messiah, and also denying him to be. We have been bamboozled for so long. They create a space for people to question their responsibilities in the havocs taunting mankind. It is so painful to see people still very blind to see how these people have given rise to a fleeting evolution to rule and destroy mankind.

They talk of a god of forgiveness and peace in the New Testament, while in preceding years, in the Old Testament, it has been an eye for an eye, which most Muslims come to accept as a belief for living a life credited with morality and virtues. The Jews are contradictory to themselves as they are to others. As for me, Hussein, I still believe the actuality of the motive why humanity obstinate too long in the dark shadow of its own misery is commonly due to the fact we tend to allow ourselves to be driven by power and faith to possess and own the Universe and everything in it—doing what it desires of it, and furthermore, contends its own perfection to be indisputable and unchallenged. We have to realize all corporations are not Jews. The truth be said, we have to unleash our rage on these people who, at present day, believe they own our souls. We have to come together in executing our plans to reconquer our kingdom on Earth. Looking around, I see nothing in the future that will become of me and you and the entire human race. If they live, we perish, if they perish, then we will live. To observe perceptibly as they cause us anguish, resentments, a feeling of chronic anger and bitterness, these are all against the will of those who believe there are things to be done to freeze it, knowing we are capable only if we unite in oneness and reach a conclusion in order to bring into existence the change we have long yearned for, using our active brain and rational thought process. Our eyes labor to bring us information, our ears labor to pick it up and transfer it, our brains labor to accumulate and ponder it, so will our hands and legs labor to enforce it. Some might lose our lives during this process of a new evolution, but not revolution as it is now."

"Some will lose connections with their loved ones. In accordance with fact, what are we living for if we are not and will never be satisfied and encouraged by what we see being done to destroy us in our very eyes? Without death, there is no life. Same, when we say without life, it means there is no death. They are both combined; it is a reason we live and die. Physical and spiritual are bind together to represent man—and that is truly the nature of it. Seeing your image in a mirror, does that not occur to you why man lives? Seeing yourself, your other self in a mirror—that appears to be your other life, which is death. And the other self is what you stare at in the mirror. We will assume it is both (birth and death) that merge together to form human. It is not that I do not appreciate and respect Jesus Christ for his every miraculous work and also his teachings. I do. I champion the course of his sacrifices to bring transformation into the world. Looking at it clearly and drawing a meaning from his teachings we see that when we propose to deflect from the Old Testament to the New Testament, we are plunging into a different philosophy from our ancient beliefs: pulling ourselves from darkness into light—and that was precisely what materialized in the Bible. Jesus Christ's Sermon on the Mount about loving one's neighbor as we love ourselves, forgiving our enemies, and praying for their repentance, were all remarkable one can see it as a transformation from what people were accustomed to, that you have to kill your enemy first before he comes to kill you. His teachings were all about love and forgiveness, and it was to reestablish the affiliation between man and his maker and nature, to achieve and secure peace on Earth, to eliminate greed and restore love within families, within societies. I tell you, if we could associate with this basic principles of love and compassion, we will all arrive in our dreamland."

"I know, in general, many people have rejected his claims of being the son of God—but who can truly grasp the metaphorical meanings of his claims. Looking to the Bible, we see he preached in parables and believed people, who are as wise as he was, might derive some meanings from his parables. He sensed the people of the world needed education in thinking. He was a philosopher and poet. Howbeit, the people who wrote the scriptures were also poets, and what do poets do? They exploit their own selves—their struggles, their understandings, their wisdom, their existence, their inwardness, their observations—and ingeniously apply them to their ambitions to write. And when they put things down, they wind and turn from one direction to another, taking it upstream for the unwise to comprehend. They are philosophers with more natural tendency for creativity. The tranquility and calmness of the poet is to be equated to a stone burning in fire. Jesus, if he existed, was what a god would look like. It does boggle my mind to see this very innocent man has come to live among humans, and was a Jew, if in fact the story told about him was true. His teachings apprise us to understand the God we seek is within us, within our fellow beings. Then, it is a question to me how these Jews were able to come up with stories like that?"

"That has been so edifying and illuminative, Hussein. I owe you a lot for the supports you have rendered to us throughout this period of adversity that we refer to as a curse. You have been a light that I look to in so many cases. I think of how to emulate your style. I think of how I could renounce my role here and come in your company to reach that wonderland that all the time you have rhythmically preached about. I am honored to be considered a friend. I know I do not deserve it. Thank you once again." The caliph, having said that, orders for some food to be served among his new friends and Hussein, the man that tries in every way to help him alters his beliefs to value human lives and not chase after vengeance.

"Let me tell you what I have learned from your admonitions of tolerance, peaceful, and harmonious coexistence with our neighbors and God and nature. It explains in precise the rational motive love is the basic principle of morality and uprightness," states the caliphate.

After then, the food is brought to them. He begs all of them including the Jew, a traitor, all, to eat and dine with him, with no pity, no fear, no favor attached to it. He instructs his men to drop their weapons and celebrate a new era of peace and brotherhood with their former foes and victims of assault. "The factual fact is that I see not one reason we have to be treating each other as enemies when we can live peacefully together and eat and drink in merriment. Why all these troubles and the life of danger that humankind has come to rely on?" He stands up and serves everyone there with food and drinks before sitting himself down to eat with them. "As I was saying, Jesus Christ's Sermon on the Mount about love is a theory I could well expound in order for it to be comprehensible for the unenlightened. It is without a shadow of doubt to say, he with love in is heart must loveth so the heart of another and loveth so the one that created both. Therefore, he that loveth another, loveth also himself, and loveth his creator."

"Very true," intrudes Tyson, but this time, with a smile on his face. And thence he presses on, "We have to guarantee ourselves, engage in discussions necessary to exit from a room engrossed with madness, a room engrossed with hatred and violence. We have to spread our knowledge across the border before it fades away, and then, not permit our hearts to be troubled. We will continue to share the brightness of our brilliance against the darkness of their ignorance. They are ignorant even if they assert to know it all. We will follow that hearts of ours to wherever they intend to place us. The honey that death makes, we will taste, lay our hands in history when it collapse and await fate to bring forth the peace that has long crumbled in the drifting waters, so prophesied those wise men from the east. I understand very well why you all have decided to take on this journey. So am I, and so is Hussein. We are in this together. Hear how they have said we are free, and we are still chained down by the authorization of their system. I tell you, we are not free. Nevertheless, we will regain our freedom, and we will do it peacefully and wisely to obtain that freedom that they promise to give to us that is ours. We will put ourselves in danger. Yes, we will. Danger, itself, will not cease to exist, it will not cease to reappear in our every action and daring. So also we will not be exhausted of the energy and wit to elude it. In as far as our hearts are not maimed with vicious intentions, we will hold all the cards. But if they succeed in finding a desirability to alter their ways and abandon the odd ways, then we will compromise. If not, we will 'render to Caesar what is Caesar's, and to God, what is God's.' They will not, in pretext, layout rules for a compromise and break the same rules in effort to make rest of humanity a tool. We will not allow what they have been perpetuating to be a sequential designed process to exploit and render others invalid. We will incline to our principles—to create an ideal society, one which is embellished with education, equality, solidarity, freedom, and hope for all. We will desist from further conformity to their will to perpetually make of us a device to facilitate and achieve their means. They pronounce fluently and clearly to the public how we are all one, how we are a team, yet we remain a subordinate functionary, we remain expendable resources. To be a team, to merge in oneness and to work on an objective in reconciliation to bring about peace and unity, there has to be a foundation. For a team will never be as good as the foundation. The foundation of reconciliation can only be built upon love and compassion, which is despairing to them, for greed sleeps and rules deep in them and make them rather bear the evil and the consequences that follow. They relish the outcome of the curses that will come upon them to dream in the desert and never return home to their maker."

All of them, after having heedfully listened and watched Tyson, the rich American supports and incites the sentiment to annihilate the system of the world whereby many are starving to death, while others derive pleasure from the sweat of their fellow men, labeling it civilization. They all rise to their feet from where they sit to enjoy their meals. They clap and scream his name more than a dozen times.

"Tyson! Tyson! Tyson! Tyson!" On and on.

"I apologize for all my wrong doings, and I hope you all that I have offended...that are still here would look into your hearts to see if there is a space where forgiveness can emerge," says the caliph as he shed tears and covers his face with his palm and ten fingers.

"Stop crying, man," says Tyson and the rest who swiftly go closer to hug and pamper the man said to have masterminded hundreds of terrorists around the globe to assign themselves into committing atrociousness—slaying and shooting non-Muslims and Muslims alike, all in a prospect of revenge.

It is that he feels so remorseful for all his deeds, all his devotion to malignity, all his melancholy. In otherwise, it is his soul, however, weary and troubled by his own observations of how the world is being manipulated by the chosen ones...that has led to his own commitments to vengeance in order to rebuild and reinstate a just and fair condition for his own people he thinks he cherishes. Towards his concerns for faith to remain within him and within other Muslims, he has developed an idea to tackle the oppressors and vandals, but, at the same time, tackling his own ghost who rests upon his mind to publicly and shamelessly guide him astray. He graciously repudiates and despises those people who have come in the name of civilization, who have come to lecture them on how to eat, think, speak, and act, claiming it is a pathway to arriving in a free society. These people that have become his foes, are the same people who wittingly have sowed a seed of danger that has mistakenly fallen to the moisture land, mistakenly grown to become their lamentation and prompt all (humanity) to devolve into chaos, till the end of time, begets more and more asinine and severe penalties.

But all of a sudden, it appears he is touched deep down in his heart immediately Hussein and Tyson unveil their speculations and suppositions to him, and over and above, declare their supports and align themselves with him in a struggle to put an end to the world system of injustice and inequality. He has thought he and his fellow Muslims are the ones seeing what others are unable to perceive with the naked eyes—seeing good and evil presented to revive the destructive manner that bears the head of the world in its hands. He has fallaciously with determination adjudicated to make their sole recourse to be to seek vengeance for themselves, measure for measure, an eye for an eye, a tooth for a tooth.

Precipitously, while they still feast, rejoice, reconcile, recount various past events, and also outline and summarize what next their aspiration is to be, they could hear as large numbers of firebombs falling on top of the very haven built underneath the earth—a dungeon constructed in the middle of a desert and covered with sands and grasses to reveal a beautiful natural landscape, with no one able to trace a life in there. It is the American airstrikes. The noise of planes could be heard as they drop bombs everywhere in the desert, destroying everything man-made and natural, destroying the spirits of the many Mephistopheles and martyrs. They are bombing everywhere, using sophisticated machines to drive the bombs underground that the devil himself could feel the unrest and tumult. It is destructive, it is a precarious scene only malignant spirits could thrive and survive, it is a reflection of the new world and its technological determinism. Everywhere in that desert is bombarded. The haven they are all dining and making merry and harmonizing, there, which is twenty feet built underground, are seen shattered—caused by the blast and fire effects of the bombs shed on the desert by the United States Air Force. Everyone there in that beautiful and well-equipped house, are scattered and disposed of a position.

At the very instant, twenty three of the guards lay dead, while the caliph, Hussein, Tyson, George, the Jew, and a few guards are all still alive, but suffer a grave injury. The whole place is profusely destroyed. While they all lay down with no one to rush to their aid. George, who manages to get to his feet, advances straight to where one of the gun of the guard lay flat. He picks it up and advances sluggishly to where the caliph also lay unconscious, unable to move an inch. He raises the AK47 gun up and points it to the caliph, about to fire at him. Tyson also manages to raise his and opens his eyes to experience what an act his brother is about to execute. At first, he seems confounded and thinks what he sees is unreal. But when he attempts to take a better look, he sees his brother, George, is about to shoot the hell out of the caliph. He is not emplaced to accept a forgiving proposition. Recalling how they have severely tortured and mocked him and the Jew, he wants to kill him, he hates him; he wants to be the cause of his death, and as well, the sole witness.

Tyson sees them both, he sees how his brother, advancing sluggishly with his wounded and broken arms and legs, still pointing the gun at the caliph. He screams loudly from the distance where he lay low on the floor, entreating, for his brother to pardon the caliph for all his misdeeds in the past. He would not cease calling his name and pleads for a new resolution to precede. He wants to hear his brother say he has forgiven him. But George would not lend his ear to him, and as he becomes progressive and highly intense in his advancement towards the caliph to shoot him down, one of the guard, who is tremendously hurt and could not move an inch, except to pick his own AK47 and raises it up, fires directly at George, only to save his caliph—to show his last loyalty to him. Although, George does abruptly retaliates and fires back at the guard and also fires at the caliphate, leaving more three people dead.

Tyson could bear a witness to this very scene of horror and outrage that has occurred in awake of a cursed day that he has previously supposed to be marked the most graceful and frolicsome day of his life—seeing he could wondrously convert a terrible monster to become a good person, a role model. He wants to change his ways of thinking into something that brings joy to the world instead of his pursuit of power while lying to his followers that their God is preparing a place for them in Heaven. He thinks he has perceived how victory shines its light across the Universe, overcoming evil and restoring the lost faith of mankind.

Before falling to the ground, after the gunshot, Tyson sees his own brother, George, how he screams. He screams loud and utters his last words:

"I have done my best to defend the greatest nation on Earth." After saying that, he laughs and fall down.

To Tyson, it seems his brother has laughed the mythical misery and sufficiency of his childhood, his boyhood and adulthood; it seems he has laughed the notion of an imminence of danger his own country pleases to embrace; and it seems he has laughed his wit out to avoid the imminence of inferno that he probably would see himself in a moment. Tyson grasps it is a concept so special to his brother, so pure, so unadulterated—a concept he would die for, a concept he has died for. It is far behind what he thinks of all what have fomented troubles and brought his brother to that desert of evil. It is patriotism, it is very much comparable to fanaticism, or worse if well-defined and construed. It melts into his heart and seizes it with grip—to see the world shrugging off an issue like this. It destroys a nation, it destroys a community, it creates division among humans. It is not only it disburses an attitude of self-importance and pride, it doubtlessly supports and aids hostility and bloodshed. When some people intensely become attached to their deep feelings of who or what they are identified to be, it does not only become a burden to them, but a burden to the whole society where they live. Having an identity you can consistently defend and support could lead you to separation, a separation from others, and sometimes, a separation from yourself. Separation, and when it is based on superiority complex, it reduces the steep pedantic caliber of that nation and brings it into a disarray.

After all that have materialized. After all the bombs dropped on the very house they assembled, Tyson conceives it is time for him to move on and be oblivious of his past life with his brother. He has to accept life the way it appears to him, not trying to change the course of nature.

So, after he manages to uplift himself from where he has fallen down and covered with muds and dusts caused by the explosion of the bombs, he stares up to see who are still alive and who are not. He raises his brother up to see he is breathless. Thence, he moves closer to where Hussein lay flat, covered by scattered bricks and muds and dust. He removes everything from his body and draws him closer to himself. When eventually he is able to get him out to the corner of the building that was still untouched by the bombs, he sees he is still alive, but very much unconscious and could not utter a word. He speedily runs for the water virtually covered with dirt. He takes the water gives it to him to drink. But unfortunately for him, he realizes his friend, his brother, his compeer, is not having the innate capacity to open his mouth, not to mention he could sip a drop. Hence, he sprinkles some of the water on his body and rubs him with it. He keeps rubbing and sprinkling as he screams and yells for him to be heard. He scuffles for more jars of water he could find, and brings them closer to his friend, then push ahead with the sprinklings and rubbing until at a time he sees his peer opens his eyes bit by bit and smiles faintly to him. It seems to him the gods and goddesses together with the Universe have refused to allow him into their wonderful world and settled on sending him back to life to take on his obligation.

It is a joyous moment for him; it is a wonderful experience; it is absolutely amazing; it is impossibility that genuinely becomes possibility amidst confirmation, and amidst supernatural phenomenon that myriads contemplate if it exist. He sees himself holding his peer and kissing him, kissing every part of his body sheltered with dusts and muds. He loves him; he loves him like he would never love his dead brother, George. He loves him like he loves himself, or more; for he is half-side of him—they are one of two souls. He genuinely is a replacement of his brother, George; he truly is what George will never be or has not be; he truly is the one that helped him through the pathway that leads to discoveries, that leads to eternity.

Chapter 15

I t is Kadosh, the same lad troubled with the countless problems engulfing the world. He is undeniably enshrouded in a situation reachable by discomfort and anguish. He is battling in his heart how it comes to be there have been too many unrests around the globe, in the intervening time, there are more unrests in his own heart. Arriving in Europe to be faced with disappointments and despairs. He finds himself in a great distress because of the unhealthy state of affairs he has thrown himself into—seeking refugee protection in a country where he seems not to be welcomed. Every a night and day, his heart burns, his hope of surviving fades away, only to be superseded by varieties of appointment and degradation and confrontation from the country's Ministry of Foreign Affairs, the Refugee Council, and the social workers. Although, tolerance, forbearance, and endurance are to perform an indispensable character if there would be any means he is standing a chance to live there, this he knows quite well. Wherein, the more he attempts to do what is right to be done, the more he is mystified, the more he is provoked and elevated to a level of fury and acrimony.

There arises that mélange of speculations and reflections, tragedies and comedies, wholes and halves. It is easier to tear a house down and start to rebuild it than to assist and raise a stranger. So far as it gives the impression of being more pleasurable and entertaining to tear the house down and rebuild it than to assist and raise the stranger. It seems, thus, disheartening to people of the world to assist others, while it brings us to success to mock and humiliate them. It is not that caring for a dog or other pets is not profound and proving how altruist we are. What if I cannot regard and care for a fellow human being the way I would pets? What does that make of me? A philanthropist, a hypocrite, a sentimentalist, or a narcissist? Human is human. An animal is an animal. Has it not be said we can all live together by the same people who also believe there has to be a limit in everything we do to help others?

Someone once said, "A community of supports is necessary to help a survivor reach safety and peace."

In contrast, the notion of everyone for himself or herself is what majority of us have come to endorse. To come to look at a vivid account of this matter of contention, it sounds as if humans are still not poised to re-engage in activities that could help us reestablish relations within ourselves, to walk towards reconciliation between all humans and nature—the restoration of the interpersonal bond between people of different kinds—and that indeed poses the greatest threat to humanity and our surviving chance on Earth. It is like campaigning to encourage people to support how to develop concrete mechanisms for stronger economic policies to enhance growth, then, at the same time, drawing rigid and solid plans on how to continuously build more nuclear power plants to supply more tons of carbon dioxide into the atmosphere. When shall a fool admit he is a fool? He will constantly and courageously find a way to defend himself, asserting how he knows it better than anyone does.

Kadosh fancies a world not fit for him to live in the near future in a place where he has been rendered a helping hand—the very place he populates and hopes to live the rest of his life. When he thinks of applying for an expulsion to be taken back to his country, he summons everything to his mind—his past life—how he could be killed by some group of terrorists back there. How will he start life over again when he is not having a relation or family there? Even in the place where he is been born, and also the place he previously departs to set out on a dubious venture to Europe, are places where no one has a right to healthcare. He has never been entitled to be treated in a hospital without him paying with all his possession. Right away where he now lives and still grumbles and whines and protests, he could have medical treatment, he could have medications—all free—though paid for by the country's social security system and the Refugee Council. He is given a place he could sleep every day before the asylum procedures come to an end—that is before the Refugee Council and the Ministry of Foreign Affairs make a decision on what to do to him. But it is comprehensible, it is coherent, and it is unclutter they are going to send him back to his country, in as much as he does not acquire the asylum status to be granted acceptance. He fathoms it is not of the country's interest to guarantee any standard of protection for him as a refugee. He observes how other refugees he has come to meet there struggle and strive so as to make it to stay in the country. Those, who in fact, are granted refugee status because it is obvious to the world how their countries are torn apart by wars, are paid reasonable amount of money every month, and it is said they could be assisted in every form till death. They are almost having equal rights as the citizens. Some of them who have this opportunity six months forthwith after they arrived in the country, are mocking those who have stayed and waited for many year, many who have waited up to ten years and more. They spend the money given to them every months in purchasing cars, clothes, and shoes, making phone calls to their friends and families, inviting them to come join in the lottery. This fulfillment, uncommon in many countries in Europe, is seen put into practice in this very country. For that, many are pouring in from different parts of the world with majority of them from the Middle East, forcing the country to become stricter and harsh to these strangers who are seen ineligible for asylum—commonly referred to as "economic migrants." The Eastern Europeans are the ones more penalized by the strict laws. They too have seized on great opportunities prior to this time in exploiting the country, bringing with them their families to seek refuge only to benefit the money and health care rendered to them, inviting more friends and relations.

To Kadosh, he sees it as a means of self-destruction for people to lumber and wander around the globe for a purpose that produces unquestionable responses, but nonsensical. It is stimulating a sense of intervention in the world's problems inside of him. It is propelling him to validate the many errors made by many immigrants, himself included. He tries to find a way to distinguish between happiness and mere affectation, solely to approach and arrive at a point where he catches the glimpse of the absurdities that characterize the issues of migration. He sees himself come into a hole of rabbit to kill a rabbit for dinner, and being careless of the danger that he might encounter. He sees himself trapped along the alleyway to reach his own indefinite time yet to come. He is confused and frustrated, seeing what he sees as self-imposed afflictions. People could leave their families and friends in search for a better life in a world that is not fit for them, or they are not welcomed, and will never be, as expected, come rain, come sunshine. There are things worth more than attaining the life we crave, the life which tantalizes us with dazzling and celebrated time—that as well absorbs and removes the ingenuity and dignity we possess within us. Not that it is not benefiting in some many ways, but the price to pay in order to attain that life is not worth it. It is simple as to ask anyone who has thrusted himself or herself into that life if faithfully they have encountered it well. It is frustrating and makes us see others to be so mean to us when we cannot achieve our goals and are being left abandoned. Worst of it, it has destroyed the lives of many individuals, who come to realize what we intended is far different from what we are presented. Thus, if that the truth be said, we would prefer we all cleave to a new strategy to eliminate poverty in our own place, rather than walking on dreams unreachable and unfitting. Not having to blame others for our own problems. We must understand that we can regulate and stabilize our situations by first putting the blames on ourselves and taking responsibilities.

Yes, it is typical the land where myriads of these refugees come from are places devastated by war, corruption, oppression, and neglects. But if we do not endeavor to obtain the necessary plans to unravel and resolve these issues on our own, then who do we hold responsible for failing? We should have to engage in collaboration and partaking in events to elevate and empower our communities, not withdrawing from it and heading to a distinctive insignificant direction to find a better life.

What we do we do for the next generation, we do it to create a better world for our children and their children. When it becomes a conflict we have to violently entangle in, we must retreat, then reinforce and apply wit and plan of action to tackle it peacefully, but we must try. By not trying makes us so weak and foolish—to leave our own land to be humiliated and disregarded by other people in different places.

There again, Kadosh has experienced everything. He has made an effort to persevere and live like others, no matter how critical and painstaking it is—his fear of being deported back home sooner or later, his inability to cope with the new society or integrate. Day after day, the situation worsens and he becomes more perplexed and appalled. At a time he devises a new system, a new talent for chasing women, since that has become his only option to be able to remain in the country and not be deported. It is ludicrous and non-essential to him how he could run after different women at the same time, doing everything he could to win their hearts in an effort to effectuate a marriage event to sustain his stay in the country, while these women also capitalize on his situation and make him a sex toy. Holding the belief a secure, steady, and sincere conscious will embody and exemplify the best path to success, he tries to be truthful and plain to these women, while they decline to accept his decent and honest life. On the contrary, they are in favor of those who would trick and use them in reaching their goals. To him, it is unfair and baffling. Perhaps, he would not allow that to change who he is. He would not alter his lifestyle to gain the world. He would not be compelled to live a life full of deception to work his way up the ladder. There are more desirable things ahead of what is affront of him. Doing what is wrong to hurt people so as to live in a country is against his will, against humanity. How sad and hurtful to see a young man runs after women of his mother's age, and yet being neglected, for they conceive it is not for love, rather, for the document. And no matter how he tries in every aspect to justify his motive of how he sincerely cares about them, they are all disposed to follow the rules. Some who would have make any attempt to say: ' "it is ok, let them see how it will end."' They too have become afraid because of too much pressure laid upon him to get married or else he would have to return to his country. No threat is as frightening as when you are being pressurized to do anything. It is ludicrous, frankly, it is.

He sees it happening, he sees it happening to immigrants around the globe, he sees how many who, at the initial time, enter the country they have been innocent as newborns. Until after a period of time when they are gradually transformed into thieves and drug dealers, for they are never given any financial support even as they notice the setback in their lives and the fashion it wavers and shakes, while at the same time others in the country, living standards turn higher and higher. It seems the vilification they are vehemently subjected to is not what they have wished for. In that form, they have to discover a perilous flight route that would get them to live like the people they see every day. For work, it is forbidden for them in as much they are illegal. What is left for them on the table is to thrive in delinquency purposefully to elude dubious and critical situations, and then uplift their own spirits. Although, many who have come have intentionally and bravely come for drug dealings. Despite how many are caught and imprisoned, others would not surrender. It is as if the country is enthroned with money to assist the youths to attain a dream of self-destruction with drugs. It is all drugs, drugs, drugs, and drugs.

It disconcerts Kadosh to see how the little kids are mired in confusion and not knowing what to do with the money given to them by their government. It disconcerts him to see 13-year-old boys and girls hold a full packet of cigarettes and smoke with contentious mood along the street with no one to caution them. It is not out of a mere feeling of jealousy that he gets upset and wants to slap the hell out of some of them, rather than how he sees them with great opportunities and privileges to study and gain degrees. The money is there, and it is unwittingly poured on them to destroy themselves while they feel it is part of enjoyment. It strains his heart to see how the foreigners are more eager, aiming on a serious attachment to studying to have qualifications for work, as many of the so-called natives consume and drain away their time. It is all fun, it is entertaining to him, espying how humans could live with pride, conceit, and egoism, thinking there is no good reason to be fretful of what would occur in the future. It is like gambling and relishing the money won, forgetting someday time might bring tough luck. It is all a way he could elaborate on a system not meant for everyone except for the indigenous people and the integrated immigrants. It is a thing of chance, like a lottery, like saying, ' "many are called, but few are chosen.'"

There are list of countries more favorable, but few Africans and Eastern Europeans. The people who are very much pledged to bigotry and unfairness are not even the natives, but the others who have migrated from other parts of Europe, or their parents have done so: the Portuguese and Serbians are the worst—for the fact they fear others have come to take their chances away. Then, there are the Greeks, Italians, Spaniards,

French, Dutch, Germans, Belgians, Britons, Americans, Swedes, Russians, Austrians…etcetera. They too have come to explore a better future, perhaps to live and die there. However, they have come and been treated probably as second-class citizens at the beginning. In consequence, when they come up with advantageous circumstances, they become even more proud and mean to others that are new. It is like a thing injected in every one of them, regardless of their race, creed, or background. Worst, the Africans. It is all good, good for Kadosh, good for mankind to ponder on the reasons poverty has separated itself from wealth, the reasons some feed on the blood of others. Money brought to these countries by the corrupt governments of other poor people are spent in their presence, in spite of how they are still derided. Is it that those who come across with fortune are far associated with goodness and intelligence than the ones who are faced with hardship? In this very country, one has to learn to always hear both sides of every story. We have to understand crime can be a product of the law, and as a lack of social benefit. People are obligated to refrain from the lifestyle that embraces goodwill, to be preoccupied with the practice of misconducts. It is all about money, money, and money is running around the brain and mind of every male and female—citizens and immigrants. It is money, it is worth dying for. In an attempt to regard and worship money and make it all we desire, we become a hostage to that same money until the day we lose our breath.

When these immigrants look around them and understand they are being mocked and inflicted penalties for becoming a burden, their internally generated revenues become enviousness, which is the outcome of their being disregarded, ignored, and unfairly treated. They would have to do whatever it takes to subsist and flourish like the people in the country. They have to sell drugs to destroy the youths who are so much in need of it and could never live without it. It appears to be a retribution from their own points of view. They are in supposition of paying for what has been bought long ago from them in their own lands. Thus, they are quite oblivious they are in a foreign land, and are to succumb to the country's temptations and pressure, or even succumb to death. One thing being understood or misunderstood is—to suffer and bear is a better thing to do than to be brave and daring to start a fight you can never win.

When we battle in predicaments, when we observe how unfairly we are being treated, or how we are being oppressed, thus far, we keep calm until our oppressors become wearied and capitulate to reverse their course. It does not show a kind of weakness in not intending to start a battle with the oppressors. For even if we are to fight, we must not do it the wrong way, we must not allow anger to control us. To fight is not to involve in violence act, but to raise our voice for the Universe to hear us. Another thing is what if we use violence and lose? By then, we have idiotically and stubbornly demand permission of more mockery and punishment to be brought upon us. So, it is better to endure, to be patient, and exercise perseverance, then await how the gods who watch us all will shoot back. Wherein, while eagerly waiting, we have to continuously raise our voices and lay out some plans of action that would definitely alter the situation for us, without having to shed a drop of blood. We have to do something. We have to try in every way to alter the situation. By fighting does not mean we have to shed blood, it means we have to strive.

Kadosh, who has visited almost all the museums in the country, and have done a lot of research to know things about the people and the properness for their attitude, pride, and passion. He learns they have long suffered in the hands of their neighbors. They have been invaded and conquered several times by different empires and countries, and yet they would not relinquish to continue to be whom they are and live the life they desire. You could imagine a small country becomes so rich they can now say to their neighbors who have wanted them to be their slaves.

"'Look, we are on our own, and we do what we want.'"

It is obvious and insane how money has become a god in this land. And money is good, it is good to spend. Everyone will worship it, everyone will practice it, everyone will live it, and as well, everyone will make you love and discern the importance and value of it. What is so prevalent is the luxurious life everyone is willing to accept: there are challenges and competitiveness in who drives the best car, who wears the best dress, who lives in a good house, or who has the most beautiful man or woman, and this is often practiced by the natives, and also the foreigners. It is all competitiveness. Then when it comes to the aspect of acquiring knowledge to produce and create with imagination, the people are unconcerned. Instead, they tend to learn the different languages around the continent, which is good and bad. Good, because it is for communicating, and communication, which is the exchange of information, ideas or thought from one person to the other. Bad, because they have to spend much time learning languages and avoid doing research in different field of studies. That you fall in love with people, for the fact they have assisted you in a way your own relations have never been able to. To state it clearly and delicately, you have to give back to the society. Then it becomes a moral obligation for you to contribute to the improvement and elevation of the foundational principle. You have to give everything that you have—including your prescience. If the truth be said, will it not be far reasonable and advantageous if the country decides to prompt the citizens into investing much time and energy in some kind of developments in art, in science, and in technology, rather than learning different languages? Instead of funding projects to include more languages to be spoken—like adding Portuguese language to the country's official languages, the funds can be laid on better projects, for instance, the development of a University Teaching Hospital, which the country does lack. The banking and financial sector which are very important to the country's economy must not be overlooked, but we cannot rely exclusively on that. There has to be a call for people to embrace ideas that yields creativity, productivity, innovation, and invention. What about sport facilities? The money is there, so why not spend it on projects that will ensure a better future? Very few people Kadosh has met with possess that high degree of intelligence, and when you meet with them, they seem smart and have well-traveled, or have migrated from somewhere. The indigenous people, those who are cultured and tasteful, are never in any aspect disposed to journey through the passageway, nor sojourn in a land where they might encounter some unknown illegal aliens, not to mention that they are willing to engage in conversations with them. It is that it is the people's culture to mind their own business and never interfered in other people's lives. So it is said that everyone minds his or her own business. This, most people who are new there assert to be a thing done to exhibit pride. It is still our pride that helps create that distance between us. However, how could Kadosh ever recount the life he lives in this very land, looking to evaluate the circumstances with criticism, when ipso facto he has benefited enormously from the very people and their system? When in point of fact, they have rendered to him a life the government of his country has never for once thought of rendering. They have demonstrated a measure of capacity in providing for him a place to sleep and also feed him for all the time he is given a valid authorization to live there. They have provided him with free transportation to everywhere in the country throughout the time he is permitted to live there. They have provided him with free medical treatment and medicines whenever he falls sick. They have even sent him to the nearby country for an eye operation when he nearly goes blind with complicated cataract. They have paid for his education throughout his stay in this land—trying to make him learn the many languages freely. As they have done for him, so also they have done for every immigrant who have come to seek refuge in their land. They do their best to assist them, providing them with the basic amenities of life—which they are being deprived by their country's governments. All this have come to constitute to what has compelled them to fall in love with the country and want to live the rest of their lives there. But when they are humiliated, disrespected, and rejected, outrage and umbrage have both come to wipe away all the good done for them. Although, many have said it would have been preferable if they are allowed to work and earn some money, instead of sleeping at home or running around the country. They could save some little money should in case they are to be sent back to their countries of origin, so they can start a new life back there. Not that they would not want to return home, but money has become a thing no one can live without as dictated by the system. Better not help people than make fools of them. Yes, it is true to say it is something about pride. Pride is playing a leading role in everything everyone is doing. All these things are impetuously clustered together: it is pride, it is wealth, it is threat, it is impecuniousness. It is obviously delirious and preposterous the way we permit the wealthy people to proudly pose threats to the wretched. It is the way of the world. It is how it is. It is how it has always been.

Intrinsically, who would be in a position so high she would not be proud, seeing all she has been able to accomplish? Looking into the depth of the whole matter, to explain the characteristics of controversy, to spot the authenticity, principles, and factualism. We will note that we the strangers tend to express too much of dissatisfaction in every aspect of situations we live through. We look in the direction of the negative aspects, without having to bring the whole picture to mind in order to exercise contemplation. We sometimes, wrongfully or thoughtlessly, frame in our minds that we are the victims. But why do we have to eat the food we condemn? Would it not be more appropriate we refuse the food instead of condemning it with our thoughts and words? For instance, if we could understand it better than how we draw conclusions from our own points of view. If we could draw a comparison between what we eat and condemn and how we beg for assistance from our neighbors, and yet criticize them for not doing enough. It signifies how we should rather be considering our governments responsible for our ordeal and condescension, yet we put every blames on people who have come to our aids when we are in a deep mess. The truth be said, if the westerners refuse to assist the many refugees they receive every day, no one will hold them responsible. But that they believe human beings have rights to live and enjoy social and economic developments, and to fulfil their promises and criteria, which they have set for themselves, that humans have the rights to live to their potential if assisted—the so-called human rights. They too have undergone circumstances more precarious and urgent, and they have fled to different parts of the world to seek refuge and shelter. For that they have learned lessons, seeing into other's adversities and taking it to be theirs. We all must learn. Though, none is perfect, and we must admit so. But we must blame our governments for exploiting us, disregarding us, causing us grief, and forcing us to flee our lands. Why should a twelve-year-old boy leave his parents to journey through the hot desert, through the deep seas and oceans, just to search for a better life in a land he knows nothing about? Our governments are our problems. They are the ones letting us down.

Kadosh have come to understand something about these people who have come to accept people from every nation to live with them. He believes if anyone takes time, efficacy, and rapaciousness to look back to their history, we would see they have the rights to be proud. Looking from where they have come from, how their ancestors have suffered in the hands of their greedy neighbors by being conquered and humiliated. Yet, they have decided not to look back in anger, they have welcomed everyone to join in relishing the good life, and also to help build and secure the small, but mighty, nation. It teaches us a lesson to not pay evil with evil, but instead forgive even if we will never forget. Pride comes from a low extraverted thinking if we will accept the truth—how we see the world around us. Although most of us are being pushed to adopt it as a decree. Nevertheless, we see how we think we are wise to punish our neighbors who would later become our savior.

Then again, we can say the funniest thing to do can as well be the weirdest thing. This is how to explain everything to the wise ones, this is how everything happens in this land. The manner in which many of these immigrants strive, tax themselves in order to come up with success, in order to obtain a residence permit to live legally in the land, for they know if they are being rewarded with it, it would be that automatically their lives would be transformed into honorable and happy mood. The social benefits in which they would be welded. The privileges they would be given. A good life. A real good life. Some have gone to an extent to committing suicide when they could not. Some have even jumped on a speedy train, injuring every part of their bodies. And at the same time, there are those who fortunately pluck the ripened fruit, with documents in their hands, with all the benefits, they would not settle upon living and maintaining an appropriate work life, getting a job, getting education without any payment due, instead they have to engage more in drug dealings. Very funny indeed. Those who are willing to work their lives out are deprived of it, while those unwilling to build and repair are issued every opportunity of a lifetime. Very funny indeed. In the terms of rating the country, it will be seen as a small, but mighty, country. It is a place every nationality around the globe have come to assemble to work and live, and freedom is the mark of the land that bears its witness in the sight of the Universe to track progress and consigns it to posterity.

O' Luxembourg, O' sweet land of a dream, how he loves to fit in, how he loves to be a part of it.

It came to pass that Kadosh has received an email directed at him by the Universe, assigning him to a task of commencing to inculcate the people around him with a sense of an exigent compunction and to legitimate a cause to return them to their maker. After that, he would have to depart from that land where he inhabits to a land not far from there—the very place where they are to execute their grand plan in saving the world, if solely they will be able to fill the bill. And he is to travel to Paris, where revolution has once taken effect—the city of Légalité, Egalité, Fraternité. There, he is to meet with Lakota, Hussein, Tyson, Shiromi, and Aadita—and they all are to meet in a very big mansion built in the outskirts of Paris. They are to meet there and will be instructed on what next step to take to get the message to the whole world.

At first, Kadosh thinks it is going to be a problem if he vacates his asylum procedures to accost a situation he very much prepares for. For some months that have passed, he has had a dream of how his soul has traveled to the wonderland where the gods and goddesses dwell—where the Universe has spoken to them and set them on a journey to return to Earth to heal the wounded soul of humanity.

He knows it is a call, a call he cannot decline. He has to run away to do the will of the Universe. He has to follow the instruction, do what is right for humanity, alternately to waiting for his asylum to be granted. Which is more meaningful and considerable—his stay in the country where there is no chance for him, or his call to heal humanity?

He sees himself fed up with the whole notion of clinging to other's faiths and beliefs. He is sick and tired of adhering to a cause that avails and certifies opprobrium. Tribulation, the way he perceives it, is a fruition of a great exertion for accomplishment. Thus, driven by success, and unable to live a life suitable and divine. What is one to accomplish if the truth be uttered when you are an illegal alien in a foreign country and sitting in a public bar with the natives of the land, hearing on television of how immigrants from Africa and the Middle East are coming to invade Europe, and at the same time, immigrants from Mexico and other South American countries are struggling to get to the United States, and in Australia, people from Thailand and other neighboring countries are losing their lives in the sea, all for the fact they aim to cross into Australia on boats and canoes? It sure does prompts confusion, it prompts degradation. All these run around Kadosh's brain and mind. He sees how people complain and vilify these immigrants. Not that he does not comprehend the situations in these civilized nations—the frustration they too have to meet with if they are not heedful and do the right thing at the right time. Yes, it is true these illegal immigrants come into their countries with complications, burdens, and disturbances. They come to perpetuate the population. They come pleading for assistances, pleading for treatments, pleading for everything to stand a future. They come certainly without finance, but only to demand and demand. They come with no family to call on. They come prepensely for better welfare. Most unfavorable, they come, bringing different rules and regulations along, bringing different cultures along—some which are not in compliance with the culture of the indigenous people. Some, they come, bringing their religions with them and forcing them on the people who own the land—by so doing, causing chaos and unrests. Meanwhile, the natives who would always want to preserve those moral values of theirs, become frustrated as well. But, if the truth be said, from the beginning of time these people have been on their own in their lands, living the lives that suits and soothes them when these civilized people leaves to hunt for them, preaching to them of how to live life and how to die. This should be seen as the price of colonialism. It is all greed—the want it all that led to all these. They have gone there with intent to exploit them, to purchase them as slaves from their chiefs and kings and warlords who have been tricked into committing these acts of evil. They have gone there to make of them tools and bring them abroad to be used as cows and horses in working in their plantations to generate wealth, and to develop their cities.

How could one now lay complains of invasion when, in fact, we were the ones who started it all? We have to be careful of what we wish for. It would have been better if everyone lives on his own and they live a life that is suitable for them, rather than forcing them to live your own way with no intention of providing them the materials to do so. In a context like this, we trace back to the time when humans were humans and do esteem and regard humanity and nature; we trace back to when men were governing themselves and were as free as birds in the air; we trace to that time when we were not ruled and controlled by machines. That time of primitiveness, these Africans, Indians, Aborigines, and other tribes were all living their primitive lives in their own dark world, and were satisfied and vivacious. Until the Arabs and Europeans came with their ideals, ideals of civilization, ideals on how to live, postulating to be the givers and takers of life, bringing to these people different cultures and traditions on the basis of showing how more superior and wise they are, solely to exploit them. They came, assuming to be next to the supernatural being they call "God", saying the light was needed to snuff out the darkness.

The Indians were on their own when forced out of their land, then occupied it. So were the Aborigines and other tribes who peacefully inhabit their land, not calling for anyone for enlightenment. Looking back to the horrible events in the past can bring too much sad memories. But we have to accept the fact that it will not be so easy to forget that past, for if we do not look to it and merges it with the present, we can hardly define and shape our future. We have to comprehend the cause and the consequences of our every deed. Tolerance can play a vital role when dealing with issues. We should move on, but walk along the right track and permit the guidance of love and compassion.

Chapter 16

In the city of Paris, there are all those who come from every part of the planet with different backgrounds, and share the same values and visions. It is the scheduled time for the mission set for all by the Universe to be carried out, the time for the message to reach the four corners of the Earth.

There are all assembled in a big mansion in Cergy, a town just a few kilometers around the outskirts of Paris. It is a wonderful day in the middle of spring, as they arrive in the house formerly bought and paid for by Tyson.

There is Aadita, who appeared to be the beautiful angel Lakota has chased after and has been invited for a coffee in Paris. When eventually they meet to talk about politics and other crucial issues clogging mankind's progress and his apprehension of the Universe and everything there-in. She is able to attempt the very disclosure of who she really is to him. Lakota, whose eyes confuse him of what he experiences, is so remorseful for not able to capture her image in time. He thinks he has met the woman of his life, but wholly to meet his partner in a mission to heal humanity. Instantly, when she utters her name out to him, he knows precisely who she is, and walks closer to hug and kiss her, while the people around observe them both in astonishment as they squawk and speak languages unknown to them, as they say the words said to them by the Universe.

Then, there is Shiromi, who has been born and raised in Tokyo, Japan. At the age of 16, he has moved to Canada to live with his uncle. There, he has attended a computer-science and engineering school in one University of Toronto, and is later offered a job at a computer company in the U.S. There, where he is, he is earning enormous amount of money, receiving paychecks, and lavishing on himself and friends.

It is not until the day he becomes drunk and rush to hospital for emergency treatment. At first, the doctors and nurses all believe he is never going to survive the critical situation he has placed himself by going to drink and inhale cocaine, and mistakenly inhaled something poisonous that badly affects his brain. Although, he has been in coma for six months. His breathing tube has been taken out and left on a nasal device throughout these days and weeks and months. Everyone who knows him believes he is going to be seriously disabled even if he survives. But, all of a sudden, two days after six months he has been there, he opens his eyes and speaks to one of the doctors, who speedily flees the room he is admitted, going out and uttering words and sounds in a shrill tone and calling the names of the other doctors and nurses to come. It is so unbelievable when they all rush to meet him in the room, smiling and feels very at ease. It is something related to supernatural phenomenon, it is a prodigy. One of the nurses who is dedicated to praying and always praying for him, succeeds in seizing on this opening in order to protest and contend the existence of a supernatural being she calls "God". She also affirms it is Jesus Christ who has intervened to reveal his miraculous work to the nonbelievers. And, in the course of all these, Shiromi has been in the wonderland with the gods and goddesses and has returned to Earth, for him to take on some obligations, to not only heal himself, but to heal others.

After all that transpire while in hospital, he has come to quickly realize how dearly life is, and it enables him to evince his ability to submerge himself into a whirlpool of vulnerability and perils. He is forced to disembark from the ship of thoughts and code-breaking, and then, unfalteringly centers on disseminating the news of an end chapter to the story that has been foretold, to show the world to the people, extending the teachings of the Universe to them so as for a change to be observed, if not, a terrible wreck will be welcomed.

In the big mansion where they are all gathered by the universe. They could do whatever they want there. They could cook and eat and drink anything they want and need—all paid for and delivered by Tyson, who is worth more than ten billion dollars and has made himself, and all his wealth, available to sponsor the teachings of the Universe to reach the whole world. It is a very big mansion with twenty-six rooms, each different and worth upgrading. Like a hotel, every room has a bathroom and a toilet. The compound is fenced in, 1000 feet by 1000 feet plot of land with gardens and parks. Every room has unique interior designs and large collections of pictures and paintings. In the compound there is a lawn tennis court, a football field, and a table tennis board where they could play tennis and swim in a nearby swimming pool. A beautiful and comfortable house to live in, and Tyson has spent four million euros in purchasing this very house for all.

When they have all finished with touring the house and have a dinner together. Some have gone to shower and dress themselves to return to the big hall designed for holding meetings and discourses to reach accord and making decisions to alter the mindset of the people of the world that has been intoxicated with evil acts, solely to achieve objectives and reach goals, all in the name of money—greed's terms for destruction.

This time of spring is when people begin to experience warmness and sunshine. At this same time, this very time, the world is enthralled by the beauty of fear and despondency. The world is in a bad mood that describes its own bitter ends. The belief, the confidence and expectation that the world would be at peace and achieve the unachievable, easily becomes a mere illusion, and this illusion is seen broken into pieces. That the world would be saved by fasting and prayers by religious people, and also by scientists and astronomers, are mere fairy-tales, a sheer lunacy. The world is in grand trouble envisioned long ago but unseen by majority even as it unfolds and manifests.

The most powerful nations on Earth are at war with themselves, a verbal war. They are willing to fight each other, but none is willing to commence. Granting all these, they are mobilized, teed up, and primed to hit the ball. On account of who should be leading and who should not they could all point fingers, cast themselves in doleful secrecy and idleness. It is they who dictate for others on what is right and wrong, yet they are tearing their souls to save and destroy the world just as they have already destroyed their own animating principle.

Firstly, it is a cyber warfare, and it is so intense and maniacal. They routinely troubling each other, the chief reason, no one knows. To other people, it is thrilling, priceless, moronic, and unthinking. It certainly might be all about money and power. And there is no one to put an end to this, no one, except to watch as they permit themselves to invade their own sanity in order to apprehend if normality is written in it, then, to distinguish between simple and hard.

At that hour when Lakota, Kadosh, Tyson, Aadita, Shiromi, and Hussein are all together and commence with their discussions of the world and its innumerable problems that seem really threatening to the soul of mankind.

It is Tyson, who raises the motion. "Firstly, we have to talk about money and how it has come into the world that it now becomes the driving tools to reach anywhere."

"That is a good thing to start with," responds Kadosh, who has fled from the small country to come to Paris to be loved and regarded by the people that matters, people who know his worth and usefulness. "And if I could dig a little bit deeper, I would say, we could trace the history of money to thousands of years ago when money was made of bronze and in use in some parts of Asia, like China during the Zhou dynasty, and also in India. Before then, cowries were in use and first manufactured there in these places between 700 and 500 B.C. Then, there was a time when silver coinages were later brought up to serve as a medium of trade. But, in recent days, it has become a unit of account. It has become a drive for contesting and for challenging. It has become an element to drive us into competitiveness. Aforetime, it was meant to be a tool to promote social progress and aid people in gaining better standards of life. But, in current time, our affiliation and dependence on money is increasing and increasing, and it has become our dissatisfaction and grief. We have made this money a controlling element in every aspect of life. We have made it to be the one and all passage which every bargain, every transference, every exchange, every compact, every contract, every covenant, and every deal must all pass through in order to be valid and integrated."

"You are very right, Kadosh. It seems you have been with us in the desert when we previously discussed this very issue of money as the primary source of every of humanity's problem," says Tyson, recollecting how they have all discussed this same issue in the desert.

"Yes," retorts, Kadosh, standing to keep account whether he is being taken seriously as his voice raises with sarcasm. "I tell you this, if money has not been the issue, humans would be living just normal, we would all be living with love and compassion in our hearts."

"Very true," adds Aadita, also standing from where she sits. "That is how they have been able to invent brain and mind control techniques to manipulate we humans. They have done so with the creation of this paper (money). And since they are humans and have been able to create it, we are more than them, we possess the power more superior than theirs, and we can, as well, destroy it. Yes we can, we can."

"Yes, we can! Yes we can!" All hail as they uplift themselves and join in the chanting.

Tyson is acutely amused with what he witnesses. He knows he is not alone. He sees himself feel whole with these people. He appreciates them. He hypothesizes their presence is of a good significance in returning mankind to its maker. He stares deep at them, and with a calm and soft voice, utters these words, "Believing in the power of thoughts and intentions. Believing in the instructions of the Universe—the desire to pursue whatever we wish to achieve on Earth for the sake of humanity, to pursue the great concerns over the great cause of healing, healing the soul that has been badly brutalized. In balancing potency with desirability, I say to you, we will be flushed with success. I say to you, I will spend all I have to ensure guarantee and present activities to express our true nature. They will bear witness and many will be indoctrinated and instigated to join in the evolution. I tell you, we are there already in the wonderland as gods and goddesses. This battle is ours, and we will be victorious."

"Yes, we will," all repeatedly hail.

Tyson, who is the oldest of all and poised to help ensure things are not misunderstood, so as to have a comprehension of the way in which the evolution is going to be realized. He uplifts himself again and looks around, examining and studying everyone minutely to see if any is about to say something. When none of them utter something, he sits back on his cushion, and proceeds with what he is about to say while standing. "You see, all these questions and discussions about money may be considered simultaneously too placid and disturbing to think about. It is a thing we cannot, with reasonable and pious observance, administrate its evasion, even if it happens we become the rulers of the world. Even supposing, it now appears to be an idea created by men to run, to override, to crush other people and take control of the world. In essence, it is true. We see how it is portrayed in paper and metal to serve a purpose to govern people's lives. It is "we the people" like we say in America, who have enabled this. We approve of it for us to be made subordinate functionary, making us entered in a realm of the absurd. You see, it is the intent, the consciousness surrounding this money that turn it sweet and sour—which implies, it is how we follow it. Money serves two purposes: it suppresses, and as well, it elevates. And, it has served both. If we use it wisely, all will be well. Then if we use it foolishly, we await the repercussions. Some say if we abolish the use of money we will create a better world, we will establish equality among humans and among nations. But I tell you that is not the issue."

"Then, what is the issue," requests snappily, Shiromi, who has been thinking about this issue long ago and figures out the only way man could live in peace and harmony is to utterly abstain from the touch of money.

"Ok, I will tell you now," answers Tyson, taking a walk around the place they are assembled. Looking closer to his dearest friend, Hussein. He entreats him to courteously assist him in delivering the lecture. "Yes I can help you do that. Nonetheless, I bet you can do a better job, brother," he says to him as they both look into each other's eyes and understand what should be done. "The issue is that the problem of the world is far extended to the four corners of the globe. It is not a problem of one person, or one race, or one religious belief. Honestly, it is a problem of the world. And, it is simply that we humans prefer to cultivate the notion of ordinary pleasure. By so-doing, we become oblivious of what precisely is the principle of life. Many of us do not know the purpose of life, and it shows signs of how we do not care. That everyone of us here fathom how we possess the building capacity to expose the reality of life to others and inspiring them with words and actions for them to follow to put an end to the lethal adversary eating our souls. We have to do our part as the Universe has instructed, we have to bring the news to them, the good news needed to transform them to look away from that fatal jeopardy and stare into the light of hope. Our politicians are our problems. They rule us. They take charge of the provocation of hatred amongst humans. They cause conflicts around the globe. Every time we see ambitious and worried politicians being guided by expediency rather than the principle of life—not to know why we are living and what we are living for. They put in front everything that practically contributes to their self-interest. They do everything they want. They do and adhere to this way of life and luring others into it. Now, is it not time for us all to say to them that enough is enough, for the world actually does not belong to you people alone?—it is for us all. And we are discontented with you dictating to us of what is right and wrong, we are weary of your ideals."

"I get you right, Tyson," obtrudes Aadita, rising from her seat and walking from one end of the extravagant monastic parlor to the other end. "You are, in the sense, referring to our political elites and mercenaries that live among us to be the major impediments restricting our progression to reconstitute serenity and tranquility in our world. Secondly, you are saying every individual has a role to play in the uplifting of humanity. That is true. But, I suggest we are not going to open our arms to accept that concept of letting money be our soul provider, because if we do so, we are conclusively defending the right for them to prolong and affix to the ideal that will extend and dignifies capitalism. As we all ascertain, that if capitalism outlast, then man will see his destruction come to accomplishment. To me, I do consider we introduce any way that will substitute capitalism. Money and capitalism are constantly going to be hand to hand—they are birds of the same feathers that flock together."

"You have clarified it all, Aadita," says Shiromi, as he maintains an upright position, and he adds, "Money is the root of all evil and will continue to be."

"All well said, my compeers. I do concur," says Tyson, walking closer to hold Aadita by her hand and bringing her closer to Shiromi, calling out for the others, still sitting, to come join in the reunion. "But, there is something we must remember. We must remember that capitalism has done more harm than was intended which is meant to generate profit and to validate a degree of competitiveness."

"Then, for what reason do we have to engage in such competitions that we no longer see our fellow humans as we see ourselves? We have been torn apart by the beliefs which frantically facilitate struggling and resentment in an effort to reach our goals, in an effort to acquire possessions, thereby, compelling us to be killing each other. The people in control give us that money after much exhaustion, they give it to us as a tool to drive us, to move us to anywhere they wish, but in return we give them our souls," articulates, Kadosh as he walks away from the rest of them to return to his seat.

"That is true, Kadosh," replies Tyson, seeing himself as the only man left alone to defend the system he so much understands to be a doom to humanity, but cannot be eradicated. "You see, capitalism has rendered to mankind great advancement in science and technology which are what we see beautifying our world and making it more comfortable for us to live in. The problem is not money. The problem is humans who furnish themselves with unnecessary material things, with a belief they are entitled to have it all for themselves—which takes them to resurrect in greed and lament the end time. You see, when people begin to apply this vision of love and compassion for their neighbors, then the Universe will open its heart wide for mankind to enter to receive the blessings that await them. There, they will see the light shining and never run away from it again. It is not that we will have to reject the fact that when people possess more than enough, they become proud. They do, and that pride itself has to a great degree contributed to more competitiveness that has led to productivity, confidence, and accomplishments. Hence, these things are good in developing societies and nations as I have previously outlined. But, there also comes pride that has led to arrogance, egotism, and subjugation, which have led man to all these predicaments. Since we are naturally drawn to this pride, it becomes a part of every individual. In the real sense, when there is love, pride will find no way to excel. We have to acknowledge we are faced with a problem of separateness among ourselves and that is the basis for our hatred and conflicts. Love is the only remedy. Love, as I believe, is what we should be living for. It is true that we have permitted ourselves out of the wheel of nature and humanity. We have separated ourselves from humanity, and it has only resulted in everyone becoming afraid of their neighbors. We have purchased and paid for fear. All we need now is oneness, all we need is love. Love as I have read in the Bible, says: Love is patient, love is kind. It does not envy, it does not boast, it is not proud. It does not dishonor others, it is not self-seeking, it is not easily angered, it keeps no record of wrongs. Love does not delight in evil but rejoices with the truth. It always protects, always trusts, always hopes, always perseveres. Love never fails. But where there are prophecies, they will cease; where there are tongues, they will be stilled; where there is knowledge, it will pass away."

Lakota, who has read history and studied a bit of mythology and religion, is not prepared to let his ears to all that is said to edify him of the meaning of oneness and the good outcome of it. Then he uplifts himself to express his own version of the subject-matter, and also his perspectives. "I do agree with you, Tyson. You deserve credits when you said we all need each other to survive. It is true that love is the remedy. Even so, when it comes to 'oneness' as you have earlier mentioned, I do see it differently from my own point of view. To respond to what you have said, I believe people of the world indeed do necessitate a cure to the cancer of hatred—we need to accomplish that mission to abolish that ideology of hate. All the same, first, we have to understand that as we make plans on coming together to resolve this issue, many are also planning to continue to dissolve this brotherly and sisterly love. They do not want us to unite and live peacefully together, instead, to lure and assist us to keep killing one another simply for them to profit. What I am indicating is that since, via domestication and indoctrination, we have come to embrace what we have been taught and now acting along with it. So, when we talk about 'oneness' we have to recognize the fact that it will be a goal that will be unachievable. Elaborating on the topic of that oneness, which denotes unison or agreement, I practically believe this refers to a 'oneness' where one sees his fellow human being submerges and drowns in an ocean, and with a great desire, he lends a helping hand. That is compassion. But when it comes to thought, feeling, or aim, then I do reason that it would be more harmonious and desirable if we are being left alone to sort this out—and that is freedom—which certifies that a man, with obligation, enabled to do his own reflection and consideration of which way is best for him to walk along. The truth cannot be affirmed by fiction is what many still cease to ascertain. We must understand everything is included and allowed to live according to its true nature. It is for the good of humans for everyone to be permitted to admit his own weakness and follow his own will—people must be allowed to choose their own fate, and not being imposed some ideals that are not in accord and will never be with their mind, will, and feelings; it will never suit them no matter how they try."

Staring at everybody, Lakota presses on, "My aim is that we can be separated and still love and care for each other. It is true that if the Arabs and Europeans have not travel to other continents to interfere in these people's ways of life and colonize them with the intent to transform and bring them into civilization, these people categorically would have been living just better. Since civilization surfaced itself or has been forced to, life has become more complex for human beings. Though, we are still foolishly unaware that complexity of existence has increased and it is still increasing. Now everything is interconnected. What affects me will surely affects you—and it is what causes global economic crisis—antecedent, which contributed to the Second World War. Civilization, I understand has for certain, incorporated man into his doom; it has driven us so far that we have replaced natural environment with man-made things. There was then when people were original and unrefined and energetic and were minding their own business in some corners of the world with no one to instruct anyone or emphasize the concepts and themes of a progressive reform. In primitive time, people live day-to-day with their families. They were poor though, but they could farm and harvest foods that sustain them. There were no electricity or phones or television and people could form a strong bond with their families and communities. These original and ordinary people make their own things by their hands, and the world was calm and quiet—no machines, no carbon dioxide to fill the air, and no leaving home to go to work with time condition in a daily routine to come home exhausted while pile of bills await them. Just good and happy life. Until men started to invent new systems to govern themselves and enforce them to live according to their wishes, according to their rules. Then, taking their civilizations to places where people do not have it, expanding imperial frontiers, achieving stunning military victory, spreading their beliefs and values to bring law and order to people whom they regard as primitive and dangerous, using them as slaves, using them as super exploited labor.

"In a very real sense, we all could classify and submit our understandings on the theme the Jews when inventing their biblical stories, attest the first humans have eaten from the tree of the knowledge of good and evil, that, which symbolizes the beginning of a composition of good and evil in order for man to live appropriately to his preference, but initiating a project of separation between him and his maker. From then on, after the separation, man has become an ardent lover and worshipper of the pursuance of knowledge—the knowledge of everything—good or bad. Man has come to know more than he needs to. He learns and attains skills in all he has never perceived, acquiring and accumulating knowledge—like in mathematics, philology, astronomy, astrology, numerology, philosophy, science, art, apocalypse, and symbolism, etc. To the extent, he has acquainted himself with spirituality, calling his own ghost, returning death to life, attempting to explore the mystery of death and life, attempting to find a meaning to all that is seen and unseen, all that is known and unknown. But, to be sincere with ourselves, what treasure awaits us if we find a possibility to explore death? A place no one has ever visited; a place no one dares to pay a visit, knowing there is no returning. See how we intend to engineer and actualize our own extermination. To advance ourselves and find a discernment to the meanings of everything, which, in actuality, is not there. We have perpetuated and condescended acts that yield tragedies more than happiness. We have come to relish the way we plunge into imagination—doing hard-thinking and obscuring ourselves from the light and grace of nature, just to compound our predicaments and losing our exquisite moral sensibility. Why should we administer in a cogitation like that? See now how a lot of perpetual religions are being unveiled and conducted in darkness and many in power are all involved. They are involved in the various aspects of these religions which affiliate mysticism and blood-shed. Civilization, when people started to acquire the aptitude to build, improve, and extend it to the four corners of the Earth, they have known already it is power they seek in order to rule others. All those who initiated it were trading in lucrative goods within themselves, and at a time they decided to extend it to different parts of the world. Though, they did engage in battles with themselves, upgrade and enhance ideas to strengthen their military power, and also to improve their curiosity in every other things."

Chapter 17

Some days have passed, followed by weeks, followed by months, after they have met for the first time in a house located on the outskirt of Paris to liberate humanity from the great tribulation it is been placed. Multifarious activities have been successfully carried out, plans have been developed and fulfilled. Still, there are many more to be done to ensnare the hearts of men for a reunion of all souls. The utter captivation of the human inner self is an essential aspect of the reality, and it is clear and coherent. Considering this theme of reunion of all souls from every aspect of life, infiltration in every governments around the globe is needed and it is to be the chief source for an approval to ascend to the peak.

Tyson, whose businesses are being controlled by his CEOs and managers in the U.S., is, in recent times, residing in Cergy. He has in every possible way made efforts to assure his comrades of the need not to be too cynical. He wants them to abjure all of their held ideas, concepts, beliefs, and perspectives, allowing a new flow of energy to be examined and stored in a collective individualism. He understands it is beliefs, egos, and fears that separate humans, and to face the situation with a resolution, is to abolish it entirely. He has applied his mind and brain intentionally to acquire knowledge and understand the cosmos. Reading books, he has come across a man saying:

"We are a global network of neurochemical reactions. And, the self-amplifying circle of acceptance and acknowledgement sustained by the daily choices in our interactions is the chain reaction that will ultimately define our collective ability to overcome imagined differences and look at life in the grand scheme of things."

What he has read indeed energized him to conceive a future where everyone could live together—embracing love and compassion to create a world with the absence of fear and conflicts, and to be fully redeemed with peace and harmony. He believes it is the government and the people of every nation that have to bring about this change by engaging in activities pleasing to all. The society must be well formed to set up unshakeable future for all. Thus, the governments must, with obligation, not be allowed constant validations to oversee. Self-awareness is to be the key to open the door of reconciliation for all. Enlightenment would have to demonstrate its existence.

So, he has starts with the assistance and guidance of his comrades, spending money on well-read and comprehensive politicians. They are building schools, hospitals, and homes for the needy, and also feeding them. They organize and support a secret society for a purpose to infiltrate all the governments of the world. And, it is Tyson financing everything. Since nothing could be done without money, they forcefully embrace the system and put money ahead and spend it to bring into reality the change they so greatly crave. "Bring the change that you want."

Although, all those who are nominated as candidates and are campaigning vigorously to be elected, are doing so in pretense, wittingly showing their supports for the old system—to emulate their predecessors and vowing not to shift the paradigm.

Thence, most of them are winning elections and being sworn in government departments, parliaments, congresses, and overall offices. They are illuminating the world—bringing people to the light—enlightening, and making them awake. They participate and partake in events that bring the citizens together, building bridges to link everyone, analyzing and justifying their rationale for the extermination and breaking of boundaries between the governments and the citizens, between cities, and between countries. They expose to the common people the secrets of government aims and purposes. They begin to employ their witty and pure minds into assisting all and pointing to the stars far east to reach where the Messiah is been born, coming to redefine democracy and what it stands for—which is a system involving the distribution of political powers. They were detailing democracy and notifying others to understand it as a form of government in which all eligible inhabitant are permitted to participate equally—not regarding to color of race, gender, or religious faiths and traditions—this government they would say, could be either directly or indirectly. The direct government which is when the inhabitants directly vote for a bill to be passed. And then comes the indirect government which is through elected representatives who then propose, develop, and establish the laws by which the society is run. This democracy said to have originated from the Greeks, signifying, "rule of the people," which, in modern time, is equally referred to as, "power by the people." This democracy is said to empower the inhabitants to have their say in the government, to promote the principles of social equality and respects and regards for all individuals within the community. And on top of that, they make people understand democracy must be conducted peacefully under equitable electoral system—and it must all be for the favor of equitable distribution of wealth and income.

These newly elected government officials are transforming the world. They are mentally and physically disposed to maintain their stability in the creation of a new world different from the odd ways people have been governed and ruined. They are scrupulously, and with tranquility, initiating an exciting expansion of their movements and the vitality of it to arrive at the turning point for the world to either retreat, or advance in a new direction of evolution. They do so with the aid of modern technology, emboldening and inspiring the common people to enhance their imagination, to test the validity of their ideas—to reshape the planet and the living organisms in it. To the common people they have profoundly help alleviate their constrictions and tensions, they as well entrust their sincere hearts—balancing equation between rich and poor, bringing the gap closer than it has ever been. They take absolute control of the banks, regulating the up and down of volatile stocks. They are able to confront and survive the great economic crisis, by effecting the adaptation necessary that involves social engineering and an evolution of business management principles that increase and expand trades and businesses as unemployment rates around the globe also become lowest, and it is three percent, while work-force participations near record high. They cautiously drive the world into a realm of education and human development, all in a lifestyle characterized by virtue and morality, characterized by empathy, characterized by a dream to heal rather than to cause harm. They advocate the need for forgiveness and reconciliation, helping people realize and uphold the dignity of humanity, helping to eliminate the production and sales of arms, to eliminate instability that is always fueled by inequality and injustice. Nuclear weapons are completely eliminated everywhere around the globe. And there is no one placed in a state of preparedness to depart from their countries of origin to anywhere except for a visit or the person chooses to do so on his or her own volition, not when immigrants invade other countries—in the sense, migration is no longer a primary issue to burden people with—since people seem contented with the lives they live at home, practicing their own culture and religion and tradition. Then, it is man drawing nigh to nature, trembling into it, embracing it. It is man refraining from the misconception of nature being a foe to him. It is man accepting nature as a home, understanding it to be his closest guide and confidant to accomplish his goals of affiliating himself with the Universe. There is going to be a fundamental change soon. Change is about to happen. Change is happening. They are fostering and strengthening real bonds and connections between humans, between man and nature. Evolution is taking place, and it is said to be the only route left to heal the world, and mankind living in it.

Yes, it appears the people of the world have come to adopt a new ideal—a new system—where the rich and the poor see themselves as one, engaging in contests on who shows more compassion and love to his neighbor, merely to be laureled, in lieu of the former and odd ways that widely and unreasonably attracts contentions against one another in order to attain and maintain supremacy. It has become a different planet— where people have chosen to adopt an ideal to live by, a way of common law of property first initiated by Pythagoras—where people share and share alike—own nothing—own everything. It is a world of equality, justice, education, and harmony. It is a world free of greed, power, fear, and poverty.

This, at the initial time, is the reason he has found it so formidable when he meets with his comrades in Cergy, Paris. He has always known there must be a way to deal with issues. The very first time they have met, he sees himself alone, contrast to the belief which predicts the destruction of mankind in the direction of rebirth. He could not help imagine a world where civilization would not be noticeable. It seems his heart is being hit by a tremendous and unusual tempest. He could see his fellows, his comrades, flip-flopping around the place, pacing nervously, and acting like lunatics. They have been grossly offended with his own opinion to think civilization is a blessing rather than a curse. They have been exceedingly enraged with the world and everything beneath. They are against civilization and its continuous existence, and they endeavor to find a way to forcefully help people emerge from it. Their experiences are readable in their eyes by anyone who may venture to come closer to give heed. Their appearances, their deep consciousness reflect a motive notable for annihilation. They seem dragged into cynicism and are fed up with all about rebuilding humanity and the world it lives. It has all made him so passive, attracting him into a world left in disarray.

He, Tyson, not that he is not sharing the same idea of a sudden and quick change, unless we intend to meet our doom. He believes in a change, but let us not forget the old sayings: "Rome was not built in a day." He is still under the impression that man must return to his maker. He is still under the impression that if the Universe would have to overlook men's evil acts of the past and present, it would refuse to accept any proposal for a survival. But, except on one thing, he tends to see it differently when it comes to making a change even if he has to stand alone. He believes in evolution and transformation in governments, societies, and individuals. He understands we humans of this generation are not to be responsible for the undesirable outcome when it comes to how man strains his relationship with his maker. The problems have long ago commenced by our forefathers. Perhaps, our consistent failure to reform and reestablish that relationship has solaced our criticism. For him, he could favor civilization and, as well, favors primitiveness. He could be one or the other depending on how people approach the concepts.

In Kadosh, he could see something very peculiar and magnificent. He envisions a world where they could both save humanity. He fathoms he let he his head spins to his fortune begets. In the season whence hope sleeps he reaps the seed sown long ago in the depth of grief. But, in the context and course of the matter, lays thence in his bosom the soul of his own dagger. Howbeit, his hunger favors the accursed trouble that grossly scuffles and blows in a bubble. Waking up to see his vision drifts away in a thousand miles whence sorrows in his heart with a capacity filled. He bleeds deep down to hisself to return in the arduous journey and dies in a place where man and god first encountered in a grace instilled; to create faith and beauty and horror. He is saying to the world, "Arise O' citizens. Arise," to these words let thy ears down, let them down and do not awake evil in a sleep where it is been crackdown. These words marked by streaks. Hear the wind how its trumpet blows, but be not a foe; for its rage is as destructive and uncanny and thick. This strong imagination bear thee a woe; if then crudely endeavors whatsoever to dispel. Beware! This dominance around the globe is unfold. You and I, they dominate, they control, they manipulate, they own. Dich und ich, toi et moi, tu y yo, lei e io, a device shall we be known. Let not that fear be so predominant in thy heart to propel thee to flee the danger of art. Thou shall thy voice uplift and thy words withhold. Do it with a relation of affinity like a story untold.

Chapter 18

I t happens the world has reached a brink of evolution. It has achieved recognition of a beautiful and peaceful place for humans to seek refuge. However, it has taken many—the mischief-makers by complete surprise in a way all these have come to be. They are furious and expressing feelings of dissatisfactions and resentments, seeing everyone treated equally—a system they detest so much, and have for long, ruled against. In point of fact, to them it is strange how this possibility egress from the obscure side of malevolence. They cannot in life accept this defeat. They will do everything within their power and beneath so to reinstall the system that is auspicious and inspiring to them—which upholds and guarantees differences between individuals and cause an immense gap to exist between the wealthy and the poor. People must be honored and respected while others must be born to be their subservient, to be their instruments for facilitation.

This world is for us, not for all—that they recommence and steadily publicize by means of propaganda. They have to bring the world back into their control, into their possession. They will never propose permission for the world to repose. They will never accept a compromise—to let all enjoy the fruits of their labor. They want a separation of individuals and a system that enhances the rise of craziness and deceit that can alter the ways in which fate can be redefined. They are these people—they are the patriots, the fanatics, whose core beliefs are very strong and deep, having been attached to identity. They are these people—the nationalists—who firmly hold on to customs and traditions and would not let others come to change their orthodox mindset—to modify their views of politics, economics, and culture. They will not stick with forbearance to drive into power again. They will not relinquish their struggles to torment others and extort from them. They are eager to let the ball roll back to their court in favor of proceeding with the gambling games. They will not relent. For them there is a place for complacency on conflicts and wars.

To start with, these people, with insatiable nature, these people, having the excessive desires to possess more than what they actually need, are launching and running their own vigorous campaign to return the world to where it has shown its absence. They profess publicly about beliefs in the supernatural being—asserting they are in a clear mission, with a vision to return the world to the living and true God by condemning this new system that favors all to be so reprehensible and blasphemous. They have labeled the rulers "anti-Christ" and claim how profoundly precarious the system is to humanity. With the wealth they have long concealed from the world, they cast in a rapid advancement, acquainting with people and showering them with uncountable luxuries. Since they are able to fetch vividly to their minds the indications for their prior defeat to be infiltration, they too start using the media as their propaganda. They are influencing the world again with their religious teachings and practices, showing movies and plays in their own favor and smear the characters of the good leaders, distracting from distraction by distraction to distraction, distracting people's attention from the reason why we live in this world. And because these people are notable for their strong belief in reaching the four corners of the world with luxuries and entertainment, they are able to gain ground and spread their messages with the assistance of their followers to every part of the globe. These people are from different ethnic and racial categories. They are around the globe. They are in control of everything that exist here on Earth. They falsify claims of how the new system that is winning approval because it is advantageous to all—to be communism—which they indeed expound as authoritarian and dictatorial. And in a gradual manner, they are able to reconquer their empire and draw a red line for the peasants.

After when they seize power again and regroup their teams to impose law and order to control humanity, imposing the most repressive and severe restriction on people. They commence in building more religious buildings, naming them sacred places for worship. Those who would not abide to the rules and regulations are thrown into jail to rot and die. Gays and lesbians are summoned, judged, and subjected to penalties. Although, they are making remarkable accomplishments in advances in lethal technologies and yet, posing some qualities of being moral, idolizing the odd cultures and ideals to exploit the common people. And those common people likewise have forgotten churches, mosques, synagogues, and temples have all for long been the powerful institutions on Earth. They forget these institutions are corporation, and they will remain what they stand for. They are a bureaucracy. They are everything that the modern capitalism is—yet, they preach that the love of money is the root of all evil.

In the course of time, everything works out fine for these controllers and manipulators of the world. They improve in every aspect of technology and perpetuating the expansion of their empires. The power they possess is misguiding them to hurt, provoke, and magnetize others to believe in everything being taught to them—and this is widely spaced to tremble on a wave of perplexity and complexity in Tyson and his comrades.

And Tyson gets his team together—afterwards that they lost interest in the deliberate efforts to bring about the change they so yearn for, they reach a final conclusion to escape from the city where they were being chased around for having conspired to infiltrate the governments of the world, their government. Tyson and his comrade's inabilities to lay immense fortifications to subsume the system and the people they have bestowed their supports to hold on to power for longer period is more than a frustration. Now, it is horror and death chasing after them. They would either abscond, or welcome what materialize.

Via investigations and thorough checking, that it is revealed in a manner in which Tyson has generously invested all his money, together with the help of his compeers in an attempt to transform the world and make it a better and peaceful place for humans to populate, a wanted poster of them is issued everywhere in the world. Placed in a wanted list, mortification opens its mouth wide to swallow them. They do not seek to catch them alive to be prosecuted, but they want them killed; persecution is how they will avenge.

Tyson, who have come to carry out his own investigations and discerns how the world is being run by politicians, entrepreneurs, entertainment industry high society, and religious features and dignitaries. He is bewildered and feels rueful, instantly mourning the end of humanity. He is unable to find a place in his heart to forgive the world for its misdeeds. He has attested to an event which thus exhibit an exposure of a celebration of evil. These are the people on top—celebrities with money and fame—people who could spend millions of dollars in one night—immorality, drugs, and alcohol being part of their lifestyles. Still, they are the ones influencing the governments, socially and politically. They are the ones to decide who runs the country and who would not. They could get away with murder and still live to the fullest in the society with no one to question their abilities. It is shocking when Tyson for the first time arrived in a secret society he is introduced to by some other billionaires who used to be his pals. There he witnesses how the politicians, those who own and control banks around the globe, celebrities, brokers and other elites amass to decide where the world is heading to—exhorting people to hold on to it as a "New World Order". It is stupefying and horrendous, seeing this.

After when he narrates some of the stories to his compeers, Lakota refuses to carelessly consume his time to do a different thing, for he is willing to depart from their hideout in Europe to go live in the Amazon forest where he could be safe and bring to creativity all he has been told. He wants to draw a picture of everything in a novel that will be read in years to come, probably after the end of the first Adams in the Garden of Eden. He must do it. He must bury his hand to the pen in order to express that desire of his—meant in a way to recount a transformation his heart bears. He has to join in the circle of those willing to pioneer an alternative way of living. He has to trigger a debate across the globe on the issue of poverty, which has long been successfully ravaged by those who relish the pursuit of wealth and ignore the interests of the common people. He has to be a parcel of the ones bringing a liberation of the world from those who beam and suppose everything to be a game, a game, which prompts others to join the money stampede to enrich the rich further and impoverish the poor more.

Chapter 19

A nd it came to be that the people in power have decided to expand their beliefs and culture to every part of the world, as far as they possess everything they consider adequate to fulfill their desires. The more the expansion of their empires, the more the invention of war machines and technologies. They impose strict laws and dictate to others on which way to incorporate and heed. They were enlisting young men and women into army and having them swear with Bibles, Korans, Torah, and other religious books that they would fight and die for their countries. It is a symbol of patriotism. It is a verification of showing how superior some are over the others. It is a vindication of their principles and creeds.

In the course of the perpetual deployments of military tanks, artilleries, and troops around every borders in order to measure out threats to other nations who intentionally withdraw from their policy and are recalcitrant and fail to comply to ideas seem noxious to them—showing no acceptance to be governed and policed, to be dictated to, using force and power and influence. Thence, there arises a conflict that is beginning to create "fear" in every individuals. There is fear everywhere—the fear of my neighbor coming to kill me; the fear of how my neighbor practices a religion quite distinct from mine, which means he must be a terrorist, or the other man has a black, dark, or white skin color, and he is not fit to live in my neighborhood. This fear is everywhere. There is the fear of the Chinese taking over the global economy and preserving a progressive expansion of their own empire and keen to wile the world into communism if fortunately becomes so powerful and rich. There is this fear of terrorists attacking us in our hometowns for the fact they hate freedom and liberty, and also hate innocent people and constantly plan to kill us all. Yes, there is this fear of other races coming to be more superior and smarter than my race and be in command of the world and everything in it—and that to us, is unacceptable, unthinkable, verboten. There is the fear which never allow a perception that everyone deserves to be at peace with who and what they are as long as their behaviors and attitudes are not unlawful and vicious, and they are not tormenting any of us. But, intrinsically, if we have to rethink, will it not be comely and just and harmonious if we pass how judgements on people regardless of their sex, color, national origin, ethnicity, creed, disability, or sexual orientation?

In reality, we are having more to be preoccupied and deranged about. We are having these hazardous and afflictive situations we are grappling with…and yet, still unable to escape the impasse. For instance, we are having a situation where people are criminalized for blasphemy to draw them to their religion again. There is a situation where many people from Africa, Asia, Middle East, South America, countries buried in poverty and wars, becoming too fanatic, harboring hatred in their hearts, chanting death to the west, blaming them for their miserable situations, instead of looking for a way to sort out their own problems. There is a situation of North Korea being ruled by a little boy, a dictator, who seems mentally deranged—thinking of posing threats to its neighbors. Although, all these are a result of the Japanese sequential appearances in combat with Korea, invading and conquering the country for years ago, and after, it has been the Russians who introduced communism and dictatorship to them. There is the situation of Russian leaders annexing neighboring countries with its military influence, spying on every countries with a proposed course to weakens their power and restore its country's old glory, threatening the west with nuclear capability, making every Russians to be referred to as "spies" and "dangerous", so people better be careful when they demand a visa to visit their country. Quite frankly, it would have been prominent and more appropriate if the Russian leaders have dedicated more time in growing their economy, and focusing on the country's welfare and the well-being of the citizens, instead they are working tirelessly to weaken American potential in the world, they are working on how to change American ambitious plan to spread their ideal of democracy across the globe with their military and economic power because they see it to be erroneous as it creates more problems and destabilizes these countries. They want to become a hindrance to every of the west projects because they cannot find mutual ground of understanding with them, because they see clearly how America and its allies continuously and proudly disregard and undermine their capability, while at the same time, build their empires with imperialist policies. They want to confront America and its allies because they see how much NATO poses a threat to them. These Russian leaders believe the only way to come out successfully is to find a way to be respected and regarded, and they are doing this, threatening the world with a nuclear war. There is a situation of the Chinese expanding their military power. There is the situation which is a continuous dishing out of public funds to corporations and big businesses while everyone keeps silent. There is another situation of Iran ruled by the laws implemented by theocrats, and is completely prepared to increase its military spending and also fuel wars around its region, with an orderly conception of becoming one of the world superpowers—in finance, technology, and military. Then, there is the U.S-led strategies to arm and finance some of the rebels to fight against their dictatorial regimes, creating troops that beget terrorists, breeding them, guiding them, and then, eliminating them after the mission is over and restart all over again and again. There is the situation of how the Jews and the Palestinians will be able to live side-by-side with each other, as the Jews are killing them—and at the same time, accusing them of terrorism, transforming the Holy Land, a place of different beliefs and faiths: spiritual homeland of the Jews, where the Christian Jesus is believed to be crucified, where the Muslims prophet Mohammed has visited heaven—now has been turned into a cursed river that floats into an ocean of bombs and blood, destroying everything that seems holy and replacing it with terror and horror. There is the situation of the Germans, after the Second World War and the Cold War, they have come to unite, and as well been able to look deep into their hearts to find a space in it to create a better relationship with their neighbors, and making friendly ties and trades with other race and religions around the globe. They have been able to develop a sense of tolerance and diversity. This promotion of relations with other countries they have come to see to be very beneficial to their economy and also to their stand in the world's affair. They have come to embrace immigrants and tolerate them more than every other country in the world. But, there is a thing to be looked at in all these that have transpired in a time so very few and fast. There is a need for scrutiny, there is a need for questions to be raised. Looking back to history to expand our experience with the manner they have always crave power because of the country's familiarity with wars, being the source and cause of the first and second world wars when millions of lives were lost. What is making the Germans vest their interests and desires to increase the population of the country and forcibly unite Europe? Is it simply on a cause to build an economy? Is it on a cause that will lead the world to the right direction? Or, it is on a cause no one knows nothing about or cares to dig deep to know. Then, there is the situation of the corrupt and insane leaders in Africa and other developing countries, mismanaging the people's wealth, siphoning their countries treasury and banking it in private banks in Europe and in the U.S, while the peasants starve to death as wars and conflicts devour nature and mankind with no one having the guts to carry-out an investigation, or else that person is indeed delightful to dig a grave for himself to be buried. Another unstable and perilous situation of terrorism spreading to the four corners of the planet—whereby young men and women are being brainwashed to join to destroy, not that the recruitments are done by use of force, but, voluntarily, people are willing to append themselves to violent groups that their intentions are to afflict the rest of humanity with unrest.

There are dangerous situations we have met with and survived because of the plenteous options and decisions we have cunningly taken. However, have we not learn to note with our fortitudes, cooperation, and determinations we can heal ourselves and the planet we inhabit again? Instead, see how we have created "fear".

See how this fear is created and becomes part of the individuals. Although, it may seem anomalistic and discretional to say that many among us still are unknowledgeable to capture how we are the cause of our everyday problems.

Looking to the sources of "fear", and how it has come to be so imminent to humans, we understand fear can be classified as rational and irrational. The rational, which is appropriate, and the irrational, which is inappropriate. This fear, which is the dark side of every human could be encountered through danger, evil, or pain. Fear is so powerful we found ourselves imposed by force to devolve upon a powerful ally inside of us, a spirit of confidence and resolution to overcome and conquer it—which is to say, fear is ominous and vile to man. So, why then do we have to think of creating this fear? Why then do we have to build our society on fear? Now, are we not supposed to be developing the natural instincts to love and follow positivity in the Universe throughout, seeing how we could be living much better—embracing empathy and erasing fear—simply by supporting fairer distributions of goodness for all? On the contrary, we plung into our own doom by creating a world that allows the flow of obscene money to override the impulses of democracy which its outcome is to further divides us. We should be loving and receiving love, doing so through adaptation and education. But, see how we now act and think via distrusts and fear. They make us divide ourselves, and we follow the unfounded dogmas which they have instilled in us. And, in spite of all these, they care less about us, apart from making us swim in a pool of gloom, using us as their ladder to climb to reach where they benefit, whether through wages or debts. Yes, it is true we do not acknowledge how for long there has been a tremendous expansion of unregulated capital in the world, thereby deregulating currencies—and it is a way of increasing corporate profits—the crumbs permitted to ordinary people have to be taken away. Everything would have to go to the rich. This is, in fact, causing a despair within the ordinary people, and politicians are backing the corporates— the same politicians being elected by this same ordinary people. Which is to say democracy has become hypocrisy. Are we not beings of energy and vibrations? Why is it now that we cannot think? Do we not strongly believe we were all humans and still are if we believe we are? Although, religious institutions and the so-called governments have come to make us think distinctively. They make us look to individual necessity of survival, when we should be assisting and caring for our neighbors, when we are having more than abundant for ourselves and to spare and share; they create ideas and feelings that permeate the system and our societies, edifying us of what is right, and what is wrong. Perhaps, their notion mainly is to achieve distinctions and earn honors, to be seen as gods and goddesses as they behave and live in a good manner appropriate to their statistics. They want to own everything from natural to man-made; they want to rule and conquer the world, while they unceasingly and carefully observe, with joy, as the peasants suffer and lament. Yet, they preach and advocate to us of a better world we would be living in if we confide and rely on them. Will it not be of a profound absurdity if we approve and conform to these forms of ideologies that permit some people to find fortunes in other's misfortunes?

So, it happens rivalries that exist between the many biggest and most powerful nations on Earth are creating tensions day-in, day-out, and it is leading to the onset of nuclear defense system. More and more nuclear weapons are being designed and produced. Massive numbers of nuclear warheads are built and displayed on televisions in order for one to menace and deter the others to submit to its prime demands. Trade between these nations are blocked due to tough sanctions imposed by one on the other. It is a moment of tears and panic. It is a moment characterized by grotesquery and intense feeling of repugnance. It is the moment when all who championed and partook in the apotheosis of the ideals that constitute and procreate additional capacity to shatter and dilapidate, are then projected into lamentation. And this is the moment for the general world population to bid farewell to the planet Earth. It is the time of apocalypse, and it is drawing nigh, it is arriving in our very eyes for us to bear witness of the old prophecies.

Out of frustration, desperation emerges. It is a desperation to fight a war so for some to convince their counterparts of how powerful they are. Regardless, many are still very doubtful of the nearest indubitable and subtle catastrophic event that is about to supervene. They believe it to be something conventional, something typical. But, how could we be so blind we cannot even see we have reached the end of time? What real substantial solutions have we to tackle this theme of returning to where we come from? Within the context of serious conversations, we all are in accord that humanity has gone too far, we are squarely aware our intense ambitions have led to extreme competitiveness—which has resulted in hurting one another so to survive. We witness the many dimensions this phenomena— the lack of respect and reverence for all lives. Now, it is a system we too have invented and cannot contend: It is hard to obey a policeman. Law-enforcement officers are recruited to abuse their power of responsibility like a weapon to brandish. We realize in a flash of prescience how the lovely ship we all board is sinking, not certainly because the numbers are overbalanced by the size, but because we prefer conclusive settlements to live with greed, to put more load on one end where we are not standing and watch it sinks while rejecting the notion to assist the people on the other side, forgetting we are onboard the same ship—which, without a shadow of doubt, will sink from one side before it finally drags the whole ship to the bottom of the sea. We are idiots, we are fools who believe we know everything, whereas we know nothing.

This is the beginning of everything, the beginning of the end of the first Adams and a rebirth of another. Rumors of the world coming to an end—this is a reason for the lack of information, or the reason for excessive information. The story is realizing its shortcomings. The world superpowers who have once pledged allegiance to save the world from a terrifying calamity by engaging in talks and commitments, signing Arms Reduction Treaty, to steadily reduce the dangers of nuclear weapons, to disarm and dismantle nuclear bombs. But for the fact all are struggling to let power be in their own possession and dictate to others, they are forced to withdraw from the Treaty, instead, repose their concentration more on developing new and more sophisticated and advanced nuclear-powered multipurpose submarines. They are designing and building more nuclear weapons. These countries have contemptuously drawn themselves into a pervasive arms race.

However, the might of a nuclear weapon was first exhibited to the world during the Second World War, when the Americans dropped atomic bombs on the Japanese cities of Hiroshima and Nagasaki, killing and wounding more than 225,000 people.

As the U.S. continues to increase its presence in Europe and threatening Russia, deploying ballistic-missile destroyers to bolster NATO's anti-missile, then Russia, out of frustration of a weaken economy and lack of supports from its allies, they have started sending warnings and threats to the neighboring countries who are to suffer the consequences, and as well pulling out from the Arms Reduction Treaty they were committed to with the U.S. Which is to say, another cold war is about to surface, or something worse than that is erupting, problem is erupting. They are both playing games with nuclear weapons, or they think it is always going to be so if they mock other people's intelligence, or they seemingly lack the mental capacity to discern the aftereffect of this game they play.

Nuclear weapon notable as weapons for mass destruction; a nuclear device no larger than traditional bombs can devastate an entire city by blast, fire, and radiation. These weapons, after the destructions of Hiroshima and Nagasaki, have been detonated over two thousands occasions for the motive of testing and demonstration. Thus, countries known for the possession of the weapons have increased to thirteen, and many more are willing to have it. The world nuclear-armed states have come to possess a combined total roughly 18,000 nuclear warheads, with the U.S. 8,000 and Russia, 7,900. Where are we heading to? The whole situation, this situation is only leaving us to be lying asleep in delusion when we could be standing erect in reality. Death and fear have become names that take us to live in a cold and harsh world. Our fantasies of a beautiful and peaceful world have been lost to pride and prejudice, lost to power and neglects, lost to greed and distrusts.

Chapter 20

Arriving in an obscure part of the world—a place no one would ever imagine to be safe for a man who have toiled in the middle of nowhere and somewhere in efforts to acquire wealth, and has acquired it enough to feed a nation. Tyson and his compeers see themselves living in this dark quarter where light seems to be a constant bitter enemy. They have furtively eluded the bereavement that trails them, using a private jet arranged for by some of Tyson's main pals who are still in government and having access to provide him with anything he requires of them. During when a search for them is carried out, they have first smuggled themselves in a car and have gone far to live in the southern part of Spain. From there, they left Spain to arrive in the rainforest of Amazon in Brazil—a place also close to Columbia and Peru. There, they have contended against some drug cartels whom they briefed a little explanation of their predicaments and have been pitied and assisted to reside in the most hidden and stimulating part of the world.

It is translucently reckoned the most vivacious, naturalistic, and feasible time of their lives, rediscovering the sanctity of the inner bliss. They are close to nature and everything that pervades it. Their misery is accounted to solace and fondness—and fright and dismay elope to an unthinkable environment. There is a plausible theory that recounts adventure and nature as the source of the beginning of life and death, and this is near validity and factuality. Happy they are, taking this narrow path to the place where the sun shines and the flowers bloom and sing songs not a soul comprehends. How their affection and adoration for nature set on them the flame that burns that never quenches, burns with delights and bliss that proudly begets in them a tradition for love and peace all alone in the woods, as they clap and chant and dance...Oh, how happy they are to witness this day!

Living in this rainforest with the natives, who are uncultivated and backward, they too have come to stumble upon peace and tranquility. They eat everything cultivated by the natives, and as well, assist in farming and hunting. They could go to a nearby river to swim and play, to sing and dance with the natives. They Are at the point of returning to life and normality, treasuring every little or big thing they meet. They could sense the relation between humanity and nature, reasoning on why they are both in necessity of each other; they could perceive the various species of animals in the forest, terrestrial and aquatic: lizards, spider monkeys, golden lion Tamarin, sloth, giant anteater, giant river otter, glass frog, Amazon pink-river dolphin, side-necked turtles, alligators, etc. And, by bearing witness to this form of life, they all draw a conclusion to further bring to completion their firm commitment to help humanity return to nature, for they see that is where home is, where hope is. Tyson, who have always affirm strongly civilization is to be man's only hope in returning to his maker, in returning to home—has come to acknowledge the certainty and conviction for a-no-need for people to seek knowledge and wisdom which are truly found in nature. The meaning of life is solely when we live, not when we possess. He instantaneously savvy a pure effective motive this forest is destined for them to populate. His heart is replenished with joy and hope, knowing the Universe is behind everything that has happened. They could go fishing and hunting, returning to where they lay and sleep every day without bothering about tomorrow.

Lying awake in the middle of the night in a small hut built with bamboo sticks and leaves and muds from the mixed sand and water, Hussein looks through some of the clothes he has brought with him to see if he is still in possession of a letter once written and sent to him by one British brunette lass whom they have both studied long ago in London. It is a love poem to share the intimate relationship they have. Despite the fact he has for long forgotten about this intimacy due to his too much devotion to be a part in the healing of the wounded souls that inhabit the planet Earth. But he could not help forget her pretty, angel-like face. He could not help think if she is the one to lead him to the maker. So, he begins to regret his actions for deserting her far and moving on to engage in a battle that seems uncertain if he would come out victorious. He loves her. He loves her like he has never loved anyone before. He has made a solemn promise to live his entire life with her, and never to hurt her. Now, he could sense she has been hurt. She would definitely be in wait for that love they both share. Hence, he brings out the letter, uncloses his heart, and reads to himself.

LOVE, TOO BIG A WORD.

Completely paralyzed he lays
Heart bleeds, blood helplessly afloat
Like a waterfall and for so many days
Still in a far distance hope shroud in a coat
Then from mountain torrent she slid into a serene valley
The valley where love accord both a meeting and a mingling
With both souls enchant progress in calmness
So innocent, much experienced comes stableness
Heart to heart they strive
Heart to heart they drive
Credulity awakes a bond tied and the seed of love watered
Goals achieved and dreams attained
And around the globe they walk and stumble and tremble
But constantly heart to heart they strive
But constantly heart to heart they drive
Love to them a religion, love to them the one and all
Love too big a word
Mean it when you say it.

While Hussein is still awake and reading the love poem and pondering, there arrives Tyson, who also has felt something strong for him and could not utter it, except to remain as a compeer that both have a burden to bear in the wake of knowledge and light to reach to the world.

"Hey! Brother, why are you not asleep?" asks Tyson, walking closer to see what is wrong, taking away the letter from him to read while Hussein relaxes and goes calm and mute. After he is done with the reading, he puts up a question to him again, keeping the letter in his grasp. "Did you really love her?" Tyson demands.

"Yes, I still do. But the issue here is, will I ever see her again?" Responds Hussein, still very relaxed as he utters the words and drops of tears protrude from his eyes, falling down through his cheeks.

"You do not need to do that, Hussein. I know you love her. I have never had a woman who love me because I have been too busy striving to achieve wealth. That same wealth, some women have attempted to take away from me and have taken advantage of my goodness to them. You see, love need to be share, whether romantic, empathic, or friendly. You cannot keep it to yourself, for that would seem basically interpreted in a very uproariously ironic circumstance. After doing a few research to weigh in on this theme of love, I have arrived at a suspension of disbelief, that loving oneself is first and also the greatest of all love. However, I have also seen deep into it, to grasp, in clarity, that without we permitting it to flow to another being, or say, extending it to another soul, there is truly not anyway we will be able to feel that love. It remains a burden to us. It is only when we share it that it now revert and reestablish within us."

"You are very right my brother. The truth is that it is not allowing that love be a part of us to share to others that is a problem. Then, what if the people you are sharing it with seem not to merit it? Or, they capitalize on that as you have previously mentioned. Then, intend to use you for loving them?" Hussein demands, looking into his brother's eyes to see if he catches a glimpse of what he is insinuating. He wants to know if he feels something for him.

"Yes, you are right. Nevertheless, we have to keep doing what is right in the sight of the Universe that sees it all, we have to keep allowing the flow of love. How does love flow from one if he is not loving another? Where is the love flowing to? Is it not by loving others you feel good about who you are, or what you are, knowing you are indeed having love within you that you share, and it is being returned to you? Love, I certainly believe is sharing, not to retain in possession. It is ignorance that causes man to be unaware of his true self—of what are fundamental and what are not. The world needs love, and the people are utterly ignorant. Not knowing is a problem."

"Not knowing is a problem...I tell you, knowing is another. Many who think they know, literally know nothing as they have imprudently put into services what they know in creating more havocs and destructions. Sometimes, I can see my mind in a maelstrom of hopelessly emotion when taking a good look into this subject-matter. Which have made me come to a conclusion: no one knows the right thing to be doing, as the right thing can be the wrong thing, and the wrong thing can also be the right thing!" articulates Hussein.

As they discuss this substantial form of a subject-matter so relevant and genial, Aadita walks in, sits closer to the both of them and stare into their eyes, moving her head from one direction to the other, swiftly adding to what she has overheard put into discourse. "Let me commence from here. If Christopher Columbus is so respected and commemorated in the U.S. and some other European countries, why is Pythagoras not taught to children and commemorated?"

No one said a word in response to her question. Then, she continues, "It has nothing to do with knowledge whatsoever, but enough to do with greed that has ruined man and his fate. People are heedless of the terrible consequences that will erupt if they remarkably desire to proceed with the ideology that constitutes and aids people to tango and boogie in iniquity to achieve all that is vanity. They are incognizant, even if they relentlessly feign to know everything. Because if they know, they would know they must return to their maker. They would not need anyone to edify them on that."

"Well said, Aadita," replies Hussein, and he continues, "Not that they do not know. Without a shadow of doubt, they do. It is because their knowledge is based on materialism that we see it so. I tell you, when knowledge is based on virtue and morality, we will see how humans will live very close to achieve placidity and armistice. Knowledge well used, precipitates advancement and represents truth. To replenish our hearts with knowledge is not to besiege problems, but to do it, with the intention of identifying ourselves as more superior than others, classifying ourselves and creating separation—which only yields conflicts and wars. They forget generosity only result to prosperity. Selfishness always extend its guilt to violence and hatred. See what is happening in the Middle East. The Arabs are separated than every other set of people in the world. They all want a piece of themselves—for example, Iran. They see that nation as a threat. All these are for the fact that Iran, if becomes too rich and powerful, will abstain from them and decries their objectives in that area. Iran on his own is evil, seeing itself as the last man standing for the Arabs and their creed. In another way round, the Saudis and others envy Iran and its advancement in technology and science. They fear Iran. They all envy themselves over there—the Sunnis, the Shiites, the Kurds, and all others. No one likes anyone except himself or herself. It is the problem plaguing the world that cannot be mowed down. It is the problem of greed and distrusts, and it is the obstacles to peace and prosperity. Self-serving. Of course, you see all of them serving their own interests. You see the Europeans, Americans, Chinese, Russians, Africans, South Americans, all and all—they are literally oblivious the pit they dig, will be where they will be buried. They do everything, everything for interest. The African leaders, who, in actual fact, should be seen as the greediest. When the Europeans and Arabs started with their slave trade, they never did it by force. Instead, they enticed and used the warriors and kings in Africa to chase and bind their own people and be bargaining and retailing them to the buyers. Who are we to blame? For the fact that the Europeans and Arabs took advantage of their ignorance, then, we can consider them responsible for this very atrocity done to mankind. However, see recently how these Africans still regard and handle their own people. They siphon their countries money from their treasury account and run it to the banks in Europe. It is absurd. It should be a thing unheard of. And all these are a result of how people tend to possess everything. This has simply warrants us to struggle and fight to attain power in order to protect our possessions. This is insanity; it deserves a punishment to be inflicted on man's objective to seek what is not there. To kill to have things to impress others; to feel proud and powerful in the presence of others. We gain nothing, we lose all. If we die, then all is gone. We can never be free if we do not pay our dues, and who do we pay them to? Of course to humanity and nature. That is to whom our dues have to be paid. To be free, we have to free our consciousness, and we have to free it from greed. Then, taking a look at the conflicts between the Zionists and the Palestinians, it is all greed and power. Of course, no one is saying all Jews are morally bad in principle. Seeing what has eventuated in the Middle East for some years now, many people have come to clearly and completely comprehend the terrible tragedies that have befell the Palestinians there and the Israelis inaccurate portrayal of the story. The Israelis have made themselves two-faced, treacherous, and distasteful. They comprehend all the enormity of lying to the world and causing havoc to their neighbors, and if they proceed in this manner, it will only make them a laughable matter instead of the heroic role they love to play, and the good people they tend to be. Even if the Palestinians and other Arab countries initiated this problem by not allowing the Jews to create their own state when they demanded for it, but, is it not yet time for people to live side by side without bloodshed? Instead, Israeli government has continuously build settlements in occupied Palestinian territory."

Shiromi, Lakota, and Kadosh, who are propelled to wake up from their sleep due to how disquiet evolve over the tenacious debate. They walk straight to where Aadita, Tyson, and Hussein sit and engage in a formal discussion on the theme of the various problems the world is faced with. When Tyson first see the three of them walked in, he knows things would unequivocally get heated. He knows the tension and anxiety are about to be shrouded in a circle of intellectual property with rumpus and augmentation of facts and furies. He senses all of their energy to be in high gear. So, he opens his arms to embrace them one after the other as they walk in to tie in this brilliant conversation.

And when they have all embraced and kissed each other, having decided to make fire with woods and sit around it in a circle. Commences Lakota, who has started writing a new book with the collaboration of Shiromi.

"I think I overheard all of you discussing about how Africans are soaked in the waters of greed that they cannot afford to assist their fellow Africans, rather than to steal from them," he says.

"Yes, that is what I am saying," defends, Hussein.

"That is a fact, brother," says Lakota, as he draws closer to the fire to feel its warmth. "In the real sense, I guess we all conform to the sole truth, which explains how these people in Africa, the Aborigines, the Indians, or other people who have been uncivilized prior to the arrival of their colonial masters, have been living happily in their remote environments just as we are now and happy with our lives. When these strangers came, these primitive people at first embraced them wholeheartedly, seeing them as saints. They were heartily friendly and congenial with them. The strangers were enamored, as they would do to their own brothers and sisters. Only at the end to be brainwashed, exploited, and driven out of their own lands. Tracing history, we understand how these people were treated and manipulated was wrong and evil. To define it with ambiguity, I will tell you, it will not be an easy task for these people to propound their adherence to this form of life that has been forcefully imposed on them. A conscientious effort to abide by this principle that does not affirm their own beliefs, is constantly going to be disastrous. It will never suit them no matter how they strive. When we talk about corruption and greed, it were all customs and beliefs copied from their masters. Guess no one knows what a heavy burden it is to pretend to live like a different person. To imitate is to see yourself bamboozled. These barbarians never knew or heard of Jesus Christ and Muhammed before the scriptures were preached to them, yet they were enslaved and colonized by those same scriptures. In these primitive people's hearts, they were wealthy, snobbish, and complacent as we are here tonight. It was their masters who revealed to them how foolish and barbaric they were, therefor, bringing new ideas to steal from them, to turn them against each other—which they too learn from as they tasted both sugar and salt and could distinguish between the two. Now, they have chosen that same route to exploit the nearest people to them. Or, let us analyze on a recognized symbol of how humanity should be governed and ruled. Let us consider the panic, lies, madness, caprice, gossips, killings, conflicts, and wars involved in a given moment of circumstances—and it is the thing universally referred to as democracy. In practice and reality, it is not even democracy we have. In some parts of Europe, like the Scandinavians, we might say it is imminent. But, in the U.S and other parts of the world, especially in Africa, it leads the poor directly to adversity and poverty and enrich the rich. It could be referred to as plutocracy and oligarchy."

"In-between the lobbyists and corporations who purchase politicians with their money, and in return not to fight against their special interests, the banks and film industries now control the government, the thirst and hunger for wars. And yet, the Americans vision is about spreading this democracy throughout the globe. When we cannot deal with the issues of gun violence in our own country, we want to travel abroad to lecture others on how they could clean their roads. Democracy is supposed to make human life better, make us to be contented, prosperous, tranquil, solicitous, and ensure us safety, instead it has become a contrivance to enslave mankind and repel it down into a motion of intensity and fierceness. See how we have devoted ourselves to technology and allowing it to dominate our lives. How can we find peace? How can we find our maker? People accelerate to relinquish contacts with the real world because they are tapped into social networks and websites, they are suffering from addiction to chatting online. They no longer care for their families and friends in the real world. They prefer to cling to their ghostly friends, and by so-doing some become victims of scamming. Porn causing a far adamant effect on teenage boys and girls including their mothers and fathers. People now lack the understanding and courage to confront transgression and wrongdoing, believing only by violence we thrive in achieving peace—which signifies we have to do it based on the law of an eye for an eye—as a doctrine we have to accept in order to outlive. Does it really matter if one is gay or lesbian? Everyone has the right for a choice. But why should we consistently endeavor a modification of everything, including the unchangeable? Why should a man think of bearing a child? It is all a matter of technology and the madness it begets. Women as child-bearers, have achieved the most enormous gift of nature, and for that sensibleness they are subjected to be good in child up-bringing. Good music and art are no longer what we treasure and uphold, instead, we credit and adulate music without meanings that are filled with sex and drugs and alcohol. Oh, what a world that we now live in. If this is what civilization looks like, then we would have to rethink. We would have to unlock a room for reorientation."

After Lakota has finished pouring out his own perspective of history and the various critical situations humanity is faced with at present time, he sits mute and unfit to wait to suffer the glares and stares around him.

His eagerness to leave to a different environment is pressing on him. Meanwhile, when he looks into the eyes of Aadita, he could not help resist her, and that forbids him from uplifting his head once more.

They have both liked each other from the first day they met. They cherish each other's potential in carrying out activities. In the meantime, neither of them could utter it, making them come to see themselves as brother and sister. She has come to love him more for a reason best notable to the both of them. Everyone there, she admires their general abilities and intelligence, but she admires him more because of his special, creative aptitude. She has read some of the scripts he is has been writing and finds it interesting and inspiring. She believes in him, knowing his writing could bring a change to the entire world.

As they remain silent and calm, it sounds the last discourse of Lakota has explained everything all that they needed to hear and have inside them to preach to the world. Then, it is Tyson who has the willingness to push on with the subject-matter and speaks his own perspective for others to listen and also learn, for it is to all, an opened space to learn and also edify one another.

He continues, "What baffles me most is how Americans could be spending more than half a trillion dollars in the military, which is more than half of the yearly budget. That amount of money is doubled the money spent by rest of the countries around the globe in their military, yet the Americans remain the most fearful people when it comes to security, simply because they have made too many enemies around the globe. People in America do not feel safe. They are afraid of terrorists coming to attack them. They are afraid of Iran, Russia, China, Pakistan, and even Mexico and Canada. They are afraid of everybody. And to say, the world might need 30 billion dollars to eradicate and eliminate extreme poverty and hunger around the globe. If we can spend almost a trillion dollars in defense, why not erase poverty from its presence? What are we waiting for? Is this greed and power what we intend to live for all our lives? Why not make things easier for ourselves by using the wealth to benefit the globe. Why can we not do the right thing and be positive rather than cause havoc and become negative? Fear has become our everyday life. I am American. I have been born and bred there. I come to admit how that country has become a threat to the world peace and prosperity even more than the terrorists have. Half of the world population detest and dislike America for their vision of bringing the world together to be one. They all think America is a threat and the cause of the major problems engulfing the world—from spreading democracy to dragging the world into a state of disorder, a state of confusion. America portrays itself as the king of the world, the controller and decider of human destiny. Ruling with its power and driving the world into a goal no one knows nothing about, doing so, and doing with sensation adjoined with hypocrisy."

"On the other hand, we should also comprehend America is not a nation that started on its own. It is a nation has been built with a combination of all nations, primarily from the Europe continent, and as well, the slaves brought from Africa. Perhaps we should note even slavery was not started by the Americans. It all began in Europe, even in early time before they discovered other continents, they have started enslaving themselves. The Arabs were also very cunning, traveling to other parts of the world, using religion doctrines in exploiting people who were seen to be ignorant. America, with ingenuity and imagination, the people have come to formulate ideas, invent new policies of government—to bring the system of capitalism in progress and aligned it with democracy for the whole of humanity to learn and adopt. That is where the problem lies, and it is a shame for one to dictate to others, while stoutly reproving dictatorship. Nonetheless, the stories we all recognize very well are those that states it is done out of greed and the struggling for power. It is due to competitiveness and how to exhibit pride in one's identity—all these, which actually started in Europe. The Europeans are to find fault with...for all the calamities mankind has fallen. They have always believed in the strife for power. For that, they have waged innumerable and disastrous wars against themselves and later came up with the ideas extended to everywhere their empires were in the world, constantly believing themselves to be more superior in race and subtleties. They believed every other race must be subdued and obligated to copy their own rules and ways of life. They traveled to every part of the world where they were never invited, in a course to invade, to colonize, to exploit, building their own empires there—and thereby destroying these people's cultures, beliefs, and religions. To this day, many people still argue this, and they assert it was for survival of species. Both continents—Europe and North America still are the best when it comes to assisting and providing for others. They can do better to be able to turn everything around if only they are willing to lead the world towards the right direction. It all depends on the choice we make—either to make the wrong choice or the right one to heal our wounded planet, to heal humanity. Tell it to a fool we are not endowed with intelligence and are to be considered responsible in every dangerous situations we find ourselves. In the same way we strive to acquire knowledge and initiate a reflection on religion and its history, then we come to recollect the manner in which Christianity as a religious institute was falsified for personal gain. Verily, with Christian religion, peace, love, and compassion have thrived and arrived to be in general existence within communities, states, and worldwide. Meanwhile, in the past, this same religion was also said to have pervaded every cities and nations with violence and hatred. It was branded a vehement attachment to frailty and villainy—for instance witchcraft trials, the crusades, the inquisitions—all these were shrouded in a shadow of holiness. The religion was noticed in the support of slavery, Christian terrorism, forced conversions, violence against Jews, women, and infidels. The Christians many attempts to stop people from looking into a new way of life is what led to many secret societies being formed and organized, which have become too superior and are now ruling our world. Some of these secret societies have been able to look to occultism as a way of achieving power, like Hitler and his compatriots did, which led to more than 60 million people losing their lives during the Second World War. It is not that anyone is complete of his or her nature. No! Perfection cannot be pronounced when it comes to human nature. Completion originates when the positive merges with the negative. With both sides learning to accept and embrace the same theory, and doing so with comprehension, the Universe will point its light to lead the way. This is true that we have all engaged in wrong-doings in one way or another, but in our willingness to admit our mistakes and never to repeat them, that is when the door of hope for a reconciliation and progress becomes open."

Chapter 21

Some months have passed and they are still in the rainforest, living their lives to the fullest with the natives who enjoy their companionship. Things are easy and life is good and meritorious. Each day is all fun, brimmed with joy, excitements, and fearlessness. With the natives they cultivate crops and do their fishing in the river. They assemble themselves, cook and roast meats and smoke fishes, then they dine together.

On a sunny afternoon, as some swim in the river, while others dance and sing on the bank of the same river. The birds in the sky are happy and full, singing loudly, and making melodies. It is a beautiful day all humans thus would account as enthralling, seemly, groovy and pleasurable. It is so beautiful a day that one is bound to question nature if the gods and goddesses have come to visit the planet Earth from their land of immortality. It is a strange and wonderful day and could be felt to the bone. The sky seems bluer than it has always been, making everything look unfamiliar to them.

As they treasure trove themselves in that state of serenity, tranquility, and peace, their minds are free from disturbances and provocations. They are full of delights as they watch nature displays its suitability and utility. It is at this time, suddenly, all of their attentions are magnetized by the explosion of water from under the river to the sky, as if a mighty rock has be thrown in. It is simultaneously filled with fright and amusement.

They could evidently and transparently get their eyes full as the waters splash upward and downward, and afterward, it is the appearance of El gran maestro which comes into sight, but accompanied by the goddess of penitence. They are both boosted into the sky by the waters that exploded from the underground of the river. The entire incident is to leans in a mystery; it is absolutely correlated with a power that goes beyond a natural force; it is a testament of the presence of the immortals amidst humans.

Watching as El gran maestro and the goddess of penitence appear and walk on top of the river towards them, they all remain stable and upright, watching a scene that creates wonderment and admiration. And when they both ultimately walk to the end of the river and stand on the bank with Aadita, Hussein, Tyson, and Kadosh, hymns are recited in honor of the god and goddess, follow by affectionate embrace. When Shiromi and Lakota who are still far from them, eventually drag themselves out of the waters to join the company, the unabridged state of affairs becomes more dazzlingly beautiful and humorous. Shiromi could not help resist the sight of the goddess of penitence. They both at the same time raise their heads and smile broadly at each other. With no time to waste, they run into each other and lapse into osculation while others watch and cheer and chant. It is reckoned a glorious and marvelous day for all as everyone embrace and chat, shrugging off any doubt of being capable of undertaking the dubious task to save the world from its condemnation.

After some minutes have passed, El gran maestro is incapable of allowing the meeting and mingling discount the time for him to explicate his real motives for descending from the land of the immortals down to Earth. So, he instructs them to lend their ears to him.

And he says to them, "We the immortals have done our part of the battle. In the contest, we have come forth victorious. However, we still have more than enough to do because when we destroyed those monsters and demons in the land of the dead, some of them have been able to board an escape flight to descend to Earth. Now, they have come in form of humans and are completely in fit condition to infiltrate humans, advance their ideologies to first demonize those who seem not to be in accord with the doctrines, then mutilate them. And, if they are unable to write a success story in doing that, then they would have to set the world itself ablaze. Albeit, the Universe and all the gods and goddesses would not be concerned or take a position that would permits any interference in this particular event. What I am implying is that the end of the world is at hand! Alas! These humans are to take their own responsibilities; they are to carry their own burdens. If they wish to reengage with humanity and nature, then they will be fortified to overcome all the obstacles. But, if they take a decision to proceed further with their hearts of stone and prolong a time that will result in destruction and death to be welcomed, that too is their own issue to deal with. It is all a choice for them to make. The ball is in their court now. And again, I repeat, the end of the world is as imminent as it has never been. As for you all, our sincere appreciation for the wonderful tasks you have engaged in. You are all saints already. To be named a saint, there is a certain series of steps involved, and these steps you have all taken. You are already saints, even when people pass their judgments on you and condemn you. There is none without guilt or sin. But, who is of the Universe, is of the universe, who is of the monsters, is of the monsters. Go into the world. Do the best you can, and the rest, let the Universe take control." After he has says this, he turns to look at Kadosh, and utters, "Do not forget to break the code." And when he finishes saying that, he uplifts his head up and looks into the sky, while the goddess of penitence joins him, and they both ascend into the sky and disappear behind the cloud.

After when El gran maestro and the goddess of penitence have left, the whole of them could not move an inch. They sit near the river in silence and ponder and speculate. They all want to do something to save the world from this cataclysmic event about to invade and entrain man. They want to be a part of history in the healing. How could they do this on their own when it appears the Universe itself is fed up with man and his ways of deception and craziness and foolishness? Their consciousness is bothered. Their minds are conceived with miscellaneous information and ideas. Perhaps, none is able to come out with a tangible solution to a problem grander than their mental toughness.

They are still all there, sitting and doing their lateral thinking and reflection puzzles in a manner so deliberate and composed. Lakota is the first to debut a proposition on a step to take. He proposes he travels to London, England to publish his book. Since they have all read the manuscript and are indeed confident the book will alter people's view of the governments, look for an indispensable measure to help reclaim the power they possess from them. He outlines his plans and strategy of getting there and what topic he is to engage in when it comes to using gracious vibes and impression for people to gain his confidence. Money is going to be an austere wholeness for his massive plans to come to accomplishment. Although, he visualizes his appearance there will be of a great contribution to spread the message far and beyond. He would have to do this. He would have to interpose himself in between survival and accomplishment. No matter what comes, he would have to do it; he would have to do it for humanity—to express himself forcibly in order for it to de facto grasp the consequences of its immediate failure to reconcile with its maker. He would have to bring a gracious change to the world before it gets late to see darkness wipe away everything that has been built from the beginning of time. He has to chase these enemies far away into the forest of no man's land. He has to impart knowledge to people so to prompt them into an evolution.

The next day, after saying and doing everything. Everybody have agreed with his plans and departure. Tyson is able to get in contact with one of his pals who also has arranged their escape to the forest where they have come to make a home, pleading for his every assistance. Lakota sets on the journey with Aadita, and they both left the forest of Amazon, hugging and kissing their comrades, and the natives who have come to be their only neighbors, and finally, bidding them adieu.

Reaching Sao Paulo in Brazil where he meet with the man Tyson instructs him on how he could be of assistance to them. After spending two days in a hotel, he and Aadita eventually board a private jet to take them to London. A prior explanation has been given, which means the man assisting them knows everything and has exercised a staunch and skeptical disapproval to the idea at the beginning. Meanwhile, they have also been able to come to a conclusion not to plunge into this menacing itinerary. But, for the sake of humanity, some would have to lose their lives, but not their souls. They would have to be the lambs to be sacrificed for others to live. If they are not doing it, their godliness crown will not be granted to them to be worn. They have to do it. They are fated to do it. What is done to heal humanity is done to please the Universe. And the Universe sees it all.

At long last when they arrive in London, Aadita and Lakota are smuggled into a car driven into a compound of a very big mansion in the outskirt of the city, South West London. After some few days, the book is said to be put into publication. And when it is done, without delay, it is considered one of the best-selling books of all-time. Although, avalanche of money is pumped into publication, translation into many languages, and marketing to expand sales. Abruptly, people are flooding stores, hectic to get a copy. Those who have read it state their approval and proclaim the qualities of the content. It is a book unambiguously written to bequeath to people intellectual and ethereal insights. It is about the world and power and greed. It is about a change of the system from within. It is about cooperation to stage events that favor expression of protest to oust the greedy dogs in and around the globe. It was about kindness, compassion, evolution, education, humanitarian, diplomacy, understanding, integrity, tolerance, love, forgiveness, and communication amongst humans. It is a book millions of people have been anticipating and patiently wait for it.

Meanwhile, the name of the author is shrewdly concealed, made to merchandize under a false name. The more people read, the more the sales barrage, and the more people acknowledge what is happening around them. People have come to sense the truth that surrounds the world and what plunges it into chaos. And they ought to quickly execute a shrewd and diplomatic intervention to keep the world safe from the demons and monsters that have fallen down from the land of the dead onto Earth.

And it reaches a time when people start to figure out how relevant it is to bear the pains and adversities by retrieving from unnecessary commodities: people cultivating their own food, sewing their own clothes, rearing their cows, sheep, goats, and poultry at home, abstaining from materials only necessitated in order for others to see a vivid impression of one's image and personality. They drastically reduce their demands for everything, boycotting corporates, the banks, Wall Street Stock Exchange, and all that crap, and the observation of the outcome leads to the origin of an economic decimation and displacement that becomes widespread, which, in actual fact, is a fall of the empire that has been built by the greedy dogs.

While others relish the good outcome of their too much sacrifices, some set off in wrath, and their enthusiasm is intense, in a revengeful profile. They are distressed by their apparent lack of progress and profiting. They have to do everything to make sure the perpetrators of this very acts of altering people's mind to revolt against them pay for the damages. Henceforth, investigations are carried out, and when at last the substantial evidence they discover is attached to a book written by one author under a disguised name—which seems to has led to this immense impairment in production and sales that resulted in a collapse of their empire, they spontaneously order all copies of the book to be burnt and banned. At the same time, a search is carried out for Lakota and Aadita, who are already disguised, still living in London where the book is first published. Day after day, more searches are made and books are burned.

As the common people could not proceed with the tolerance of humiliation and intimidation, they take to the street and everything ripens into unrests everywhere around the globe. The unrests are not of race or religion, but of the disparity between the rich and the poor, for all who have read the book, all who understand the importance, come to have a discernment of the fundamental reasons the world is experiencing wars, conflicts, hunger, bigotry, hatred, racism, sexism, and violence. They have to put an end to all this garbage. They have to do so or they all would perish in the end. Times and situations metamorphose into inordinate misery and vicissitude for the governments and big businesses. Every day, people would march and protest peacefully for their voices to be heard, and it is going on and on and on. With the police brutality putting a halt to this, it is broadened into an act of revolution to change the political system of every country.

In the context of this incident, Lakota and Aadita are on the run to a place they know not, but they conceive in their hearts they have painted themselves into a corner. Lakota is worried about his future if ever it occurs he comes out of this entanglement alive, and yet, he is more worried about Aadita. He knows they are both going to get caught and be killed. Even if they disguise and are hiding in a remote village they inexorably supposed not a soul could trace their whereabouts. He could visualize how they are caught and made to pay with their lives. He knows it is suicidal for them to have gotten themselves captivated and become too obsessed with a burden too difficult for them to bear. He foresees the powerful forces at work, and he fathoms he would prevail if he navigate and push ahead with instincts and intuition and not be against them. He has to maintain his focus on the truth and those aspects that align with his soul. He sees how his strong belief in the divinity he has long created in his mind is proven true to him by revealing itself through the Universe he still has never seen, yet understands it to be responsible for creating and shaping every human fate. In a way the immortals manifest themselves into humans and return to immortality is, to him, about to be seen as reality. They have taken this burden upon themselves to save others, to bring a change to a world formerly seemed crumbled by greed and the strife for power, in a world where egocentricity has become suited in the center of virtue and uprightness. The role every life plays matters to the Universe, and this, the world comprehends not. If good could thrive and supersede evil, all shall be well, but if not, the end of man is nigh. Man has brought upon himself a tragedy that cannot be willfully erased from vision. He must be in preparation to meet and confront the troublesome state of affairs that flares before him. Those who have encountered death and evil regret the incident on which they have done so. But those who have not encountered something similar, assert it is a normal way to live and die. Death, as a mystery, would not appear in a possible way to favor the goodness of it. Any a soul lost, if lost in grief, is doomed to be lost repeatedly. Since the world rejoices in a condition of transgression and relish the breeding of more transgressions, woe unto men. They have caused their very soul to die. They have induce mystery in life, and in death. They tend to play the role of a master, whereas it would have been best if they lay down and sleep in serenity and reasonableness without any request of who is who, or who wins, or whom do we see as the head and tail.

Chapter 22

It is in the forest where they are assembled to bid adieu to their two comrades who have been shot with an air rifle in a village in some part of England. It is said many bullets have been shot at them by one of the villager who veritably has never been seen again after he has shot and unmasked all their disguised costumes from, to be sure he has killed the right vagabonds. Their bodies have been later discovered by the police and brought to the city of London where people mourn and weep for days before the bodies are finally laid to rest. It is said there a revolution has started in every part of the world. Citizens of every country have come to see the killing as a way to shut them up. They start to fight with their governments and prompting unrest everywhere. And, as violence becomes involved, it begins to escalate into uncontrollable situation that extend into a direction of conflict and war. The deaths of Lakota and Aadita are seen regrettable by the greedy dogs capable of executing their plans to assassinate them. It becomes a gigantic problem with no common resolution. It is sequential, not seeing an end, troubling to the greedy dogs, who are on the verge of losing everything they have tried to protect, which intrinsically are things acquired through gross and dubious tax practices and exploitation of the peasants.

Henceforth, as Tyson, Hussein, Shiromi, and Kadosh, all gathered in await of their dead comrades to present themselves prior to their final ascension into the kingdom of the immortals, they observe as El gran maestro, accompanied by Lakota and Aadita, all descend from the sky and land in their very midst as they have been when they meet for the first time in the wonderland where the gods and goddesses dwell. They are clean and pure, and their robes smell of mints and incense. They embrace affectionately and exchange greetings and kiss everybody, and after some minutes Lakota and Aadita were seen again as they ascend with El gran maestro into the sky with no time to delay, waving to them as they disappear into the cloud while others shed tears of joy, seeing their compeers transformed into immortals.

Some days after Lakota and Aadita have ascended into the kingdom of the immortals, Kadosh wakes up early in the morning, screaming. When his compeers arrived to demand of what is happening, he narrates a nightmare he has had. It is a nightmare provided with instincts that erect grotesque horror. It is about how in the middle of a state of riotous confusion, there appears a helicopter flying in the sky, and not far away from humans standing on the ground. On board this helicopter is Kadosh, handcuffed, and two other American soldiers—one of them, an expert, in the shooting of microchip implant into the heads of every human being. According to what he hears them both discuss, it is said to be an obligation for every human being living on the planet Earth—solely to be able to control them, make them eat their ideas, purchase products, and act as instructed. The microchip is to silence the uprising of those who have taken to the streets to protest for their voice to be heard, making it a power of good to oust their governments.

As for Kadosh, he fathoms the end of humanity, he fathoms the greedy dog's anger and frustration for having lost the game they play with the ordinary people. So, their vengeance is tremendous and prominent. They have to offer a relentless protection over what they deem belongs to them. They have to hold on to greed and power which they have sacrificed so much to attain.

Then, after a while, Kadosh is dropped down. When he attempts to alert people of what he has instantly witnessed, no one lend their ears to him. And, all of a sudden, he sees the same helicopter flying towards where he is standing in the midst of already violence disorder. Since he conceives what is about to ensue, he commences to run in a headlong and disorderly haste, alerting people on his way of the effective consequences of what is about to take place that they all know nothing about. He is still running and running, and there are many people out on the streets, waiting for the helicopter, totally unware of the services in which it is intended. Kadosh perceives how the microchips are being shot from the helicopter to the forehead of every humans waiting to be saved. It is eerie and ruthless and rancorous. He sees it as it is being done. And when he eventually meets someone he has known long ago and tries in every way to notify him, he uplifts his head to see the helicopter near him, and they push ahead with the shooting while he dodges them. They would not relent, only to continuously shoot while he dodges and runs out of the crowd where all of them have previously been targeted and are having the microchips in their brain without knowing it. After much strenuous efforts to escape them, at the end he has to concede defeat and comply with their will. Thence he observes as they shoot it directly into his forehead and penetrate into his brain, from there to his mind—impelling him to be senseless and unconscious. However, deep in his heart, he could see he still possesses that extraordinary power to save others, yet he could not save himself. He observes in a dim light as he is taken into the helicopter again and driven away.

"This is not a nightmare," says Tyson, after having listened to his compeer narrates the whole horrific nightmare.

"Then, what is it?" Requests Shiromi.

"To me, I am not seeing it as a nightmare. Instead, I am seeing it as some kind of intuitive understanding, a manifestation of a supernatural reality. It is known as "epiphany", which many Christians refer to as a "revelation" from their God. There are people who are tied to seeing visions," answers Kadosh, staring at Tyson to see if they are both in the same frame of mind.

"Veritably true, my brother," says he, Tyson, staring back at Kadosh. He continues, "I do believe this dream we supposed to be a nightmare is a vision. It seems to be a kind of mental image produced by his own imagination, an image he has long conceived in his mind, and it is attached to a natural force. All we need now is to understand it well, and with a good interpretation, we can derive a meaning from it."

"You are right, Tyson," answers he, Kadosh. "You see, at the time we come across some serious complications that virtually halt our climbing to the mountain of fire when returning to Earth from the land of the immortals, I have had a vision that helps me break a code and come to find a solution to how we could advance to reach the peak of the mountain. You are all aware of that, are you not?"

"Yes, we are," reply, all of them.

"So, I guess this is the time for me to do the same here. El gran maestro has said to me twice to break the code. This is the code to free humanity from the bondage they have been held. I tell you now, it is all about calculation. It is a process involving a solution for a problem. We have to study the relationships, the measurements, the properties, and the quantities of sets using numbers and symbols. The whole thing is mathematics. You see, we learn man is his own God he thinks has created him, so also when we refer to Satan, or the devil as they call it, we can as well learn man is his own devil he has created and thinks has been created by God. Observing it in a clear form, we are conscious of what is happening around us in our society today, which brings us to the fact the world is going to be destroyed by the same man himself, not God, as the scriptures has said. Man has created and built everything in it, so he will also be considered responsible for the destruction. Man is his own God. And that is the reason we see in the Bible, in Genesis, God, who is also man created the world, and in Revelation, he too destroyed it. Lurked behind the invented stories of the Jews of how the world was created and how God and Satan came into existence, we derive a metaphorical meaning from it. Now, we have to do our own calculation, but we have to use a mathematical formula in solving this problem. Come to look at it, we are aware that knowledge as many believe, was the forbidden fruit that caused man to die. Of course, if we look at it very well, we will see that, theoretically, knowledge yields wisdom, which has empowered man to achieve his goals in advancing and developing a place he calls home. From another point of view, if we look at it well, we will see that it is not the knowledge that led him into tribulations, instead, it is his greed. Greed is man's problem, and it is man's Satan that perpetrates evil, while knowledge is man's God that perpetrates good. Greed goes with evil, hate, darkness, and despairs, while knowledge goes with good, love, light, and hope. It is all calculations, it is all mathematics, the purity to reach man's dreamland. Mathematics, in the real sense, is the pure language everyone can understand. It is numbers; it is not like a language spoken by a particular group of people; it is the universal language, and it is the pure language. Then, another thing, this mathematics has to be applied in an abstract form conveyed via a process of drawing conclusion from fact or evidence. This process is referred to as 'reasoning'. Man indeed requires reasoning, deep thoughts to outlive and outlast, to understand himself and fit with the Universe, fits with nature, his surroundings. Thoughts create reality, and this is the truth about knowledge. It provides us with the adequate power and energy to study, to gain understanding and become aware of anything. It is 'awareness,' which is the light to lead mankind to its maker. It is the body of truth. But, there is a misconception, when knowledge now becomes an ideal created to control people's mind for a reason to assemble them to become one, a vision to place on people the belief we can seek the truth and reach Heaven on our own, while at the same time, taking what belongs to them and making them slaves. This ideal being created and made into laws, implemented to rule and govern all humans around the globe. We are driving too rapidly and farther than required. Do we not see this from every corner that we seek using brain and mind control techniques to manipulate human beings?"

"I sincerely agree with what you have outlined. But my question now is, how do we protect the world from the nullification which is about to force upon it?" Asks Tyson, looking very furious and wants so much to halt the tragedy about to occur on Earth.

"Yes," responds Kadosh. "Another vision has been revealed to me right when you asked that question, Tyson. A nuclear missile is about to be launched from underground, right in the U.S. by some unknown enemies who have been born, bred, and still live there. Now, let me narrate some parts of history to all of you. There are myths that seem forgotten, or have not be unveiled to many who preferred not to show concerns with the issues irksome and tormenting humanity. It is a combination of myths. For more than a decade, these particular people have been building that nuclear bomb in their own house, in an estate owned by one billionaire who, in fact, is a member of the U.S congress. They belong not to a race or tribe, but to a religious faith so strong and influential. You see, these very people have infiltrated the U.S. politics to an extent they now have a say in U.S. policies and law making. They own the largest amount of the Federal Reserves in the U.S. and around the globe. They have been financing wars for centuries. In fact, they have funded both sides of every war since Napoleon Bonaparte. They have been the backbones for many countries in Europe when it comes to borrowing money to fight wars, until when America was founded under the act of liberation through struggles and engaging in war with their colonial master, the British. So, America has become a trusted partner who could help bring their vision into reality and make them achieve their goals. Money has been their weapon, and it still is. Due to the problems that have occurred some months ago… that people have come to completely acknowledge how they have been manipulated and have taken a decision as they reach assent on a course of revolution. There has been the fear of the powerful people losing all their wealth. Therefore, they have come up with a plan to divert people's attentions from the current issues to how Russia and China have become the major threats to the U.S. security. They have decided to launch this missile that will kill thousands—which is planned to infuriate the U.S. to destroy Russia and China with the nuclear missiles deployed formerly in the nearby countries. These same people are also residing in Poland and Japan. They have been able to build another nuclear bombs there in their house, underground. And, immediately as they launch the one in New York City, they will as well launch the one in Poland to attack Russia, and also the one in Japan to attack China. That means, a nuclear war has been declared by those countries with the many numbers of nuclear arsenals."

"What are we to do to stop it now?" demands again, Tyson, unable to sit to lend his ears to Kadosh as he coolly and introspectively effects a depiction on how the world is going to start a nuclear war, which everyone grasps is to be the apocalypse long been foretold by many prophets and scholars. "There has to be a solution to it." Tyson requests of Kadosh, to think, to find a response. His eagerness is to do anything to save humanity from the calamity that is about to surface.

"We have to break the code before it is too late," says Kadosh.

"What code?" Retorts, Tyson, watching others as they remain calm and confused, not knowing how to intervene in a matter so complex and troubling.

"We have to leave this place now to our different directions. Some would have to be in Warsaw, Poland within forty-eight-hours, while others would have to be in New York within that same time, and another in Japan in order to defuse the bombs with one particular number. There are numbers of buttons. All anyone needs to do is to press one button, the accurate number. If mistakenly another number is touched, there will be an alarm, and anyone caught at that scene does not need to be told what he will be facing. We have to decipher a code and get a number needed to save humanity"

"What number is that," demands Tyson, restless and frustrated with everything.

"It is the sum divide by the count. That is how to calculate the mean value. This is the formula we are to apply here. We have to count from 1 to 10, and we also have to add 1+2+3+4+5+6 till 10; then, the sum if divided by 10, we come up with an answer which is 5.5. By rounding number to the nearest whole, we come up with an answer which is 6. So, number 6 is the number needed to defuse the bombs.

"But before we have to plunge ourselves into this dangerous task, we have to be fully aware we are endangering ourselves and bound to meet death. I will frankly offer my counsel to all of you. Please, do not go there with the heart to pardon anyone because of how he or she might look. You have to make sure you are going there in an effort to defuse the bombs, so, no matter whom you come across who tries to stop you, lend your ears to nobody."

"If I may ask, why is it that this particular people have come to be able to take control of the world and everything in it, and yet, they still intend to destroy it? How have they managed to meet with wealth and power so easily? Demands, Hussein.

"It's a long story, Hussein. If we are to continue narrating the story we would not be able to put forward our plans to halt their progress in executing their own plans. But, let me brief you about these people. It is about the misty and gloomy elites of international bankers who are furtively controlling the politics and economy of the whole wide world. Money is the root of all evil, we all know. So, it is the source of all wars. These people motives in the beginning indeed have not been to cause wars, but rather to make profits. They have long associated themselves with the monarchs and aristocrats in Europe, possessing wealth enough to control the minds of the entire Europeans and extending it to the Americans. When people chide and curse Adolf Hitler and his admirers and supporters, they will consign to oblivion what precisely was the driving force for him to cuddle the Eugenic ideology. After many researches have been effectuated, we have come to trové that it was an Anglo-American ideology that he drew inspiration from. Although, he has always regretted the Germans losing the First World War and becoming poor and destabilized. He has always loathed the Jews for the fact that he witnessed other Europeans like him persecuting them. In the sense, he tried to emulate the Americans. He tried to know where the strength of the white race lies. He learnt that the Americans were determined to accomplish the long time vision of many white people, which firmly promotes and endorses the white race to be the most supreme race in all race. Meanwhile, there was already segregation in America, and Hitler was appreciably in favor of it. Albeit, the Americans were doing it on their own, not knowing it was to be copied by a radical Nazi movement, or they knew, but never thought Hitler was ever going to become the onus that would seek their own destruction. We should always be careful of what we teach others. What we create, is what is coming to destroy us. Before the Second World War, did we not see many in Europe in supports of the fascist movement? Even in Britain, King Edward the 8th openly gave the Nazi salutes and also visited Hitler. The Anglo-Americans did goad and back Hitler. They financed him, they also financed the fascist Franco in Spain, and Mussolini in Italy. A lot of them accede to commercial dealings with the Nazis before and during the war and benefit slave labors, and that swiftly fosters Hitler's accession to power. Many Jews as well, at the beginning, did play an important role with funds from their banks and industries. Although, Hitler did spur and embolden majority of the Zionists in Germany in efforts to wittily bolster their returns to settle in Palestine. So many top military in the German Nazi were Jews, including Alfred Ernst Rosenberg, the Latvian Jew and also a German philosopher and was an influential dialogue of the Nazi party. Then comes the question, why did Hitler detest the Jews so much he decided to wipe them out of the surface of the Earth? Some historians and scholars believe, in time to come, he drafted them as the enemy of white European society. He was afraid of them just as the Egyptians were during the time of their Exodus. You see, the ratiocination here that I am intending to enlighten everyone about the past is that, if we know our history, we will know there is no means whatsoever how we can save the world. Everything, every message is all concealed in a bottle. And to get it out, then one would have to break the bottle, which also if broken, will result in another form of evil to bechance the nearest species to inhabit the Earth. The truth is concealed, and there's no one to reveal it. Though, in accordance with the Jewish scripture, one man, who was a Nazarene that tried to do so long before civilization erupted. What happened to him? He was nailed to the cross of Calvary. They crucified him for they claimed his teachings were incoherent and did not correlate with theirs, and yet he asserted they worship the same God. He was revealing the truth, and principally against 'usury' which he denounced as against the rules of humanity, as against their doctrines, as against the laws of the prophets. The act of loaning and charging interests at an illegally high rate—which is banking, is the bottle where the message is been concealed."

They are all subsumed in a series of perplexities that have developed tout de suite as they heed the phrase, 'We will know there is no means whatsoever how we can save the world',—which, in actuality, signifies everyone is going to perish for the misdeeds of some few people who think of only gaining the world to see others shed tears. At the moment they would have to do everything in their every effort to quench the fire about to be set ablaze. But they also have to characterize everything by a combination of intense focus and confidence, or else they will lose the battle. So, they allow a disposal of themselves to their faiths, readjust and make a detour around the forest until they eventually see themselves in the place where two single-engine light transport aircraft are already waiting to fly them to Sao Paulo, there in Brazil. Then, from Sao Paulo, Kadosh and Hussein are smuggled into another private jet directed to Poland, while Shiromi is to be smuggled into the one heading to Japan, and then Tyson is to board another one heading to New York City.

While on the flight, Kadosh and Hussein sit all alone, discussing how the Egyptians might have felt the same way Hitler did about the Jews, for the simple reason they have both chastised them for nothing. Meanwhile, the two pilots fly the plane and also talk to themselves. Then, abruptly, Kadosh begins to sense something strange about to come into effect as he conscientiously listens to his heart beats. He could sense the nearness of the Universe. He is seeing clearly as the Universe opens its arms to receive him into its bosom. He forthwith understands he is never going to make it to Poland. Perhaps, the immense capacity with which this vision has tossed itself to him, is enough for him to acquiesce to the call of death. In his life he has never felt like that aforetime. He is so unhappy and agitated that he desires to depart from his own body and jumping out of the flight from the sky to fall down with his soul, while he leaves his body on the flight so not to cause it a damage. And, as this feelings of death continues to develop inside of him, he too has to allow the development of the feelings of honesty to comply with the request. And when he does, they correspond.

All at once, one of the pilots walks out from the cockpit and points a small caliber handgun at Kadosh and Hussein who have almost fallen asleep.

"Wake up, you morons!" he yells at them.

As they manage to open their eyes, they could see him pointing his gun and telling them, "You assumed you can stop us from executing our plans of destroying the world. We built it, and we will destroy it. We run the world and everything in it. We feel it is time for us to do what we want with it. And there you are, the six of you, trying to change our plans. Our intention is only to instill fear, not to destroy everything. We have succeeded in eliminating two before and have since been tracing the four of you and never been able to attain a good outcome. Now, it is our time and you are never getting out free from this." He starts to shoot instantly as he finishes with his speech. And that is the end of Kadosh and Hussein. Their missions on Earth have been fulfilled. They could see their souls departing from their bodies and ascending into the wonderland to join with the other gods and goddesses.

It is all done. Missions have been accomplished. At the very time Kadosh and Hussein have been shot to death, Shiromi has been shot as well by one of the pilots onboard the flight, which he has been taking to Japan. He could see how his soul departs from his body, and all of a sudden, he sees the goddess of penitence opens her arms to receive him as they both hold each other and he could experience deep pleasure; he feels entirely exonerated, revived, and incentive. He could feel the both of their hearts beat, and are susceptible, wide, and clear. He could feel how they both breathe and it makes him feel alive. There is strength, there is connection, and there is healing in this intimacy of a god and a goddess.

Lastly, it is Tyson onboard another flight heading to New York. He is lying in one of the leather flat-bed seat on the luxury private jet. Like in a dream he opens his eyes to realize someone dressed up in an expensive suits sitting close to him. It is a friend he has known long time ago when he has first become a billionaire, and has been welcomed to the billionaire's club in New York City.

"Hello Tyson," he says to him, offering his hand.

"Hello Charley." Tyson responds, also reaching out for a shake.

Then, he puts up a question to him. "Tyson, can you still recall how we used to invest our money in buying shares in different companies, invest in stocks, bonds, mutual funds, exchange-traded funds, and other different investments? You used to be good in that real estate investment trust and all that stuffs I still recollect. You have made pretty good money. You know about everything, you know how we used to make stock market plummets when it is already near the U.S. presidential election. You know how we use banks to serve as an institution to store and reserve money, how we lend money out to people in need to invest in businesses, to start their own corporation. You knew how we accept bills of exchange, convert domestic into and from foreign currencies, all, in efforts to bring about sustainable economic growth and further improvement in labor markets. Why have you come to turned your back on us? Why have you come to be the enemy who eats and sleeps with us? You have done a lot, Tyson, you have done a lot, and you deserve to die."

"As for death, I am not bothered. All I beseech of you is please spare the world for the sake of that God you have mentioned to me several times—that God that you serve and love so much."

"Stop talking about my God. That is not the issue here. All I need you to do is tell me how you have come up with this credence that has driven you so mad to relinquish the good things of life and hold wretchedness so tightly in your arms and legs. What has changed you? What vision has been revealed to you, so I too can follow you to where you intend to go? But, believe me, you cannot save the world anymore. It has been said and done. The demons have come down to Earth to be in charge of everything. They have decided to first destroy the planet in an attempt to instill more fear in humans. Not that the whole world is going to be destroyed, but it is that we want America to teach Russia and China, and all these other countries a little lesson. We know they are not prepared to bow down to Baba if they are not dealt with. So, relax your mind. This is how the world goes, and there is no way you can alter it, nor would you be able to stop it. It is how species survive. Take a look at the animals in the forest, the fishes in the waters. They all feed on each other. The bigger and stronger ones feed on the smaller and weaker ones. It is nature, it is not man's ideal things seem to become bad for some. That is how we have been able to develop so fast and advance in every aspects of life."

"You are right, Charley," says Tyson. "But do you not see what we have done to the planet? What about all these dreams and visions we promised the next generation? What about how we have made peace a nightmare for them, made conflicts and wars what they are now to be born into. We have betrayed our mother nature. We have impaired and ravaged the bonds between humans for only one reason—to benefit. Now, tell me, if we both die, are we not going to leave everything behind?"

"Yes, Tyson. I am quite frankly aware of the meaning of what you intend to advocate. But there is no one who has come to die for another man's sin. Everyone would have to suffer for his or her own transgression. Or, probably you have forgotten my religion teaches me it is only God who has the right to forgive, nobody else. And, moreover, he is the only true God."

"Oh, do you truly believe in that God?" Demands, Tyson. "If you believe in that God, would you not make him see you show love and compassion to all of humanity, making the world a better and peaceful place to inhabit? Is it not pleasing to that God you believe in who will lead us to that paradise we want? Why has it become so difficult for us to do what is right instead of destroying each other? Of what essence is it for us to be preaching doctrines, fasting and praying, reading holy books, and asserting we are righteous only to paint pictures for others to see while we are not demonstrating this in our actions? If we save the world, are we saving it for ourselves, or saving it for our children and children's children? Causing wars only aggravate problems. Imagine how starving refugees are fleeing their countries held in wars every day, and are all running to civilized countries, which also has become a burden people there cannot contend. If we can believe what is most important is not what we see, but what we feel for each other, life would be understandable, and all will be happy and rejoicing. The mystery about life we cannot understand, but we understand it is better for all to be included in the fight against the enemies than a few to get themselves in it. They will lose. The bigger the strength, the more likely the victory."

Charley, the man who has worked so hard to ensure the elimination of a friend he has once knew and transacted so many businesses with, but has become his enemy because he intends to fight for humanity rather than caring for himself alone. Here they are, the both of them. He has thought of shooting him for the first time and never thought of engaging in any kind of a discourse with him. He has been able to investigate and meet with people who know Tyson and his comrades are in the Amazon forest. At first, he has said he wants to go inside the forest with his troops to search and terminate all of them. But he has been advised to lay low like a wolf patiently for them to come out on their own. And the same people whom Tyson has trusted so much and have been working with him to deliver messages and transport them to anywhere they wish to travel in the struggles to help humanity survives the difficult test laid ahead; these same people have betrayed him by working with Charley and the entire billionaires who seek Tyson's elimination.

Now that he has come to know him better and bind a comprehension of his motives for the intervention, he knows it is stronger than anything fabricated or formulated by any human; it has empowered him to think of saving the human race. He acknowledges he has permitted affection to influence his desires. He could not blame him for this. It is not of human to comprehend how it is beget in us and nurtured to become a thing we cannot control. Empathy is what he sees it to be—the entering into another person's feelings. To grasp that feelings. And this power is so extraordinary that he changes one's mental vision of a series of events. It comes naturally and helps define who we are as humans.

He walks straight to meet with the other pilot. Then, returning to where Tyson is already bind with some automatic belts that jotted out of the leather flat-bed seat that he was still lying. Then, he discloses everything to him. "Your comrades have all been shot dead by the instruction of the ones on top, the Commanders in Chiefs. I am so sorry to let you know that."

This instant, Tyson starts to cry like a baby. Something that has never happened to him before. Even when he lost his both parents, he has never felt this way. He could imagine or he thinks he sees it openly and brightly how Hussein, Shiromi, Lakota, Kadosh, and Aadita, all in their appearance, looking to him from above, smiling and cheering. He is willing to be with them, he is willing to be a god, for humans are wicked, and living on Earth is not worth it. He could be a god and be free like his compeers who could now hover around like angels. He want to be free. To live is to be held in bondage, and to die for humanity is to be free and cheerful. He shed tears and screams.

"This cannot help, Tyson. You and I have to leave this flight right now, or else we will be dead in a few minutes time. The other pilot is about to commit suicide when I informed him about you. He does not want you free. But there is a parachute here that we are both to use to fly away downward into the sea. Please, take my counsel. I want us to both live. I wish I have never done any of this. Life cannot be reversed. The only thing I can do is to be a part of your vision if we succeed."

"What about the bomb?" Demands Tyson.

"I told you it is not to destroy the whole world. Please, let us leave."

He unbinds the automatic belts and gives him a parachute to wear, while he too wears the other one. Then, there arrives the other pilot, who holds a rifle in his hand. He waves to them not to jump out of the aircraft or he is going to shoot. Perhaps, it is too late for that. Charley could not listen to him. Instead, he pushes Tyson and exits with him as the pilot starts to fire a wide range of his fully automatic rifle. They descend from the sky, accelerating due to the force of gravity pulling them down. At once, they could hear the explosion of the aircraft. While still in the sky, Tyson could see everything overtly and translucently with his eyes, how the other gods and goddesses including El gran maestro, hovering around like angels, singing songs of praises. They are cheerful and feel alive and comfortable. They are staring deep at him and worshipping him. When he opens his eyes, he sees he is still with Charley in the sky, as they both keep descending, holding themselves while returning down to Earth. During the last part of the descent, they open the parachutes and land unconsciously in the sea.

Chapter 23

The wind smiles its waxen face of horror, blowing steadfastly from east to west, north to south with its gradual expansion of terror that melts with the explosion of terrible and viperous waves, which possess a nature of vice, which in carnage craves. Suddenly, a flashlight appears in the amused sky and covers the sun coloring pages. Everywhere then with the sparkling light so brightened, showing itself from the cloud like a light born of fireworks to create spectacular galaxy collision images. As all humans shocked and aghast, their heads uplift to witness a true consternation that tears their very souls dry. Into the clear and beautiful, blue sky, in New York City, a nuclear missile has been launched perpendicular to Earth hurl and consent to a rebound. Same in Kremlin, same in Beijing to all human's observations compound. At the very outset, prediction cries its very heart out to mankind, but gracefully badly crunched. Inexplicable, the scene seems as various detonations of the destructive bombs carry the mightiest, the mightiest, the mightiest magnitude of noise; sound a clamorous and grumbling thunder. The gods and goddesses their hands wash away clean, very clean, after transformation occur that divinely walks the saints right to pleasure superiority in the wonderland. An accord orient in good effort to reach to turn their backs on humans to be thrown in a predicament unescapable, to be scourged for disobedience. Now, see how it happens, see how the detonation of the nuclear bomb rock the whole city, extirpating thousands of humans. Immediately after the blast, the bomb mushroom cloud rises more than 20,000 feet above the ground level as everywhere becomes cloudy, murky, smoky, dusky, and obscure. People stampede crazily and hopelessly from one good direction to another bad one in every attempt to cunningly develop an escape route to nowhere. Buildings and monuments and tantalizing fragrances watering down to tamper and crush the many a people more. Tiredness and weariness and frustration and fear and despairs battle the hearts of men as they horrendously scuffle to dare into perilous journey with oaths sworn to rejection and ferocity and insensibility. Human bodies blood spurting out, dead bodies everywhere you with a possible awareness turn your view; tremendous mountain of heat tour its way into their hearts, into their bones, into their blood, into their souls. Thirst and hunger thrive and draw conclusion to proceed, to advance, to capitalize. Now, not anywhere to turn a view without it meet with human bodies burnt from the fingers to the head, and to the toe; the skins peeling, falling, dropping, melting, and red muscles exposed. All humans equally alive, equally deceased. Shattering, crashing, a wide range of destruction spread its dominion to every a part of the planet. This instantly actuates the trees and flowers and all other plants in stumbling and plunging to inferno along the devastated pathway that leads as the air they breathe they breathe in faces turned doom and gloom. Wild animals, domestic animals drain in tears and bleed their sorrows full; birds in the sky storm through the air, darting forth and back and downward to Earth all tumble, and at the other side of the cities, observation carried out of how seas and oceans and rivers on wild beast and blood and muds and gas feed. Fills everywhere you look to with chaos, with destruction, with danger, with death. The air and atmosphere than the view more unfavorable, more polluted, more terrifying, more deadly. It is horrible, this scene is horrible that for those whose eyes bear witness, they are dead before death calls them. A tale that cannot be told. A tale need not be told. For any who hears it, cast his imagination into a raging fire. It is all about life and death; it is all about the issues of succession and power; it is greed; it is all about possession.

As the inherent conflicts and tensions between these powerful nations deepen into a realm of uncontrollable rage, tantrum, and disaccord, more nuclear missiles they continuously with desperation launch to their confirmed and suspected foes and rivals directly from different countries engrossed. Partly or fully involved in this catastrophic war situation, every country becomes. Those mistakenly caught in the crossfire, in the worse ever tragedy they are immersed. Then it is all fighting, all due to the lack of distrust. That emerges, conspiracy from corners all around: Russia standing tall in a bombardment to create extermination of Germany and the nearby European countries, while the U.S. with a kind of tender rage, Russia and China in bombardment comes to wholly share a concentration, and also bombarding Mexico who secretly allows Russia a space and time in the building and installing of some nuclear bombs underground in their country. They are all bombarding one another. To an extent, countries in Africa are supplied nuclear bombs by Russia while some others are aided by the Americans. No one is confiding in the other person. It has become a nuclear world war. Germans bombarding Russia, France bombarding Russia, Italy bombarding Greece, Iran bombarding Saudi Arabia, China bombarding Japan, Malaysia and other nearby countries bombarding themselves. Russia and Mexico bombard the U.S. from behind and Brazil bombarding Argentina and Uruguay while some others near them are also bombarding Brazil. It is anger and madness that have swallowed the hearts of men in a world abandoned to its destruction by the Universe. It is horrible, it is awful, it is sickie, it is dreadful, it is mind-blowing, and no one is mentally disposed to smooth the path to achieve peace. It seems to be something mandatory for them to cave in to psychopathy, lunacy, mental derangement, stupidity, psychosis. It seems all are intoxicated with some of kind mixed potion of the product of a paroxysm of rage, of vengeance, of wrath. They all want to explore the land of the dead and see if it is a better place to populate than the Earth. They all want to feel that physical suffering, the mental suffering, the affliction, the trauma. Since their visions are in essence embellished with bewilderment, they want so much to quench the fire that burns within them. It is unthinkable what crop up and how it suddenly mellows to become so disastrous. It is happening, it is an obscure nightmarish vision long foretold. It is the voices of the good working men and women who have constantly suffer oppression that the gods and goddesses have come to hear and pay attentions, constraining them to abandon these people to be chastised and incarcerated in a domain of commotion by their own evil acts. The sweats, the agonies, the vexations, the grudges of the slaves have all been amassed to become a retribution to the wicked. The wicked shall know no peace and tranquility. It is a sad story to tell, a sad story of the end of a wicked world and a new beginning of life to be brimmed with the attractions of natural beauty—in which love and compassion is to retain a crucial position. It is happening how the gods and goddesses take observations of everything humans experience and could not change a thing, for they have vowed to allow mankind be the controller of its destiny. It is happening how the demons and monsters who have fallen from above, unto Earth, how their spirits are hovering in the sky around the globe, and they witness how humans are intertwined with a condition of suffering, with a condition of distress, with a condition of pains. But all they could put up with is to uplift their voices and sing in amusement, mocking all that are burning, all that are dying, and all that are tormented. It is happening, as these monsters raise their heads up to see the gods and goddesses, they fall down to worship them, imploring forgiveness and renewal of hearts. They have no option, except to repent of their transgression and come live with the Universe.

Chapter 24

After many weeks have passed, Tyson could see himself lay awake by the seashore in a place he knows not, a place he has never in life thinks exist. He is thinking through his head, he is eager for a systematic examination in order to come to his senses, in order to have a discernment of how he has arrived to be stunt with this amazement in front of him. From afar he could see another body, either dead or alive. He whirls, crouches, and struggles to uplift himself and lingers, advancing towards the man on the ground. Ultimately, when he reaches, he discovers the man still breathes, and he is the same man they have both descended from the aircraft using the parachutes; the man is Charley. He is filled with a great dismay how this has come to happen—that the man they have both successfully escaped death, the man who has saved his life after being lured to do so by his words of wisdom, apparently has become the same man he sees lay almost dead, one of his leg being bitten off in an attack by some strange animals. Tyson could not help stare at his face and witness the pains this man undergoes, taking shallow breathes, deeper and deeper.

"Oh, Charley, what is amiss?" he cries.

"What has happened to you?"

"You do not have to worry much about me, Tyson, because I am never going to live. Anyway, I am so glad you have made it alive. You have done your best to save humanity. You are a great man. I wish I have known all these will occur from the beginning when I and my crew start planning on how to instill fear on people in an attempt to regain our lost empire."

"I don not think you should have to bother yourself with that for now. I would have to do everything to ensure you survive."

"You do not really need to, because there is no way you can. The world has been destroyed. What we have thought to be a mere intention to create fear has become what destroyed humanity." He manages to raise his water resistant Apple 20 thousand-dollars wrist-watch for Tyson to calmly see what has been recorded, how the world has experienced a self-destruction by the use of nuclear bombs. Meanwhile, as Tyson watches the motion picture of the entire world engaging in destroying themselves with nuclear bombs, he shed tears. It occurs to him not to forgive this man, Charley, and his crew for having gained a favorable outcome in luring the world into that situation of horrible, mass destruction. Whether to forgive him or to add up to his pains, he could not form a judgment. He too is in a confused state of mind.

"I know you are speculating on whether to let me die or help me. Intrinsically, you cannot help me anymore. I am dead already, but there is one thing for you to do. I entreat you to forgive me, please do."

"I forgive you already," responds Tyson, still shedding tears and mourning the souls of the innocents who have lost their lives.

"Let me quickly enlighten you about the mysteries of the existence of man and his complications. My crew and I have known you and your comrades have been able to decipher the code and have the number to deactivate the bombs. They knew you and your crew. They knew you could save the human race. But their intention, as I said before, is merely to create fear and not to take the world into a direction very critical and dangerous, as it later turns. That number (6) was to be converted to numbers 666, which we all knew you will be able to get when it comes to the time for deactivation. The numbers 666 was the anti-Christ numbers; the number of a man associated with the beast. It was said to be an evil number, which many Christians believe is coming to destroy the world before the final return of Jesus Christ as depicted in the book of Revelation in the New Testaments. Most people used that number as they liked and saw it as something irrelevant, they joked with it and not knowing what it implied. And of course, many scholars had attempted in doing their thorough research, even with joint efforts, to come with a reasonable significance of it. But I tell you from what I have seen and known, there were many things like images, objects, data, information, and facts that connect humans to evil. Sometimes they come to success because of our strong beliefs in them. Albeit, religious stories about creation were all myths; they were stories invented to control our minds, to create fear in order for humans to look into their hearts and find places in them to employ conducts agreeable and gratifying to other human beings. The scriptures, many were not able to exert a cloudless comprehension to see them as phrases written that literally denote a kind of idea applied to another to suggest a likeness or analogy between them. They were metaphors which appeared in our sights and were swiftly transformed into different meanings and inserted into us to become knowledge. We have to understand the meanings of the scriptures. We have to be able to interpret them accurately like we interpret dreams, if not we will misunderstand them. We, the Jews, studied enough that we decided to help the world with our knowledge, to make the people of the world esteem and deem themselves as powerful as the gods and goddesses they have created. With our prodigious aptitude, we were able to tell these stories and making it so meaningful. We did everything for humankind, and yet, they charged us with force accusations, asserting we know nothing other than being money lenders. They persecuted us. They detested us. They all wanted a piece of us—Muslims, Christians, Pagans, Buddhist, etc. It was true many Jews including me were money lenders, and that was something that remained an obscure secret to the outside world of the Jewish community. Our belief which can be read in our religious books manifests and allows people to pass their judgements on what factually our intention was, if not to unite everyone. We believed human dignity did not depend on the place of one's birth, nor is it limited to one region. We also believed the greatness or worth of a person is not measured by his or her outward appearance. And to confirm all these, you can read something like this from the religious books written to guide us to attain life that is worthy.

"I quote, 'Then God said, let us make man in our image, according to our likeness; and let them rule over the fish of the sea and over the birds of the sky and over the cattle and over all the earth, and over every creeping thing that creeps on the earth. God created man in His own image, in the image of God He created him; male and female He created them. God blessed them; and God said to them, be fruitful and multiply, and fill the earth, and subdue it; and rule over the fish of the sea and over the birds of the sky and over every living thing that moves on the earth.' What we tried to explain is, now, since Adam was created in God's image, and he is the common ancestor of all mankind—that means all humans are equal and are the descendants of Adam. Therefore, Adam was our father, and Eve was our mother and they were the only people who gave birth to us all. When we assert to be the God chosen ones, we intended to make people see us differently and respect us for the insights we were able to acquire. Then, there came the problem: we were having different sect of groups claiming to be Jews. We had the Zionists who indeed were not real Jews even if they claim to be, and their religion was Zionism. Unlike the Jews who were practicing Judaism. Something people outside the Jewish community did not know is there were always a big fight between this two different sects within the community. The Zionists held the power of the nation. They were into politics and wanted a destruction of anyone who stand on their way to regain power and to be named the chosen ones of God. Unlike the real Jews, very simple people who believed in their daily lives and prayed to God for themselves as well for others.

It was true what I am telling you. The Zionists were not real Jews. They only came to infiltrate us, to make the world see us differently, to label us names not fit to our beliefs and faith. These people wanted to reside in the Holy Land, and wanted to do so with all their might and strengths. They wanted to rule the world and make it hell for others. You see, all these started long long ago when the Knight Templars first came to fight for the Jews in the Holy Crusade and Jihad wars. But, truly to be said, many Jews were not in support of this idea, because they were living their good lives there. They even backed and bedded the Palestinians, who truly inhabited in that land at that time. The Jews never wanted war and consistently believed it was not right for them to own the country. After then, after that holy war, the Templars unearthed and stole most of the relics belonging to the ancient temples and fled away to Europe with them. Some, they even refer to as the 'Holy Grail', which they asserted was a hidden secret of knowledge, while others asserted it was an object. Who knew what they found? I guess no one. Meanwhile, many of us were still presuming truly it was what they later transformed into something evil as the numbers 666, the mark of the beast."

"Knowing much about the Jewish community helps one understand the differences in every sect; likening this to the Sadducees and the Pharisees in the time of the said Jesus Christ, whom many firmly believed to be the Lamb of God that came to take away the sins of the world. The Sadducees were different people. They were these aristocrats—the wealthy class who were much concerned with politics and the wealth of Israel, while the Pharisees were the minority middle-class businessmen who were close to the poor people and were devoted to their religion than playing politics. But these two different people would not believe Jesus, even when they knew he was telling them the truth. Their objection to his doctrines was because he was preaching to people to presuppose man as God and God to be man. He was saying he was from the father, the father sent him, he was God, also the son of God, and also human. All these were seen to have amass to a prodigious contradiction to Jewish beliefs. Everything he said that should have been believed to be truth were all expressed in paradox. To the Jews, a lot of what he said was blasphemy. To the Jews God was above all things. He is the ruler, the creator, and always in control. And the Torah was the book of laws given to us by the prophets, so there was no need someone like Jesus coming with words of illusion to enlighten them. The least satisfactory of all was when Jesus branded them hypocrites and harshly expresses his strong disapproval of their many ways of lies and deceits. In the terms of how greed had long been a crucial issue no one ever found a solution to, he entered the synagogue, cast and threw everything away that they were using in transacting their money lending. And that swiftly drew their attention to him. They quickly grasped he has not come to only preach his Sermon on the Mount, but to turn their people against them by revealing the truth about life to all. And that was a clear motive for his crucifixion. Hence, it is to this day that all the stories, which were invented, were for the good of humanity, for people to fear and respect God and also their fellow beings. The Egyptians, Babylonians, Greeks, Romans, and other empires had their own stories invented as well. Jesus, as the book wrote about him, should not have been a man we would have taken his words for granted, for there were meanings to them. We would have all be living in a peaceful and better world with his doctrines. He is the greatest of all saints and prophets. He is you, he is me, he is everyone, he is God; he is the Universe and everything that has lived. He wanted us to have faith in humanity, and if we have done just that, fear would have been swallowed. He knew it all, he saw it all. If the people of the world had followed the scriptures and took his preaching to heart, we would not be killing ourselves. But there were those too proud and greedy to allow that eventuated, so they decided to stem the progress of the Sermon on the Mount, they decided to continually use the scriptures in committing great atrocities in the name of Jesus Christ so to frustrate others not to look to it as the right option in choosing which way to return to the maker. And these people were the class of the numbers, 666. The numbers were a representation of the ruling class in the modern world. The numbers were used in a conspiracy to control humankind. It was all a conspiracy theory, and the inner circle was never been able to be scattered as history itself remained."

"I do not know if you get it well. They were the elites, the powerful people in every nation. And they were all having one common goal, perhaps with the lack of trust and confidence in each other. I tell you, I was one of them. These people were controlling everyone. Let me state it discernibly. When had the greedy German politicians trusted the English? Or, when had the greedy English politicians trusted the Germans? Or when had the English decided to forgive the Americans for their revolution and coming to take the power of the world from them? Or, when had the French loved the English that much? When has Japan referred to China as a friend? When has Russia trusted Turkey? When had Mexico relied on Brazil or Argentina? When had Nigeria believed in South Africa? We are talking about the greedy politicians of the powerful countries in the world who implemented the protocols and extended it to all parts of the globe. They were the ones who believed it was fair and safe to spy on each other for the lack of trust, organizing different forms of Secret Agents. You might have thought the CIA to have been the most powerful Secret Agent in the world, but I tell you, there were stronger and powerful ones owned and financed by other countries in the west. The fact that America developed more sophisticated and advanced technology brought them to the spotlight. Talk about the Israeli spies, they were spying on everyone, including America who was protecting them. In the sense, there was enviousness, there was pride, and all these were so secret among each other. Everyone was fighting for his or her self-interest, not to rely on a neighbor who might downplay them the next hour. It was funny though. The world was a mess, and there was no way it would have become better, for greed and the strife for power have long dominated the hearts of men. It was only the west led by America that could have been able to restore humankind if they had walked along the path to achieve the objectives of the Declaration of Independence, which states as follows: 'We hold these truths to be self-evident, that all men are created equal, that they are endowed by their Creator with certain unalienable Rights, that among these are Life, Liberty and the pursuit of Happiness'. The world would have become a better and peaceful place if not what the Declaration of Independence was meant for was later not what it came to represent at the end. All these were a problem erupted in greed by the man known as Alexander Hamilton, who was the first Secretary of Treasury, going far to introduce the nation's financial system that brought us all into capitalism, a way worse than what the intention of the Union fought against that was practiced by their former colonial master. And all these he did, misinterpreting Adam Smith's Wealth of The Nation that he drew inspiration from. Meanwhile, in the contest, a man was left behind—a man who fought hard with words and actions for the independence, and that was Thomas Paine whom history forgot, for the fact he wanted something different from others, and spent all his life not pursuing power or money, on the contrary, he attempted to change the course of history that will enable all men live equally. Although, he did belong to the group to spread the New World Order. Maybe that was the reason he never excelled after all he did for humanity. So it was, that Jesus Christ's purpose on Earth was to teach, to restore the world, and he was crucified by the Pharisees—for they knew he was the man that came to show the way to the divine, for they knew he was not exceedingly upset with the thieves, the adulterous, the foolish, the beggars, or the stubborn ones, but he was upset with them for asserting to know it all when actually they now nothing; he was upset with them for wanting to possess and retain power, he was upset with them for their hypocrisy, he was upset with them for their false preaching of a supreme God that made them the chosen ones."

On the spot, as Charley refers briefly to the numbers 666, the mark of the beast, he slowly closes his eyes and dies in silence. Tyson spots himself in an entire devastation. He could not help shed tears, and stand the grief that boils inside his heart. He is alone again, alone in a world trembled and placed in darkness and despair. He could not help bring to reality all his desires to heal humanity, to save the world and make it a better and peaceful place. His vision is gone, his dream has been badly impaired. It is all gone and he is been left all alone by himself in the whole world.

When he could not move himself or take a walk to anywhere he knows, he lifts his head up to the sky and screams so loudly the gods and goddesses in the wonderland are able to hear him and descend to Earth to answer his call. And from a great distance, he could see them walking closer to him. Closer. Closer. And, all of a sudden, what he sees are some group of native people who might have been populating the nearby forest. He tries cleaning his both eyes to see if he has mistaken them for humans, he tries to see if his sight is not deceiving him. He closes his eyes once and twice again to open them in order to see if his perception is wrong. But all remains the same as he sees them, he sees them all naked—males and females. A beautiful little girl is walking towards where he is. She is walking closer to present him a beautiful bouquet of carcuma flowers that smells really good as he receives them from her and smells them. It is good. The flowers are performing an oracle of the natural gift of nature. They are breathing life into him, issuing him an assurance to witness and experience how everything moves accordingly to their natural rhythm with the mother, Earth. It is him reaching for the flowers, reaching to the little girl, reaching to the other grown up men and women, who have come to receive him back to life. It is him seeing himself with the natives in a land where nature could communicate with humanity, far from the place where he has been born and bred; it is in the forest of Nicaragua, near the Caribbean Sea. He is there, witnessing the balance and harmony that his heart craves. He is quietly witnessing how nature is calling him back to life.

Chapter 25

I t is about 6:00 a.m. Tyson wakes up from a bed in a corner of the cell. He could force a broad view of the small room he is as he gradually opens his eyes. At first, everything seems completely dark. Then it becomes dispositioned in a steep regulation of blurriness. It is dim and a bit unclear. Finally, it spares gleams of light. He lays awake, facing the upper interior surface of where he is. But when he attempts to cast his view around the room to examine everything there, he speedily notices he is locked up in a cell with a grown man whom seems to be fed up with his life as he raises his head and counts the ceiling tiles. The man is white. He is naked with the entire body tattooed with Nazi swastikas. He looks pale and very serious, his eyes turning to fixate on him. When Tyson tries again to blink his eyes to see he is not dreaming, he finds it is real, he is in a real world, and apparently, with Adolf Hitler himself in a cell. Where in the world is he? It is incomprehensible, and he could not demand that from his cellmate because it is his first time meeting with the most vicious man that has ever lived on Earth, been thought to be dead long ago. How he has stupidly managed to find himself in this place, is a mystery. It is more than a mystery. He is troubled, but he is not alone in the world, or perhaps he is dreaming the world has been destroyed, or is he in a psychiatric hospital? All he speculates is how he has come to see himself locked in a conflict within his own heart with array of evil forces marching to inflict him with adversity. And he starts to communicate with himself, looking to the ceiling tiles, not bothering to know if Adolf Hitler, whom he sees there, or any other person is hearing him, and he is saying, "Why is this a burden that has come to trap his own self upon my very peaceful soul? Is this not a substantial evidence I can find insights within? But being myself more than the testimony put forward this day to all, doubtful it might be when narrated. I say, it has deepened my abstract thinking; it has prolonged proportionately my desire to create a dissimilar world of my own tragedy, my own malicious mischief, casting myself in a shadow where the situation appears to be complex and precarious, flying in wonderment, peering into an abstract world that steams double bubbles. That I have to undergo the process of transformation and purification in order to fulfill my purpose on Earth, just as the Universe, as I read and understand, will fulfill his purpose against the wicked. Taking this lessons, I wholeheartedly surmise it is to help construct some kind of scientific explanations; to shed some lights on the exploration of micro-macrocosmic form. All men are created equal, and must live equally. I forbid you to rule out any kind of spiritual and human supremacy along the path of evolution. O' Mahatma, lead me through, I entreat. Looking through the waters of my eyes, my disbelief and sadness that rejoice their souls in solitude, arousing my cynicism, which is for the sake of humanity. This, which signifies and contradicts the entire system that humanity has begot itself. This, which the individuals cannot comprehend, will never comprehend. This, which only concentrates on recognition and pride and greed and lust and atrocity. It is true to say I so much share a belief that enlightenment can carry the hope of mankind further; it can sink us into a realm of supernatural existence within our souls. It is not that we have driven too far to that high level of wickedness and butter our bread with farfetched and asymmetrical hate and blood. But that when we failed to take ourselves through that acknowledgement of the things around us. If this be the truth, my fellow mortals bid me well to proceed more distant in time and space with this conscious choice and hypothetical proposition of mine. If not, let the hands that build also be the hands to destroy. Verily, I see man has fallen steep into a dream enclosed by iniquity he can no longer uplift his head in order to see what is surrounding him. He desires so much to lay in wait for trouble and die in his own bloody bed buckled by bad behavior. My worriment and state of exaltation have both intertwined that I come to fear time more than I fear the devil itself. I come to fear time, believing it is going too far away from me, and I cannot right my wrongs before dawn. And when it is dawn, bad things might protest and present themselves before me. Darkness is evil, this I know well. The light that leads my way is fading away. O' madness! O' madness! Why have you driven the world into your world? Is there still time left for us to conquer this madness? O' time! O' time! You are my friend, you are my foe. Time. This time. It spurs me ups and downs; it channels my thoughts from death to birth, from birth to death. I wish I can stop time. I wish I can reverse time. But I only can reflect and contemplate on the whirlwind that carries it to my world. I only can perpetuate the circle of insanity that rolled into my stubborn head. I only can walk on top of the muddy scene that dissolution and gross misconduct appear to cling to, the muddy scene the planet we inhabit. I only can breathe the air of time which have ceaselessly stood on my way to not allow the inflow of emotion which sweeps around me. Click, clack, the clock counts. Ding, dong, the bell rings. But slowly, and with pace, the time accelerates as it reaches dawn, as it brings horrors, hopelessness, conflicts, and wars. It moves around us. It drains away the good nature of mankind. It appears like a man who reaches his place of work to commence a hard day joy of pain. And it fades away like a woman whose breasts have fallen down, rejected by young lads, her only remaining days seem to watch as the new generation suits the society. I see everything wrapped in a shadow of time. Time! O' time, I cannot catch. Time! O' time, give me the masterpiece so I can express myself easily and fluently in English language, for me to be deliberate and specific. Yes, I can see a gross human right violation. Or, what about executives who award themselves big pay rises? I can see people, mostly politicians, spewing venomous hatred. I can see the evil spirits chained to my own ghost, and immediately as I set myself to flee, they have all chased after me, clinching to my bone and flesh, sucking my blood, eating my flesh, and all I do is to scream endlessly, with no one to hear me from underground where I possess my possession. That for long I have disclosed my heart to some strange powers that have forbidden to let me live and be on my own, for they have cluster their fists into my hollow heart.

Chapter 26

I t is after when Tyson finishes uttering these strange words to himself that he looks to the man sharing the same sanctuary with him—and he finds no one there. He is still in a locked room. Then, he understands there is something going wrong. There is something needed not to be said that has been said. Something needed not to be seen that has been seen. He tries to piece everything together to know what it is that is wrong, what exactly he is doing where he finds himself. Yet, he could not get to the bottom of it. Although, images and information that will not be stemmed by any means that still reflect inside of him are profuse and frightening. He could still visualize humanitarian and economic disasters, the displacement of people and facilitation of the rise of evil acts. He could still see there are no known practice that could lead to a feasibility of any activity focused on joint efforts to resolve conflicts around the globe. He is imagining, he is speculating, he is contemplating on these issues, these issues of how people shattered by wars and conflicts make every attempt to flee to inhabit places they feel could be safer. What will the future be? What will it be for the natives of these places they are fleeing to, and to them the foreigners in the many years to come? What will it be for the fact that many could never conform to other's culture, other's perspectives, other's rule of life? Or, has it all occurred for humans to find a way to learn to live together in harmony and think of reconciliation rather than separation? Yet, a human being born of a woman would bind him or herself up with a bomb to kill others, and at the same time dies. Suicide bombers are multiplying. Why is it that we cannot sit and dig deep to know what in fact has led to people having this kind of ideology of hate? It is all baffling and terrifying how we could continually buy to the notion of "if you cannot beat them you better join them."

In a world we live in, we complain every time of corruption, of slavery, and how destructive is the system, yet we trail the path of constant ignorance which only makes us to resist and permit the elevation and amelioration of what we bear witness. Technology has become the god we all worship. It is true we believe more in machines and robots, we have given them our jobs and we are left with none, we endow with the feelings these machines and robots are our future. Of course they are, just as they are our destruction. Machines and robots have done so much good to mankind. They have contributed to the advancement of mankind and the society. But they have done more damages and are poised to do more, to send man to his doom, for they too have come to lost faith and beliefs in mankind. Now, how long, how long shall we perpetually lay foundations for those whose beliefs are that people of the world must continuously wander aimlessly in search of wealth, in search of glory, in search of their souls? Now, how long, how long shall we keep up with the notion that the media will control our lives, our politics, our marriage, our justice system, our everything? Do we not see they are destroying the human race by painting pictures and exhibiting images distinctive from the actual ones?

Well, metaphorically, it might signifies when Tyson looks around, he could only perceive the major problems engulfing the world and it is driving him into a confused state of mind, looking for an answer to a question thrown to him long ago by the Universe on the reason why can't we be wise enough to do what is right that is beneficial to all instead of creating a culture characterized by mistrust and fear? Now, is there any means to stem the advancement and extension of ideals positively meant to stimulate conflicts and misfortunes? Treating others as expendable resources, will that commission us to smooth the path to peace? When will the change come? That change we all hunger and thirst for, that change of the hearts and souls, that change of evolution that will take us all to the wonderland where we all dream to be that is here on Earth?

Or, maybe it seems we care less about ourselves and the future for the next generation. It happens he, Tyson consistently fret over issues not supposed to be a burden to him. But it is so absurd to see how we live in a world where people launch themselves into legends by fighting wars, by creating fast moving and sophisticated armies, war machines and weapons to terrify others purposefully to fulfil their dreams of ruling over them. Whereas, money spent on war machines is enough to feed the whole world. It is heartbreaking when he sees people in countries involved in wars and conflicts fleeing to every other parts of the world to seek refuge in order to be able to live a life free from repression and force—and that has become a burden to others who are lamenting, not knowing how to confront the crisis. Howbeit, these are all the consequences of some who feel they have the right to do whatever they want by invading other countries, just like the U.S and its allies execute their plans of the invasion of Iraq, just like France started bombarding Libya and was finally aided by Italy, Britain, Spain and the U.S. See how we want our world to be. We create monsters, we create terrorists that have become awful problematic issue to deal with. Why should we not heed to take extreme precautions when it comes to dealing with international conflicts? The Middle East problem has become a problem no one can resolve because they have come to see themselves divided by democracy and theocracy. They would have been better off with their culture and ideas if people haven not come to preach to them a new way of life that is necessary. The grandest of all these problems is when we are not in good terms with one country because we seem panicked by their drive and tenacity both in economy and defense, then we turn to their neighbors and arm them with weapons, asserting it is to help them defend themselves against others who pose threats to them—aided and abetted by our governments we assist in building them, assuring them with strength and capacity. Then, in the long run they take advantage of it to develop and expand their defense mechanisms. It has happened before and it is still happening. We all have allies who detest our allies, the other detests the other, and the other detests us, and the other is our ally—in the long run we supply arms and weapons to those we think are our allies who will later become real foes. Do we not get tired of all these wars we fight every day and lose? Do we not think there could be another way out in dealing with issues so critical? If we keep repeating what dropped us the first time into holes full of miseries, we should be deemed morons, ignoramus. Better animals than humans if we cannot find a way to sort things out, if we cannot find a way to love and treat our neighbors in a way that is conforming to acceptable standard and abstain from greed and power and lust.

Tyson is wondering, he is wondering why it has to happen not only the wicked would be punished for their misdeeds, but also the good people who never help alter the evil acts in the beginning. It is painful; it has become to him a mystery he has never comprehend, and will never been able to. The existence of a supernatural being we know nothing about if factually if it is true, this to him has created the right moment for man to conduct a proper investigation and exploration to ascertain if divinity is real or it is a pure myth.

It is true it has necessarily become a tragedy we do not conform to how the society is, nor do we comply with it on account of how the system is driving humanity (the society) to a state of despair and unto death. And even as many in the society acknowledge this, yet they become more firmly proud to embrace this system. Is it the bane of human existence, or it is a modest contribution to the fulfilment of the prophecies of the prophesiers that man will be destroyed and reborn for a new beginning?

What exactly is the freedom we desire so much? Is it when our thoughts are being controlled? Is it when they can tap into our communication systems and knowing everything we communicate? Is all this the birth of freedom, or the end of it? For security purposes they say they do it, since the terrorists have made Earth a place not safe and fit for all, adding to the problems. If only we could adopt a complete new way of strategic thinking embodied and propped by the right system, by the right process, the right skills, the right technology. If only we could be able to know how to choose between the nature of power and the power of nature. No one wants to utter the truth because of the fear of death or not being able to achieve their dreams which is attached to wealth. But everyone wants to lie and deceive so to live and abstain from wretchedness. Now, do we not notice the more we become civilized and advance in the exploration of celestial structures in outer space by means of continuously evolving and growing space technology and also improving our ways of life and working towards achieving every of our objectives to live better lives in the society, then, the darker the hearts of men? Indeed what we all cherish most is to see people smile. Yes we see them smile, and always smiling on a troubled planet.

Take my hand that hand to hand we walk to play in the moonlight
The spirit in me I will not demean but only to let leap
To the outside world where I crave to witness the energy to reap
Let's not override to meet with the traffic that holds a red light
My whole heart and soul I will constantly render
For you to dress with a love so tender
The air we breathe I believe must not be bought
My love your love will heal my soul
And give us back all that we've sown
While we experience the sunshine that lives
We will abstain from the ambitious plan to steal and corrupt
And let peace be unto us all.

www.ingramcontent.com/pod-product-compliance
Lightning Source LLC
Chambersburg PA
CBHW050342190726
48284CB00007BB/2119